Warning: Christians and people who are easily offe

Jesus and Mary: Messiah! The Greatest Story N

By Eleni Lee and Judith Rebecca Namwebya

Introduction

Jesus Christ was a magician. But not a very good one. Not that anyone really cared because he was devastatingly handsome. "Love thy neighbour" he said. And, ladies, he practised what he preached. Jesus and his disciples earn extra cash doing a stand-up act on lazy Sabbath afternoons. But the act wasn't going too well. Until they met Mary, an escaped African slave girl. Mary was a dancer. She was tall, glamorous and hot as hell. But Mary was not all she seemed…

Messiah is a roller-coaster of a Rom-com of Biblical proportions. Zombies, witches, battles, dinosaurs (yes, dinosaurs) – it's got the lot.

Warning: Messiah contains blasphemy and scenes of a sexual nature. Christians and people who are easily offended should not read this book.

Warning: Christians and people who are easily offended should not read this book

Jesus and Mary: Messiah! The Greatest Story Never Told.

Prelude

Battle of Phillippi. Greece. 42 BC.

Cleopatra and Mark Anthony looked from the summit of the hill onto the battle raging in the plane below. There were Roman standards flying while guards, messengers and cavalry dashed back and forth. There were several tents including Cleopatra's exotic marquee. Cleopatra was bewitchingly beautiful.

Mark Antony looked worried. The dust from the battlefield was rising. In the distance the shouts and cries of war were audible.

"What happened?" Mark Antony asked Cleopatra.

"A storm," she replied. "It wrecked my fleet. And my governor, Serapion, he defected when he thought all was lost, like the cowardly dog he is."

"So they know our plans?" asked Mark Anthony. "We are done for. We cannot break their battle lines. My troops will begin to desert when they see the battle is lost. Brutus and Cassius will prevail. One will become Caesar."

"I can still deliver victory to you," said Cleopatra. "But the cost will be high. What price will you pay for victory?"

"Anything!" replied Mark Antony. "Deliver victory to me and you will be my Queen. You and I will rule the world."

"So be it," replied Cleopatra, turning and leading her entourage into the marquee.

…

Cleopatra stood before three breathtakingly beautiful warrior maidens in the marquee. Two were African. One was European. The four women were alone.

"Now, my Hebrew Slaves," announced Cleopatra. "You must lead our armies and break the enemy lines. Serapion has betrayed me and even now consorts with Brutus. Chastise him!"

The women turned to prepare for battle. They smiled maliciously and their eyes glowed a demonic red as they drew swords.

The sun was setting and the opposing soldiers saw a cloud of dust rising as if from an avalanche. The dust cloud rolled down the hillside, accelerating with each yard. The skies began to thunder, softly at first then louder and louder. The soldiers became nervous, and the horses began to whine. Suddenly the irresistible force of the three warrior maidens' shields collided with the front line like battering rams. Soldiers, horses and weapons were tossed everywhere. Huge warriors were cast high into the air along with arms, legs and decapitated heads. Cleopatra's army cheered and followed the three demonic maidens through the gap in

Warning: Christians and people who are easily offended should not read this book

the enemy lines and began to fan out as the enemy soldiers started to panic and flee. The three invincible she-devils slashed and chopped all who approached them – a gap appeared before them as the opposing soldiers backed away behind a shield wall, terrified. The she-devils looked up and smiled. Their eyes glowed red as they pointed their sword towards the enemy headquarters where Brutus and the traitor, Serapion, gazed down.

…

"My lord," cried Serapion to Brutus in the opposing headquarters. "We are undone. The omens!"

"Talk sense, you superstitious fool!" shouted Brutus, angrily. "We have the advantage. We outnumber them. We hold the high ground. Their reinforcements are lost. They cannot break our lines. We grow stronger and they weaken before us. They will soon flee."

"But the omens, my Lord," cried Serapion, in fear. "The Queen. She has released them. The Valkyrie. The Angels of Death."

"You talk in riddles." shouted Brutus. "Be gone and take your cowardice with you."

Serapion fled in fear. He heard thunder and looked up. The skies had begun to darken. A great storm could be seen blowing in from the sea.

…

Serapion's head was on a silver shield in front of Cleopatra's throne as the doors swung open and the warrior maidens swept into the throne room in Cleopatra's Palace, Cairo. Several huge Nubian warriors followed the three warrior maidens. Cleopatra and Mark Antony sat on twin thrones. Cleopatra was heavily pregnant. There were huge piles of gold bars and coins in the middle of the room.

The three warrior maidens approached the twin thrones. They saluted Cleopatra who smiled back and waved in acknowledgement.

"My three most valiant servants," said Cleopatra. "Take these worthless baubles and trinkets as a reward for your service." She pointed to the huge piles of gold. One of the warrior maidens glanced to a Nubian warrior. Immediately the warriors began to collect the treasure and move it outside.

Cleopatra kissed Mark Antony, who was sitting beside her, and then summoned the three warrior maidens onto the balcony. "I would speak to you alone, Mary, Jezebel and Delilah."

The three warrior maidens followed Cleopatra onto the balcony. It was night.

"Behold the Sign," announced Cleopatra pointing to the sky. The three looked up to see an unusually bright star lighting up the land some distance away. "As is foretold, the star marks the birth of the Messiah. Go now. Find this Messiah and destroy him. He will be born in the Kingdom of Judea. Go to my friend Herod the Great, King of Judea, and make as slave girls

Warning: Christians and people who are easily offended should not read this book

until you find this Messiah. I have sent messengers to Herod. He will expect you. Make this Messiah renounce his God. Make this Messiah admit he is a false Prophet, a liar and a hypocrite. Then the world will be deaf to him."

"We can use the dark arts to kill him here and now," said one of the African warrior maidens.

"No, Mary" said Cleopatra. "Our spells cannot injure his body. He can only die by the hand of man. He is protected by the Angels."

"How many angels?" asked Mary.

"All of them!" replied Cleopatra. "The entire celestial host protects him. Now go. Approach this Messiah unbeknownst and in disguise. Deceive the Angels. Let them not know your true intentions until you know him. Use all your powers – everything I have taught you. Bring this Messiah to his knees and expose him. We will do the rest."

"As you command." replied Mary and Jezebel.

Cleopatra looked round. "Where is Delilah?" she asked. Mary and Jezebel, the two African warrior maidens turned to look. Delilah was no longer with them. Then they heard laughter in the throne room.

Cleopatra, still heavily pregnant, stormed back into the throne room followed by Mary and Jezebel. Delilah was sitting beside Mark Antony giggling and playing with his hair.

"Begone, foul temptress." shouted Cleopatra, scowling at Mark Antony as she remounted the steps to the throne. Delilah dashed away, grinning. Delilah followed Mary and Jezebel out of the throne room. The doors of the throne room slammed behind the three warrior maidens as Delilah turned briefly and waved to Mark Antony. Delilah turned back to find that Mary and Jezebel had stopped in the corridor and were standing scowling at her. Delilah grinned sheepishly. Jezebel looked away. She noticed a Roman Centurion eyeing her. Jezebel smiled at him. The Roman Centurion made an obscene gesture with his tongue. Jezebel blew him a kiss and waved him over. A few seconds later the Centurion was hurled out of a Palace window and fell five stories to his death.

Warning: Christians and people who are easily offended should not read this book

Part 1 – The Magician

Magdala, Judea, AD 30

The people were milling round the sandy expanse near the village. A few Roman guards had been posted to keep order. It was afternoon and there was nothing much to do. Several hermits and preachers, some wearing loin cloths, were plying their trade. The preachers were standing on promontories or soap boxes professing, or wailing, to small gatherings. People kept moving between the preachers to find one they liked. A couple of overweight and extravagantly dressed Temple Priests were observing the preachers to ensure there was no sedition – and to collect the fee for the licence to perform in public. Each Temple Priest was followed by a few useful-looking minders.

Suddenly a man shouted from the middle of the crowd "Help! Somebody Help. My father. He is dying."

People hurried over to watch. They surrounded the man who shouted. He was wailing loudly and tending to an older man, who was lying supine on the ground, foaming at the mouth with only the whites of his eyes visible. His skin was grey, and he appeared more like a zombie than a man.

"Woe is me," moaned his son. "Why are the good always taken so young? My father still had so much to offer."

"Make way!" commanded another voice. The rapidly expanding crowd parted as Peter pushed his way through.

"Have no fear," said Peter. "Jesus Christ is here!"

"I do not believe this!" said an onlooking Roman soldier to his companion as they watched the scene in disgust. "There has to be a law against it. That has got to be some sort of blasphemy. What does the Temple Priest say?"

"Ten shekels a turn and no questions asked, thank you very much," replied the other soldier, shrugging his shoulders. "At least that's what I hear."

Fortunately, the Centurion happened by.

"Excuse me Sir," said the soldier. "This is sacrilege."

"That would be an ecumenical matter," replied the Centurion.

"What does that mean?" asked the soldier.

"I have no idea," said the Centurion. "But it comes straight from the Fifth Floor. You just stand down, soldier. You know what they say: when in Rome."

"But we're not in Rome," the soldier pointed out.

Warning: Christians and people who are easily offended should not read this book

"Precisely!" said the Centurion. "These people are a set of Godless heathens," he added with contempt, and walked off.

…

"It's a miracle," said the son as Jesus attended to the rapidly recovering zombie. "My father is raised from the dead. Hallelujah!" The crowd cheered and clapped as Jesus and the zombie bowed and made their way off.

The son furtively handed a purse to the Temple Priests as he passed. The Priest slipped the purse into his robes and then briskly made off.

"A Star is Born in Judea this very day." announced Peter to the modestly sized group of assembled villagers that had been drawn to the commotion. He and Judas shepherded them towards a large rock. "Roll up! Roll up! Roll up! Come ye – come ye - one and all. Come round. Bring your friends. Come hither to witness the Man, the Miracle, the Legend, the Idol, that is Jesus the Master of Illusion! Come and be astounded - you won't believe your eyes as you watch him make grown men vanish – heal the sick – and even raise the dead. Gentlemen you will be amazed by the Messiah of Magic, children will be enchanted by the Duke of the Dark Arts, and ladies – you will be bewitched by the Viscount of Voodoo. And, ladies, just remember – Jesus is performing here for one night only!"

Jesus appeared from behind the rock. He was devastatingly handsome.

"For my first trick," Jesus began. "I need a lady."

"Don't we all," shouted a man from the audience. His wife thumped him as peals of laughter erupted.

"A lady, any lady." said Jesus as the laughter subsided. His assistants wheeled a coffin sized box from behind the rock and stood it upright. A few hands went up half-heartedly from amongst the audience.

"Ah, young lady." announced Jesus, indicating a girl milling round amongst the throng. The girl looked surprised and embarrassed. She tried to hide.

"No, no," said Jesus. "Don't be frightened. It's all perfectly safe."

"Go on," said a man amongst the throng. A couple more joined him. She reluctantly came forward.

"Now, dear," said Jesus. "What's your name?"

"Grace," she whispered.

"Speak up," shouted a man in the audience.

"Grace," she said, still hardly audible.

"Ladies and Gentlemen," said Jesus. "I present you with the Amazing Grace."

Warning: Christians and people who are easily offended should not read this book

One of his assistants had opened the vertical coffin. Jesus stepped over and led Grace towards it.

"See!" Jesus reached inside and banged the sides and back of the box.

"Solid as a rock," Jesus confirmed. He waved his hands. His assistants turned the box round. Jesus pounded the sides and back from the outside.

"You see," said Jesus. "A perfectly ordinary solid cabinet. Would any member of the audience like to test it out?"

"Here," shouted a man. A burly man stepped forward. Jesus waved him towards the cabinet. The volunteer conspicuously banged the inside of the box and then the sides and back as the assistants span it round.

"Nothing unusual here!" he pronounced, and then he slank off into the crowd, narrowly avoiding a man wielding crutches.

"Now don't be scared, Grace," said Jesus. "Step inside the box."

"Are you sure it's safe?" asked Grace.

"Safe as houses," said Jesus.

"Our house fell down last week," said Grace, suddenly in a clear and audible voice. The audience laughed, warming towards the act now.

"This trick is perfectly safe," said Jesus. "I haven't had any accidents in…in weeks." The audience laughed.

Grace stepped into the box, with a suspicious lack of reticence considering her earlier shyness.

Jesus closed the box and he and the assistants made great play of turning the box round and banging the sides and lid.

"Ta dah!" Jesus sprang the box open once more to reveal an empty chamber.

A few men in the audience led the rest in applause. Other villagers, who had been milling around, overheard and began to make their way over.

Jesus quickly closed the box again. Once again, he and the assistants made great play of turning the box round and banging the sides and lid.

"Ta dah!" Jesus sprang the box open once more to reveal Grace, this time wearing a different, more colourful outfit, and equipped with expensive looking costume jewellery.

The audience gasped. Now they were hooked. Some began to shout over to their friends and relatives. People began to wander over from all around.

Warning: Christians and people who are easily offended should not read this book

…

As the act ended.

"Goodnight," said Jesus. "And wherever you go – may your God go with you."

The audience began to disperse. Some members crept quietly behind the rock to join Grace.

A man who had been collecting money from the audience came over and handed a bag of coins to Jesus. Jesus weighed the bag in his hand, raised his eyebrows and smiled. He handed the bag back to his colleague as they both set off behind the rock where most of the assembled troop were now standing. There were two cabinet boxes, one of which had been used to make Grace disappear, and assorted clutter and props which several men were packing.

"Tough crowd," said the man, counting coins into the bag. "But we didn't do too badly."

"It's only a small place," said Jesus. "Not much entertainment here. Especially once the preachers have run out of steam."

"God bless those preachers," said another man who was helping pack. He had been one of the men leading the applause earlier. "They pack 'em in like cattle and we milks 'em. It's just a shame we can't get 'em before the church collection. That way they would have more money to give us. Preaching! Now there's a job!"

"Jesus. Don't be in such a hurry to open the box," Grace, suddenly interrupting. "You have no idea how hard it is to get your clothes off in that coffin."

"Maybe you should give us a signal," said the anonymous man who had 'volunteered' from the audience to check the integrity of the cabinet during the performance, and was now helping pack the props.

"Perhaps she could knock on the sides or something?" said the man formerly with the crutches, now miraculously healed and packing props.

"It needs to be a signal that won't just sound like something falling about inside," said the man who had previously encouraged Grace to become part of the act.

"And there's another thing," said Grace. "You spin the box far too quickly. It makes my head spin. And I tore some of my outfit. And mum says I shouldn't be wasting my time here performing with you anyway. It isn't seemly. Mum says big brothers shouldn't be taking advantage of my size. Just because I'm small."

"You're a runt," said Joseph, a boy who was with the troop. Grace kicked him.

"Mum is such a killjoy," said Jesus. "And you're not a runt."

"I'm almost ten and I'll soon be too big to fit in that coffin," shouted Grace.

"Trouble in Paradise?", a disembodied woman's voice suddenly rose-up.

Warning: Christians and people who are easily offended should not read this book

"Who said that?" asked Jesus. The door of the second cabinet opened and a stunning ebony girl stepped out.

"You called," she said.

"Wow!" said the Boy Joseph. Grace kicked him again.

She reached a glamorous hand towards Jesus, who appeared dazed but automatically shook it.

"False bottom?" she commented, glancing into the box. "Pretty good. But I've seen it before."

There was a pause as Jesus, and the other men, stood bewitched.

Grace kicked Jesus.

"Where…" whimpered Jesus, startled. "Where have you seen it before?" he repeated more forcefully this time.

"All sorts of places," said the newcomer. "Herod's palace, Athens, Cairo."

"You've been to Cairo?" asked Grace.

"You could say that," replied the newcomer.

"Have you met Cleopatra?" asked Grace.

"Grace," said Jesus, recovering his senses. "Cleopatra has been dead for over thirty years."

The newcomer smiled. "I'll tell you about her later," she said to Grace. "She died of a broken heart you know. Very sad."

"My name is Jesus," said Jesus. "And this is Peter," he continued waving towards the announcer. "And this is my little brother Joseph."

"Pleased to meet you," said the Boy Joseph, stepping bravely forward and presenting his hand to the newcomer which she shook politely and laughed along with Jesus. "That's my kid sister, Grace," said Joseph. Grace squinted at the newcomer, becoming irritated at all the attention her rival was receiving.

"And I'm Judas," said another man appearing from the mob and standing next to Jesus. Judas passed Jesus a gourd from which he had just taken a swig. Judas held the money bag.

"Ah," said the newcomer. "You are his double for that trick. You two do look alike. At least from a distance."

"It's a curse really," said Judas. "Being as ugly as him."

"I wish I was cursed like that," said another older man.

"You must be the dead body," said the newcomer.

Warning: Christians and people who are easily offended should not read this book

"Almost as dead as that 'One Night Only' gag," said the older man.

"The ladies like it," said Peter. "At least, they do once they've seen him."

Jesus lifted a gourd to his lips and took a drink.

"Yes," replied the newcomer, eyeing up Jesus. "He is rather cute."

Jesus spluttered and sprayed the wine all over the newcomer. All the men laughed and made crude noises and gestures.

"I am so sorry," said Jesus, reaching forward. He stopped himself when he realised he couldn't actually help without touching her inappropriately.

"Forget it," said the newcomer. "I'll just take these rags off and let them dry in the sun." She began to untie her top.

All the men made even more vulgar noises.

"Grace," said the newcomer, just before untying the first strap. "Be a dear and just nip over there and bring me that bag. I have a spare top in there. Just in case."

"Bah!" shouted several of the men.

"What did your last slave die of?" mumbled Grace, as she waddled over to collect the bag.

"Grace," shouted the newcomer. "I'm just going behind this rock thing to get changed. You come round with my bag and help me. Oh. I've got something in it for you." Grace suddenly cheered up.

The newcomer strode elegantly towards the rock.

"Now boys," she said seductively. "No peeking!"

All the men made even more vulgar noises.

The newcomer disappeared behind the rock and Grace quickly followed.

All work had long since ceased.

Jesus cringed.

"You're in there mate!" began Peter. Followed by howls of laughter and abuse and similar comments from the rest as they took it in turns to wink, rub his hair and prod him 'knowingly'.

"I'm not deaf," rang out the protest from the newcomer from behind the rock.

"Are all boys that stupid?" Grace could be heard to ask.

"Yes," replied the newcomer. "All of them."

Warning: Christians and people who are easily offended should not read this book

"Shut up!" said Jesus to the men, who had quietened down but were still sniggering. "Get back to work."

Jesus edged toward the rock, making sure everyone could see he was averting his gaze and not attempting to 'peak'.

"Hello in there," he said. "What's your name?"

"Grace, you idiot," shouted Grace in reply.

The men all began laughing again.

"Not you, her," said Jesus, irritably.

There was a pause.

"She," replied Grace. "Is called Mary."

"Well we wonder if she would like to join us for supper," said Jesus. "We've done rather well today. Despite this being a one-horse town."

"'She'," said Mary, emerging from behind the rock in a belly dancer's outfit. "Would be delighted to join you this evening."

The jaw of the collective group hit the floor. Jesus stared. Then averted his gaze.

"And 'she'," continued Mary. "Is a professional dancer. And 'she' would be pleased to join your act, seeing as how your beautiful assistant, The Amazing Grace, has just tendered her resignation."

Jesus looked at Grace.

"It's OK," said Grace. "I resign. Look what she gave me," Grace was sporting a jewelled tiara that looked suspiciously like it contained real jewels.

"I better just consult with my colleagues," Jesus replied.

"I'm in," said Peter, immediately.

"Me two," said Judas.

"Me three," said the boy Joseph. Grace kicked him - he was ignoring her and her new tiara.

"Any objections?" shouted Jesus. He did not wait for any replies.

"Congratulations!" said Jesus. "You're hired." He reached out and shook her hand once again.

"Incidentally," he continued, moving closer so he could whisper. "The Box Office hasn't been too good lately. And we owe this guy a load of bread for hiring out some of the gear. So

Warning: Christians and people who are easily offended should not read this book

we don't know if we can pay you. But my dad has a spare room so maybe you could stay there for free, food included, until things pick up."

"Are you trying to get her to stay in that broken up old barn?" asked Judas, deliberately loudly.

The other men began to jeer and make vulgar noises. Jesus scowled at them.

"It's a bit of a fixer upper," he said, quietly. "But I am a carpenter. So I'll have it all sorted in a few days. You can stay with Grace until then."

"She cannot," said Grace, loudly. "The barn is a wreck. And you're the worst carpenter in Jerusalem. And there's no space in my bed."

"She'll just have to bunk up with you," said Judas to Jesus, loudly.

More jeering and vulgar gestures.

"Ignore them," said Jesus. "My dad will help. He's good with his hands."

"Like father like son," added Judas. More jeering and vulgar gestures.

"I would be delighted," said Mary, graciously. "Now I must get changed again." She strode gracefully back behind the rock.

The men all began to snigger again.

"Mum isn't going to like this," said Grace.

Suddenly everyone stopped laughing.

Warning: Christians and people who are easily offended should not read this book

Dancer

"Dancer!" shouted Jesus' mother. "She's a whore. Don't you know anything? It's one of those euphemisms."

"Keep your voice down, mum," replied Jesus, flustered. "She'll hear you."

Jesus and his parents were sitting round an old table with food spread around it. The other children were in the next room, pretending not to listen.

"What if she does," protested Jesus' mum, now quietly. "I'll not have a whore living in this house."

"Technically she's in the barn," said Joseph, Jesus' father.

"That's so typical of you," snapped Mary, Mother of Jesus, to Joseph. "Always taking his side."

"You're on your own son," said Joseph, losing interest in the argument and taking some food.

"She'll be good for the act," said Jesus.

"We got loads of money yesterday," added Joseph the Younger, from the room the next door.

"Get to bed you," shouted Mary, Mother of Jesus. "You don't be listening to this. This is adult talk." She lowered her voice. "I want her out of here tomorrow!" she said to Jesus.

"Aw come on mum," Jesus protested. "She's got nowhere else to go."

"She's got plenty of places to go," said Mary, Mother of Jesus. "Especially where she's been!"

"Tell you what," said Jesus. "Let her stay until the next act. And if you still insist, then we'll get rid of her."

Mary Mother of Jesus scowled.

There was an uncomfortable silence.

"Just until the end of the week," she finally agreed. "Then I want her straight out of here."

"Great mum," said Jesus. "I'll fix up the barn. The roof leaks like a sieve."

"Whoa there, son," said Joseph interrupting. "Firstly, if it rains after you've fixed the roof, she'll drown for certain. Secondly, you ain't going anywhere near that place while she's in there. Me and Grace will go over and try and fix something now. But that place is strictly out of bounds for now."

Warning: Christians and people who are easily offended should not read this book

"Strictly out of bounds for the duration," repeated Mary, Mother of Jesus. "You're not to go within a hundred paces of the barn. In fact, we'll send Rebekah over. She can stay there and keep guard."

"No rest for the wicked," said Joseph the Elder, standing. "Rebekah! Grace! Front and centre. You're taking first watch."

Rebekah and Grace, who had obviously been listening, trooped straight in.

Mary Mother of Jesus scowled again.

"Here," she said to the two girls. "She handed them some of the food, and a water jar. I expect she'll be hungry."

"Do you think she'll give me a tiara, mum?" asked Rebekah. "Grace got one."

"Don't be rude," scalded Mary, Mother of Jesus. "She's a guest here. She doesn't have to give us anything. Actually," Mary paused. "I have an old dress." Mary stood and made a move towards the door. "I'll go and dig it out. It's a bit more modest than her current wardrobe so she'll look more like a lady…" "…and less like a whore," she whispered under her breath.

…

"Sorry to cause all this trouble," said Mary to Jesus, the next day. They were sitting on the beach. Grace was standing by the shore throwing stones.

"It's no problem," said Jesus.

"Your mum thinks I'm a whore," said Mary.

"No, she doesn't," said Jesus.

"Yes, she does," said Mary. "I heard everything."

"Awkward!" said Jesus.

"I don't blame her," said Mary. "That's what people always think. But what should I do? I can't help the way I look. Or the places I've been," she added looking downcast.

"Why not get yourself a husband?" asked Jesus.

"Is that an offer?" asked Mary.

Jesus looked embarrassed.

"What would your mother say?" asked Mary.

"Point taken," said Jesus. "Hey, do you want to see something amazing?"

"Sure," said Mary, brightening up.

Warning: Christians and people who are easily offended should not read this book

"Come," said Jesus standing. He led her a few steps down the beach. "Now stay there," he ordered.

Grace looked round and smiled. Grace began wandering over.

Jesus strode across to the water and wadded in up to his ankles. Then he continued wading. Suddenly Mary noticed he wasn't sinking into the water. Jesus continued for several steps.

"Oh my God!" exclaimed Mary, amazed.

Grace had reached her by this point. They both watched: Mary in disbelief, Grace utterly unimpressed.

Jesus made several magical gestures. Mary clapped. She waved for him to come back.

"There are some rocks just beneath the waterline," Grace explained, impassively. "You'll see them in an hour when the tide goes out. He does that to impress all the girls."

Jesus began walking back, suddenly slipped and fell into the water entirely submerged.

Mary startled and she and Grace began to run over.

Jesus reappeared, this time the water was up to his waist.

"Don't panic," he shouted. "It was deliberate."

Mary sighed with relief.

Jesus waded out of the water.

Mary Mother of Jesus appeared behind them. "Doing his walking on water trick again?" she said.

"I'm very impressed," said Mary.

"Except for him falling in," said Mary, Mother of Jesus. "They are mighty slippery. Those submerged rocks."

"I gather," said Mary.

"I've brought you something else to eat," said Mary, Mother of Jesus, handing a basket over. "You look like you need a good meal. Far too skinny by half if you ask me."

"Why thank you," said Mary, taking the basket, gratefully.

"Come on Grace," said Mary, Mother of Jesus. "Time you ate."

"Can't I stay here and have the picnic?" protested Grace. "She might give me another tiara."

"I'm sure she's run out of tiaras," said Mary, Mother of Jesus, leading Grace up the shore by the hand. "They don't grow on trees you know."

Warning: Christians and people who are easily offended should not read this book

"What's in the basket," asked the soaking Jesus.

"Guilt offering," replied Mary. "I think peace has just been declared."

"I knew she'd go wobbly in the end," added Jesus. "She always does."

"Is that so?" asked Mary, indignantly. "And how many other girls have you brought back here to live?"

"You're the first," said Jesus, pulling his wet tunic over his head and tossing it on the sand. "Well, the first one this week."

"Goodness!" said Mary, staring at his rippling bare torso. "I can certainly believe that!"

Warning: Christians and people who are easily offended should not read this book

Doubles

The next show. Two of the upright coffins were set up right behind Jesus. The coffins were several feet apart. They were both standing in front of a wall. Their doors were wide-open, and they were empty. There was a solid wooden pole mounted vertically between the coffins which was securely driven into the ground.

"Before your very eye," announced Jesus before the assembled crowd. "I will transport myself in the blink of an eye through time and space itself."

"You mean between those two boxes?" shouted a heckler.

"Behold!" exclaimed Jesus. "A mind reader." The audience laughed.

Jesus made a great play of theatrically demonstrating the emptiness of both boxes. He closed one and stepped over to the other, measuring each stride. He nodded to one of his assistants who began a drum roll.

"Before your very eyes," he shouted to the audience. "I shall disappear, re-apparate yonder and then miraculously return."

He stepped into the box and slammed the door closed. Immediately the door to the second box flew open and he stepped out. Bowed quickly to the applause. Stepped back inside and slammed the door closed. Jesus re-emerged from the first box once more. He left it open and demonstrated once more that it was empty. He closed the door.

"Now for my next trick," he began.

"Open the other coffin," shouted the heckler, who was actually a plant.

Jesus opened the door of his own 'coffin'.

"Not that," shouted the heckler. "The other one."

"You mean that one," asked Jesus, pointing to the second box.

"Yeah!" shouted the heckler. "There's someone in it."

"God forbid," replied Jesus.

"Open the bloody coffin!" shouted the heckler.

"I warn you," said Jesus. "Interfering with the dark arts is a dangerous business."

"Open the bloody coffin!" shouted the heckler.

"I give you all fair warning," said Jesus. "I take no responsibility for the consequences."

"Open the bloody coffin!" shouted the heckler.

Warning: Christians and people who are easily offended should not read this book

"What do you all think?" Jesus asked, playing with the audience. "Shall I open the Pandora's Box?"

"Yeah!" shouted several. "Get on with it!" and similar invectives.

Jesus stepped over.

"You have been warned," he said, seriously. He moved closer to the second box and paused, nervously.

Get on with it!" shouted the audience and some began to boo.

Jesus held up his finger. "Be silent, my friends," he started. "Now watch closely." He made various gestures and movements around the second coffin, playing for time. The audience had quietened and were increasingly curious now.

"Three – two – one," he said slowly.

Suddenly there was an explosion and dust flew from behind the second coffin. It collapsed as Mary exploded out in her extremely revealing dancer's outfit – a woven crop top and hot pants – which she dispensed with quite rapidly to reveal a cloth of golden bikini.

The startled audience quickly recovered and began to clap as Mary paraded up and down the makeshift stage, she made a point of stroking the spear of a Roman guard who was standing just off stage. She bumped and ground and shook her booty for a period of minutes, increasingly to the fury of the wives of the male audience members. Mary ended her first appearance with a pole dance. By this time the audience had doubled in size and included several Roman guards, who had been waved over by their brothers-in-arms.

Mary ended her act by stepping into the second coffin, which collapsed as soon as she slammed the door.

The audience burst into rapturous applause.

Warning: Christians and people who are easily offended should not read this book

House calls

"We're millionaires!" shouted Joseph the Younger, dashing straight into the house and throwing a heavy bag of coins onto the table in front of Joseph the Elder. Jesus and Mary entered, followed by Judas.

"Is that the whole take?" asked Joseph the Elder, picking up the heavy bag and looking impressed. He spilled the coins on the table as the children gathered round and eagerly began to pretend to count them.

"No way," added Judas. "That's just Jesus' share."

"And Mary's," added Jesus, modestly.

"Damn!" said Joseph the Elder. "We can pay the bills for the whole month with this. Even that shylock."

"It was her," interjected Joseph the Younger, enthusiastically.

"By her," said Mary Mother of Jesus. "You mean our guest."

"She just stepped out of that coffin thing," said Joseph the Younger. "And started wiggling in that dancing dress. And they all came running."

"We had to put on an evening performance," said Judas. "Full house. Standing room only. Even the Romans turned up."

"It sounds like you're a big hit," said Mary Mother of Jesus.

"Well," said Mary. "I do have experience. Anyhow, I can move out now."

"Go next door," said Mary Mother of Jesus to Joseph and the other children.

There was an uncomfortable silence as the children left. Mary Mother of Jesus pushed food towards Judas who sat and began to eat.

"I have had some rather unkind thoughts about you," said Mary, Mother of Jesus.

"You don't have to explain," said Mary, blushing.

"Yes, I do," said Mary, Mother of Jesus. "Father!" She prodded Joseph the Elder with her elbow. Joseph the Elder looked uncomfortable and had been trying to avoid eye contact.

"What my wife is trying to say is," mumbled Joseph. "Well, I've fixed up the barn. And you can stay there until you're ready to move out."

"Or find yourself a husband," added Mary Mother of Jesus. Joseph sighed with relief now he had formally invited Mary to stay as the Master of the House and had completely discharged his responsibilities.

Warning: Christians and people who are easily offended should not read this book

"Jesus tells me that you don't have a father," continued Mary, Mother of Jesus.

"Well obviously I had a father," replied Mary.

"I think what mother is trying to say is that your father deserted you," said Jesus.

"Exactly," said Mary, Mother of Jesus. "So you are an orphan. And I will not be seen to throw an orphan out on the streets."

"That's very kind of you," said Mary.

"So it's settled," said Mary, Mother of Jesus. "Mary will stay as an adopted member of our family."

"I am overwhelmed," said Mary.

"It's our pleasure, daughter" said Mary, Mother of Jesus. She paused. "But the barn is still out of bounds to all boys. Especially you," she stared at Judas, who sniggered.

…

The next Sabbath.

A woman approached some of the Roman guards while Mary was dancing.

"This is obscene," she complained. "Why don't you do something?"

"Well now," replied the officer, calmly. "It's a serious thing, putting folks on trial for obscenity. There is such a thing as freedom of expression, especially in art."

"Art?" complained the woman. "That's porn. Not art."

"You shouldn't be too quick to judge," replied the officer. "Hey boys, what do you think?"

"Art!" they replied in unison as they leered at Mary's dance.

"You're a disgrace," said the woman. "You should drag that houri in front of the judge."

"We need evidence for that," said the officer. "We can't just go around just arresting people whenever we feel like it."

"How much evidence do you need?" demanded the woman. "Use your eye."

"That's what I am doing," said the officer. "Gathering evidence. Hey, boys" he said to the soldiers. "Have you seen anything obscene?"

"Oh no!" said two of the leering soldiers. "But there's still plenty of time left," added another.

"You see," said the officer. "There are no witnesses. Let's just roll with it and see how things turn out!"

Warning: Christians and people who are easily offended should not read this book

"A curse on the lot of you," said the woman, storming off. "Men are all the same," she grumbled as she sloped off.

"You boys haven't paid," said Judas, to the soldiers.

"We're working," said the officer.

"I can see that," said Judas. "Its two shekels a gawp. Each."

"Damn your eyes man," said the officer. "That's more than I get paid in a month."

"A likely story," said Judas.

"Clear off," said the officer. "Or we'll arrest you for obstruction."

Judas leaned closer to the officer. "You know," Judas said. "For twenty shekels I can arrange a wardrobe malfunction. If you know what I mean. Those clothes she's almost wearing. They're very delicate. The straps could snap at any minute – with the right help of course."

"Erm," said the officer. "Let me consult with my colleagues." He beckoned to the other soldiers to come round him. "Get your money out boys," he whispered to them in the huddle.

...

There was a disturbance in the crowd. Some people were fussing over a girl. Everyone turned to look. The act had to pause. Jesus was curious. He walked through the crowd, who parted for him, assuming that he had some authority as he was the headline act. Mary and the others followed him.

A girl was laying on the ground, convulsing and foaming at the mouth. She spasmed and was turning blue. Jesus pushed the others away, who were relieved that someone else was taking responsibility. Jesus knelt by the girl and tried to straighten her neck. She suddenly stopped convulsing and went limp. The girl's mother suddenly pushed her way through the crowd and knelt to cradle her daughter who opened her eyes and looked round, still confused.

"It's a miracle," said a man. "A Miracle!" the audience whispered to each other awestruck, as Jesus stood, bewildered.

"What did you do?" asked Mary, in a whisper.

"God only knows," whispered Jesus in response. "I just touched her, and she woke up."

"Keep it to yourself mate," whispered Judas. "We can cash in on this big-time."

"You really have no scruples, do you?" asked Jesus.

"Absolutely none," said Judas, grinning.

"God give me strength," added Jesus, sloping off through the crowd to try and restart the performance.

Warning: Christians and people who are easily offended should not read this book

...

At the next performance.

"Do you make house calls," asked a man. Jesus was chatting with Judas in the Preaching field. The others were setting up their props several yards away.

"How do you mean?" asked Jesus, turning to the man.

"My brother," he said. "He is gripped by a great malady. He's been rolling round in agony for days. He keeps clutching his stomach. He says he's possessed by a jinni. We've tried everything. Everyone knows you are a great healer. Could you come and attend to him? We're desperate."

"Where do you live?" asked Jesus.

"About two miles over there," said the man, pointing hopefully.

"That's too far," said Jesus. "We're on in half an hour." He began to walk away.

"I'll give you ten shekels," said the man.

"Lead on!" said Jesus, turning and following him immediately.

...

A man was lying on a bed, writhing in agony. He was exhausted. He could barely speak. His wife was wringing her hands as she sat next to him, mopping his fevered brow.

His brother rushed into the room excitedly. Jesus followed with Mary and several others who they had had picked up on the way, and who had nothing else to do.

"Look!" said the woman to her husband. "It's Jesus, the healer, they've brought him to heal you." The dying man did not acknowledge them and continued to moan and roll around.

Jesus knelt before him and put his hands on the man's stomach as he rolled round. Mary knelt next to him.

"What now?" she whispered.

"Frankly!" whispered Jesus. "I don't have a Goddamn clue! Let's just wing it."

Jesus closed his eyes as if in deep concentration and held his hands on the man. Jesus mumbled under his breath making incantations.

"We need some hogs-bane," shouted Mary, suddenly jumping up.

The woman dashed into the yard while the onlookers watched Jesus. They were entranced. The woman returned with a handful of weeds.

Warning: Christians and people who are easily offended should not read this book

"Now boil some water," said Mary. "And grind that stuff up and make a compress," she instructed. "Put it on his stomach when it has cooled down and then pray for his recovery."

"Ah!" Jesus shouted as if in pain. Jesus suddenly went stiff and fell on all fours. The onlookers gasped. After a few seconds Jesus stood up. He was looking pained and breathless.

"It is done," Jesus said, after a minute. "I have cast out the demon. Your husband will be well tomorrow if he is a true believer and has done no ill by his neighbours."

"Hallelujah!" shouted Mary. "Praise the Lord!"

The onlookers and the wife joined in with the "Hallelujahs!"

Jesus blessed the man, the house and the audience and left briskly with Mary in tow. The man continued to groan and roll around.

"What happens if he dies?" whispered Mary as they marched back to the show ground with the crowd of onlookers running along so they could keep up.

"We'll be long gone by then," whispered Jesus. "I'll send Judas back tomorrow to collect the money. If he lives."

"Aren't you worried?" asked Mary.

"The Priests would take his money, whether he lived or died," said Jesus. "At least I'm doing a no-win no-fee thing. Most folks get better after a day or so whatever happens. My dad had an attack of the same last year. It's a question of playing the odds."

"Let's hope so," said Mary. "You're a real charlatan you know."

"Thank you," said Jesus. "Perhaps I should become a doctor."

…

"My Lord!" said Jesus to Mary, later the next day as they walked along the beach. Rebeka was running in front. "You were superhot yesterday. Those guys all had their tongues hanging out. Especially after that wardrobe malfunction!"

"You're too kind," said Mary. "It's amazing how that strap just snapped off. You'd think someone had unpicked the threads."

"You know," said Jesus. "Does it make you uncomfortable? You know. Having all those men leering at you."

"You get used to it," said Mary.

"I guess you do," said Jesus. He paused. "You don't have to do that. Not if you don't want to."

"What about the act?" asked Mary.

Warning: Christians and people who are easily offended should not read this book

"Well," said Jesus. "You're just standing in for Grace. Now that she's too big. And doesn't want to go in the coffin anymore. But Grace didn't dance or take her clothes off."

"I don't take all my clothes off," added Mary.

"No, I meant, you don't need to you know, reveal yourself so much in that dancing outfit," spluttered Jesus.

"I know what you meant," said Mary, punching him, playfully.

There was a pause.

"Would you like me to take all my clothes off?" she asked.

Jesus was suddenly speechless.

"Erm," he stuttered.

"As part of the act, of course," added Mary.

"Erm," Jesus stuttered once more.

"I'm sorry," said Mary. "I've embarrassed you. Forget I said anything."

"Cripes!" said Jesus.

"Sorry," said Mary, again. "I have a bad habit of speaking without thinking."

"Apology accepted," said Jesus, clearly shaken. "We will not speak of it again," he added, regathering his composure.

"Then everything is alright," said Mary, smiling.

Warning: Christians and people who are easily offended should not read this book

Coloured dress

The act had just finished.

"Bless each and every one of you," said Jesus. The crowd began to disperse. Jesus noticed an attractive, slightly older lady in a colourful dress at the front of the crowd. She was watching him intently. Jesus smiled at her. She smiled back. Suddenly another woman hobbled forth on crutches.

"Jesus!" the lame woman announced. "I suffer a great illness. My legs. They are possessed by an evil spirit and no longer obey me. I cannot walk these five and twenty days." The crowd began to assemble round her.

"Oh dear," whispered Judas to Jesus. "Let's bail."

"It's too late for that" whispered Mary. "They've all seen her. We'll look like a bunch of frauds if we run."

Jesus looked bewildered and stood, dumfounded, as the woman hobbled purposefully towards him.

"Cast out the evil spirits within me," she demanded. "Heal me preacher!"

There was a standoff as Jesus and the woman stared at each other in silence.

"Do something, idiot," whispered Mary to Jesus.

Jesus sprang into action. He boldly grasped the woman's head and held her shoulder.

"Get thee out, Satan!" he commanded. "Leave this good woman. Torture her no more." Mary and Judas fell to the ground on their knees. Many of the onlookers followed suit.

"Get thee out, Satan!" repeated Jesus, even lounder. "I command thee by all that is Holy. Leave this body and return to the darkness from whence ye came."

The woman screamed and fainted, falling backwards. She was caught by onlookers who were eagerly watching from behind. They held her. Her crutches clattered on the ground. Suddenly the woman recovered and stood upright unassisted.

"I am cured," she said. "Cured!"

"Hallelujah!" shouted Jesus. Mary led the onlookers in a chorus of Amens and Hallelujahs.

"What did you do?" whispered Mary to Jesus.

"I have no idea!" said Jesus. "I just improvised. Judas, is this your doing?"

"Not guilty boss," whispered Judas.

The other woman in the colourful dress had been watching the commotion.

Warning: Christians and people who are easily offended should not read this book

"You are truly a miracle worker," said the woman in the colourful dress to Jesus, interrupting his conspiracy. She was almost middle aged, quite attractive and unusually well dressed.

"God works through me," replied Jesus, trying to look credible.

"I am but a poor widow," said the wealthy widow woman. "But I invite you to share a simple meal with me and my servants if it pleases you."

"May I think about it?" said Jesus. "I must attend to my brethren."

"I will leave a servant to bring you," said the woman, clearly impressed with Jesus.

"Who's she?" asked Mary, as soon as the woman was out of ear shot.

"I have no idea," said Jesus. "But I intend to find out. In fact, I'll make it my top priority."

"You dirty dog," said Mary, punching Jesus playfully on the arm and laughing.

Jesus smiled back at her. "Man cannot live by bread alone," he said. "Don't worry. You're still number one!"

Mary laughed even louder.

"What's happening?" Judas asked Mary, as Jesus strolled off, whistling in the direction of the lusty widow.

"It's Jesus," replied Mary. "I think he's pulled!"

"With who?" asked Judas.

"That woman in the bright dress," said Mary, glancing over towards the woman who was strolling away, occasionally glancing back to make sure Jesus was following discreetly.

Judas stood side by side with Mary. He squinted as he peered at the lusty widow from a distance.

He paused.

"Nice!" he said.

"Oh! You boys," said Mary, punching him and laughing.

…

Early the next morning Jesus was striding down the street whistling.

"Ah Mary," he said, brightly, as he saw her. "A good morning to you. And what a beautiful morning it is!"

"Where were you last night?" Mary asked, smiling back.

"I had business," said Jesus.

Warning: Christians and people who are easily offended should not read this book

"Business with that widow, I take it?" asked Mary.

"I'll never tell," replied Jesus.

"You look like you've just won the lottery," said Mary. Jesus pulled out a purse and waved it. He looked rather pleased with himself.

"Where did you get that?" asked Mary.

Jesus smiled knowingly.

"Oh My God!" said Mary. "You're a gigolo!"

Jesus, grinned.

"You are a disgrace!" said Mary. "Taking advantage of that poor lonely woman. And taking money from her after you have used her."

"You're one to talk," replied Jesus.

Mary suddenly stopped and looked away, obviously hurt.

Jesus paused and then realised.

"Oh no!" he said, stuttered. "I didn't mean it like that."

Mary still looked upset.

"I'm so sorry," said Jesus, pleading. "I wasn't thinking."

Mary looked him in the eye. Then she looked over towards a shop. The shopkeeper was just opening it up. Mary looked back at Jesus.

"That's a nice dress," she said, pointing to the stock which was now visible in the shop.

"Do you want it?" asked Jesus, relieved that the atmosphere had thawed.

"Well, only if you want to get it for me," said Mary. "It does look very expensive"

"OK," said Jesus. "I can afford it. Anything to make you happy."

"By the way," said Mary. "Are there any shoe shops round here?"

Jesus looked at her and scowled. He handed her the entire purse resignedly.

"Let this be a learning experience," said Mary. "There is no amount of money Man can earn that Woman cannot take from him, and spend. So endeth the lesson."

…

"You know that trick with the water?" Mary asked Jesus as they were setting up the act.

Warning: Christians and people who are easily offended should not read this book

"The one where you swap the boxes while I'm tearing up the cloth?" said Jesus.

"Yeah," said Mary. "I was thinking. We get a lot of stick from the lady punters because all the men are leering at me."

"I know where you're going with this," interjected Judas. "Mary could spill the water down her front. And then she would have to take her top off."

"You are a very sick individual," said Mary, ignoring his suggestion. "Although…I could trip and spill the water on you, Jesus. Although I'd probably need a bucket."

"For why?" asked Jesus.

"It would give you an excuse to take your top off," said Mary. "And you could put the wet top in the box. And then we can magically pull out a dry one. In fact, you could pull out a multi-coloured one. Although none of the ladies will notice that bit."

"And why not?" asked Jesus.

"Because they'll all be ogling your hot buns, you moron," replied Mary. "And best all, it will all look like an accident. Something for the ladies! Make sure you turn round when you've taken your top off as well."

"One bucket coming up," added Judas.

…

Warning: Christians and people who are easily offended should not read this book

Dead Sea

"Hey Jesus," said Mary. The show had just finished. "May I introduce Stephanie, maid in waiting for Mary, Matron of Galilea."

Mary waved at Stephanie who reached out and shook Jesus' hand. "My mistress has seen you more than a few times," began Stephanie. "Unfortunately, she is consumed with a fearsome malady and suffers pain in her back so great that she can barely walk. She asks if you could come and lay your healing hands on her."

"Well, I don't know," replied Jesus. "We may have a show this evening."

Mary leant over and whispered in his ear, "She's paid fifty shekels up front." Mary wiggled a purse.

"Goodness!" said Jesus. He shouted to the others: "Sorry boys. Show's been cancelled due to unforeseen circumstances."

"What's her name, these unforeseen circumstances?" shouted Peter while some of the others jeered.

"Philistines!" retorted Jesus. "Lead on," he ordered Stephanie.

...

It was getting late. A woman in late middle age was lying on a couch. As soon as Jesus, Mary and Stephanie entered she began moaning.

"Woe is me," she moaned. "I am cursed. I am but a poor widow whose husband died just two days past. It is my heart that is broken." She rolled around, grimacing.

"This is Jesus," said Stephanie. "And his er...assistant."

"I apologise to you both," moaned the woman. "I suffer a great malady. The Gods have abandoned me. I suffer a living Hell. It would be better if I were dead."

"Now it can't be as bad as all that," said Jesus, attempting to be comforting.

"Ahhh!" cried the woman. She tore off her robe and lay face down on the couch. She was naked and somewhat overweight. "Apply your healing hands: exorcise the demons within me or kill me now and end my pain," she commanded, dramatically.

Jesus looked across at Stephanie who was now brandishing an expensive golden jug with a spout. "Massage oil!" she mouthed to Jesus. Jesus grimaced at Mary.

Jesus knelt and began to massage the woman's back as Stephanie and Mary sympathised.

...

Warning: Christians and people who are easily offended should not read this book

A couple of hours later Stephanie was leading Jesus and Mary down an ornate corridor within the villa.

"It's far too late to find your way home," explained Stephanie. "My mistress won't hear of it. Stay the night and we will organise a carriage tomorrow."

"Are you sure it's not an inconvenience?" asked Mary.

"It's usually best to do what the mistress wants," said Stephanie as she opened the door of a bedroom. "Miss Mary," she said. "This can be your room and Mr Jesus," she pointed across the corridor. "You can sleep in that room over there." She smiled at them and left. Mary stood in the doorway of her room.

"I'm bushed," she said. "I thought that awful woman would never let us go. Every time you tried to stop she began moaning and rolling around. She didn't look to be in that much pain to me."

"You are very insensitive," said Jesus. "Pain is not just physical. The poor woman has just lost her husband."

"He probably ran off," said Mary.

"Ok," said Jesus. "I'm in the room opposite if you want anything."

"Ok," said Mary, turning. Jesus moved slightly forward so he was just blocking the door.

Mary turned to close the door. "I thought you were going?" she asked, squinting at him.

"Sure," said Jesus. "I'm going to that room there. Just across the corridor. That's where I am. Just in case you need me."

Mary looked Jesus squarely in the eyes and waited.

"You know," said Jesus. "It's only across the corridor. It's a bit silly really. Wasting two rooms." He peered over her to look inside. "I mean your room is huge, like a villa on its own. I bet two people could easily stay in there and no one would even know."

"I'd know," said Mary.

"Aw," said Jesus, trying to look pathetic.

"Goodnight!" said Mary assertively, pushing him out of the doorway and then closing and locking the door.

...

An hour later Mary was suddenly roused by a scratching at her door. She climbed off the bed, took a lamp, and crept over.

Warning: Christians and people who are easily offended should not read this book

"Psst," she heard. "Let me in." It was Jesus whispering. She opened the door a fraction. Jesus pushed his way in. "Where's your bed?" he whispered, furtively looking round and spotting the bed.

"And I thought romance was dead!" said Mary, sarcastically. Jesus dashed over to the bed and began to climb under it. There were footsteps in the corridor and a knock at the door.

Mary opened the door, bewildered. Two female servants were standing outside looking harassed.

"Does this belong to the young man?" one asked, holding up a sandal.

"I think so," replied Mary, taking the sandal.

"Have you seen him?" asked the girls.

"No," lied Mary. "Not for hours."

"We're all looking for him," said the girls, scuffling off and leaving the sandal.

Mary was still holding the sandal. She closed the door and locked it. She turned to look at Jesus who was now peering from under the bed.

"I thought you had gone to your room?" asked Mary, angrily.

"I got lost," said Jesus, emerging from under the bed. "Pass me that," he said. Mary threw the sandal at him.

"Yes, Cinderella, you will go to the ball," she snarled. "What happened? Did her husband come back from the dead?"

"No," said Jesus, putting the sandal on his foot. "He came back from the Dead Sea. He's the commander of the garrison there. Hey, does the window lead into the street?" Jesus jumped up and went to look out of the window.

"I suppose," said Mary.

Jesus opened the window and began climbing out. "Come on then," he said to Mary.

"What's this to do with me?" asked Mary. "It's your mess."

"Yeah," said Jesus. "But you introduced us. And you took the money."

Mary paused and thought.

"Shit!" she said. "You've got me pimping for you now."

They both climbed out of the window and set off down the darkened street.

"Where are we going?" asked Mary.

Warning: Christians and people who are easily offended should not read this book

"Just down here," said Jesus, leading her. "There's an inn along here. I know the landlady. I've done her a couple of favours."

"Good," said Mary. She thought for a second. "Exactly what favours?"

Jesus looked at her sheepishly.

"What are you like!" exclaimed Mary as they scurried off. "You do know people get stoned for adultery?"

"Yeah," said Jesus. "But what ya gonna do? Who wants to live forever?"

They reached an inn. They went round the back and Jesus knocked on a window. Suddenly a door opened. It was obvious that the door was not the guest entrance. The landlady appeared. Her face brightened when she saw Jesus. Then she saw Mary and her face fell.

"Can we come in?" asked Jesus. "We're in a bit of a fix." He pushed past the landlady as she stepped aside in the doorway. "This is my friend Mary," he explained.

"Yeah!" said the landlady, wearily. "Friends with benefits!" She closed the door.

"Mind if I go upstairs and take a look outside," said Jesus. "I just want to make sure no one is following us."

"Like her husband?" asked the landlady. "Help yourself, you know the way," she added, sitting at a table, and taking a drink. She beckoned for Mary to sit as Jesus skulked off up some stairs.

"So what's your story?" she asked Mary.

"I'm living with him," said Mary then startled as the landlady raised her eyes. "No," said Mary, flustered. "Not in the biblical sense. He's converted a barn for me to live in. There's no funny business going on."

"A barn conversion?" asked the landlady, curiously.

"That's it," replied Mary.

"He does a lot of conversions," the landlady added as she relaxed. "He's converted me once or twice." She sniggered.

Mary looked at her and began to snigger too.

The landlady passed her a glass. She slid over to Mary. "Has he tried to convert you yet?" she asked.

"He's tried," said Mary.

"But he ain't had any success yet?" the landlady asked.

"No," replied Mary. "But it's not without want of trying."

Warning: Christians and people who are easily offended should not read this book

"Good for you," said the landlady. "Treat 'em, mean. Keep 'em keen."

They sniggered.

"Hey," said the landlady after a pause. "Do you want to know a secret? It's not really a secret. But just amongst us girls."

"Go on," said Mary, intrigued.

"He may look like an Angel," whispered the landlady. "But he's a Demon in the sack."

They both fell about laughing.

"What's so funny?" asked Jesus, suddenly reappearing.

"Nothing!" said the landlady. "I take it the coast is clear."

"Yeah," said Jesus.

"I'm off back to bed," said the landlady. "You two can stay here. Make yourself at home." She stood up and then headed for the door. "Delighted to meet you," said the landlady to Mary as she closed the door behind her.

"Sleep tight," said Mary to the landlady. They waited for the landlady to get out of earshot.

"Is there any woman in this country that you haven't slept with?" Mary whispered to Jesus angrily.

"No," said Jesus, flustered. "I mean yes…I mean…"

He paused.

"What was the question again?" he asked.

"You are incorrigible," said Mary.,

"Why thank you," said Jesus, clearly flattered.

"Fornication and Adultery are forbidden by the Ten Commandments," warned Mary.

"Well," said Jesus. "I see them more as guidelines really."

Mary looked at him in disbelief.

"I must have got the wrong guy," she said, shaking her head.

"What?" asked Jesus.

"Never mind," replied Mary.

Warning: Christians and people who are easily offended should not read this book

Dance

"Yo! Dog!" said Judas, walking in on Mary and Jesus in the kitchen. "I've got this great idea."

"Does it involve me wearing a bikini?" asked Mary.

"Only if you want to," replied Judas. "The thing is, I thought it would be good to have some audience participation. You know, like when they do that thumbs down thing with the gladiators. It gets everyone going."

"I'm listening," said Jesus.

"Well now," said Judas. "I just happened to meet these guys and they do an act. It's real classy and it's been a big hit. Nothing to do with girls in bikinis or anything. Anyhow, they're leaving town soon and going back to Spain or somewhere and they said they can teach us the act and we can do it round here, for a small fee of course."

"Do we need any music or accompaniment?" asked Mary.

"Nah," said Judas. "You can just beatbox."

"I'm not sure about this," said Jesus.

"Yeah," said Mary. "Your suggestions always involve someone taking their clothes off."

"Come on," said Judas. "Help me to help you. It's a real class act. This will make us all big stars. You'll be headlining at Caesar's Palace before you know it."

"Ok," said Jesus, reluctantly.

"Great," said Judas. "You won't regret this. It's called the Macarena. It's Spanish for twerking or something. Absolute class."

Warning: Christians and people who are easily offended should not read this book

Holiday camp

The audience were just ending their attempt at the Macarena.

Jesus was dancing next to Mary on the stage.

"Do you have any idea what the words mean in that song?" he asked the audience as the others left the stage.

He paused – there was no reply.

"Here's a sample," he said. "'I am not trying to seduce you… They all want me… They can't have me… So they all come and dance beside me… And if you're good, I'll take you home with me.'"

Jesus spoke to the audience: "Tell me folks: was I good?"

"Yeah!" shouted several of the audience.

"So sister, Mary," Jesus asked. "Can I take you home with me?"

"Where do you think I've been staying the past month?" replied Mary.

The audience hooted with approval – at least the guys did.

"You know, I've been hearing about King Solomon, he of the mines," said Jesus. "They say he had 700 wives and 300 concubines. And he was meant to be wise? If I woke up and I had 700 wives, I'd know I'd have died and gone to Hell. Can you imagine going shopping for shoes with 700 wives? I went shopping for shoes with my sister and I was praying for death after three hours. And what's the deal with 300 concubines? I mean 700 concubines and 300 wives maybe. Even then, it's still a bit heavy in the wife department. Hell – I don't know what they were putting in his food back then, but I want some. Anyhow, we can be thankful that, now we're civilised, we can only have one wife. Well, one wife at a time."

Even the women in the audience approved of the sentiment.

"Now for you viewing pleasure," announced Jesus. "Sister Mary, our very own Queen of Sheba, will be doing another dance based on a bible story – this time it's the Garden of Eden, before they invented clothes – and do we have any snakes out there?"

Raucous hooting from the crowd.

"But first…" said Jesus.

Jesus did a torn paper trick to the boos of the men.

…

The show had just finished, Judas came running up to speak to Jesus, Peter and Mary.

"You'll never guess what!" asked Judas, grinning

Warning: Christians and people who are easily offended should not read this book

"By the look on your face, it involves an obscene profit," said Mary.

"Only the market rate," said Judas. "Plus my commission. Now here it is. The leaders of town council came to me earlier and said there is a retreat, a bit like a holiday camp, a few miles up the coast and they feel really guilty for neglecting the people there – not doing their neighbourly duty and all that – especially as some of the residents have been there for years. So they've put together a collection and wondered if we could put a show on for the camp. Just to appease the guilty conscience of the town's folk."

"I smell a rat," said Mary.

"No no," said Judas. "That's all there is. Just one show. Best of all we can do it midweek like a matinee. And, even better, they feel so bad about the whole thing they've paid up front. I don't know about you but I'm up to my eyes in debt with the Shylocks and this will pay off the whole thing."

"Same here," said Peter. "My share covers everything that I owe."

"It's like manna from heaven," said Judas. "All the boys are on board. I've already been round."

"What do you think," Jesus asked Mary.

"Well," said Mary, suspiciously. "It beats working for a living."

"OK," said Jesus. "I'm in."

"Great," said Judas. "We'll all meet up Wednesday morning at my place and go over."

…

Wednesday lunchtime.

"It's a fucking leper colony," said Mary as they all approached the 'retreat'.

"Didn't I mention that?" said Judas. "I'm sure I did. But there are so many leper colonies 'round here I might have overlooked it."

"Group huddle," shouted Jesus. "Gather round."

The troop gathered round.

"Not you," said Mary to Judas. "Stand over there by that tree and think about what you've done."

"Yeah," said Peter. "And here's a rope to hang yourself." He threw Judas a rope as Judas sloped off in disgrace.

"OK," said Jesus. "It turns out this holiday camp is the district leper colony. But most of you have taken the cash from the town council…"

Warning: Christians and people who are easily offended should not read this book

"…And spent it…" said Peter.

"So what's the deal?" said Jesus.

"I don't have a choice," said Peter. "I can't give that money back. I've paid off the shylocks and it's all spent."

"Same here," said Paul.

"Me too," said the others.

"So it sounds like we're going to go through with it," said Jesus. "I mean how bad can it be?"

"We could all catch leprosy and die horrible deaths," said Peter. "But even that's better than facing those Shylocks and asking for another loan."

"OK," said Jesus. "Those who want to go through with the show raise your hands." Everyone put their hands up – some rather reluctantly.

"What do you think, Mary?" Jesus asked.

"There's a rather nice dress I've been wanting," she said. "And with your share as well as mine I can get it tomorrow."

"Where does it say I have to give you my share?" said Jesus.

"Look," said Mary. "You're going to give me your share sooner or later so I'm actually saving you time."

"Fair comment," said Jesus, resigned to the fact. "OK," he shouted. "Someone cut Judas down. It's on! Best foot forward."

"Cool!" said Joseph the Younger. "I bet some of their ears have fallen off. And some have no noses. Do you think they keep the bits that have dropped off and they'll show us?"

"OMG!" said Jesus. "No chance. Not a chance in Hell. You aren't going any further. Not another step. Now you turn round and go straight back home. And for God's sake don't tell mum where we've been. Just say it was an adults' only show."

"Bah," said Joseph the Younger. "Can't I just come a bit further and peer over the hill tops. From a safe distance?"

"Not even that," said Mary. "Now scram. Go on." She waved for him to go. Joseph the Younger sloped off.

"And don't you dare tell mum where we've been," ordered Jesus.

"OK," replied Joseph the Younger, walking off.

"Not even if she begs you," shouted Jesus.

Warning: Christians and people who are easily offended should not read this book

"OK," shouted Joseph back.

"Not even if she's lying on her deathbed and it's her last wish that you tell her," said Jesus.

"OK," shouted Joseph in reply.

…

Jesus and the Disciples did their act. Mary had finished a song. There was polite but restrained applause from a large number of people who were sitting a safe distance from the stage. Most of the audience had covered their heads and their faces. They were watching intently.

Jesus took the stage. He was moved. Jesus began speaking: "Looking out at you all, my friends, I cannot help thinking of the rich men and the temple priests and those others who are fearful of coming here. For what does it profit a man, if he shall gain the whole world, and lose his own soul? What do you think? If a man has a hundred sheep, and one of them is lost, doesn't he leave the ninety and nine, and go into the mountains, and seek the one that has gone astray? And if he finds it, he will rejoice more over that sheep, than of the ninety and nine which did not stray. It is not the will of your Father in heaven, that any one of these little ones shall perish. So where are the Priests and the rich men and Scribes and the Pharisees. Anyway, now for a magic trick." He took out some parchment…

Jesus left the stage after his magic trick and Mary took over.

"Good crowd," Jesus said to Peter. Jesus looked out in the crowd and suddenly saw Joseph the Younger, peering over a rock and sniggering at the lepers.

"Oh shit!" said Jesus. "Is that Joseph?" He pointed. Peter looked over.

"The little sod," said Peter peering out. Suddenly Joseph realised he'd been spotted and dashed down out of sight.

…

Mary and Jesus were strolling along the path home that evening. They had almost reached the barn. Jesus looked up. Mary, mother of Jesus, was running toward him from the big house. She was waving a cane. Jesus looked round. He began to feel nervous. Mary, mother of Jesus, got closer.

Suddenly Mary, mother of Jesus, exploded: "I'll kill you!" she shouted at Jesus, waving the cane in the air. "I'll kill you. I have no son. Taking him to a leper colony. Get out. Never come back."

Jesus set off briskly in the opposite direction. Mary, his mother, caught up with him. She began to beat him with the cane. Jesus ducked and ran out of range. Mary, mother of Jesus, gave chase, cursing at him. Eventually she chased him into the lake. Jesus had to wade out several feet from the shore to avoid her assaults.

Warning: Christians and people who are easily offended should not read this book

"You are no son of mine," shouted Mary Mother of Jesus from the shore. "I found you in a barn. No son of mine would be so stupid as to go in a leper colony. And you took your own brother with you. I disown you. I curse the day you were born. I curse it! Go from here. Never come back. I don't know you. Begone, child of Satan!"

She threw the cane at Jesus, then turned around and stormed up the beach.

"Avert your gaze," she told Mary. "He may take on other forms." She stormed back to the house.

Mary approached the lake.

"That could have gone better," said Mary.

Jesus waded ashore.

"Come on," said Mary, leading him away. "You better stay with me. You can tell everyone you spent the night with Judas. I'm sure he'll cover for you."

They crept back into Mary's barn.

"Hey," Jesus asked Mary, later that evening. "Do you think Solomon really had 700 wives and 300 concubines?"

"Don't be stupid," replied Mary. "He had five wives, one for each day of the week. That way he could get his weekends off."

"And concubines?" asked Jesus.

"Just for emergencies," replied Mary. "You know, when he was away on wars of conquest, or touring his Kingdom, or had a few days off in Jericho to chill out. Anyhow, that all changed when The Queen of Sheba turned up. Then he chased all his wives and concubines out of the Palace and banished them. Yeah. Call me a baboon with lipstick, would you? Anyhow they got off lightly. Some people thought they should be buried alive. But if Solomon had a fault, it was that he was too soft. He never got over her, you know, The Queen of Sheba."

"She sounds like an amazing woman," added Jesus.

"That's what they say," said Mary, smiling.

There was a pause as Mary and Jesus sat on the bed.

"It's getting late," said Jesus.

"It sure is," said Mary.

"I just wondered," said Jesus.

"Wondered what?" asked Mary.

"Well," said Jesus. "If you, you know, do you want some more money?"

Warning: Christians and people who are easily offended should not read this book

"You mean to give you a good time?" asked Mary, suspiciously.

"Maybe," said Jesus. There was a pause. "Now, if we had an arrangement tonight, roughly how much spending money would you be wanting. For a good time?"

"Ten gold coins," replied Mary. "And not those crappy, gold-plated tin ones with the Star of David on. The big ones with an Eagle on the back and SPQR stamped all over them."

"I can't afford ten sovereigns," said Jesus.

"Well, I'll give you an introductory rate then," said Mary, smiling. "Eight gold sovereigns."

"I don't have that either," said Jesus.

"How many gold coins do you have?" asked Mary.

"None," said Jesus.

"Well it looks like your shit out of luck then," said Mary.

"I have twenty shekels from today," replied Jesus.

"OK, sugar," said Mary. "You can hold my hand for an hour. Come on."

She pushed him onto the bed, and they lay next to each other holding hands. After a minute Jesus rolled over and tried to snuggle up.

"Hey," said Mary. "Spooning is extra. Get back over there. This bit in the middle is no man's land."

Jesus rolled on his back again.

"You know," said Jesus. "I gave those twenty shekels to the lepers."

"I know," said Mary. "You can have this on account but next time it's money up front."

"I shouldn't have asked you to do things for money should I?" asked Jesus.

"No, you shouldn't!" replied Mary. "And I hope you feel suitably guilty now."

"Yeah," said Jesus. "I'm sorry."

"Sorry doesn't cut it, baby," said Mary. "But seeing as how you risked a long agonising death to cheer up those lepers today, I'll overlook it this time."

"That's nice of you," said Jesus.

"It was your dick talking, wasn't it?" asked Mary.

"Yeah," said Jesus. "Sorry."

"What's the stupidest animal on earth?" asked Mary.

Warning: Christians and people who are easily offended should not read this book

"I don't know," replied Jesus.

"A guy with a hard on," said Mary. "Anyway, my arm's aching. Roll over and face the wall."

Jesus rolled over as directed. Mary cuddled up to his back and put her arm round him.

"And don't get any funny ideas," said Mary. There was a pause. "What's this?" complained Mary, punching Jesus' arm.

"It's my shoulder," replied Jesus.

"It's too bony," said Mary. "I can't get comfy. What with your bony shoulder. Are you sure you're not deformed?"

"No," said Jesus. "I can't help how I'm made."

"Well you're too bony," said Mary.

There was another pause.

"You're breathing too loud," complained Mary.

"I can't help breathing," protested Jesus.

"Stop it," said Mary. "You sound like a sow giving birth."

There was another pause.

"You don't snore do you?...."

...

Warning: Christians and people who are easily offended should not read this book

Good Samaritan

Mary and Jesus were on the beach. "Come on," said Mary. "Dance for me baby."

Jesus tried to moonwalk but fell over.

"Perhaps we started a bit too hard," said Mary. "Try this." Mary walked like an Egyptian.

Jesus made a passable effort.

"This is even easier, it's called the Zombie," said Mary. "Come on. Do it with me." Mary demonstrated the Monster Walk and Jesus gradually picked it up.

"Look," said Mary. "A little dancing will tie up a few minutes at the start of the show and it's a lot easier than trying to make up gags. Any reasonable attempt at a soft shoe shuffle goes down well with the audience. Especially if they can see you have two left feet. I mean. It's not as though I'm asking you to take your clothes off at the same time."

"Perhaps that would be easier," said Jesus.

"Maybe next week," said Mary. "Come here." Mary took hold of Jesus in the classical ballroom hold. "Right hand on the small of my back. Not on my bum. Down there is tiger country!" She adjusted his grip. "Now you're meant to lead. But seeing as how this is your first time just try and follow me. Here we go: Slow Slow Quick Quick Slow."

Jesus was hopeless. Mary uncoupled. "Just watch," she said. "Slow Slow Quick Quick Slow." Mary demonstrated the steps. "Honestly, this will get you out of any fix on a dancefloor."

She demonstrated again.

"Isn't there something easier?" asked Jesus.

"You could stand still," said Mary. "That's about the only other option. Anyhow, this is the absolute basics. Judas can do it. In fact, that boy is quite funky."

She demonstrated the steps once more.

"Now you", she said.

Jesus had a go and made some sort of attempt.

"Not bad but needs some work," said Mary. "Now with me." She put his hands in the ballroom hold.

"Slow Slow Quick Quick Slow," she said. They made some slow progress up the beach.

"There," said Mary. "It wasn't that bad, was it?"

Warning: Christians and people who are easily offended should not read this book

"I'm getting the hang of it," said Jesus, smiling.

"Great," said Mary. "Now all we have to do is add some timing, grace, poise and flare." They were still in hold.

"Am I that bad?" asked Jesus.

Mary laughed and put her hand on his face. "Don't panic. I've been doing this for a long time but it's all new to you," she said. "Everyone knows that white people have no rhythm anyway. All you have to do is to take one step at a time and not fall over. Actually, let's not over complicate things. Just take one step at a time. Forget about the second bit."

They paraded back down the beach in hold.

"Excellent," said Mary. "Let's take five. That's what they say in show business when they mean you can have a break. And usually a smoke. Dancers all smoke like chimneys you know. It's to keep their weight down."

They both sat down on some rocks.

"I've decided to make my act socially relevant," said Jesus.

"Sounds hilarious," said Mary.

"There are too many gags about fat women and gay men and making fun of Philistines," said Jesus. "It's politically incorrect. There must be an alternative."

"Alternative comedy, eh?" said Mary. "That's easy. Just do the usual lines but say 'fuck' between every third word."

"Sounds a bit controversial," said Jesus slightly phased.

"You bet your big fat cock it is," said Mary. "Who were you going to stick it to?"

"What do you mean?" asked Jesus.

"If you are doing alternative comedy," said Mary. "You have to stick it to The Man. Or The Woman. Or someone in authority who is not a member of a minority group. Which means that you're not reinforcing stereotypes, but it also means that the people you are humiliating hold all executive power and can have your tongue cut out."

"Just for saying 'fuck'?" asked Jesus.

"That's about the size of it," said Mary. "Of course, you could say the 'c' word and then it wouldn't just be your tongue they'd cut out."

"On reflection, I think I need to move towards alternative comedy by easy steps," said Jesus. "Perhaps a children's act or some suggestive limericks."

Warning: Christians and people who are easily offended should not read this book

"That's the spirit," said Mary. "You could do both at once. Observe: 'Mary had a little lamb. She used to call it Billy. One day she threw it in the air and caught it by its willy.'"

"The establishment will be quaking in their boots when they hear that, you bad ass bitch!" said Jesus.

"Try this one for size," said Mary. "Mary had a little lamb. She bought it in Medina…"

"I get the drift," interrupted Jesus.

"Mary had a little pig," continued Mary. "It used to squeal and grunt…"

"Whoa there tiger!" interrupted Jesus. "Sometimes less is more. You know, you are quite good at this," said Jesus. "Perhaps you could do some stand-up?"

"Nah," said Mary. "They won't like that. It shatters the illusion. Guys like strippers to be vacuous fuckwits. If you tell gags they start to feel insecure. It challenges their fantasies – especially that they can seduce you with simple lies. They cannot objectify you quite so easily." She paused, "You know it's a lot easier for black people to do alternative comedy than you white folks. We just say the 'n' word in every sentence. That sort of insightful political commentary really challenges the existing order – you can feel the very fabric of society crumbling in front of you. Anyhow, enough sedition and biting satire for now. Back to the Cha Cha Cha – let's dance."

"I already know one dance," said Jesus. "It's called the Hava Nagila." Jesus demonstrated the traditional Jewish dance with his hands held high.

"It's been done before," said Mary. "But maybe we could add a twist. You know: some drum and bass in the background. I can imagine some hip hop in there as well. You'll have to call yourself Jay-dog instead of Jesus though. Maybe Jay-Ice or Ice-Jay or Jay-Z. On second thoughts Jay-Z would be sad and bogus. Anyway, leave it with me."

…

Jesus, Mary, Judas and Peter were heading toward town for the show. Peter pushed a cart. "The other guys with the props will be there by now," said Peter. "What's this?"

They came round a bend and saw a man lying by the side of the road. He was badly bruised around the head and neck, and he was bleeding and partly conscious. Some torn clothes and some of his possessions were strewn about. His dog lay close-by – it was dead and had been stabbed several times.

"Hell fire," said Jesus. They all dashed over.

"He's been robbed," said Judas.

"He's lucky to be alive," said Peter. They knelt by him.

"What shall we do?" asked Peter.

Warning: Christians and people who are easily offended should not read this book

"We can't leave him here," said Jesus. "Come on, we can put him on the cart." Jesus and Peter began to help the injured man onto the cart.

"This isn't good," said Judas. "That's why they call this place the Bad Lands of South Damascus. Lots of bandits up there in the hills." Judas and Mary began scanning the nearby hills. Judas couldn't see anything, but something caught Mary's eye. She said nothing.

"What are we going to do when we get him into town?" asked Judas.

"You can spend some of that money we earned you," said Peter. "And get him fixed up."

"I'm as poor as a church mouse," said Judas. "If debt was a puddle, I'd have drowned in it by now."

"What do you spend all those donations on, the donations that you collect with malice from the punters?" asked Jesus.

"That money doesn't even cover the interest," said Judas. "I have negative equity. My investments are so toxic they could kill a herd of elephants."

"Well get some of those elephants to pull this cart," said Jesus, beckoning Judas to take hold of the shafts.

"We should try and collect some of his stuff as well," said Peter, collecting some of the clothes and oddments which were scattered around.

"What are you looking at?" Jesus asked Mary. She was staring at the summit of a nearby hill.

"Nothing," said Mary. "I thought I saw someone. But it was just a vulture. Probably come to carry that dead dog off."

"Why did they have to kill the guy's dog?" said Peter. "It makes me angry. Killing a dog. If I find the guys that did this…"

"Let's hope they don't find us," said Judas.

"They'll have made off by now," said Mary. "I have to go over here," she continued.

"It's a bit dangerous," said Jesus. "With bandits around."

"Yeah," said Judas. "One of us should come with you. In fact, all of us ought to come."

"No," said Mary. "You can't do that. The bandits will be miles away by now."

"One of us should go with you," said Jesus.

"No and no," said Mary, definitively. "I'll be fine. Just a minute or two. Do I need to draw you a picture?"

"Ah," said Jesus, suddenly enlightened. "My bad. You just run along but be quick. And shout if you see anything."

Warning: Christians and people who are easily offended should not read this book

"The thought had crossed my mind," replied Mary as she briskly wandered behind some rocks.

…

Over the brow of the hill five dirty, cruel faces were watching.

"Let's get out of here," said one.

"Nah," said the leader. "We outnumber those guys. And it'll take days before the Feds come from that town. They don't have any muscle there. It's a real pit."

"Did you see that black girl?" asked another desperate robber. "She's one fine looking bitch."

"Let's hang around here," said the leader. "I've seen that lot before. They'll be putting on a show in the town. And then they'll be coming through this way again with all the cash. We can knock 'em all off and then we can teach that dog a few new tricks." They all sniggered.

"Watch it," said one of the gang. "She's coming over here."

"I'm quaking in my boots," said the Leader. "She's only going round that rock to take a piss."

A second later, Mary appeared behind them. They heard her and turned round.

"Hello, baby!" said the Leader. "You move fast." They all stepped down from the brow of the hill and surrounded her. One of them pulled out a vicious looking knife.

"I am under some time-pressure," said Mary. "So let's just by-pass the foreplay."

She returned to Jesus and the others two minutes later. The vulture began licking the blood which oozed down the posts on which the five bandits' heads were impaled.

…

Jesus and Mary pulled the cart to Naomi's House. They had already unloaded the props and the other members of the troop were assembling the stage for the act.

Jesus knocked on the door. A tall middle-aged woman answered.

"We were told you may be able to help," said Jesus. "This man's been attacked on the road and robbed."

"Sure," said Naomi. "Bring him in."

They entered the house. The injured man had recovered consciousness but was still delirious. He could walk with help. They put him on a bed. Three young women appeared.

"He seems to be recovering," said Naomi. "I'm Naomi and these are my three daughters. My unmarried daughters."

Warning: Christians and people who are easily offended should not read this book

"Oh mum," said one. "You're embarrassing us." She left to get some water for the injured man to drink. The other two stayed in the room and eyed up Jesus and Mary. One of the girls began trying to attend to the man and make him comfortable.

"You see all the thanks I get," said Naomi. "My husband died years ago, and I had to raise these three daughters on my own. So I run a house for the sick. But it all costs money. And I'm not having any success marrying them off because they have no dowry. Incidentally, you don't know any rich bachelors, do you?"

"If only," said Mary.

"Well if you hear about any, give me a call," said Naomi.

The injured man began to come round although he was still rambling.

"He seems to be getting better," said Naomi. "Now I know that money is such a vulgar subject. But we have to eat. Do we have any idea who this man is and if he has any money?"

"He was robbed," said Mary. "If he had any money, they took it."

"He may have a family," said Jesus. "In fact, he was probably on business so he must have some income. Let me have a quick word with my colleague here." He beckoned Mary to speak to him outside. They left the room.

"What do you think?" Jesus asked Mary when they were out of earshot.

"You can't just leave him to die," said Mary. "But those girls can't look after every waif and stray they come across or they'll all starve."

"Do you think we can sweet talk Judas out of any cash," said Jesus. "From the collection?"

"He's a total hard ass," said Mary. "And he's up to his eyes in debt with the Shylocks. But if we all chip in a penny or two it will keep our friend there for a couple of days and then things may sort themselves out."

"OK," said Jesus. "We'll go in and tell Naomi and her daughters that I'll come back later and give them a few shekels to cover tonight. And when we get back to the boys, you can take up a collection."

"Why me?" asked Mary.

"They like you," said Jesus. "You can be more persuasive than me. Especially with guys. In fact, you can go round the audience with a plate and try your luck with them. If you look pathetic enough, you'll probably raise enough cash to keep him for a month."

"You mean you want me to flaunt myself to a load of dribbling idiots to get them to part with even more of their cash?" asked Mary.

"Yeah," said Jesus.

Warning: Christians and people who are easily offended should not read this book

"OK," said Mary. "Just checking."

"It's for a good cause anyway," said Jesus.

"Fair enough," said Mary.

At the performance later that day, Mary and two of the Disciples had perfected the sand dance. The dance wasn't particularly sexy, but it was well received, and Mary had more clothes on than usual.

Jesus took the stage.

"What a great audience," he said. "Now, here's a public safety announcement. We picked up a man outside town who was beaten and robbed earlier today. So we want you all to be careful because there are bandits around. If anyone is travelling back to the city let's all meet up here after the show and go together. Now, the beautiful Mary, who has come directly to us from her hit show on the West Bank, will be coming round the audience to collect money for the unfortunate victim who is still fighting for his life at the House of Naomi. All donations will be generously received. Remember: do unto others as you would have them do unto you. Incidentally it's rather hot today so Mary may have to take some of her clothes off to keep cool especially if she has to carry all that money you are about to give her."

Judas interrupted. "Great news!" he shouted from the front of the stage. "The Feds have found the five robbers. What's left of them anyway. And for only two shekels per person, I have been granted exclusive rights to take you to view their grizzly remains. Adults only. Those with a nervous disposition are advised to stay away."

The men in the audience began to cheer.

Jesus began to do a trick with disappearing jars – one of which accidentally escaped from its cover in the middle of the act and smashed on the floor. Mary sidled up to Judas who was looking very pleased with himself.

"I hope you give that money you are charging to Miss Naomi," she asked.

"Of course," said Judas. "Some of it, minus expenses and handling fee. Wooden posts don't grow on trees, you know."

...

The act had just finished.

"Judas!" shouted Mary. "Front and centre."

"Bah," said Judas, sloping over.

"How much money are you going to get for taking those ghouls to see the bodies of the five robbers?" asked Peter.

"I don't know yet," replied Judas. "Maybe six dinars."

Warning: Christians and people who are easily offended should not read this book

"Right," said Peter. "Jesus is going to the House of Naomi and he's giving her half of the collection we made today plus three dinars. So when you have your ill-gotten gains from the tour of death, you can put three dinars in the bag for us to divide up later in the week."

"But I had to do a deal with the Feds," said Judas. "They have to keep the vultures off and sight seers away until we've all had a good look. It's a crime scene, you know."

"Crime scene my ass," said Mary. "You stump up three dinars. And remember, there are plenty of pointed wooden posts just desperate for heads."

"How did you know the heads were on posts?" asked Judas.

"A little bird told me," replied Mary.

Judas reluctantly put some coins into the money bag that Jesus was holding.

"Right," said Jesus. "I'm off the drop this money before I get mugged. You boys can set off home."

"To hell with that," said Joseph the Younger. "Once we finish here, I'm going with Judas to see those dead bodies. He says they're all green and crawling with maggots."

"Stop swearing, you little sod," said Joseph. "You're too young to see headless bodies. But I suppose it's educational seeing what happens to outlaws, just don't tell mum."

"Coolio!" said Joseph the Younger. "Do you think they'll let us keep one if we pay the guards. I can show it to all the kids at home? A genuine severed head. That would be awesome!" He wandered off with Judas.

"You want some company?" Mary asked Jesus.

"I better," said Jesus. "They looked pretty dangerous, that Naomi woman and her three daughters."

"Yeah!" said Mary. "A good-looking boy like you. Anything could happen."

They set off.

"Does it happen often round here?" asked Mary. "People getting mugged?"

"Not really," said Jesus. "Firstly, there isn't much of a point – most people don't have any money to mug off them. And any outlaws round here are going to get spotted and rounded up double quick. It's a different story up in the hills though. You wouldn't want to go trekking up in the mountains without half a dozen legionnaires. People tend to do long-distance trips in conveys."

"Like a caravan?" asked Mary. "With camels and Bedouins."

"I think so," said Jesus. "I've never seen a caravan myself."

Warning: Christians and people who are easily offended should not read this book

"I was in a caravan for a while," said Mary. "Those rich Bedouins have luxury caravans complete with four-poster beds and kitchens and baths and with their own fully equipped harem."

"And were you in the harem?" asked Jesus.

"Can I trust you to be discreet?" asked Mary.

"Yeah!" said Jesus. "What was it like?"

"Being in a harem is the only way to travel," said Mary. "You have to look nice, so you don't need to carry anything – they have loads of slaves and camels and donkeys for all that. So you just sit around wearing silk and do the odd belly dance. Of course, the old goat might need to be serviced every so often. But the rich guys have so many concubines that your turn only comes up once a month if that. But it's exhausting work for the boss while he's running a caravan, so he's pretty worn out come sunset. And slave girls are mainly there so the boss can show you off to impress the other rich Arabs who come to visit from the towns."

"How did you get into that line of work?" asked Jesus.

"They sold me?" said Mary, dismissively.

"How much?" asked Jesus.

"More money than you can imagine," replied Mary.

"I can imagine quite a lot," said Jesus.

"Two thousand camels," said Mary. "That's double the going rate. But I'm worth it."

"What happened then? How did you get here?" asked Jesus.

"Herod was a bit short of dancing girls," said Mary. "And the Sultan was short of camels. So they did a swap. But Herod gets bored pretty quick. I mean he's scandalised the entire nation by trading his last wife in for an upgrade. And he got bored of me. You see, dancing girls are a bit like expensive ornaments, and they have to upgrade every year to the latest model to stay in fashion. So he let me go."

"Just like that?" asked Jesus.

"Not quite," said Mary. "Now I'm going to tell you a real secret now. So you must promise not to tell anyone."

"My lips are sealed," said Jesus.

"I was actually sold to Herod's dad, just to confuse things he was also called Herod, Herod the Great. He died an agonising death," continued Mary. "They still call it Herod's evil. And they thought I had put a curse on him."

"Did you?" asked Jesus.

Warning: Christians and people who are easily offended should not read this book

"Nah," said Mary. "Well maybe just a little but he didn't die of it. Anyhow, they were all lining up to have me burned but some Priest leapt in to say that they should watch out or I'd put a curse on them and there would be plagues and all the first-born children would die and all that hocus pocus stuff that Moses laid on the Pharaohs. And seeing as I was brought from Egypt originally, they all panicked and so they got an angry mob to chase out of town and they called it a banishment. Case closed."

"It still sounds a bit suspicious," said Jesus. "There's something you're not telling me."

"Actually, the Priest was on my payroll," said Mary. "You see, one of my little jobs in the Palace was to help the chambermaids in the bedrooms. So I helped myself to some of the cash that King Herod so carelessly left lying round. Then I split the loot with the High Priest, who was quite sweet on me, and he helped me smuggle it out of the Palace. No one is going to search a slave girl who is accompanying the High Priest on his rounds. And when the balloon went up, I told him he could have all the gold that I'd ferreted away, and I'd even marry him if he got me off the hook with the Inquisition. The loot was all hidden at his place anyway."

"So why didn't you marry him?" asked Jesus.

"His wife found out," said Mary. "The pig hadn't told me he was already married. Then she chased me out of town. Frankly I'd rather take my chances with the angry mob next time. So that's why I'm here. What about you?"

"I was born in a stable," said Jesus. "I grew up and here I am. The country's worst carpenter but its greatest magician."

"And lover," said Mary. "Or so the girls say."

"Oh you girls," said Jesus. "We're here now."

They knocked on the door and went inside. Jesus gave the money they had collected to Naomi who took it into a room to count. The injured man was still confused but appeared visibly better.

"What's your friend's name?" one of the daughters asked Mary.

"He's called Jesus," said another daughter, giggling. "He's a famous magician."

"And my name's Chloe," said one. "And this is Deborah, and this is Eve because she's the oldest."

"Is this your girlfriend," Chloe asked Jesus.

"No," said Mary, to prevent Jesus being embarrassed. "We're just friends. We perform in the act together."

There was a pause.

Warning: Christians and people who are easily offended should not read this book

"You know our mum keeps wanting to get us married," said Deborah. "But we don't have any dowry. Anyway, we aren't that bothered about getting married. You know, we can still have gentleman friends."

"That's good to know," said Jesus.

There was another pause.

"We hear there's a dancing girl whose clothes keep disappearing in your act," said Eve.

"Surely not all her clothes," said Jesus.

"Do you make her clothes disappear?" asked Chloe.

"If only I had that power," said Jesus.

"You could come back later," said Chloe. "Perhaps you can make my clothes disappear."

"Be quiet you little whore," scalded Eve, although she clearly did not mean it.

"You just want his clothes to disappear," retorted Chloe.

"You're both a pair of sluts," said Deborah.

Naomi came back into the room.

"You are very generous," said Naomi. "That will keep him for at least a week. Now we won't keep you any longer. Goodnight." She shook Mary's hand and kissed Jesus on the cheek, rather too long for decency's sake.

They made their goodbyes and Naomi showed Jesus and Mary out.

"Do chicks always hit on you like that?" asked Mary as soon as the door was closed.

"It's not my fault," said Jesus. "It's a curse really. And they're impressionable young girls. I'm not interested. I still have some scruples. Anyhow, it's getting late, and I need to see a guy in town about a job. He's called Frazer. You can come too. He wants an extension built. Why I don't know 'cos he's already got loads of space. I think it's because his neighbour got a conservatory, and his wife wants to keep up with the Joneses. Anyhow, if we're lucky he'll give us dinner and we can stay over. He was asking about you last time he was here."

"Sounds like a plan," said Mary. "I presume he was asking about my previous experience."

"Something like that," said Jesus.

….

Dawn was breaking. Jesus crept down the street and quietly slid the window open. He climbed back into the guest bedroom of the House of Frazer and slid to the floor.

"Morning," whispered Mary.

Warning: Christians and people who are easily offended should not read this book

"Argh!" shouted Jesus in surprise. "How did you get in here?" he whispered, after composing himself. Mary was sat in a chair in a dark corner. She was fully dressed.

"I heard you slip out," said Mary. "My room is just next door and that window creeks. And I was just curious as to where you'd been all night. How are your scruples now? Did you leave them with Naomi? Or was it Deborah?"

Jesus looked Mary in the eye sheepishly.

"Or was it Eve?" asked Mary. "She certainly looked keen to get her hands on your scruples."

Jesus still looked sheepish.

"Go on," said Mary "You can tell me."

"Deborah," said Jesus. He twiddles his thumbs. "Deborah and…"

"OMG!" said Mary. "You bad, bad boy. I hope you weren't going to say Naomi."

Jesus looked at his feet. "I'm not proud of it," he said. "It just seemed like the right thing to do at the time. And you know, she caught me in the corridor outside her mum's room and…"

"What is wrong with you?" said Mary, in disbelief. "How can you live with yourself?"

"I just got caught up in the moment," said Jesus.

"And to think," said Mary. "I almost got burned for being a witch and you're the Devil incarnate. It's so unfair."

"Sorry," said Jesus.

"Oh that makes it all OK," said Mary. "You are a wicked, evil boy." She began hitting him with a cushion. Jesus hid his face in his hands.

"Yes," said Mary. "You should cover your face in shame. What am I going to do with you?" she stopped hitting him.

"So you just nipped in to see where I was?" asked Jesus.

"You aren't going to be any use to me for anything else," said Mary. "Are you? Come," she said, standing. "We can lie on the bed and then we can watch the sun rise soon. It will be romantic and there won't be any of that funny stuff, not for a few hours anyway, knowing what you men are like."

Mary led Jesus to the bed and lay next to him.

"If anyone catches us together, they will gossip like fishwives, and they are the worst gossips of all," said Jesus. "Our ears will burn."

"Have you been on Mars with your head in a bucket?" said Mary. "Don't you know anything? Everyone's already saying that I'm your floozy. I'm far too old not to be married

Warning: Christians and people who are easily offended should not read this book

and they take one look at me and they're consumed with jealousy, not just the women either. Of course, the irony is that you're bonking every other woman with two legs and a pulse except me. But let them talk. It makes them happy."

There was a pause.

"Mary," asked Jesus. "What was it like being a slave girl in the palace?"

"You get three square meals a day, although you have to watch your figure, and you have some chores but otherwise not too bad," replied Mary.

"No," said Jesus. "I meant the other stuff."

"Ah!" said Mary. "You mean all that degrading sexual stuff. Let's face it, slave girls aren't just there to look pretty. You've been wanting to ask that for a while, haven't you?"

"Yes," said Jesus. "But I'm shy. Does it upset you to talk about it?"

"I'd rather not," said Mary. "It feels as though those things happened to someone else."

There was an uncomfortable silence.

"Do you think badly of me for selling myself?" asked Mary.

"I don't think you had a choice," said Jesus.

"That's true," said Mary. "They say it's better to die in honour than live in sin. But they're wrong. You do what you need to do so you will survive. I was born into sin. It was normal: something we had to put up with. It didn't seem strange or wrong."

There was an uncomfortable silence.

"Do you want me to tell you about Herod the Great?" asked Mary.

"Sure," said Jesus.

"I was his favourite," said Mary. "Actually, he never laid a hand on me, unlike all those other pigs in the Palace. But he didn't like being alone, especially at night. You see he was always frightened. He didn't show it. But he was frightened of losing his wealth and losing his Kingdom, and in the end just losing his life. He told me about how he had to be strong and ruthless so people would fear him, especially the rich and powerful people, because that was the only way he could survive. But he was paranoid – everyone seemed to be plotting against him – and a lot of the time he was right. But when he got older, he used to talk to me. He said he was really frightened of what would happen in the afterlife when he had to account for his sins, and they were really really big sins, and how he could never make it right. He gave me my freedom long ago. But where was I going to go? It was his idea that I steal the gold and bribe the Temple Priest. Herod knew that guy was a rat. But he told me to hide the stolen gold at the Priest's Palace. That way, when Herod died and couldn't protect me, the High Priest wouldn't dare have me executed, or I would tell everyone where all the King's stolen

Warning: Christians and people who are easily offended should not read this book

loot was hidden. Herod made the Palace Guards promise to keep me in the Palace and protect me from assassins, even after he died, so the only way to get rid of me was to have me banished. He put it about that his curse would fall on any man who tried to harm me and, seeing as he died in agony, that had some credence. Of course, by having me banished it meant that I couldn't go back, and cause trouble and I would keep my head down and my mouth shut so as not to draw any unwanted attention. So in the end they had to let me go. The only thing Herod asked was that I prayed for him. He said I would be the only person on Earth who would ever mourn him. Herod the Great built loads of temples and palaces. But when he was dying, he told me all his wealth and power could not protect me or save him."

"What did he die of?" asked Jesus.

"He was poisoned," said Mary. "Probably on the orders of one of his sons. I know who did it, but it doesn't matter. It was written in the stars."

"Don't they have food tasters and guards all over the kitchens to stop kings being poisoned?" asked Jesus.

"Sure," said Mary. "But food tasters only taste food, not the golden goblets that kings use. You just line the cups with the poison if you can get to them."

"He sounded to be very lonely," said Jesus.

"Yes," said Mary. "It was very sad. I miss him a little. He was always good to me. One of the guards was a bit too friendly with me once and Herod had him flayed alive. No one bothered me after that. Look! The sun is rising. Let's go outside and watch."

They left the house and went to watch the sunrise.

Warning: Christians and people who are easily offended should not read this book

On the beach

"Have another go," said Mary, watching Jesus trying to moonwalk again. They were on the beach. It was morning. Jesus lost his balance and fell over.

"I think we're approaching this from the wrong angle," said Mary. "You're too worried about the steps."

She walked up to Jesus, who had brushed himself down. She took hold of him.

"Now I'm going to try and teach you to tango," she said, putting his hands into position. "Think of this as less of a dance and more like hard core pornography."

"Goodness me," said Jesus.

"Stop this," said Mary. "We're just pretending. And you've done much worse with one of those lusty widows."

"True," said Jesus. "But we had the lights off."

"Concentrate," said Mary. Moving his leg. "You have to make sure that you can't get a fag paper between our inner thighs."

"Be gentle with me," said Jesus. They took a few steps in hold.

"Yeah," said Mary. "I think we've found your idiom." She uncoupled from him.

"Show me your chest," she commanded.

"Show me your chest," said Jesus.

"OK," said Mary. Starting to pull up her dress.

"No," said Jesus, flustered. "I didn't mean that. Why do I need to show you my chest?"

"Because you have to shave it, of course," said Mary. "In fact, if you want to tango properly, we have to wax your chest hairs."

"We've got lots of wax," said Jesus. "To make candles and to help the wooden runners slide."

"Brilliant," said Mary. "This evening you can come round, and me and Grace will wax your chest. We'll enjoy doing that. It doesn't hurt a bit. Not in the slightest. In fact, you'll barely even notice we're doing it."

"I'm looking forward to that," said Jesus.

"You should," said Mary, grinning.

"It does sound a bit kinky," said Jesus.

Warning: Christians and people who are easily offended should not read this book

"We'll probably have to throw a bucket of cold water on you afterwards," said Mary. "To calm your inflamed passions. But it will be well worth it. With a bare chest you can do tango and all sorts of things: the paso doble, the rumba, even the salsa. It's all in the hips. And the chest of course. Which has to be waxed."

"Do you have to wax your chest?" asked Jesus.

"No dear," she replied. "I have to wax my legs. In fact, we could wax your legs as well if you want. I expect you'll be crying out for us to wax a bit more of you when we've finished with your chest."

"Sounds great," said Jesus.

"Do that trick with the pebbles," said Mary.

Jesus picked up a few pebbles. He took one in his hand, held it out and then made it disappear. It reappeared as he opened the other hand.

"That's a different pebble," said Mary.

"Of course, it is," said Jesus. "I didn't have time to get two that were the same."

"Ah," said Mary. "I see."

"Of course," said Jesus. "You were watching the wrong hand."

"Can you do it with coins?" asked Mary.

"Even easier," said Jesus. "But folk get a bit narky if you make their coins vanish."

"For the love of money is the root of all evil," quoted Mary.

"That's what they tell me," said Jesus. "But I've never had enough to know." They sat down.

"I heard about all these Pharaohs and Kings and Emperors who get murdered for their money," said Mary.

"It's a dangerous business being an Emperor or a King," said Jesus.

"It certainly is," said Mary.

"How much do you think it costs to have a King assassinated?" asked Jesus.

"They do say a king is worth his weight in gold," said Mary. "So an average king weighs about 200 pounds. That's about eight gold bars in old money. Thinking about it, I'm surprised any last longer than a few weeks. I'm in the wrong business."

"Would you assassinate me for eight gold bars?" Jesus asked.

"Hey, give me two bent nails and some loose change and brother, you are going down," replied Mary.

Warning: Christians and people who are easily offended should not read this book

"I'm worth more than that," said Jesus.

"Go on," said Mary. "You're the eldest son. So what are you worth, assuming you inherit all your father's vast Empire?"

"There's a dozen goats, and some tools, and an open front villa by the sea, rather compact and rustic I admit," said Jesus.

"If I were an assassin," said Mary. "Do you know what that would get you?"

"Go on," said Jesus.

Mary nipped him.

"Let that be a lesson to you," said Mary. "You can have that on account. But if it bruises you owe me another six goats. Enough of this diabolical scheming." She dragged him to his feet. "You, my boy, are about to learn the most demonic dance step that Satan, in his wisdom, has gifted to mankind. Performing this move in public has the death penalty in at least a dozen Kingdoms. Before the sun goes down today: you will shake your booty."

…

"What do you mean a hundred shekels?" shouted Peter.

"It says here," said the bailiff, pointing to some parchment. "One hundred shekels to be paid today or we can take possession of your stuff, especially the boat. Don't blame me. I'm just doing my job."

The bailiffs were two heavily looking men.

"I only borrowed fifty," said Peter. "And that isn't due for another six months."

"This says different," said the bailiff. "At least it would do if I could read it. Reading is not my strong point."

"Nor me," said the other bailiff. "But I'm good with numbers and that boat must be worth at least fifty shekels. Now, do you have any cash, or do we take the boat?"

"Of course, I don't have any cash," said Peter. "A couple of loads of fish and maybe some loose change but that's it. But I don't owe you guys shit."

"We aint' going anywhere until you pay," said the bailiff. "And we're going to have to search the house and make an inventory of your stuff. Although that probably won't add up to more than five shekels total. I mean the building itself ain't worth more than two bits. Your boat is the only asset worth a damn."

"Show me that agreement," said Mary. She was standing next to Jesus and watching the fun. They were all standing around the boat which had been pulled up on the beach.

Warning: Christians and people who are easily offended should not read this book

"Here ya go darlin," said the bailiff, smiling. "Them squiggles. That's called writing. And it says he has to pay his debt today or else. But seeing as none of us can read you'll just have to take our word for it."

"It says here," said Mary, reading the parchment. "The agreement made this day, in the Most Holy Temple of Jerusalem, between Shylock the Damned, and Mark, son of Philip, fisherman of Nazareth, for the loan of thirty shekels to be paid back to afore mentioned Shylock the Damned within a year starting 1 August, sixteenth year of the Reign of Emperor Tiberius. May his Empire last a thousand year as the Gods worship and protect him yardy yardy yah."

"You evil witch," said the Bailiff. "Like you can read."

"If you don't believe me, summon the magistrate," said Mary. "He'll tell you the same thing. You boys have the wrong man. Mark the fisherman is two miles up the coast. And the debt ain't due for another four months."

"I ain't buying it," said the Bailiff. "This guy here still owes us one hundred shekels today."

"Tell that to the judge," said Mary.

"The bottom line is you ain't moving anything," said Jesus. He stood next to Peter as his brother Paul stood by them.

"Now clear off to that dragon's den you came from and bring the right form next time," said Mary.

The bailiffs whispered to each other.

"My associate here is going off to the nearest town to bring along the magistrate," said the bailiff, as his colleague set off, cursing. "Then we'll see who is right and who is wrong. And don't be surprised if the magistrate reads the riot act as well as that bloody form. Oh yes. They'll be big trouble. Them magistrates don't like having their time wasted. Especially on a Saturday when the football is on. And don't say I didn't warn you. Now I'm going to have to wait here because we know your sort. You'll be changing the registration on that boat the moment our back is turned. Or sailing off into the sunset. So the boat stays here on the beach with me."

"We're staying here with it," said Peter.

"That's good," said the bailiff sitting on a rock.

"Yes, it is," said Peter, climbing on the fishing boat.

"Then there's no problem," said the bailiff.

"No there isn't," said Peter.

"Then that's good," said the bailiff.

"Yes, it is," said Peter. "No problem at all."

Warning: Christians and people who are easily offended should not read this book

"None whatsoever," said the bailiff.

There was a pause in the standoff as both parties tried to think of ways to outdo the other with more witty put-downs.

"Would you like a drink?" Paul asked the bailiff.

"Yes please," said the bailiff. "That would be very kind of you."

Paul set off to the house.

Jesus and Mary sidled up to Peter on the boat.

"The other guys have left already so they can set up the show for tomorrow," said Jesus.

"You better get going," said Peter. "It's miles. You won't be able to get there if you don't leave today."

"We can't just leave you here," said Jesus. "You need the extra muscle when that guy gets back with his mates."

"He'll bring a magistrate as well," said Mary. "To keep things nice and legal. But he's brought the wrong form."

"I didn't know you could read," said Jesus to Mary.

"You never asked," replied Mary.

"That form is in Greek," said Jesus. "What else can you read?"

"Hebrew," said Mary. "And a bit of Latin, that's all the rage now, and Persian on a good day. Sanskrit and some Chinese but only the Shan and Zhou dialects. My Quinn is a bit ropey. And Egyptian of course – that's the best one. You can do all those spells and curses in Egyptian. It's a bit heavy going though. What with having to write on the stone slabs with hammers and chisels."

"You are really amazing," said Jesus, impressed.

"Oh you," said Mary, grinning. "I'm blushing now."

"I can barely read the time," said Jesus.

"I was thinking," said Peter. "We can actually cut out a few hours in the journey if we sail across the lake. That way we'll easily be in time for the show tomorrow and the other boys will already be there."

"Let's see what happens," said Jesus. "You may not even have a boat by this evening."

…

A few hours later.

Warning: Christians and people who are easily offended should not read this book

"Let me see," demanded the Roman centurion.

"We were waiting for the magistrate, your honour," said the bailiff. They were all standing by Peter's boat.

"Well he ain't here," said the Centurion. "Because he's watching the footie. And he can't read Greek for shit anyway. Show me the form."

The bailiff handed the Centurion the agreement.

"And this is Mark, son of Philip?" asked the Centurion.

"No," admitted the bailiff, sheepishly. "This is Peter, brother of Paul."

"And it's August now?" said the Centurion. "And here's me and the entire civilised world thinking it's March." He threw the agreement back at the bailiff. "Go on clear off, you got the wrong form," he pronounced.

"Any chance of setting up a monthly repayment plan?" said one of the bailiffs hopefully as they skulked off.

"Sorry about this, Sir, Madam," said the Centurion as he left. "We just can't get the staff."

"Sorted!" said Jesus.

Peter looked at the sky.

"I don't like the look of those clouds," said Peter.

"Me neither," said Paul.

"Come on," said Mary. "Where's your sense of adventure?"

"Yeah," said Jesus. "Get the wind behind your sales and we'll be over the other side in a jiffy. When the boys arrive, we'll already be waiting."

"What do you think?" Peter asked Paul.

"I wouldn't," said Paul.

"I'm going," said Mary, climbing into the boat and saluting. "Set the main brace and weigh the anchor. Avast me hearties. Trim the sail and catch the fair wind while she blows, ye scurvy dogs."

"What is she talking about?" Peter asked Paul.

"I think she just wants us to push the boat off the beach," replied Paul.

…

Warning: Christians and people who are easily offended should not read this book

Jesus, Mary and Peter were sailing across the Sea of Galilea. They were moving quite quickly. The wind was blowing a bit too fiercely for Peter's liking and the waves were looking threatening.

Peter looked worried. "I begin to think this was not my best idea," he said as he manned the rudder. "We'll make for shore as fast as we can. But we'll be out for at least another hour. Just pray that the storm doesn't blow up."

"Aye Aye, Captain Pete," said Mary. She was on the prow of the boat enjoying herself hugely.

"Do we have to do anything?" asked Jesus.

"There isn't much we can do," said Peter.

"I like the cut of your jib," added Mary. "Hey Jesus, come behind me. I want to lean over the front."

"It's called the prow," said Jesus.

"I want you to stop me falling in while I take the air," said Mary. "It'll give my hair a blow dry."

Jesus stood behind Mary and held her waist while she leaned off the bow. Her hair blew in the wind, which was becoming a gale. Suddenly a big wave came over the bow and soaked them all.

"Empty the fish out of those buckets and use them to bail the water," said Peter. "I'm going to take the sail in."

Jesus and Mary began bailing water half-heartedly. Peter was beginning to panic. He quickly collapsed the sale and took down the mast.

"Hold this," he told Mary, handing her part of the sail. "I'm going to try and cover the boat with the sail to keep the waves from sinking us. I'll tie it to the cleats. You just hold that corner. Jesus, you just keep bailing."

Peter managed to tie the sail to cover part of the boat. However, things were becoming desperate. The boat bobbed on the waves and the rain began to come down in sheets. A storm had blown up and rumbles of thunder became audible.

"I've never seen the weather get this bad so quickly," said Peter as he began to bail along with Jesus.

"Isn't it terrific," shouted Mary. "We three fighting the elements. Neptune, I curse thee!"

"We're in enough trouble already," said Peter. "Without you bringing the wrath of the sea God on us."

Warning: Christians and people who are easily offended should not read this book

"Actually, Neptune doesn't exist," said Jesus. "Small point but there is only one true God. Those others are all false Roman Gods. I wouldn't normally mention it, but it seems unusually relevant now."

"Ask whichever God you want to save our asses," shouted Peter. "And bail faster."

They continued to bail as bolts of lightning flashed in the skies above them. The boat was thrown back and forth between huge waves as the torrential rain came down.

A few minutes later Peter shouted. "If we capsize, hold onto the boat and grab onto anything that floats. I'm going to lash you two together, so you don't get washed away." He staggered over with a rope. They were crouching beneath the sail trying to hold it taught and prevent the waves flooding the vessel.

"What about you?" shouted Jesus.

"I got you into this," shouted Peter. "If Poseidon needs a sacrifice, he can take me."

Mary looked at Jesus and laughed.

"Ye of little faith," she shouted. "Come death and face me. Feel my wroth."

Jesus prayed. Mary held him and laughed.

After a terrible hour the storm began to subside. The three continued to bail the water from the boat. Fortunately, the wind blew them ashore.

Mary and Jesus jumped ashore and collapsed on the beach as Peter took a line and began to drag the boat up the steep shale.

"The boat is flooded," said Peter. "We won't be able to drag it far up this beach, and the tide is still coming in."

He walked over to where Jesus and Mary were lying, dripping wet. "I'm going to the village down the coast. I can bring some guys back to help fix the boat. The timbers are strained and it's leaking like hell. You two stay here and stop it floating off when the tide comes up. You can set a fire over there and get dry. There's still some fish in the boat."

"Are you OK?" asked Jesus.

"I'm a goddamned long way from being OK," said Peter, shaking visibly. "I almost got you drowned on account of my pride and stupidity. I need some time alone. I'll be back by midnight. If you're in a praying mood give thanks. It's a miracle we're still alive."

Peter set off, still shaking.

"It would have been easier if you could actually walk on water," said Mary.

"Damn straight," said Jesus. "But I wasn't worried."

Warning: Christians and people who are easily offended should not read this book

"No?" asked Mary.

"No way," said Jesus. "You're my guardian angel. Nothing bad is going to happen while I'm with you."

"That's kind of you," Mary replied. "I just hope I can justify your faith."

...

Jesus and Mary were sat on the beach soon afterward. They had tied the boat down and they had made a fire. They were using the boat sails as shelter. Mary stripped off most of her soaked clothes to lay them by the fire to dry.

"Don't be shy," she told Jesus, as she sat down. "You can take off your things and dry them. I've seen it all before."

Jesus paused, then took his tunic off to dry. They had cooked some fish and were eating it. Mary finished. She noticed that Jesus was glancing over occasionally.

"Well," she began. "Are you just going to look or are you coming over here to do something about it?"

"I hadn't realised I was staring," said Jesus, awkwardly.

"You weren't staring," said Mary. "But you keep looking over. Don't worry. I'm used to it. Believe me."

"Do you want me to come over there?" said Jesus.

"It's entirely up to you honey," said Mary. "Actually, it's quite nice that you give me a choice."

"I'd feel a bit better if you came over to me," said Jesus. He pulled the sail over to make a blanket. "Only if you want to. Affirmative consent and all that."

Mary smiled. She got up, walked over, and lay next to Jesus under the sail cloth.

"It's cold," she said. "You can put your arms around me." Jesus did as instructed.

There was an awkward silence.

"Ok," said Mary. "Let's get it into the open. Are you going to do it?"

"You mean 'it'?" said Jesus.

"Yes 'it'," replied Mary. "We may as well get it done with, so you don't pester me for the next five hours."

"Do you want to?" asked Jesus.

"It's up to you," replied Mary.

Warning: Christians and people who are easily offended should not read this book

"That's a bit of a turn off," said Jesus.

"Sorry," said Mary. "I didn't mean to kill the romance. Hey, you're not gay are you? I mean, I don't mind if you are. We could talk about soft furnishings and fashion and things."

"No," said Jesus. "I'm not gay you homophobic Nazi. It's just…"

"Just what?" asked Mary.

"You and me, we work together," said Jesus.

"It's a miracle!" announced Mary. "A guy who won't shag his co-worker because it might damage their business relationship. This must be the first time in history."

"It's not just that," said Jesus. "I get the feeling that sex for you is like a tedious chore – like gutting fish or cleaning the toilet. And, more seriously, if we did 'it', then things would probably get weird."

"Weird?" asked Mary.

"Yeah," said Jesus. "Things get weird – you know if you score and don't get married but have to see each other for work and things. It's awkward. You know: can we still see other people and how soon and all that? Weird!"

"What do you suggest?" asked Mary.

"Let's make a deal," said Jesus. "Let's just keep everything above the equator."

Mary laughed. "Ok," she said. "Above the equator. Let's shake on it."

"Deal!" said Jesus. Mary rolled over so they were facing each other, and they shook hands.

"You're so cute," said Mary.

There was another slightly less awkward silence.

"You can kiss me if you want," said Mary.

"Do you want me to kiss you?" asked Jesus, embarrassed.

Mary grabbed his face in both her hands and kissed him on the lips for a long time. Jesus was rather overwhelmed.

Mary paused and looked into his face. She smiled. "How's your equator now?" she asked.

Warning: Christians and people who are easily offended should not read this book

Record

The show had just finished. An attractive and rather wealthy-looking younger woman wandered over to speak to Jesus. Jesus was chatting with Mary.

"You have a long way to go home," said the young woman. "The weather looks foul. Come and stay at my house. You can have dinner there. We have lots of space."

"We don't want to be a burden," said Jesus. "Miss…"

"Mrs," said the woman. "Although I'm widowed. I married a rich man, but he was very old. I would highly recommend it. The best career move I could possibly have made. Is this your wife?"

"No," said Mary. "We're just friends."

"You're welcome to come as well," said the young woman. "The more the merrier."

"That's very kind of you," said Mary. "We accept." Jesus looked a little awkward but said nothing.

…

"Thanks for a lovely evening," said the young lady as she escorted Mary and Jesus to their separate rooms. She ushered Jesus into one and opened the door for Mary. "The maid is just there at the end of the corridor if you want anything," said the young woman, pointing to a door that had been left conspicuously open. A maid servant could be seen busying herself with domestic chores in the kitchen. Mary shook the hand of the young lady and went into her room. As soon as she had entered she heard her own bedroom door being closed firmly behind her.

A couple of hours later, Mary was lying awake on the bed. She heard a scratching at the window. The scratching became a tapping. Then she heard a whisper calling her name. She got up and opened the window. Jesus was crouching outside. "Shhhh!" he whispered. "Come on, let's get out of here."

"Why?" asked Mary.

"Don't argue," said Jesus. "I'll explain on the way."

"Here we go again," said Mary. She hauled herself out of the window.

"We're going back to the tavern aren't we," said Mary. "That landlady who you 'converted' after doing her a few favours?"

"Could we?" asked Jesus.

"If you insist," said Mary. "I thought you were safely locked up in your bedroom, alone. Did you get lost again?"

Warning: Christians and people who are easily offended should not read this book

"Not this time," said Jesus. "The mistress of the house came by and found me. And it all got a bit awkward, so I did a runner when her back was turned."

"Did her husband rise from the dead?" asked Mary.

"Nah," said Jesus.

"She was hot for your cock," said Mary. "Did you, you know, do 'it'?"

"That's not the sort of question a gentleman answers," said Jesus.

"I don't own you," said Mary. "It's OK if you did."

"Do you really mean that?" said Jesus.

"Not really," said Mary, pausing. "In fact, if you even so much as look at another woman again I'll kill both of you and burn the bodies."

"That's fair," said Jesus. "Let's just say I was a bit of a disappointment to the lady of the house."

There was an uncomfortable silence as they walked briskly through the dark street.

"It's got weird hasn't it?" said Mary.

"Yeah," replied Jesus.

"How long did that take?" asked Mary.

"Twelve hours," said Jesus.

"That's got to be some sort of record," said Mary. "What are we going to do now? You know about 'us'? Do you want me to move out?"

"Definitely not," said Jesus. "I'd just have to tag along, and it would be even weirder."

"What would happen if your mum caught us together, in the biblical sense?" said Mary.

"She'd turn you out and you would be hounded out of the village as a harlot," said Jesus.

"We can't very well get married," said Mary. "Your mum thinks I'm a black whore."

"You said that, not me," said Jesus. "I want to be very clear about that. And you are not a whore."

"That's nice of you to say so," said Mary. She thought for a while. "We could elope?"

"Yeah," said Jesus. "But I need tools and a workshop. And I'm not a very good carpenter. Everything I make wobbles except boats. And they usually sink."

"I can see that would be a problem," said Mary. "I know. Let's ask your lady friend who runs the inn. We're almost there anyway."

Warning: Christians and people who are easily offended should not read this book

…

"Hello to you again," said the landlady as she ushered Jesus and Mary into the tavern. She waved for them to sit down.

"So you're back, Jesus," said the landlady. "With your friend with benefits. What happened?"

"I had to make a quick exit," said Jesus. "The lady of the household was less than impressed with me."

"There's a surprise," said the landlady. "And no doubt our friend with benefits here is the cause."

"How did you know?" asked Mary, as the landlady began handing round some drinks.

"Come on girl," said the landlady. "He was dead in the water the moment you met him. I could see that from the way he looked at you. It's quite romantic really. Just like me and my first husband."

"What happened to your first husband?" asked Jesus.

"My second husband happened," said the landlady, laughing. "Ah young love."

"Can you help us?" asked Mary. "We're in a bit of a fix."

"Let me guess," said the landlady. "You can't marry him because you have baggage, you can't live together because his mum will turn you out, and you can't leave him because he will follow you to the ends of the Earth and you'll both starve on the way."

"That about sums it up," said Jesus. "You are very wise."

"I've been round the block a few times already," said the landlady. "Now, you have three options. Firstly suicide."

"Fair comment but maybe a little extreme," said Mary. "Can we park that idea for a while?"

"Suit yourself," said the landlady. "Second, you can kill everyone else."

"Let's put that on the reserve list as well," said Jesus. "What's option three?"

"You tell me," said the landlady. "I've done two already. What do you think I am? Some sort of agony aunt? It's your turn now."

"That didn't help," said Jesus.

"Love is Hell," said the landlady. "Why not just go to bed and hope it all sorts itself out. Perhaps one of you will die in your sleep. Anyway, I'm bushed. Fortunately, we have a couple of spare beds. You decide whether you need one or two. Hey," she said to Mary as she stood to leave the room, "You tamed the demon. Good work!"

Warning: Christians and people who are easily offended should not read this book

Part 2 The Conversion

Jesus was having supper with Mary at Peter's house. There was a knock at the door and Judas let himself in followed by a man.

"Hi, guys," said Judas, sitting down. "This is my new friend, Lazarus. He has a problem."

"Don't they all," replied Mary.

"Go on," said Judas, encouraging Lazarus. "Let it out. You're amongst friends. No one will judge you here."

"This sounds ominous," said Peter.

"OK," said Lazarus, reluctantly. "As you may know my father is a wealthy man. But he lives in Cyprus."

"He's a tax exile," explained Judas.

"This is all my wife's fault," continued Lazarus.

"Isn't it always," added Mary.

"She insists on living above her means, I mean our means," continued Lazarus. "Fancy tapestries, bigger villa, nice clothes. More shoes than you can wave a stick at. You know the deal. Now my dad's loaded. But he's a real Spartan and wouldn't give us a penny. 'What's the point in being heir to a fortune if ya can't get the latest chariot,' says my wife. 'Why can't I have nice things like all the centurion's wives,' she says. 'I may as well go and be concubine.' Anyhow, we kept going to this shylock. A few shekels here. A few there. And before you know it the bailiffs turn up. So we sends them away with a couple of goblets and a promissory note to pay the balance at the end of the month. But the shylock kept coming back. You know what they're like. Real hard asses. He wants his pound of flesh or we're out on the street. So we has this great idea. If I died then maybe the shylock would lay off, or my dad would stump up the cash so my widow wouldn't be destitute. Then she can get the cash, sell up, and we can meet up in Damascus and no one will be any the wiser."

"So you faked your own death?" asked Peter.

"Basically yes," admitted Lazarus.

"I do not believe this," added Mary. Jesus had his head in his hands by this point.

"Unfortunately, the shylock wasn't having it," continued Lazarus. "He kept coming back. Wanted a certificate and stuff. So eventually we had to have a funeral."

"Didn't the Priest say anything," asked Mary.

"Fifty shekels, no questions asked," said Lazarus. "We could even rent a budget crypt. Apparently, no one wanted it because dogs kept digging inside."

Warning: Christians and people who are easily offended should not read this book

"Oh no," said Peter. "I won't be able to get that image out of my mind for weeks."

"So we had a small funeral, immediate family only," said Lazarus. "Basically, my wife and a few servants. It was quite a nice 'do really. It takes at least four days to get here from Cyprus, you know what the ferries are like, so by the day my dad was going to get here everything would be all sorted. And I could creep out of the crypt the way the dogs had burrowed in with no one any the wiser."

"What went wrong?" asked Jesus.

"He died, ungrateful old swine," said Lazarus.

"So now, Lazarus has inherited a fortune," said Judas, eyes gleaming. "But he can't collect it."

"What about your wife?" asked Mary.

"They never really got on," said Lazarus. "My dad said she was a gold digger. So she got written out of the will."

"You see our problem," said Judas. "Mr Lazarus is a millionaire. But the problem is he's been dead for four days. So what I was thinking is…"

"I do not believe this," said Mary.

"Come on," said Judas. "There's worse things."

"Like what?" asked Jesus.

Judas thought for a while. "I can't think of anything right now," he admitted. "But give me time."

"No!" said Jesus.

"Come on man," said Judas. "We owe those shylocks a load of cash as well. Mr Lazarus here can pay that off. And it will be great publicity. We could do it after the act tomorrow."

"No!" said Jesus.

"Hey boys," said Lazarus. "I'm in a real fix here. As it stands, I got nothing. Only the clothes I'm standing up in."

"Can't your wife help?" asked Mary.

"She actually sold the villa and ran off with one of the servants while I was digging my way out," said Lazarus.

"Hallelujah!" said Mary. "There is a God after all."

"Come on," said Judas. "Say you'll think about it?"

Warning: Christians and people who are easily offended should not read this book

Jesus sighed.

"I'm begging you," said Lazarus.

Jesus put his head in his hands and thought.

"What excuse do we have to open the tomb?" he asked. "They are sealed up for a reason."

"I got this," said Judas. "I had a dream. A dream that Lazarus' soul was trapped in the tomb and needed to be released. The priest who conducted the blessing was disbarred for taking bribes and Lazarus' body must be blessed again by a holy man to sanctify his tortured soul."

"Has that priest been taking bribes?" asked Mary.

"Come on!" said Judas. "Do bears shit in the woods?"

"I see your point," said Mary.

Jesus looked thoughtful once more.

"Look," argued Judas. "If we do this then Lazarus gets his inheritance, which is what his father would have wanted, the punters have a story they can tell their grandchildren, and we get some spending money and publicity that you couldn't buy for a ton of gold. It's a win: win situation. We would be stupid not to!"

Jesus looked thoughtful once more.

"I'm not rolling the stone," he said eventually.

"Great," said Judas. "We'll roll the stone. I've got lots of big guys to help there. You just get into the crypt quick. Wave your wand and we'll do the rest."

"This is sacrilege," said Peter.

"Sacrilege pays the bills," said Judas. "See ya tomorrow. Come Lazarus. Let us discuss my agent's fee. It's usually ten percent. But as this is a rush job, and we have to be so very discreet I may need a little more. Stuff my mouth with gold as it were."

…

Jesus was kneeling by a disabled child entertaining him with some vanishing pebbles. Everyone was getting bored. Peter and the boys were digging and hammering and desperately trying to roll the boulder to open Lazarus' crept.

"It just won't budge," said Judas, in desperation as he walked past with a spade.

"Where are you going with that spade," asked Mary.

"The stone might be jammed on the inside," said Judas. "I'm just going to see if, you know, our man on the inside can help. I'll pass him this shovel through the tunnel."

Warning: Christians and people who are easily offended should not read this book

"This just gets worse and worse," said Mary to Jesus. "You look hungry," she said to Jesus. She handed him a boiled egg from her basket. "Here's one for you friend," she said. Giving Jesus two eggs. Jesus took one and showed it to the child who reached out. He did a trick and the egg vanished. He moved his hand again and it reappeared although it had changed to a brown egg now. The child laughed and took the coloured egg.

"Hurrah!" Peter shouted. Everyone began to cheer as the stone, which sealed the crypt, began to move.

Judas came dashing back. "Quick," he said to Jesus. "You gotta be first in there. Me and the boys will fall on our knees in the entrance as soon as you get inside and stop any troublemakers getting in."

Jesus stood up reluctantly. Judas pushed him. "Hurry up," said Judas. "A rolling stone and all that…"

The stone had just rolled open sufficiently for a man to squeeze past when Jesus reached the entrance to the tomb. "Coming through!" shouted Judas pushing his way through the crowd in front of him. "Do your stuff," he whispered to Jesus as soon as they reached the entrance.

"Let us pray," shouted Judas as soon as he could push Jesus inside the tomb. Judas knelt and began praying and wailing while he blocked the entrance. Everyone else reluctantly had to follow suit although many were trying to peer past him into the tomb.

"It's a miracle," said Judas a few seconds later as Lazarus hopped out, wrapped up like a mummy.

Everyone gasped and those who were still standing fell on their knees. Judas quickly began to unwrap Lazarus.

Jesus was still inside the tomb. Mary went in.

Jesus was standing shaking his head.

"That was low," he said, walking to the entrance.

"I know," said Mary. "But Judas does have a point. It's great publicity. And it gets the guy out of a fix."

"Where is he anyway?" asked Jesus. He and Mary stood in the entrance of the tomb.

"There he is!" exclaimed Jesus pointing towards Judas.

"The snake," he added. "He's trying to collect money from the crowd."

"It just gets worse and worse," said Mary. "What shall we do?"

Jesus thought for a second. Suddenly he picked up a cane.

Warning: Christians and people who are easily offended should not read this book

"Behold!" he shouted. "A demon! That man. He is possessed by demons." He pointed towards Judas, who startled and began looking round.

"Stand aside," said Jesus. "I will purify him. I will beat the evil out of him." Jesus chased Judas around the crowd with the cane.

A few seconds later Peter led Lazarus away with the crowd following and cheering.

Mary caught up with Jesus a minute later. Jesus was handling a bag of coins.

"Look how much this swine has swindled from the crowd," he said. "And that's not including the share he has coming from Lazarus."

"What shall we do?" asked Mary. Just then they passed the disabled child that Jesus had been entertaining. He was being carried by his father and his mother was following.

"For you," said Jesus, handing the mother the purse. The mother beamed in surprise.

"That was very kind of you," said Mary.

"What choice did we have?" asked Jesus. "We would be cursed for sure if we'd have kept it. That was dirty money."

"Damn straight," replied Mary.

Judas caught up with them.

"Where's the money?" asked Judas.

"Don't worry," said Jesus. "I've given it to a good cause."

"Bah," said Judas. "You have no idea how many overheads I have as your agent."

"Agent of chaos, more like," replied Jesus. "I'm off. The air is bad enough round here as it is. Get thee behind me Satan."

Jesus strode off down the hill with the crowd.

"What's he got that I haven't?" Judas asked Mary.

"You mean besides charm, charisma, good looks, and sex appeal of biblical proportions?" replied Mary.

"Biblical?" asked Judas.

"Biblical!" confirmed Mary.

"I must have some redeeming qualities," protested Judas.

"No," replied Mary. "You are more weasel than man."

Warning: Christians and people who are easily offended should not read this book

"That's not so bad," retorted Judas. "Weaselling out of things is what separates us from the animals…except the weasel."

"Listen, Judas," added Mary. "Jesus loves you, but everyone else thinks you're a total asshole."

…

That evening, back at his parent's house, Jesus seemed preoccupied. He had taken himself into the workshop and was pottering around aimlessly.

"What's wrong?" asked Mary. They were alone.

"I was just thinking," replied Jesus. "Is this it? You know. Is this the extent of our lives? Why are we here? What is our purpose?"

"That would be an ecumenical matter," replied Mary.

"I can't explain it either," said Jesus. "I just think there is more to life than this."

"Are you feeling guilty about that Lazarus business?" asked Mary.

"Surprisingly not," said Jesus. "We gave the money to the mother of that poor child. I was doing tricks for him, and he was so happy. And yet he couldn't speak, and he can't even dress himself. And we have everything you and I. And yet we're dissatisfied. There must be more to life."

"That's pretty heavy stuff," said Mary. "Why not ask one of the priests at the temple."

"I did," replied Jesus. "He said he can cure whatever ailed me just by letting him make a sacrifice. A bull for 100 shekels. A goat for 20 shekels. And doves are only 5 shekels: two for the price of one at the moment."

"That's not very helpful," said Mary.

"It was for him," replied Jesus. "Do you know how many doves they have in that temple? And do you know what happens to the cash they raise?"

"Tell me," said Mary.

"They give it to those shylocks, so they lend it back to us with interest," replied Jesus. "Ritual sacrifice. The gift that keeps on giving. No wonder all those travelling preachers and hermits get an audience. At least they believe in something besides filling their stomachs and lining their own pockets."

"Shame!" replied Mary.

"Sorry to bum you out," replied Jesus.

"That's ok," she replied. "You seem to be having an existential crisis."

Warning: Christians and people who are easily offended should not read this book

"No," said Jesus. "I'm just contemplating the meaning of life."

Mary went back into the big house with Mary Mother of Jesus and Joseph.

"How's the boy?" asked Mary, Mother of Jesus.

"It's all a bit deep," said Mary. "He's contemplating the meaning of life."

"Maybe he can contemplate doing some real work as well," added Joseph.

"Perhaps he wants to move out and fly the nest?" suggested Mary, Mother of Jesus.

"I'll help him pack," added Joseph.

"You are no help at all," said Mary, Mother of Jesus. "Go on. Shoo!" she herded Joseph out of the room.

"You know, Jesus has a thing for you," continued Mary, Mother of Jesus. "I know he can be a bit of a handful at times and he's a bit too popular with the ladies. But you're special. He can confide in you."

"I've noticed," said Mary, thoughtfully.

"I hear there is some hell-raising preacher coming tomorrow," said Mary, Mother of Jesus. "He's a real troublemaker. Why don't you two go along. That'll cheer him up. I hear this guy really sticks it to The Man. King Herod told him to stop trashing the priests and the guy done said that he should never have run off from his first wife and was gon' marry his own sister-in-law. It's what everyone is thinking but to say it out-loud. I ain't never heard of a man with such gall. He must have lost his head."

"Sounds like fun," said Mary.

"You get a good night's rest and have fun tomorrow," replied Mary, Mother of Jesus. "It will be a nice day out for you both."

…

Mary and Jesus were walking along the next day. Jesus was still preoccupied. They came to the river. There was a crowd of people. A man was standing in the water. A queue had formed in front of him, and he was submerging them in the water and baptising them to loud cheers from the crowd.

"There he is," said Mary. "They call him John."

"Let's get closer so we can hear," replied Jesus, pushing through the crowd.

"I bring wonderful news from God," shouted John the Baptist. "Is your world in turmoil? Do you want to find hope? Does life have no meaning? You can find this and answer all your questions. Come to me. Give your life to God. Let me join you in his fellowship. I will wash

Warning: Christians and people who are easily offended should not read this book

away your sins and you will be born again. You can find true happiness. Your life can have meaning again."

"He sounds to be right up your street," said Mary, sarcastically. "Let's ask him about Herod's wife when he does a Q and A." She looked at Jesus, who seemed preoccupied with the preacher.

John began preaching: "True believers come forth and receive the grace of God. Let me wash away all your sins – you will be forgiven instantly. Receive the peace and joy in your heart that no man can take away. Give your life to God so that you can never be alone – He will show you how to resist all the sins and temptations on the earth. Never worry again about your Earthly and material needs for He will meet all your wants. Your life will have meaning – through God you will discover that your mission is to bring joy and blessings to the people around you. You can be a light to those around you, rather than being dragged down by the sins of our time. You will conquer death itself – at the end of your Earthly life you will enter the Kingdom of Heaven and live there with God and all the Angels in bliss for all eternity."

Mary was bored. She began looking round.

"Who else will come forward?" John asked the crowd. "Who else amongst you seeks the Kingdom of Heaven."

"Over here," shouted Jesus. Mary looked at him with a start. Jesus strode forward to John. Jesus knelt and John immersed him in the water.

"We're in trouble now," said Mary to herself as John spoke inaudible words over Jesus and the crowd cheered.

Jesus beamed as he strode out of the water.

"Look at you," said Mary. "Soaked to the skin. You'll catch your death."

"It matters not," said Jesus. "For I will enter the Kingdom of Heaven. I will bring joy and blessings to the people around like a beacon of light. From this moment on, I will spend my life spreading the word of God."

"Come on," said Mary. "Don't get carried away."

"But Mary," argued Jesus. "The Spirit of the Lord is upon me, because he hath anointed me to preach the gospel to the poor; he hath sent me to heal the broken-hearted, to preach deliverance to the captives, and recovering of sight to the blind, to set at liberty them that are bruised. To preach the word of the Lord."

"Hell Fire," said Mary. "Why couldn't we just have gone to a barbeque!"

...

"He seems very preoccupied," said Mary Mother of Jesus the next day.

Warning: Christians and people who are easily offended should not read this book

"Leave him be," said Joseph. "He's in the workshop doing a proper day's work for a change."

"What happened?" Mary Mother of Jesus asked Mary.

"It's that preacher guy, John the Baptist," said Mary. "Filled his head with all that 'I am the light stuff'."

"They do that," replied Mary, Mother of Jesus. "It's probably just a phase. He'll get over it."

"As long as he finishes that table first," said Joseph. "It's a rush job you know."

…

A few days later Joseph the Younger burst into the kitchen where Mary, Mary Mother of Jesus and Joseph the Elder were sitting.

"What's happened to Jesus?" demanded Joseph the Younger. "He's no fun anymore. Sitting around praying and stuff. He even says smiling is sinful because it makes you look like a baboon. How he goes to the toilet I have no idea. He's such a pussy!"

"Watch your mouth boy," said Joseph the Elder, sternly. "That's your brother you're talking about."

"I have to admit, he is a bit wet," said Mary. "I preferred the old Jesus."

"Now, Joseph," said Mary Mother of Jesus to her son. "Sometimes people go through a phase of reflecting on what they have achieved and where they are going with their life, and they may seem distant and distracted."

"That's called the menopause and it just proves he's a pussy," said Joseph the Younger. "Anyway, I'm going to hang out with Judas. He may be an asshole but at least he's not a pussy."

"Rats!" said Joseph the Elder. "Mary, you were there when that wizard baptised Jesus. How long exactly did they hold his head underwater?"

"Not long enough to get brain damage," replied Mary.

"It's just a phase he's going through," said Mary, Mother of Jesus.

"He's busy composing his first sermon for this Sabbath," said Mary. "He's gone all biblical. Let's see what happens."

The next Sabbath in the preaching field the various motley crew of hermits and shamen were pontificating with small crowds of villagers moving between them. Jesus had a modestly large audience, mainly consisting of women.

Jesus began: "Beware of the priests, who love to go in long expensive clothing, and delight in salutations in the marketplaces, and in the best seats in the synagogues, and in the uppermost

Warning: Christians and people who are easily offended should not read this book

rooms at feasts where they gorge themselves. Beware of the priests who lay great fees and devour widows' houses, and for a pretence make long prayers: they shall receive great damnation."

An overweight temple priest was listening. He scowled and waddled off.

Jesus continued: "Thou knowest the commandments; Do not commit adultery, Do not kill, Do not steal, Do not bear false witness, Defraud not, Honour thy father and mother…"

Two young men were watching. One of them heckled: "Yeah, Yeah, Yeah. We've heard all this before. Tell us something new."

"Come on Harvey," said his friend. "We're only here to look at the chicks."

"Brother," Jesus spoke to Harvey. "Do not covet thy neighbour's wife, nor his ox, nor his ass."

"What did you say about his ass?" shouted Harvey.

"What I mean is," said Jesus flustered. "Do not desire your neighbour's ass…"

"Are you saying I'm gay?" asked Harvey.

"No, no," said Jesus. "Not that I would make judgement on you, even if you were."

"I don't know what passes for good manners in Gomorrah, but we don't take kindly to that sort of thing round here," shouted Harvey.

"Let it go," said Harvey's friend.

"He keeps saying I covet my neighbour's ass," argued Harvey.

"My neighbour doesn't have an ass," replied his friend.

"What does he sit on?" asked Harvey.

"A chair," said the friend.

"What's going on 'ere?" interrupted a Roman officer, followed by the fat temple priest and a few soldiers.

"It's him, your honour," shouted Harvey pointing at Jesus. "He called me a Somodite!"

"Come on you," commanded the Roman officer, approaching Jesus threateningly. "We've had some complaints. You ain't welcome here no more. Clear off!"

Jesus chose discretion above valour and scuttled away as the soldiers approached.

…

Warning: Christians and people who are easily offended should not read this book

The next morning Jesus appeared in the kitchen where Mary, Mary Mother of Jesus, And Joseph the Father and Son were sitting.

"Mother, Father," announced Jesus. "I have come to a decision. I cannot preach the Word of the Lord for I am yet unworthy."

"Bloody Hell, son, speak English," said Joseph the Elder.

"I must go into the desert and purify myself," said Jesus. "For I am unworthy. Outwardly I appear righteous unto men, but within I am filled with hypocrisy and iniquity."

"Let me pack you some food," said Mary, Mother of Jesus.

"There is no need," said Jesus. "Give the food to a poor man. For I will not eat during my time of contemplation. I must scourge my body to purify myself of sin."

"Here," said Mary, Mother of Jesus. "You will need some money." She tried to give him some coins.

"Ney," said Jesus. "These are the wages of sin. I need not gold."

"I'll have it," said Joseph the Younger, trying to take the coins. Mary Mother of Jesus scowled at Joseph the Younger and snapped the coins out of his reach.

"At least take a coat," said Mary.

"There is no need," said Jesus. "The word of the Lord will warm my heart and my body. I will go into the desert and find God."

"Can you do something while you're there?" asked Joseph the Elder.

"Surely, Father," replied Jesus.

"When you find God," continued Joseph. "Could you ask him where I put that purse yesterday. It had twenty shekels in it, and I can't remember where in the blazes I put it."

"You doth blaspheme, Father," replied Jesus, sternly. "But I forgive thee."

Joseph the Elder turned to Joseph the Younger. "You were right son," he said. "He is a total pussy."

Jesus made his way out.

"I'll go with him," said Mary.

"I wouldn't bother," said Joseph the Elder. "He'll come back when he's hungry."

"I better make sure nothing bad happens to him," said Mary, setting off. "I may be some time." She followed Jesus out. "Show time!" she whispered under her breath.

Warning: Christians and people who are easily offended should not read this book

The Temptation of Christ

Jesus knelt in the desert. He was praying. There was a stream close-by. He heard movement in the water. Mary stepped out of the stream and walked towards him.

"I want to be alone," said Jesus. "I want to be with my God. To know him."

"Your God already knows you and you know him," said Mary. "He has sent me. You say you want to be a preacher and a prophet. But my God knows you are a false prophet. An unworthy hypocrite. A liar. I will expose you to all men as the miserable sinner you are. A slave to my master. I will shame and discredit you. And then my sisters will destroy you. And your name will be a blasphemy on the lips of all men." Mary moved her arms. Some bushes behind her burst into flames. She stripped off her dress. The skies darkened and the ground shook.

"Behold," she said. "Today you will see your destiny. You will renounce your God and kneel before me to admit you are a liar, hypocrite and False Prophet before the World – unfit to profess any word other than the Gospels of the flesh, avarice and sin."

Jesus stood.

"Get thee behind me Satan," he commanded.

"Satan is within you," replied Mary. "He rules you. And this day you will accept him as Lord."

Jesus turned from her, but he could not silence her voice.

"Sinner!" shouted Mary. "Look upon me. For your desires betray you. You are naught but a brute beast with no understanding. A slave to my Lord. You will accept your destiny and burn with me in Hell." She took a switch and beat Jesus on the back. He turned in anger and grabbed her by the neck.

"Yes," shouted Mary. "Face your anger. Give in to your hatred. Strike me down. Go back to your people and your God as a murderer. Cursed! The most evil of men. Show unto them your true self."

Jesus came to his senses. He released her and knelt. Mary tore off his tunic.

"I took you in when you were homeless," Jesus protested.

"Liar!" said Mary. "Look upon me. You took me in to fornicate. You desired me. You were nothing but a slave to your base urges. You have always looked upon me with lust and never with charity, you cursed hypocrite. Would you have taken me in if I were ugly, or old, or a leper?"

Jesus was silent.

Warning: Christians and people who are easily offended should not read this book

"Answer you dog," shouted Mary. "He knows your mind. He has always known you. You have the Devil within you Jesus and he rules you. You are a but a slave to my Master. Look upon me. Gratify your lust. Admit your wickedness – that lust was ever your design – to satisfy your carnal urges - and you speak of charity. Liar!" She beat him with the switch once more.

And so it continued.

The next morning. Jesus awoke. He was lying on a mat under the sky. The stream was close-by. The sun was up. He rolled over. Mary put her hands gently on his face.

"You are in pain," she said, gently. "Let me comfort you." She kissed him. He kissed her. She kissed him more passionately. He startled. He realised they were naked. He rolled over and put his head in his hands.

"You hide your face," shouted Mary. "But you cannot hide the evil within. Your desire. Your lust. I will show you to the world as the fornicator and false prophet you are."

"Leave me!" begged Jesus.

"I can never leave you," said Mary. "I am the incarnation of the evil within you. You can never escape me. Go back to the city. I will be waiting there. Go high into the hills. I will be waiting. I will follow you everywhere. To the highest mountain. To the deepest ocean. To the Gates of Heaven. And then to the Gates of Hell. You will never escape me. I will show the world and our God the true evil within you. An evil you can never hide. You can never escape from me. You will kneel before me and beg my forgiveness for you are cursed."

Mary threw a water carrier in front of Jesus. "Drink!" she commanded. "You may satisfy your thirst, but you can never satisfy your lust."

Jesus, who was noticeably weaker now, drank the water.

"You speak of charity," began Mary. "But you turn your eyes away from those in need. The hungry. The weak. The beggarman. And you cast them out, so they do not offend your sight…"

Suddenly Jesus began to vomit. He fell on all fours and wretched.

"Your body tries to cleanse you of the evil within," said Mary. "But you will always have sin in your heart. That is the vengeance of the poor and the homeless that you knowingly ignored. Those you crossed the path to avoid and those whose cries you heard without seeing."

Jesus lay on the ground. Every few minutes his stomach went into spasm and he wretched once more. He moaned.

Warning: Christians and people who are easily offended should not read this book

"You can never expel your sinful nature," said Mary. "For you are like all men and are made of wickedness. Let us wait here while your body punishes you for your neglect of the weak and the helpless. Let the destitute and those you cast out vent their fury upon you."

Mary watched as Jesus lay wretched and sick as the sun rose and then fell on that terrible day.

And so it continued.

Jesus was weaker the next morning. Mary picked him up bodily and carried him. Later they reached the peak of a mountain. Mary threw Jesus down on the summit. "Look!" she commanded. Jesus opened his eyes. The mighty city of Cairo lay as a vision before them. "All this can be yours," said Mary. "I can give you all this. You can be King here. You can command armies. I can grant you all your wishes. I have the power. Kneel before me now and confess your sins. Confess to me and to the world that you are no prophet but a lying hypocrite. A fornicator: selfish and corrupt. Renounce your God and accept Satan as your master."

Jesus looked down at the city as he sat. Then he looked away. He said nothing.

"See," commanded Mary. She stood before him and let a multitude of gold coins drop like rain from her open hands. A huge pile of coins piled up by Jesus' feet. "All this can be yours. Confess your sins to me and the world. Accept my Lord as your master."

Jesus closed his eyes. He said nothing.

When he opened them once more Mary shouted: "Look!" Velociraptor came running towards Jesus. Jesus cried and cringed in terror. The dinosaurs stood all round Mary. They hissed and snapped at Jesus threateningly. Then the host of raptors parted. A huge snake slithered past Mary and reared up in front of Jesus. Jesus shuffled back and put his arms before him to protect himself.

"You cannot save yourself," shouted Mary. "For only I can save you now. Come to me Jesus. Give into your desires. Admit your wickedness to the world before me and your God." She paused. "You may fornicate with me," she added, seductively. "You may fornicate with me. You may fornicate with any woman you see. You will have a multitude of beautiful houris untouched by man or jinn and eternally young. All slave girls to satisfy your lust. You will have eternal satisfaction. Admit your wickedness to the world before me and renounce your God. Stand before all men and admit you are a fornicator and unworthy – a false prophet. And I will give you all the gold in the world. Riches beyond imagination. Kingdoms as far as the eye can see. I have this power. Give in to your lust and avarice and it will be satisfied."

May paused as Jesus listened but remained silent.

"What say you?" she asked.

Jesus said nothing.

"Once more I ask, what say you?" Mary commanded.

Warning: Christians and people who are easily offended should not read this book

Jesus said nothing.

"So shall it be," said Mary. "Let the darkness take you."

Suddenly it was pitch black. There was no light. Jesus could not see his hand before his face. He was in a deep cavern. He could feel the damp walls. He could hear dripping water. He listened. He could hear a distant sound. He listened longer. The sound was a howling. He realised there was a terrible beast in the cavern but a great distance away. He looked round once more. It was completely dark. Then he felt a light draft on his face. He looked in the direction of the breeze. There was a speck of light. Then Jesus heard the terrible howling. It was very distant but closer now. Jesus edged forward on hands and knees. The light was just visible. He crawled towards the light over the slippery boulders and through shallow freezing pools. As he moved, squeezing through narrow tunnels and slipping down slimy rocks into the pools beneath, the light became stronger, and Jesus began to see his way. But behind him the howls became louder. There were now several creatures on his trail – hunting him. As his vision returned, he could move faster. His strength had increased. The floor of the cave became flatter, and he was now able to run. The creatures behind were not visible but he could hear them running and growling. He dared not turn but he knew they were close. Jesus ran towards the light. The tunnel opened wider. Jesus heard the creatures roaring. He could almost feel their breath as they pursued him. He sprinted and was yards from the mouth of the cave. He could feel the wind blowing on his face and he saw the sun.

Then he fell. The floor of the cave collapsed beneath him. He slid into the void kicking and grabbing for any handhold but there was none. He was falling. He slowly turned in the air as the wind blew him. He was falling from a great height. He could see the land miles below. Through the desert the river was snaking across the plane, the mountains appeared like sand dunes – ranging into the far distance. Jesus fell helpless. The trees were not visible, but he could see the outlines of fields. He fell. The fields became a patchwork. The range of mountains contracted. He could only see a few peaks now. The land came into focus. Small houses were just visible. The ground was accelerating towards him at terrible speed now. He fell helpless. Time slowed for the last few seconds – every detail of the ground came into focus. The brush, the boulders, he could almost see the grains of sand.

Then darkness. Jesus startled. He was cold. It was pitch black once more. He moved his arms. He could feel strong wooden planks bracing his elbows. He was lying straight. He tried to raise his arms, but he could only move a few inches and then he felt the wooden lid above him. He tried to sit up, but his head hit a hard wooden roof inches above his face. He was in a coffin. The air began to feel close. He kicked with his feet, but the floor of the coffin was strong. There was no way out. He shouted in desperation. His voice vanished into the ground. How deep he was buried he knew not. He was helpless. His breath became laboured. He began to gasp. The air became hot and acrid. He was suffocating. Then he felt something cold on his face. He held his breath. There was another drop. A drop of cold water. There was a leak above him. He could see nothing and then there was a third drip. Then a forth. Then a stream. He moved his head. He felt the freezing cold water dripping on him. Then it began to spray. More and more. He felt the water begin to rise, first against his back and then it began

Warning: Christians and people who are easily offended should not read this book

to rise up his body, cold and icy. He began to kick once again. The floor of the coffin would not give. The water was becoming deeper, and it quashed his efforts as he struggled and consumed his strength. Jesus began to panic. He turned his head as the water reached one ear only to submerge the other. He lent forward with his forehead against the wooden lid. The water rose. It submerged his chest, then rose up his neck, then his chin. It flowed into his mouth as he spluttered. He began to drown. The water rose over his mouth. Then the water submerged him entirely. He thrashed in the darkness, gasping without air, his lung filling with the icy fluid.

Then there was light. Mary reached into the coffin and lifted Jesus bodily from the flooded casket. The lid had been torn off. She held Jesus in front of her. He shook and spluttered and gasped as air filled his lungs once more. She lowered him to the floor. Jesus knelt before her. He coughed and wretched. Slowly his life came back.

"Come," said Mary. They were in a cave. It was light but cold. Jesus looked around. He could see the entrance. There was snow outside. There was a small fire in the cave. Mary sat by it. She beckoned Jesus to sit by the fire.

Jesus sat but the cold was bitter. He could warm his hands, but his body was cold. He began to shiver. He wrapped his arms around himself. There was no shelter. He had no clothes.

"Fire is agony but brief," said Mary. "Cold is slow and painful. But the end is the same."

Mary paused to reflect.

"I was born of a woman when the pyramids were being built," explained Mary. "My mother was a Nubian slave adopted by the Hebrews. We were given to the Pharaohs generations before. No one knows my father. The guards used my mother, as they came to use me. You can never know what it is to be paralysed with fear beneath the weight of a fat, stinking man who penetrates your body at his will. And you are powerless. And you cannot move. And there is no revenge – no justice – it is just your lot. But at least they fed me - even after they ill-used my mother and she died. Such was my place for too many years. Then, with no warning, I was taken to the temple, I wondered if I was to be a sacrifice. Or perhaps one of the priests had spied me and wanted me for his own – to satisfy his own lust. But the Queen saw me and took me from the guards to be with her. One of the priests complained. He died that night of a burning fever. No one else objected. The Queen showed me the ways of Satan, the true God. She showed me power beyond imagination. I have lain waste entire armies. I have conquered Empires. Kings have knelt before me and begged for their lives. I have done this all in the name of the dark Lord. And he is generous. I have gold and riches that thousands of men cannot carry. But these trinkets are worthless. On my return from the conquest of the Land of Kush, beyond the fifth cataract, my Queen said I had done well and released me to serve her willingly or to go my own way. That night I found the men who had raped and murdered my mother and I burned them alive. They died screaming. That was reward enough. I returned to serve my Queen and, many years later, she has sent me to do this task."

Warning: Christians and people who are easily offended should not read this book

Mary paused. "You are cold," she said. "Come!"

Mary rose and led Jesus into the cave. They turned a corner. They were in a palace. A place filled with light. There was wine to drink and gold, and tapestries hanging, and fine furnishings and a balcony looking out onto a great city. The noise of the city could be heard in the distance.

Mary led Jesus to a bed. "Sit," she said and poured him wine. "You can drink this. It will do you no harm." Jesus drank. It was warm in the palace and comfortable. Mary sat beside him.

"The greatest joy is to see your enemies die in agony before you," she explained. "Vengeance again the evil men who murdered my mother was ecstasy – worth more than all the gold in the world. And I thank my Lord for giving me that power. I serve no man. I can make Kings kneel before me. All my wants and needs are given to me at a whim. But my only desire is to have power over men. To see them serve or tremble before me. This is my greatest pleasure. I do not hate you, Jesus. I no longer hate any man. The lion does not hate the lamb. The eagle does not hate the dove nor the spider the fly. But they must eat them because that is the order of things. And I must dominate men because that is my nature and the will of my lord. I take no joy in your suffering. Your pain has no value. Let it end. Tell me your God is dead – he has abandoned you. You are a good man but no prophet. Take my Lord Satan as your God and you can live here, like this, in comfort and pleasure. All your wants will be met. You may go anywhere and live as a King. You will answer to no man. Renounce your God and take up your true place in this world."

Jesus smiled at her but said nothing.

"Come lie beside me," said Mary. She lay and pulled Jesus close. She put her arms round him.

"You are tired," said Mary. "Sleep now."

…

Jesus woke again. The sun was rising. He was in a dry desert valley. There were no plants. The ground was stony. The land was totally parched. There was shimmering in the far distance. A few trees were just visible. Possibly a river. It was already hot. The land was silent. There was no sound. Jesus sat and listened for some minutes.

Eventually Jesus looked behind. There seemed to be a fire raging. Red and orange flames were just visible, and smoke was billowing up. There was a gentle breeze. Jesus realised the fire was moving slowly towards him.

Jesus set off over the parched earth. He walked briskly. He could just hear the crackling of a fire. As he moved the sound gradually increased. It was approaching him. The wind became stronger. He looked behind. The fire was consuming the sand and stone. There was no fuel, but the fire was still raging. Jesus began to run. He stumbled and fell over stones. He rose again and staggered forth. The river gradually came nearer. He could just hear the water. He

Warning: Christians and people who are easily offended should not read this book

saw the trees wave in the breeze. But the breeze was becoming stronger. The fire behind was moving faster and was burning more fiercely. He began to feel the heat on his neck and his back. He ran. The sweat that soaked his tunic began to dry and his clothes began to steam. His exposed calves began to smart as the fire began to scald them. The ground around him began to give off smoke. The fire behind began to roar. The river was close now. A few more yards. Suddenly one of the trees ahead burst into flames. It burned like a torch. Then a second. As Jesus approached the river, all the trees along the bank were burning and the grass on the riverbank was smouldering. His tunic caught fire. He dived. He landed in the water. The fire reached the riverbank. He waded out and turned. Sheets of flame leapt hundreds of feet into the air. But the fire could move no further. Jesus waded further out into the water as the heat began to blister his face. He knelt and submerged his head. The water was cool. The fire raged but he was safe.

…

Jesus woke the next morning as the sun rose. He looked round. He was alone on the summit of the mountain. There was a small flagon of water. His thirst was great, so he drank. Many miles away in the valley he recognised the river winding across the plane where he had begun his trials four days before. It would be a great journey, but the water was now gone, and the sun was warming the land.

Jesus staggered down the mountain bleeding and bruised. He stumbled over rocks and down into rifts. The sun rose high in the sky and the burning heat made the stones hot and scalded his feet. He took shade where he could, behind rocks or under the shade of scrub. But he could only rest for a few minutes before his thirst drove him on. He came to the foot of the mountain. The plains stretched ahead. He set off on boiling sand with no cover. The heat made the river shimmer in the distance. The hot sand burned his feet, but he had no alternative other than to lay down and die of thirst. He was alone and forgotten in this desolate place without help. Even the lizards ran into their burrows to escape the heat. Man had no place in this forgotten valley.

After several hours he reached the river and collapsed, exhausted, and slept. Night fell.

…

"You don't give me much credit, do you?" he heard Mary's voice. He opened his eyes. He was back on top of the mountain from where he had escaped the day before.

"Do you really think it would be so easy, to just walk out of here?" her eyes glowed red and demonic.

Mary grabbed Jesus. She was strong. She dragged him along the ground by his leg. She lifted him as she came to a cliff face. Mary held Jesus by his ankles, upside down, suspended above the void of a vast precipice.

"This is just the beginning!" Mary told him. Her eyes glowed.

Warning: Christians and people who are easily offended should not read this book

And so it continued.

Morning. Day 40.

Jesus, now very weak, awoke with a start. Mary threw his tunic at him.

"What gives with you," she demanded. "I've been stuck in this god-forsaken backwater for three decades waiting for you. What exactly is this message that is so important that I have to waste my time to break your worthless spirit?"

Jesus whispered.

"I can't hear you," shouted Mary, kneeling before him.

"Love thy neighbour," whispered Jesus.

"Love thy neighbour!" replied Mary. "Is that it?" Mary paused in disbelief. "You went through all that just to spread that one message!" She waited. Jesus said no more.

Mary shook her head. "A curse on you," she said. "I go to the temple to seek counsel with my sisters." Mary stormed off.

…

"I can't break him," said Mary in the Temple of Jerusalem. She was in a palatial room with Delilah and Jezebel. They wore the jewels and exotic silks of the concubines of kings. Mary still wore her plain peasant dress. Jezebel and Delilah looked unimpressed.

"I tried everything," explained Mary. "Fabulous wealth. Limitless gold. Houris without number. Snakes. Demons. The whole nine yards."

"Did you do the eye thing?" asked Jezebel.

"Of course, I did the eye thing," snapped Mary, angrily.

"How long were you out there?" asked Delilah.

"Forty days and forty nights," replied Mary.

"Forty days and nights!" shouted Jezebel. "How long does it usually take?"

"Usually about forty minutes," replied Mary, sheepishly. "Maybe a couple of days with a real hard ass."

"Bah!" said Delilah. "You're losing it girl."

There was an uncomfortable silence.

"Go!" said Jezebel, eventually. "Leave us. We will deal with this prophet. You are no longer required. You have failed."

Warning: Christians and people who are easily offended should not read this book

Delilah and Jezebel walked out leaving Mary alone.

…

Mary was sitting in the dust outside the Temple.

"Be gone!" shouted a temple guard. Mary ignored him. The temple guard strode over and hit her with his stick. Mary grabbed the stick defiantly but, to her surprise, she was no longer strong enough to wrench it from his hand. The Temple guard struck her once more. The temple guard kicked her as she scrambled away in the dust. A couple of Roman guards observed the scene and began to laugh. Mary sloped off into a side street. She paused outside a house and sat on the step. "Away harlot," a woman shouted through an open window. Mary ignored her. Suddenly the door opened and her husband, a big burly man, came out with a broom and beat her.

"Be gone, painted whore," he shouted as she ran off once more.

Mary began to feel hungry. She saw a man selling bread. She went to him.

As she approached him, he noticed her.

"What do you want?" he said aggressively.

"Please sir," she said. "I have no money."

"Then you must get some," he shouted. "I am not a charity or a brothel keeper. Clear off beggar and whore."

He stepped forward with his arm raised as if to hit her. Mary dashed away.

As she ran down a side-street, she noticed a small loaf on a windowsill. She grabbed it as she passed and continued running. Behind her she heard a woman shouting. "That whore just stole my bread!" Fortunately, Mary was fast enough to escape before the hue and cry caught up with her. She concealed the bread in her robe.

Mary found the secluded corner of a square. She furtively ate the bread. The sun was setting.

The next morning Mary awoke with a start. She was still in the square. A woman hit her with a brush. Two men were in the square busying themselves.

"Go on," said the woman. "Clear off. This is a respectable neighbourhood. We don't want tramps and harlots here. There's a brothel down the street. Go there."

Mary set off into the city streets. She wandered aimlessly. She found water in a stream. She hid her face from people. As the day wore on, she became tired and desperately hungry. Her clothes were already old and ragged. They were now muddy. She was dirty and had dust in her hair and on her face. She looked around for things to steal. She went into the marketplace. She walked past a man on a stall selling trinkets. She grabbed one and began to run but she collided immediately with another salesman who threw her roughly to the ground and

Warning: Christians and people who are easily offended should not read this book

retrieved the small, gilded statuette she had purloined. "Thief!" he shouted at her. She staggered to her feet as he kicked her away. She fled through the marketplace in panic.

She reached the river. She fell by the bank and lay fearful and exhausted.

…

The next day Mary wandered desperately round the town.

She saw several women taking laundry to the river.

"Sisters," asked Mary. "I need food. I can help you."

"Begone," shouted one of the women. "You get what you deserve. Whore. Go and starve in the gutter where you belong." The other women jeered in support.

Mary wandered back towards the town. "Do you have any money for a starving beggar?" she asked a man. The man looked sympathetically at her. But his wife suddenly appeared and slapped him. "Leave the whore alone," said the woman. "We don't want her sort round here."

Mary stumbled off. However, a few minutes later the man caught up with her and handed her some bread.

"Bless you," she said as she scuttled off.

Mary went back into the town. None of the women would indulge her. She asked for work: sweeping, laundry or washing. No one would help her, and many were fearful to be seen speaking to her. Most people ignored her and quickly walked off or continued their work.

Mary sat in a street corner and cried.

After some time, a few soldiers came by. The officer spotted Mary.

"Please sir," said Mary looking up at him. "I am starving."

"There is a house," said the officer. "Down at the end of the street. Ask for the House of Esther. They can help." He pointed down the street.

Mary raised herself and slowly walked down the street where the soldier had pointed. After several yards she became confused. She pulled her clothes up and covered her head.

"Do you know the House of Esther?" she asked a man who was carrying some goods. He looked furtively round. "There," he said, pointing up some steps to a doorway.

Mary climbed the steps and knocked on the door. A woman answered it.

"I was told I can get work here," said Mary.

The women slipped out and looked cautiously up and down the street. She ushered Mary inside and pointed to a chair in the barely furnished reception room. The woman disappeared through a doorway. Shortly, a better dressed middle-aged woman appeared.

Warning: Christians and people who are easily offended should not read this book

"What do you want?" she asked.

"I was told I could work here," said Mary.

"Who told you?" asked the woman, sitting.

"Some soldiers," said Mary.

"That figures," replied the woman. "Did they say what sort of work?"

"No," said Mary. "But I can try anything. Cooking, cleaning, whatever you need."

"We have no shortage of cooks and cleaners," said the woman. "Do you know what work we do here?"

"Yes," said Mary, shamefully. "It wouldn't be the first time. I am desperate."

"You're not the only one," said the woman.

"Or the last," added Mary.

"Open your cloak," said the woman. "Let me see you properly."

Mary stood and pulled down her hood.

"Goodness, child," said the woman. "You're African. How did you get here? Tell me the truth."

"I was sold to the Court of King Herod," said Mary. "But they became bored and threw me out. I fought with some fat sweaty soldiers who tried to use me without paying. And I am getting old, and they were bored of me."

"You don't look old to me," said the woman. "Where did you get those bruises?"

"Some men beat me in the street," said Mary. "I was just asking for food or money."

"Begging," said the woman, thoughtfully. "Rachel," she shouted. "Bring food for our guest."

"You are welcome to take this food," said the woman. "But you cannot stay here. You are an escaped slave girl. When the Romans hear of you, they will come and then we will all be starving in the streets. I am sorry. Take the food and go."

"But…" protested Mary.

The woman silenced Mary as Rachel brought some food on a plate.

"Eat and then leave," said the woman. "Go before anyone else sees you here."

Rachel and the woman left. Mary ate as much as she could stuff in her mouth, grabbed the remnants, and left.

…

Warning: Christians and people who are easily offended should not read this book

The sun was setting. Mary lay by the riverbank. Hunger had possessed her. She lifted herself up and limped back into the streets. She sat in a darkened doorway. Two Roman soldiers ambled past. She recognised one who had been laughing at her from outside the Temple.

"Hey," she said from the secluded doorway. They kept walking. "Hey!" she shouted louder.

The Roman soldiers turned. She waved them over.

"What do you want?" one asked.

"What do you want?" she said. "Can you help a lady in distress?"

"You're no lady," said the soldier, grinning.

They paused. There was an impasse. One of the soldiers looked round. They looked at each other. The alleyway was secluded. It was dark.

"How much?" asked the soldier.

"Two gold coins," replied Mary.

The soldiers laughed and walked away.

"Wait," said Mary. "Two shekels."

One of the soldiers hesitated. He turned around. "One shekel?" he asked.

"OK," said Mary. She was kneeling in the doorway. The soldier nodded to his companion who grinned and went to the end of the alley to keep guard. The first soldiers returned. He stood before her in the secluded, dark doorway. Mary knelt in front of him. "Money first," she said. He tossed a coin at her.

…

Later that night two more soldiers happened by. Mary was sleeping in the doorway. One of them prodded her with his foot. She woke, sleepily. It was late at night.

"Can you do a favour for an old soldier?" said one grinning.

"Two shekels," replied Mary, sleepily.

"It was only one earlier," said the soldier.

"I've put my prices up," replied Mary.

The soldiers paused.

"OK," said one. He glanced at the other who wandered off to the end of the alleyway.

"Get out!" shouted a man's voice. A window was flung open nearby. "Take that whore and go," shouted the man. The soldier adjusted himself quickly and dashed off. The door flew

Warning: Christians and people who are easily offended should not read this book

open, and a man and his son came out wielding a broom. Mary fled. They chased her into the main street. Mary fell. The man and her son beat her with the broom and kicked her. Some other windows opened.

"Clear off, you whore," said the man. They quickly gave up and briskly left as more windows and doors opened.

Mary, bruised and bleeding, stumbled away. She found a courtyard and collapsed in a corner. A window sprang open. "Be gone," came a woman's voice. "We don't want your sort round here." The door opened and a man came out with a stick. Mary sloped off before he could beat her. He followed her into the street and watched her stagger away to ensure she had left.

Mary found another sanctuary. This was in an alley between a stone trough and a wall. There were no doors or windows nearby. She lay in the alley and slept.

She woke suddenly. A man was on top of her. He was tearing her clothes. She tried to fight him, but he was strong. She wanted to yell but her throat was sore, and she was hoarse. She froze in fear. She lay back. He tore her clothes and forced her legs apart and raped her. She was powerless. When he had finished, he stood and kicked her. He spat on Mary and left.

Mary staggered slowly back to the riverbank holding her torn rags together as best she could. It took her an hour to reach the river. "Father, why have you forsaken me," she whispered as she collapsed there.

…

The sun rose. Mary lay on the riverbank. She looked up through her tears. She was bleeding and bruised and wretched.

A shadow crossed her face. She raised her hand to shield her eyes from the glare.

"I've been looking for you, Mary," she heard. "The guards told me where to come."

Jesus was standing over her. He held out his hand. Mary took his hand and stood. She looked into his eyes again.

"Come," he said.

"Where are we going?" asked Mary, bewildered.

"To my father's house," said Jesus. "We are going home."

Mary paused.

"But I tried to destroy you," said Mary. "I conspired with witches against you. I summoned demons and tried to bribe you with gold and armies and wealth beyond measure. I tempted you with my body. I tried to steal your soul so you would be damned for all eternity."

Jesus paused. "Nobody's perfect," he replied.

Warning: Christians and people who are easily offended should not read this book

Mary fell to her knees. "I am wicked beyond words," she said. "A sinful woman. I will be damned. I am condemned to burn in Hell."

"I can wash away your sin," said Jesus. "Come down to the river." He led her into the river. They waded into the river up to their waists and faced each other.

Jesus cupped his hands and poured water over her head.

"If this woman repents in her heart," he professed. "Then this water will wash away her sins and she will be born again. But know this. This woman was born into slavery. Her virtue was taken from her by evil men as a child. She had but one choice: to sell her body or starve. Her only sin is that she chose to live."

Mary cried as he continued to wash her. "I baptise thee Mary in the name of our Lord," said Jesus. Within a minute Jesus had finished.

"Maiden arise and stand before me," Jesus told her. Mary stood. Jesus knelt before her in the water and held her hands.

"Mary, I kneel before you and confess my wickedness to you and all the world," said Jesus. "For I chose to sin. I am a fornicator. A hypocrite and a liar. I lusted after you and committed adultery in my heart and with my body. I beg your forgiveness. For I am unworthy."

Mary took his head in her hands and said nothing through her tears.

Jesus continued to kneel. He put his arms around her waist.

"I am a most wicked sinner," he said. "But I am trying."

"Be gone, Satan," whispers Mary holding Jesus. "I cast thee out!"

Warning: Christians and people who are easily offended should not read this book

Part 3 – Land of Nodd

"Hey Big Man," said Judas, breezing into the kitchen at the Big House (owned by Jesus's parents). Jesus and Mary were eating.

"Great news," Judas began. "Our first international gig. We can call it our world tour."

"How are we going to get to another country and back in one weekend?" asked Mary.

"It's just over the river," said Judas. "Go to Jericho and turn right and you're there. They call it The Land of Nodd. And we've been hired to perform for one night only by their wise and all-powerful ruler, The Noddy."

"The Noddy?" repeated Mary.

"May the angels shower their blessings upon him," said Judas.

"Have you had any head injuries since we've been away?" asked Jesus.

"Nah," said Judas, ignoring the sarcasm. "You should be pleased. The Land of Nodd has been around for centuries – as long as anyone can remember. Before Abraham, before Moses, before Jericho, there was Noddy! It's a semi-autonomous region within the Roman Empire. You see they take a lot of refugees and asylum-seekers, so the Romans didn't really want it."

"Refugees?" asked Mary.

"Yeah," said Judas. "Adam and Eve when they got evicted. And Noah and his ark. But mainly Palestinians now."

"How could Noah's Ark be in the Land of Nodd?" asked Jesus. "It's landlocked."

"Ye of little faith," said Judas. "It was the only place Noah could afford the mooring fees. Imagine how much it costs to get a docking birth for an arc. Now I was thinking, a lot of folks in Nodd don't speak the language, because they are asylum seekers, so we need a show with more of a musical theme. Some of the boys have formed a close harmony group and you could put them on. I was thinking of calling them, 'The Disciples of Jesus'."

"Nah," said Mary. "That sounds more like a firm of architects than a close harmony combo."

"Well…" said Judas, thoughtfully. "I know – 'The Dee Jees'. Yeah – that will do it. Incidentally don't say anything about ears. It's culturally inappropriate in the Land of Noddy."

"What do you call a dog with no ears?" asked Jesus. "Anything you want, he can't hear you."

"That's precisely the sort of racially insensitive, politically incorrect comment we are trying to avoid," said Judas.

Warning: Christians and people who are easily offended should not read this book

"I don't believe what I'm hearing," said Mary.

Judas scowled and wagged his finger at her.

"Anyhow, you kids enjoy your evening," said Judas. "I gotta run. Things to do. People to see."

Judas got up and made off singing to himself: "You can tell by the way I use my walk, I'm a woman's man…"

…

The Dee Jees had just finished.

Jesus went on stage. There was a big audience – the capital city of Nodd was one of the largest cities in the region.

"Hello Noddy!" he shouted as the applause died down. There was no response and the audience looked blank.

"Hold on," interrupted Judas. He signalled and three men mounted the stage. "Translators," explained Judas. "Palestinian, Greek and Nordic. You just keep going."

"Did you hear about the shrimp that went to the prawn's cocktail party?" asked Jesus. "He pulled a mussel!"

There was a prolonged wait for the translators to speak followed by deadly silence.

"How do you make a blonde laugh on a Sunday?" asked Jesus. "Tell her a joke on a Wednesday!"

Peter and Paul laughed although there was no response when the translators had finished.

"I know you're out there," said Jesus. "I can hear you breathing." He paused for thought.

"Now for some magic," he continued, pulling out a saw and beckoning Mary back on the stage. The Disciples brought in a coffin. "I take it that coffin is for you," whispered Mary. "Seeing as you just died."

Mary climbed into the coffin and Jesus sawed her in half. But when the coffin was opened only some of her clothes had disappeared. As Mary took a bow she whispered to Jesus: "All those refugees are desperate to learn about the local culture. Tell them about God and stuff."

"You know," said Jesus, after a pause. "Commandments are like fingers. There are ten but you only need two: 'Love thy God' and 'Love thy neighbour'…Actually, you might not know the other eight. I'll go through them…"

…

Warning: Christians and people who are easily offended should not read this book

"That didn't get many laughs," said Mary after the show. "Except when you reached Commandment eight and couldn't remember the other two."

"Yeah," said Judas, sniggering. "That was hilarious."

"But they did enjoy it," said Mary. "They seemed really keen to engage with the local customs. I noticed all the kids were trying to speak our language."

"Hey," said Judas. "Where's the cart?"

"I thought we left it outside," said Jesus.

Peter came dashing in. "Someone's stolen the cart," he said.

"Bah!" said Judas. "We customised that – mag wheels and everything."

"Mag wheels?" asked Mary.

"Hey," said Judas. "Theft is covered under the insurance."

"Ah," replied Mary. "It had gold trimmings too."

"Top of the range," said Judas.

"How are we going to get the stuff back without our wheels?" asked Jesus.

"Don't worry," said an African man who had been a translator. "Perhaps a few of you can stay overnight as our guest and we'll probably have the cart back by tomorrow. It's probably some joy-riders. They'll just dump it in the streets later."

"That's very kind of you to help," said Mary.

"My pleasure," said the man. "Call me Mr Benjamin. Now, Mr Judas, perhaps you could stay with my associate, Miss Shani," he waved to a young lady, who smiled at Judas. "And Mr Jesus and his lady friend here can stay with me. Will anyone else require any accommodation?"

"Actually," said Judas. "The three of us can move the stuff if we find the cart tomorrow. The others can leave."

"If we can't find the cart," said Benjamin. "We can lend you one – anyway we often go through to the Big City so it won't be a problem bringing a rental-cart back."

…

Jesus Mary and Benjamin entered a large house. Benjamin sat down in a lounge area and beckoned Jesus and Mary to join him.

"Would you like a drink?" asked Benjamin.

"That's very kind of you," said Jesus. "What's your poison?"

Warning: Christians and people who are easily offended should not read this book

"We have some wine," said Benjamin. "But I never touch the stuff." He pulled out a rolled-up piece of parchment and began to light it from a candle. "My friend Miss Delores is making some food for us, and she'll be along shortly." "Delores!" He shouted. There were some swearing sounds in the kitchen but no reply. Jesus and Mary watched intrigued as Benjamin took a drag on the parchment and then blew smoke out of his mouth.

"So you don't drink alcohol," said Mary. "Is that a religious thing?"

"No," said Benjamin. "It's just that this is better." He handed Mary the rolled parchment.

"Try some," said Benjamin. "Just suck on it and inhale the fumes."

Mary tried the roll-up. Jesus looked amazed. Mary suddenly began coughing and spluttering. Her eyes watered. She handed the roll-up back to Benjamin as she continued to cough smoke out of her mouth.

"It takes a bit of getting used to," said Benjamin, taking another drag.

After a few seconds Mary regained her composure. Suddenly she began to smile.

"You want some more?" asked Benjamin.

"Right on brother," said Mary, beginning to giggle. Benjamin handed her the roll-up.

"What religion do you follow?" asked Jesus.

"We're from Ethiopia," said Benjamin, looking more relaxed. "We worship our own Emperor, the Rastaman. We is Rastas."

"What you doin' here?" shouted an angry African woman who had just burst through the door.

"I just have to speak in our own language to my woman here," said Benjamin.

"Hey, Babe," he said to Delores.

"Don't you be callin' me 'babe'," shouted Delores. "Where you bin' deese past tree days? And where is da rent? Ya said ya was goin' to go earn money for de rent. And dat was tree days past. And ah bet ya spent all dat money on ganja. Ya good-for-nothin' piece a-shit."

Delores did not look please.

"Hey woman, chill," said Benjamin.

"Don't you be tellin' me ta 'chill', like am some sorta imbecile, and don't have de sense ah was born wid," shouted Delores. "Where all dat money ya says ya gonna earn doin' dat rave 'ting in de field, load-a-crap. Or has ya spent it all on de ganja already?"

"Ah got some dough," said Benjamin. He handed her some coins.

Warning: Christians and people who are easily offended should not read this book

"You'se spent de rest of it on de weed ah expect," shouted Delores, hiding the coins immediately in her outfit. "Who deese two ya brought round, and givin' em all da food that ah can hardly afford ta buy, on account ya spend all da money on ganja."

"Deese is Brother Jesus and his woman, Sista Mary," replied Benjamin.

"Please to meet you," said Delores, suddenly speaking good English. "Dinner will be served shortly. In the meantime, I have to speak jive with my man here. I hope you don't mind."

Mary smiled and laughed. Mary handed Jesus the reefer and encouraged him to take a drag as they watched the spectacle of Delores taking several stripes off Benjamin, who was clearly taking no notice of her.

"Why ya bring deese two here?" said Delores. "What ya up ta? Ah hope dey ain't sellin' de ganja for ya. Ah knows what ya thinks, ya good-fa-nothin' layabout."

"Dey got dare wheels lifted by some yardies so ah done said dey can stay wid us 'till tomorra," replied Benjamin.

"Where dey gonna stay? Ya idiot," shouted Delores again. "We ain't got no space. Not wid ya brother and ma brother here and all dem other boys ya has here, from da 'hood, and all ya 'home boys'. And not one o' them pays nothin' but dey all eats like pigs so dare ain't no food in da house. And we is all starvin'."

"Hey woman," replied Benjamin. "Ay was tinking they could stay in ma bed. And ah was tinking dat ah could stay wid you."

"Well tink again," said Delores. "Ya ain't movin' ya ass back in wid me. Not since ya been who knows where de last tree days. Ah knows – ya bin wid dat Desiree whore again."

"Aw chill, Delores," said Benjamin. "Ya knows ya ma main squeeze and ah loves ya. And Ah ain't never hardly ever seen Desiree since ah met ya."

"Ya tink am stupid," said Delores. "And don't ya think ya can get round me sayin' ya loves me and all. Ah heard all ya lies before. And ya can kiss ma ass, if ya gettin' into ma bed again."

"Aw, come on, sugar," said Benjamin. He smiles at her.

Delores scowled for a while.

"Put ya hand out," said Delores to Benjamin. "Go on. Put ya hand out."

Benjamin reluctantly put out his hand.

"Take a look at dat," said Delores pointing to his hand. "'Cos that's what ya gonna be humpin' tonight. Ya ain't getting no action! No sir! Even if ya is in ma bed – God knows what am tinking, when ah should be putting ya worthless ass out in da street, where ya belong. No sir, don't ya been tinkin ya getting some. 'Cos ya aint."

Warning: Christians and people who are easily offended should not read this book

Benjamin smiled.

"And ya can wipe dat smile off ya hugly face as well," shouted Delores. "And ya not gettin' any. So don't ya be 'tinkin ya will. 'Cos ya ain't getting any. No sir!"

Delores stormed off into the kitchen.

"That's my lady," said Benjamin. "She the best woman in the world."

"Ah heard dat," shouted Delores from the kitchen. "And ya still ain't getting' none."

"This is good shit," said Mary, looking totally stoned.

"I better speak jive again," said Benjamin. "So Delores don't think I'm talkin' about her."

"Sure," said Mary.

"Dat's star dog," said Benjamin. "It's real good shit. A grows it ma-self in de garden here. How's ya man?"

Jesus had fallen off the chair and was lying on the floor with the reefer still in his mouth. He was totally stoned.

Mary slid off the chair and lay on top of him on the floor. "He's good," said Mary to Benjamin. "Hey sugar," she said to Jesus. "Delores says Rastaman here ain't gettin' no action. But dat don't apply to you. So don't ya been 'tinking ya off duty. Anyhow, Rastaman gonna get some action despite what Delores says. Ah know de look in her eye. He gonna get more action dan he can handle. He gonna be screaming ta get outta de bedroom when Delores is finished wid him. And you gonna be joining him. Mama got plans for you tonite!"

Mary took the refer off Jesus and she and Benjamin picked Jesus up so he was sitting by the coffee table.

Delores re-entered carrying some bowls of food and plates. Another young woman, probably her younger sister, followed with more bowls.

"Dis is jerk chicken," she said, putting down one bowl. "And dat's jerk goat. And dat's jerk Kingfish. And Maya, here, she got jerk rice and peas."

They put the bowls down.

"Ya is a good woman," said Benjamin, staggering to his feet.

"Ya still not gettin' any," said Delores, scowling at him, as he staggered off.

Delores and Maya stood and watched Jesus and Mary for a while.

"Go on," said Delores. "Ya can start. Benjamin done gone out ta get more ganja. He gonna be a while. Wid any luck he's gonna fall down a hole and break his neck. Den he won't bodder me no more tonight. Go on. Ya can start. Ya must be hungry havin' smoked all dat star dog."

Warning: Christians and people who are easily offended should not read this book

They watched as Jesus and Mary began to eat.

"Hey, sista," said Delores, starting to smile. "Ya got a good-lookin' man dare. Has ya got any more back home for ma-self and sista Maya?"

Maya started to giggle.

"Ah can ask round if ya want," said Mary.

"Me and Maya wud appreciate that," said Delores. "What he do, besides smoke ganja?"

"He's a carpenter," said Mary.

"He's a professional!" said Delores. "Wid a real job!" she exclaimed. "Hey. Benjamin," she shouted. "Ya stay out dare now. Ya ain't welcome here no more. Sista Mary got some home boys for me and Maya. Boys wot works – not sit around smoking ganja all day and eatin' de food dat we can't afford ta buy."

"What else he do?" asked Delores.

"He's a preacher," replied Mary.

"Bless ma soul," said Delores. "A preacher-man. Dat means we can go ta heaven. Not ta the fires of hell wid that ganja smoking useless piece a shit, Benjamin. Does ya get's paid to preach?"

"Yeah!" said Mary.

"Hey," said Delores to Maya. "You and me, we's hit the jackpot tonight, girl. Sista Mary's gonna get us some high-earning good-looking preacher-man each, from her own stash. Tell Benjamin ta kiss ma ass."

"He don't be doin' no preaching now," said Maya. "He ain't done said nothin' since he sat down."

"Hey sista," said Delores. "Wot you complainin' about? Benjamin don't never stop talkin' his nonsense. Talkin' 'bout all that stuff he gonna do and earn all dat money he gonna make, and he don't do shit! A man who can keep his mouth-shut and so some listenin' he done worth his weight in gold. Anyhow, ah bet he can use his tongue for sumtin' better! Don't ya know sista? Ah mean use his tongue where it counts – ah mean downtown!"

Mary, Delores and Maya began to fall about laughing. Maya and Delores eventually sat down.

Benjamin staggered back in with some dried grass and parchment.

He slumped down next to Jesus and Mary.

"Where ya at girl?" said Benjamin, who was now too stoned to see properly.

Warning: Christians and people who are easily offended should not read this book

"Ah's here, sat next to ya? Ya gone blind now? Ah wouldn't be surprised. Humpin' ya fist as much as ya has done, it must a damaged ya eyesight." said Delores.

Benjamin looked at her and glazed over.

"Here," said Delores, taking the weed and parchment from his hand. "Am gonna roll a joint for Maya and ma new friend, Sista Mary. And ya ain't getting' none tonite unless ya learns ta go down on ya knees and pray at da alter of da furry cup, like a preacher-man!"

…

"We aint ever coming back here," said Mary told Jesus the next morning as they walked over to meet Judas.

"How's that?" asked Jesus.

"'Cos it was too damned good," replied Mary. "Stay here for more than a weekend and you ain't never gonna want to go nowhere else."

"Did you have a good time then?" asked Jesus.

"Damn straight, how about you?" asked Mary.

"I don't remember," replied Jesus.

"I heard that!" said Mary.

"Did we, you know?" asked Jesus.

"In all the excitement, I just don't remember," replied Mary.

"Shit!" said Jesus.

"Is there a problem?" asked Mary.

"Sure, there's a problem," said Jesus. "I might just have scored with the hottest chick in history, and I can't tell no one because I don't remember."

"My heart bleeds for you," said Mary, scowling. "Look! There's Judas. You can tell him what you don't remember doing. You guys make all that stuff up anyhow so it don't make no difference."

"Yo!" said Judas. "Hit me with some skin." Judas held out his hands so Jesus and Mary could hi-five. Judas was pushing the cart.

"What is God's name have you got on your head?" asked Mary.

"This exquisite fashion accessory is called at Rastacap," replied Judas. "Mary can braid my hair and then I will have dreadlocks. And one keeps one's dreadlocks in this Rastacap."

"It looks like a giant tea cosy," said Jesus.

Warning: Christians and people who are easily offended should not read this book

"That's ignorant," Judas scalded. "You say that because you are intolerant. You dislike other cultures because you don't understand them – and their music. I am now on a mission to make the civilised world culturally competent."

"So you got the ganga concession for Nazareth?" asked Mary.

"Right on, sista," said Judas, grinning.

"Hey," said Judas. "I don't want to be a square but the Man ain't gonna like it if you're trying to smuggle half a ton of ganga across the border in this cart."

"No fear," said Judas. "Although we are carrying two figurines, both precious religious icons, that my new Rasta friends want delivered to the temple in Jericho as a gift to the High Priest."

"I hope you've checked that they're solid and not filled with grass," said Mary.

"There's a thought," said Judas. "We better check when we next stop."

"Now I think about it," said Mary. "That's probably the whole objective. We'll just say we're carrying incense, for personal use."

…

They reached the gates of Jericho.

"Anything to declare?" asked the guard.

"No, your honour," said Judas as they pushed the cart into the city.

"What's in the cart?" asked the guard.

"Props for our show," said Jesus.

"And some religious items as a gift for the High Priest," said Judas.

"It's about time," said the guard. "We got a drought here. We ain't had no pot in months. They say the priests been holding out on the Noddy and so he's put an embargo on deliveries. Now everyone's gonna get well." The guard ordered the other soldiers, "Let 'em though."

Mary, Jesus and Judas pushed the cart to the Temple of Jericho.

"Delivery for the High Priest," announced Judas.

"About time," said one of the guards, as they pushed open a door marked 'Deliveries' to let the cart through.

They were ushered into the inner sanctum, where the High Priest and his two assistants were eagerly waiting.

"Show me the pots," ordered the High Priest.

Warning: Christians and people who are easily offended should not read this book

Judas uncovered two heavy stones that were carefully strapped and wrapped in plane cloth.

The assistants lifted the stones out and placed them on the altar. The High Priest produced a knife and cut the ropes round each stone as the assistants unwrapped them.

"May the Gods protect us!" shouted the High Priest suddenly as he saw the two sculptures – they were both African fertility gods with huge penii (by European standards). The High Priest and his assistants appeared terrified. Suddenly there was a distant rumbling, then a defending crashing sound was heard from outside the temple. The priests fell to their knees. A guard dashed in.

"The walls!" the guard shouted. "They are cracking, and some parts have fallen."

"Guards!" shouted the High Priest, regaining his composure. "Arrest this man." He pointed to Judas. "Bring him and his accomplices before the Council at midday. I shall summon the Elders." He turned to his assistants: "Cover these two monstrosities before anyone else sees them," he ordered.

Judas, Jesus and Mary were taken to a cell and guarded. An hour later they were marched before the Synod in the Council Chamber. Several serious and very angry men were sitting round in a circle. Judas, Jesus and Mary were told to stand in the middle besides the two obscene statues which remained covered.

"Idolatry!" announced the High Priests. "This man, Judas of Nazareth. Has brought idols into the temple."

"I didn't know," protested Judas. "They were a gift to you from the Land of Nodd."

"Be silent," commanded the High Priest. "Ignorance is no excuse. I shall read from the sacred text." The High Priest unrolled a parchment.

"You may wish to avert your gaze, gentlemen," warned the High Priest. He nodded and his assistants uncovered the two pornographic statues.

"Behold! These idols for the wicked to worship, the Rasta demi-Gods, Marley and Bong, they are a curse sent from the Land of Nodd," announced the High Priest.

The High Priest began to read: "'When the Disciples of Wickedness, Marley and Bong, are brought together in the Holy Place then the Sheriff and Guardians of the Underworld shall be laid low. And the Four Horsemen of the Apocalypse shall be released to roam the Earth once more: Desmond, Dekker, Sly and Robbie. And the Gods of Reggae shall rule all the Land. And there will be a terrible wailing. And women shall cry. And all men and beasts and even mountains shall rock and roll into the pit of oblivion and shall never be heard again. And all this shall come to pass in the Kingdom of the Israelites.' So it is written." There was a pause while the Elders had time to reflect on the true horror of the situation.

There was a further rumbling as some more masonry fell from the walls of the city.

Warning: Christians and people who are easily offended should not read this book

"Your Holiness," asked an Elder. "Save us. What can be done?"

"It is also written that the Gods can be appeased," said the High Priest. "If he that carried the evil ones into the city, is present at a ceremony of atonement. And there shall also be three dusky slave girls, fair and pure, who are cleansed in the Holy Rivers of the Tigris and Euphrates valleys. And a Preacher shall wail bare-chested, possessed by Demons. And after this incantation the curse shall be lifted, and the Messengers shall be cast out of the city. And the wailing shall end. And the walls shall rise again."

"So shall it be," said the Elders, nodding in turn.

"Judas of Nazareth you have brought a curse on this city," sentenced the High Priest. "You are an idolator and servant of evil. You will remain here until the prophecy is fulfilled. I release your accomplices on their word that they will return and appease the Gods. Both you, and these two obscene idols, will remain locked in the vaults of the Temple without food so that you may be purged of your sin, until your accomplices return and lift the curse."

…

Mary and Jesus plodded through the desert.

"That was a total clusterfuck," complained Mary.

"If anyone else offers you drugs, just say no," replied Jesus.

"Yeah!" said Mary. "Ganga really screws you up."

"What in Hell is going on?" asked Jesus.

"It's all bollocks," said Mary. "The walls of Jericho are constantly falling down. Those local builders are useless. That's why they say it's Jerry Built. Now the Pharoah, he got Hebrew slaves to build them pyramids, and look, three thousand years later and they're still solid as rocks. I won't be surprised if they last another ten centuries."

"Yeah, right!" said Jesus. "As if the Earth will still be here in another thousand years. I mean they'd have run out of names for Emperors. What year would that be called? Fiftieth year of the Emperor Elvis or Donald the Great or something stupid?"

"I've been thinking about the dusky maidens that the Priest wants so they can appease their Gods," replied Mary. "It's all about Camel 'flu."

"Camel 'flu," repeated Jesus.

"Yeah!" explained Mary. "All the camels died in the Great Camel 'flu Epidemic last year. So the Bedouins can't bring any slaves from Kush and Nubia and all those places beyond the Great Desert, because they haven't got enough camels. So the only place to get African comfort girls is from King Nebuchadnezzar in Babylon – the land of the Two Rivers – because he can ship them in directly from Zanzibar."

Warning: Christians and people who are easily offended should not read this book

"You mean he's got the monopoly on sex slaves?" asked Jesus.

"Yeah!" replied Mary. "And don't he know it – retails prices done gone through the roof. So what that horny High Priest is doing is getting us to bring him two comfort girls back free and gratis, and without people suspecting he's really a dirty old pervert."

"May he burn in Hell," said Jesus.

"Amen to that," replied Mary.

"What's the going rate for African slave girls?" asked Jesus.

"It was about a thousand camels each," said Mary. "Them being luxury items and all. But what with the shortage and inflation and him wanting top of the range sports models and everything who knows."

"Where are we going to get a thousand camels, never mind two thousand?" asked Jesus.

"Hell if I know," said Mary. "I can stand in for one of the three. And I do have a contact over there in Babylon. Let's just keep going and hope for a miracle."

"That'll really do it," said Jesus, sarcastically. "Why not stop here and pray for a while too. 'Lord God Almighty, please deliver us two beautiful African slave girls of easy virtue to gratify the carnal desires of a perverted Priest.' That will really go down well. Why not part the Red Sea while we're at it."

"Been there, done that," added Mary.

Suddenly a small herd of camels appeared over the hill and came galloping towards Jesus and Mary. The camels slowed as they approached. They began to sniff Jesus' robe. Jesus stroked their noses as several harassed camel-herders came dashing over the hill. Jesus reached into his pocket. He pulled out what was left of a reefer. One of the camels snapped it up and swallowed it. The camels kept sniffing at him for more.

"It be a miracle," said the Captain of the herders, breathlessly. "Them beasties made off at seven bells. We thought we'd never spy 'em again."

"Pleased to be of service," replied Jesus. "Mr...?"

"Ahab, Captain Ahab," said Captain Ahab. "And this scurvy lot is me crew. We're in the camel business. Ships o' the desert ya know."

"I'm Jesus and this is Mary," said Jesus.

"A comely wench an 'all," said Ahab. "Ya best watch out lassie," he whispered. "My boys ain't seen a woman these past three months."

The herders began rounding up the camels and attached reigns and bridles.

"Where ya heading?" asked Ahab.

Warning: Christians and people who are easily offended should not read this book

"We're trying to get to Babylon," replied Mary.

"Shiver me timbers!" exclaimed Ahab. "If we ain't on the same course. The King there pays a good price for camels. He'll cross our palm with silver, especially since that outbreak of camel 'flu. You two landlubbers come along. Ya can keep us entertained. And your boy there. He seems to have a way with camels." He watched Jesus helping to calm the bad-tempered camels and harness them.

"It would be a pleasure," said Mary.

"Then it's settled," said Ahab. "Ya both come along to Babylon with Captain Ahab and his desert pirates. It's ten days plane sailing but we best travel at night when it's cool. We can follow the stars." He began whispering again: "Just be careful, these boys ain't seen a woman since we were last in port – a place called Gomorrah – I thought it'd been demolished but there ya go. And your friend there. He better watch out too. Ma boys can get some strange ideas when they been in the desert for a while, if ya catch me drift. When they say, 'There she blows,' they aren't talking about whales."

...

A few days later, Jesus and Mary were resting in a tent as the midday sun scorched the desert.

"Now Mary," said Jesus. "I don't want to make things more difficult than they already are."

"Go on," said Mary.

"You mustn't use all that witch-craft and those dark arts," said Jesus. "It's evil and wicked and you'll go straight to Hell."

"Hell ain't so bad," said Mary. "Although you wouldn't believe the heating bills. Anyhow, how come you're sure I'm a witch?"

"That's beside the point," argued Jesus. "No more spells or black magic or anything. Not even curses."

"Damn!" said Mary. "Unfortunately the Dark Lord takes them back when he terminates your contract."

"Are you sure?" asked Jesus.

"Positive," replied Mary. Which is a nuisance because we're going to need at least a dozen bottled jinnis to get us out of this fix. This ain't a three-wish sort of problem."

"And you ain't made any love potions or done anything like that to me?" asked Jesus.

"Not that I know of," replied Mary. "Why do you ask?"

"Never mind," replied Jesus.

Warning: Christians and people who are easily offended should not read this book

Suddenly there was shouting. Ahab dashed into the tent, threw open a roll of carpet and released a multitude of knives, swords and other weapons.

"Battle stations," said Ahab. "The Philistines are upon us. Arm ye selves and prepare to repel borders." He pointed to the weapons having grabbed a cutlas and dagger. He turned to make off.

Mary quickly picked out a spear and short sword while Jesus lifted a bow and a quiver of arrows. They dashed out to join Ahab.

The camels were sitting hobbled around the camp although they protested ferociously. Ahab's experienced men had taken positions in a circle between the various camels and tents. They were brandishing bows and swords.

Not far away, a half-dozen robed horsemen were bearing down on the camp at full gallop. Ahab's men were clearly nervous, but they continued shouting curses at the attackers. Just before they reached the camp, the charging cavalry turned and began to circle, looking for weak spots. Mary leaned back, took aim, and threw her spear. It skewered a man who fell dead from his mount. His horse ran off. Ahab's men began firing arrows at the horsemen.

Jesus fumbled with his bow. "Which way round do these go?" he asked Mary.

"Give it here," she said.

"I'm only a carpenter," protested Jesus.

Mary took aim and shot several arrows. Two more riders fell from their mounts. She loosed her last arrow at a giant of a man bearing directly down on them from a huge black horse. The arrow hit the horse which fell. The giant leapt from his stumbling mount and rolled over. He quickly stood and drew a huge scimitar. He strode forward threateningly.

"Let's be having you me beauty," shouted Captain Ahab, drawing his sabre and stepping forward to challenge the enormous warrior who towered over him.

Ahab pulled back his sword arm. The giant lifted his sword. Suddenly a pebble hit the giant squarely in the face. He dropped his arm, briefly stunned. Ahab did not need a second chance and felled the giant with one mighty swing.

The remaining bandits galloped off into the desert. Ahab and his men looked round. Jesus was casually swinging a slingshot.

"So they do work," Jesus said in amazement.

That evening Ahab, Mary and Jesus were sitting around a campfire.

"Shouldn't we go?" asked Jesus.

"Hold, yah horses," said Ahab. "We has to celebrate our victory and give thanks to the gods."

Warning: Christians and people who are easily offended should not read this book

Several of Ahab's men stepped forward and dropped various swords and other weapons in front of Jesus and Mary.

"That's the booty from them scallywags that attacked us," said Ahab. "That and two horses we rescued from the desert. Their owners won't be wanting 'em now. Not where they've gone. You take your pick."

"I'm not really that bothered," said Jesus.

"Get with the plan," protested Mary, grabbing a jewel encrusted dagger. "Here," she said, lifting out a huge scimitar in a scabbard. "You can use it to pick your teeth."

"Why?" said Jesus, taking the scimitar.

"Because you get to start the feast," said Mary.

"Arr!" added Captain Ahab, as one of his men brought forward a steaming piece of cooked meat on a platter.

"This is the heart of the beast," said Ahab. "You take the first bite."

"Heart of what?" asked Jesus as Mary impaled the morsel on her new dagger.

"The heart of that giant ya just felled," said Ahab. "Yah has to eat the heart of ya enemy so ya will get his strength."

"That's cannibalism," protested Jesus.

"Well it seems a shame ta waste it," argued Ahab. "Anyway, the boys will expect it. You two being great heroes and saving our souls and all. Especially the girl with that harpoon."

Jesus took the dagger and looked cautiously at the cooked heart. He wretched and appeared queasy.

"Give it here," said Mary impatiently. She took the dagger and ripped a piece of the meat from the chunk with her teeth and then swallowed it.

The men around cheered.

Jesus took the dagger back and delicately nibbled a piece while the men continued to cheer.

"You have the stomach of a lamb," said Ahab quaffing some vicious-looking drink. "But the heart of a warrior." He passed the cup to Jesus who took a sip. Mary took the cup and downed the entire contents, spilling most of it down her chin and onto the ground. The cheers became louder as they saw Mary drink. Ahab's men stood up and began to dance round the fire in celebration.

"That was a pretty good shot with the spear," Jesus said to Mary, as the celebrations continued. "Are you sure you don't have any powers left?"

Warning: Christians and people who are easily offended should not read this book

"No," said Mary. "That was just me. I suppose it's like riding a bicycle. Once you learn you never forget."

"What's a bicycle?" asked Jesus.

"Never mind," said Mary. "Throwing spears is a bit like sex. But the target is bigger."

"Ah," said Jesus, comprehending her comment.

...

Jesus, Mary, Ahab and the caravan of camels approached Babylon.

"Land ho!" said Ahab. Mary and Jesus were riding camels next to him.

"Well shipmates," said Ahab to Jesus and Mary. "We be parting company here. May ya have the fair winds and a following sea. And matey boy, ya has a winning way with camels. If ya ever wants to stow away again, ya can rely on Captain Ahab and his crew to give ya a berth."

"That's very kind of you," said Jesus. "I'll help the boys herd the beasts into the dock, I mean pens."

He geed his camel onwards.

"And where be ye going?" Ahab asked Mary, as she began to pull away.

"I just have to see someone," she replied. "You keep Jesus occupied. I'll be back in an hour."

"Aye Aye, 'mam," said Ahab.

...

"Come Mary, be seated," said the breath-takingly exotic Queen Thelema resident of the fabulous Penthouse of the High Tower in the Palace of Babylon.

"I have a problem," said Mary. "And I was hoping you could help."

"Of course," said Queen Thelema. "Helping beggars is exactly what I do. The Whore of Babylon - Charitable Foundation and Philanthropist. Forget what you might have heard about me being the mother of all the abominations on the Earth. I live to give. Although, credit where it's due, you have had your moments as well, Mary. That business with the seven plagues of Egypt. Very impressive!"

"Praise from Caesar," replied Mary.

"So what do you and that preacher want?" asked Queen Thelema, smiling.

"You heard?" asked Mary.

"Good news travels fast," said Queen Thelema. "But bad news travels faster."

Warning: Christians and people who are easily offended should not read this book

"I need a couple of dusky slave girls," began Mary.

"That would be for that twisted Priest in Jericho," said Queen Thelma.

"How did you know?" asked Mary.

"Come on dear," said the Queen. "With a reputation like mine, people tell you things. Anyway, he's been angling for a threesome for years. But he won't pay the going rate."

"Which is?" asked Mary.

"Ten thousand camels," said Queen Thelma. "Each."

"You fucking low-down, two-bit, grave-robbing, pimp-hustling bitch!" shouted Mary.

"Flattery will get you nowhere," said Queen Thelma. "I have my position to think of. And I have you over a barrel."

"Bah," said Mary, pausing for thought while the Queen enjoyed Mary's discomfort.

"A drink?" asked the Queen. "You have spent ten days in the desert. And you don't have any special powers now. So you must be thirsty."

"That would be nice," growled Mary. "Make it strong. And add some hemlock. It will end my pain."

The Queen snapped her fingers and a handsome, muscular, almost naked, male servant appeared and gave Mary a filled cup.

Mary looked at the cup suspiciously.

"Oh please!" said the Queen. "As if I would. I'm actually more hurt than angry."

Mary scowled at her a bit more.

"You won't get anything if you poison me," said Mary, taking a drink.

"My thoughts exactly," added the Queen.

"How about nine thousand camels and you give me that pretty boy you're travelling with," said the Queen. "What's his name?"

"You know perfectly well what he's called," said Mary, taking a drink. "And you know that: 1. I don't own him; and 2. He ain't for sale."

"You can't blame me for trying," said the Queen. "It looks like you have a problem then, deary."

Mary thought for a while.

"How much is ten thousand camels in gold?" she asked.

Warning: Christians and people who are easily offended should not read this book

"Twenty thousand camels," corrected the Queen. "Just because I'm a girl doesn't mean I can't count you know and you want two slave girls. Anyway, seeing as you don't have any gold, or silver, or loose change, it doesn't really matter."

"But I know a man who does," said Mary. "And he has an entire treasury. Which he will be more than pleased to share with you. If you do what I say."

"You wicked, wicked girl," said the Queen. "Tell me more…"

…

"I got the girls," said Mary as she met up with Jesus in the camel pens.

"That was quick," said Jesus. "How did you manage that? And how did you get the money?"

"Don't ask," said Mary. "But I didn't use any black magic so you can relax. Now all we have to do is wash them down in the river and get back to base before Judas starves to death."

"Losing a few pounds wouldn't hurt him," said Jesus. "Captain Ahab, do you have any idea how much they sell African slave girls for around here?"

"Second hand about five thousand camels," replied Ahab. "New from around eight thousand but sports models don't start below ten thousand. Or so they tell me. Why do you ask?"

"No reason," said Jesus.

"You got your very own sports model there, son," said Ahab. "You mind to keep her properly serviced." He laughed crudely.

"You got twenty thousand camels' worth of comfort girl?" Jesus asked Mary.

"Sure," Mary replied. "Glinda and Theodora, picking them up tomorrow when we've done the paperwork."

"I am very impressed," said Jesus.

"You should be," said Mary. "Do you want to know how I got them?"

"How did you get them?" asked Jesus.

"Don't ask," replied Mary and kissed him.

…

The next afternoon Mary, Jesus and the two African slave girls were splashing in the Rivers of Babylon. The two girls kept glancing over at Jesus and giggling. They were naked, much to Jesus' obvious discomfort.

"You know, I still have some worries," Jesus told Mary.

Warning: Christians and people who are easily offended should not read this book

"I know. I know," said Mary. "You have some ethical hang-up about selling slave girls for sex to a randy Priest to get Judas released from the dungeons of Jericho and certain death by starvation."

"What comes next after 'clusterfuck'?" asked Jesus.

"'Cataclysm', I think," replied Mary. "Anyhow, let's take one disaster at a time."

"Shouldn't we just let the girls go?" asked Jesus.

"And exactly where are they going to go?" asked Mary. "I can speak their language. They told me they escaped from starvation – there was a drought in their country. Just try and roll with me on this. Even as slaves they get housed and fed. And everybody who is anybody has slaves now – it's all the rage. The entire Roman Empire depends on slaves. Even Solomon had slaves. Your mob built the pyramids as slaves."

She paused.

"That doesn't help does it?" she asked,

"Not even a little," admitted Jesus.

"Look at it this way," said Mary. "Back in their homeland they would have been married off and have to perform sordid acts to gratify some hugely overweight tribal chief. Frankly, they wouldn't be much better off."

"Erm," said Jesus, unconvinced. "To be continued," he added. "Now to get back to matters in hand, how are we going to get back to Jericho? It's a ten day walk through the desert which is full of desperate thieves and robbers."

"Something will come up," said Mary.

"Do we need to put the girls in chains or something? For appearance-sake?" asked Jesus.

"They aren't going to run off," said Mary. "Especially in the desert. They'd die of thirst. Anyhow they quite like you because you're soft and let them sleep in beds and eat the same food as us and don't make demands of them. Hell, you even helped them clear up this morning. You need to stop that. They'll get spoiled and then they won't be any good as slaves."

"Well excuse me all to Hell!" said Jesus. "I've never had any slaves before."

"Well I have," said Mary. "OMG! I don't believe I just said that."

Jesus looked at Mary and smiled.

"Stop looking so smug," said Mary, punching him. "Right. We need to cross an outlaw-infested desert, release Judas, and then find a way to get the High Priests to free two top-of-the-range comfort girls worth ten thousand camels each. This is going to be a real humdinger."

Warning: Christians and people who are easily offended should not read this book

"What's that over there?" said Jesus, staring across the river.

Mary peered.

"It looks like a body?" she said.

The body twitched and an arm waved feebly in the fast-flowing current.

Jesus dived forward and swam into the stream. Fortunately, he was able to intercept the body and began towing it back. Then he saw something snaking across the water towards him.

"There's a fucking crocodile," shouted Mary scrambling up the bank. "Swim faster!" She and the two girls began throwing stones at the crocodile as Jesus swam as quickly as he could while towing the drowning man.

Suddenly there was loud shouting, and a company of soldiers came running along the riverbank. They began throwing spears at the crocodile and several soldiers waded in to help Jesus pull what turned out to be a boy from the water. The boy lay still as soon as they had him on the bank. Jesus knelt by him and rolled him over. The boy began to splutter, and water spilled from his mouth. There was a great commotion. A large band of panicking immaculately dressed women ran into the group around Jesus. A woman screamed and fell on the boy, who was now conscious. She pulled him to her breast and began crying and praying, while she rocked the spluttering boy. Jesus stepped back and stood beside Mary. A well-dressed older man spoke briefly to some of the soldiers and then saluted Jesus and spoke to him in a strange language.

"I don't understand," said Jesus, appearing bemused.

"Ah," said the Elder. "My Aramaic is not too good. But you understand?" he asked.

"Yes," said Jesus. "I am Jesus, this is Mary."

"Blessings up on you," said the Elder. "My name is Abarsam the Elder, Grand Vizier to the Court. The young lady kneeling there is Princess Atossa. These are her guards and handmaidens. And the boy you have just rescued is Prince Darius, son and heir to his most Imperial Majesty, The Living God, King of Kings, Nebuchadnezzar, Emperor of Persia and All the World beyond."

"Looks like we got our ride," said Mary, prodding Jesus.

…

Jesus, Mary, and the two girls were feasting in the Great Hall at the Court of Babylon that night. There were numerous dignitaries sitting along impressive tables loaded with food. Jesus and Mary sat in places of honour either side of Princess Atossa. Abarsam stood behind her and translated. Lavish entertainment was taking place. Jesus, Mary, and the two girls were decked out in appropriate garments given to them for the occasion.

Warning: Christians and people who are easily offended should not read this book

"Her Highness will send a Royal Guard to accompany you through the desert to the Temple at Jericho," explained Abarsam. "However, she does not have the authority to negotiate directly with the High Priest nor his ruler or the Roman Governor. But the ruler of Jericho and the Roman Governor are good friends with our Emperor. Upon his return from his most victorious conquests in the East, our Emperor will ensure the release of the two girls and their return to their homeland if they wish. They helped save Prince Darius from the serpent. They will be given high honour if they choose to return here."

"We'll let them decide," said Jesus.

"We need them to help us perform the ceremony to appease the Gods of Jericho," said Mary. "Or else the walls of Jericho will come tumbling down."

"I don't know why they bother to keep re-building those walls," said Abarsam. "They've already collapsed twice during my time here. They're built on sand. No proper foundations. They really need to move the whole city about five miles south where they can dig down and make some decent foundations on bedrock."

"I'll pass on your advice," said Mary.

"With all respect," said Abarsam. "It will fall on deaf ears. Who do you think runs the biggest construction company in Jericho?"

"Not the High Priest?" suggested Jesus.

"You got it," said Abarsam.

"What's all the commotion?" asked Jesus as there were cheers from the diners.

"It's the main course, at last," Abarsam. "Roast crocodile."

"Is that the one that tried to eat me?" asked Jesus.

"The very same," said Abarsam. "And as guest of honour you will take first bite from the cut of choice, the heart."

Multiple servants paraded in pairs through the feasting hall carrying the monstrous beast on several wooden trays.

Jesus looked at Mary and gulped.

"It gets worse," said Mary.

"How?" asked Jesus.

"You remember the High Priest telling us that the ceremony involves a bare-chested preacher possessed by demons?" asked Mary.

"Yes," said Jesus.

Warning: Christians and people who are easily offended should not read this book

"Well volunteered," said Mary.

…

Mary and the two slave girls danced in synchrony and sang while Jesus, bare chested and wearing silver pantaloons, leapt round like a lunatic. When they had finished their performance, they bowed to the applause of the guests in the Great Hall.

The High Priest was sat facing various senior members of the Persian guard of honour that had accompanied Jesus. The High Priest was well-pleased. A rather hungry Judas was released from his chains and the statues of Marley and Bong were ceremonially destroyed by Priests wielding hammers. Mary sat beside the High Priest along with the two slave girls as the banquet began.

"You have atoned for your sins," announced the High Priest, standing. "Judas and Jesus of Nazareth, you are free, but your slave girls must accompany me to the inner sanctum to complete the ceremony later. Now we will feast to celebrate our salvation and our renewed friendship with his Imperial Highness, Nebuchadnezzar, King of Persia." People began eating and drinking noisily. The High Priest sat.

"We are new to this place," asked Mary, sitting close to the High Priest. "May we ask Your Holiness a question? Just to clarify some things I've heard."

"Of course," replied the High Priest. "Indulge yourself. I intend to."

"Who is keeper of the Royal Treasury here in Jericho?" asked Mary.

"That would be the Satrap," replied The High Priest.

"And where is he?" asked Mary.

"The Romans took him away some years ago," said the High Priest. "He was rather a nuisance to them. So they took him off to Rome to negotiate with the Emperor. And he hasn't been seen or heard of since. The Romans want someone who is more imaginative. The sort of man who might lend them funds from the Treasury, at a reasonable rate of interest, for their military escapades. Despite what they say, the walls of the city can be quite useful, especially if there is a besieging army camped outside. They usually find it's more cost-effective to negotiate a settlement with us. We regard Roman belligerence as opportunities to invest in aggressive business ventures – and the returns on our investments have been very favourable so far."

"In the absence of the Sartrap, who exercises his functions?" asked Mary.

"That would be the Grand Wizard of the Ancient Order of Masons," said the High Priest. "In collaboration with the Governor of the Imperial Bank. We do a lot of building work around here, so the Order of Masons have a significant income from public funds. You have no idea who much it costs to maintain all those walls – especially when they keep falling down."

Warning: Christians and people who are easily offended should not read this book

"So there are two rulers, when there is no Satrap?" asked Mary.

"Only to regulate the bank," replied the High Priest. "It's important that there are two – to make sure one scrutinises the other, especially regarding decisions on the Bullion Reserves. We have a lot of safe deposit boxes and such – being as how we have such famous walls and tend to preserve our independence here in Jericho. We haven't been invaded since that Joshua chap in, now when was it, over a thousand years ago. We have the oldest established banking system in the civilised world. We invented compound interest, the eighth wonder of the world. Can you keep a secret?"

"Surely," replied Mary, nodding to a servant who was hovering round.

The servant refilled his glass as the High Priest continued his sales pitch. He rather enjoyed bragging about his city's achievements.

"We have over a billion talons in gold in our vaults, right here, just under your feet," said the High Priest.

"Goodness," said Mary. "Don't you worry about being robbed?"

"Nah," said the High Priest. "Our walls are fourteen feet thick and there are three concentric rings of fortifications, and we hire the most ruthless and therefore effective security guards in the world. Most of them are Huns. They don't speak a word of English so they can't plot against us, and they don't know what they're guarding. But they'd cut your head off as soon as they look at you."

"So how does anyone get their money out?" asked Mary.

"In the absence of the Satrap, major withdrawals have to be authorised by a Tribunal consisting of the High Priest, which is me, the Grand Wizard, which is also me (because we don't believe in all that witchcraft stuff anymore), and the acting Governor of the Bank, which is also me at the moment, while we appoint a replacement."

"How long have you been waiting to get a new Governor for the Bank?" asked Mary.

"Eleven years," said the High Priest. "We need someone with the right experience. It's a very responsible role. We've been out head-hunting. We've found plenty of heads but no one suitable yet."

"Thank you for that," said Mary. "I thought I understood those things, but I just wanted confirmation. International banking is rather a hobby of mine. It's nice to hear it from the Master. And now I must join my two friends. I will leave you in the safe hands of your two newest admirers." She winked at the two slave girls, who smiled seductively at the High Priest, one girl was either side of him. "I am sure they will attend to your every whim," added Mary.

Mary rose, bowed to the High Priest, and left to join Jesus and Judas. The High Priest grinned at the two girls and stood up to make an announcement.

Warning: Christians and people who are easily offended should not read this book

"My friends," he announced. "I grow weary. I will try and join you later although I am fatigued with worry these past few weeks. Please continue the feast."

The High Priest, followed by the two slave girls, left the Great Hall. The banqueters cheered and toasted the High Priest as he made his departure.

"Dirty old sod," said Jesus to Mary as she sat beside him. "You would think he could wait until after the festival."

"Not to worry," said Judas. "I'm famished. I can eat his share." He was stuffing his mouth with food. "Anyway, what took you so long to get here?"

"You would not believe the shit that we've been through," replied Mary. "Next time you want to get stoned you're on your own."

…

The High Priest led the two slave girls into his inner sanctum and private chambers. He sat on a divan.

"Bring me wine," he ordered the girls.

"Yes, my Lord," replied one, suddenly able to speak the language.

"Your every wish is our command," said the other, lounging next to him.

One girl filled a cup and handed it to the High Priest.

"May I ask my Lord a question?" asked the girl who sat beside him. The other went to the door.

The High Priest nodded as he drank.

"As well as being the High Priest, and Governor of the Bank," she asked. "You are also The Grand Wizard of The Masons?"

"Yes," said the High Priest. "We've combined the High Priest with the Grand Wizard because all that witchcraft stuff is ancient history. No one believes in it anymore." The High Priest returned to drinking.

"Excellent," said the girl by the door, as she slid the heavy bolts home sealing the entrance. She turned and smiled at her accomplice. Their eyes glowed demonically. "Let's misbehave," she announced as she strolled over.

…

Judas, Jesus and Mary had just left Jericho. They were pushing the cart.

"Do we really need this thing," asked Jesus who was pushing the cart.

"It's got the props in," said Judas.

Warning: Christians and people who are easily offended should not read this book

"Don't worry," said Mary. "I searched it for contraband earlier. And there was none. Except this." She pulled out a small bag containing dried grass.

"That's for personal use," said Judas, grabbing it off her.

"Well, you can personally roll me one a swell," said Mary. "And we aren't taking it any further than that hill. So use it or lose it."

"We could buy a load of new props with that bag of gold the Gran Vizier insisted we take for saving the Prince," said Jesus.

"I feel awkward about that," said Mary. "I mean, it can't just be a coincidence that the Prince happened to be drowning just where we were bathing. And that crocodile just appeared. You'd have thought they'd have chased off all the crocodiles in that stretch of river years ago, especially if the local Royalty were in the habit of swimming there."

"The Lord works in mysterious ways," said Judas, handling the bag of gold. "Now I think we should invest this. And, having been able to speak with my trusted financial advisors in The Bank of Jericho, Roman-Legions Inc. are the hot investment of the day. Word has it they're about to make a take-over bid for some Northern Island full of illiterate backward primitives who have barely invented language. The investment brochure says the fields are filled with gold and silver and diamonds and the weather is wonderful. Sounds like a great holiday destination. We should go there once it's been invaded and pacified. Investing these twenty gold dinars would be a good start to our portfolio. Apparently, we can't possibly lose with this investment."

"Lending money with interest is a sin," said Jesus. "It's called usury."

"What gives," asked Judas. "Everything is a sin. Making idols, bearing false witness, fornication, coveting asses. Why are all the best things a sin?"

"They just are," said Jesus. "You should work for a living. Not live off the interest produced by other people's labours."

"Well that undermines the entire Judeo-Roman political system," said Judas. "And we've just been to Jericho where they invented compound interest, God bless them. You ought to be more supportive of our achievements. One day Jewish bankers will rule the world."

"I don't approve of usury," said Jesus. "We should give that money away and not expect anything in return. We didn't earn it. It was just a fluke."

"I agree," said Mary. "Living off the sweat of others is exploitation. Workers of the world unite! Except slaves of course. I mean we'd all starve if we had to pay them."

"Does not the Bible say, 'The wise man doth invest his wealth to make more'?" protested Judas.

Warning: Christians and people who are easily offended should not read this book

"No, it doesn't," said Jesus. "You just made that up. It says: 'Give and it shall be given unto you'. Somewhere someone added a 'ten-fold' but I'm not sure where that comes from."

They saw Captain Ahab and his crew approaching on the track.

"Ahoy," shouted Ahab, waving to Jesus.

"What brings you here?" asked Mary.

"We're on a private charter," said Ahab. "The Queen, back in Babylon, crossed me palm with silver and said she wanted some discreet, ahem, removals men to move a ship load o' cargo. She didn't say what. But we've had to bring two dozen extra camels. Apparently, there are two damsels in distress marooned over here. Name of Glinda and Theodora. We bin told they're moving out on the next high tide. Any ideas where they might be birthed?"

"Try the Temple," replied Mary. "Ask for the Inner Sanctum."

Ahab waved and continued onwards with his large caravan. His boys looked very pleased with themselves. They were obviously expecting a sizable bounty on this voyage.

…

Jesus, Mary and Judas were following the river. They saw a large boat sailing towards them. They waved and a dashing officer at the tiller waved back. As the boat drew past them, they suddenly heard a shouting on board. There was a splash, and a young woman began swimming frantically ashore from the boat. There was a great commotion on board. Jesus and Mary waded into the water and helped the girl ashore. Her ankles were manacled, and she wore a silver collar round her neck indicating she was a slave.

"Can't you throw her back?" asked Judas as they mounted the bank. "She's trouble."

"A curse on you," replied Mary.

Sure enough the boat pulled in and the handsome officer leapt ashore accompanied by three vicious-looking cut-throats, all armed with cutlasses. One of the men had a deep gash on his face that was healing. The girl hid behind Jesus as the men approached. She spat and cursed at them in a foreign tongue.

"Ahoy there," said the handsome officer. "Second Lieutenant Chris Adams RN, that's Roman Navy, Britannic Contingent, at your service."

"Pleased to meet you," said Judas. "You're a long way from home."

"Indeed," replied the Lieutenant. "Let's just say me, and my shipmates here, had a dispute with our old commanding officer who accidentally fell overboard. So now we run an independent maritime trading operation. You know, shipping industrial items up and down the river, medicinal incense, ceremonial swords and daggers, oh. And the odd filly. Which brings me to my point. I wonder if we could have her back?"

Warning: Christians and people who are easily offended should not read this book

"Who?" asked Mary.

"That there filly you have, the one that just came ashore without docking," said the Lieutenant.

"You mean you're slavers and she's one of your cargo?" asked Mary.

"That isn't our primary business concern, but, basically yes," said the Lieutenant. "You see we picked this old hulk up for a prayer a few years ago and we've been doing the run up and down the river since then. We deal in whatever is fashionable. And since the chaps at Jericho fell out with The Noddy, we've mainly been doing religious incense. But prices for fillies, like your friend there, went through the roof a year or two ago. And this chap comes round and can't wait to unload her and another dozen. I think he was on the run. Anyway, we took the girls off his hands for a song and we're just going to drop them off up-river and Bob 's your uncle."

The girl was swearing and spitting. She became louder as time went on. The cut-throat with the scar on his face growled at her and she hissed back.

There was a standoff.

"Is she for sale?" asked Jesus.

"Ah," said the Lieutenant, in surprise. "You rather caught me off guard then, old chap. Well, I suppose she is. We tend to do wholesale. But good business is where you find it. Forty dinars and she's yours."

"We've only got ten," said Judas.

"We've only got twenty," said Mary, kicking Judas. "Show him," she ordered Judas, who reluctantly produced the moneybag and fingered some of the coins. Meanwhile some people, including a few soldiers, who were wandering up and down the road, began to gather and watch the entertainment.

The Lieutenant paused for thought. "May I have a minute with my business partners," he asked. He turned and spoke to the cut-throats.

"We can't strong-arm these chaps in front of that audience," said the Lieutenant, glancing toward the crowd that had gathered on the road. "We had better make a deal."

"Get shut of her," said the scarred man. "She gives me this memento when I gets too close, and then we chain her in the brig for four days. And then she jumps ship the first chance she gets. She's nothin' but trouble what with making them other girls mutiny. We picked her up for half what they're offering."

"Anymore for anymore?" whispered the Lieutenant. He paused. "No?" He turned around.

"It's a deal," said the Lieutenant, reaching out and shaking Jesus' hand.

Warning: Christians and people who are easily offended should not read this book

Mary grabbed the money bag from Judas and threw it to the scarred man who immediately emptied it into his hand and began to count the coins.

"Now," began the Lieutenant. "She's a little frisky, so you might want to keep the chains on. But we'll remove the collar so you can get your own fitted."

The Lieutenant glanced over to one of the cut-throats who cautiously approached the spitting girl. She took a swipe at him. Mary went to pacify her.

"No problem," said Jesus. "You can take the manacles off as well."

"If that's what you want," said the Lieutenant. "Mind you, if it were me, I'd chain her to something big, like a tree, if you don't want her running off tonight."

"We'll take that risk," replied Jesus.

"The customer is always right," said the Lieutenant. "No refunds by the way. Sold as seen. Just thought I should mention that."

"It's rather an old boat," said Judas, as Mary and one of the cut-throats were releasing the girl's chains.

"Well spotted," said the Lieutenant. "She used to be called The Leviathan, but that was back in her hey-day. Now we just call her the Jolly Roger – it has more of a family feel about it. She leaks like a sieve, but she runs high in the water which means we can repel boarders without too much trouble. She's the biggest fish in these waters. You know, the other night some scallywags tried to swim out and hijack us. Damned pirates don't you know. They're all sleeping with the fishes now!"

"So you are subject to maritime law?" asked Judas.

"Aye Aye, shipmate," said the Lieutenant.

"That means that any business deal that was made aboard your vessel would be offshore, technically?" said Judas. "And not subject to Roman laws, or taxes."

"I suppose not," said the Lieutenant, thoughtfully. "Anyhow, we've got the chains off your girl there. So good luck with your new purchase and we'll be off while there's a fair wind." He leant over to Judas. "Where are you based?"

"Nazareth," said Judas.

"We dock in Port Tiberias every few weeks," said the Lieutenant. "I'll look you up. Having said that, we're not too popular with the Emperor at the mo. So we try not to spend too long ashore. They seem to think the swords we carry aren't just for ceremonial use. Arms dealing or some such nonsenses. Heaven forbid!"

The Lieutenant and his pirates scrambled back on board the Jolly Roger and waved goodbye.

Warning: Christians and people who are easily offended should not read this book

"Well, that's one down," said Mary, digging out some clothes for the new girl from the cart. "Didn't he say there were another dozen on board?"

"How are we going to buy a dozen slave girls at 20 dinars a piece?" said Judas. "You've spent all our cash in one go."

"Where there's a will there's a way," said Mary.

"Yes," said Jesus. "Have faith."

"What do I care," said Judas. "I just hope girl Friday there appreciates me for what I done."

"What did you do?" asked Mary.

"Nothing," said Judas. "But she thinks I bought her freedom from those pirates. Which I did."

"With our money," correct Mary.

"It's an investment," said Judas. "I'm like a broker."

"Broker? You can break your neck pulling this cart," said Jesus. "It's your turn."

"Can't she do it?" said Judas, reluctantly taking over the cart.

"What does she look like?" asked Mary. "A horse?"

"I just hope she's grateful, that's all," complained Judas. "I expect a handsome return on my investment, I mean our investments, in future."

…

That night Mary, Jesus and the new girl were in a tent. The two girls were laying either side of Jesus. The new girl was asleep.

"You are sleeping with two hot chicks tonight," said Mary. "And you ain't getting any action from either. But you can lie about it to your mates anyway. You old dog you."

"But she's asleep," protested Jesus. "She won't notice whatever we get up to."

Mary kissed him. "It ain't happening," she said. "You sick pervert."

"Hey," said Judas from the tent next door. "Keep it down in there. Some of us are trying to sleep, unfortunately."

"Bah," said Jesus. "You just spoiled the moment."

"You can come in here if you want," said Mary. "Nothing's happening. You've killed the romance."

"Serve you right," shouted Judas. "Why does he get both girls?"

Warning: Christians and people who are easily offended should not read this book

"Because he knows how to respect boundaries," said Mary. "Well, some of the time. Anyhow, you can come in here and then you can lie to your mates and say you had a foursome. You'll probably do that anyway so you may as well get it partly right."

"I'm staying here," said Judas. "If I come in there you won't respect me in the morning."

"We don't respect you in the evening either," said Mary. "Or the daytime, or the night."

"Bah!" complained Judas.

"Sleep tight," said Mary and Jesus. "Don't do anything we wouldn't."

"Chance would be a fine thing," replied Judas.

…

Mary and Jesus woke the next morning to find several armed men pointing spears at them. They raised their hands. Suddenly, girl Friday dashed in, closely followed by an elderly man and a girl.

"I'm Teuta," said the girl. "I speak your language. This is Joni, she says you freed her from the slavers."

The soldiers lowered their weapons and Jesus and Mary quickly stood up. The elderly man tearfully embraced Jesus. Judas appeared from outside. He was smiling to himself.

"I suppose this is the King of your country?" asked Mary. Jesus was overwhelmed.

"Oh no," said Teuta. "Mr Gentius is father of Joni. He is a poor merchant. We are from Illyria. We come down here to find Joni who was kidnapped by slavers some weeks ago. We found the slavers a few days ago just North of here. We have brought them alone. Well, we have brought their heads. While they still had tongues, they said that they sold Joni to some pirates. But we see that you freed her. We are very grateful."

"Can we ask what sort of poor merchant is Mr Gentius?" suggested Judas.

"He is very poor," said Teuta. "He only owns twenty silver mines. We have brought a reward. It is not much. Only 300 libra."

"How much is that in pounds and ounces?" asked Mary.

"Let's just say we're going to need another cart," said Judas, grinning.

…

Mr Gentius insisted on a feast to celebrate finding his daughter, to which some of the local villagers were invited, as well as Jesus, Mary and Judas. Judas enjoyed counting the silver even though this did take a period of several hours.

Two days later the Illyrians were packing to make the long journey home.

Warning: Christians and people who are easily offended should not read this book

"You know," said Judas to Jesus and Mary. "With your current rate of return on our investments, if you can 'invest' this windfall we should get enough money back to buy the entire Port of Jaffa – lock stock and barrel. Just a thought. Speculate to accumulate sort of thing."

"Ahoy there!" they heard a voice. As they looked round, they saw Second Lieutenant Chis Adams at the helm of his boat which was pulling towards the bank.

"Ahoy," replied Jesus and Mary. "How goes it?"

The Lieutenant remained on board as his cutthroats busied themselves securing the boat. He shouted over the side.

"The darndest thing," said the Lieutenant. "We just got to Jericho and, would you believe it, the Governor of the Bank has had some sort of mental breakdown and shipped all the treasure off to Babylon. They say it's part of a tax avoidance scheme. Anyhow, no one has two beans to rub together in Jericho – at least not in hard currency. So we're out of luck with these dozen fillies and wondered if you want to take them off our hands. Same rate as last time."

"We'll take the lot," said Mary.

"Good show," replied the Lieutenant. "How will you be paying?"

"Silver bullion," replied Mary.

Judas fainted.

"That will do nicely," said the Lieutenant. "I'll just come ashore and have a look at the loot if you don't mind." "Mr Gilgamesh," he said to his cutthroat deputy. "We can start unloading the cargo."

"About time too," moaned Gilgamesh. "Having a woman aboard is bad luck."

…

Jesus and Mary waved farewell to Joni, Gentius and his party including the dozen former slaves that Mary had purchased and freed.

"See you back home," shouted Judas from the deck of The Jolly Roger as it set sail down river. "I have some business to discuss with the Lieutenant here. We need to recover some of our losses, you know."

"Why don't you join us?" shouted the Lieutenant. "It's plain sailing down to Galilea."

"No thanks," said Jesus.

"We had a bad experience on a boat once," explained Mary.

Jesus and Mary waved to Judas who waved back along with Second Lieutenant Chis Adams.

Warning: Christians and people who are easily offended should not read this book

"At least we don't have to push that god-awful cart anymore," said Jesus to Mary.

"Actually, it's broken," said Mary. "Judas tried to load all that silver on it and the axle snapped."

"I'll fix it when we get home," said Jesus. "Doing some joinery would be a welcome change from all this excitement."

"We're not home yet," said Mary. "Plenty of things could go wrong on the way."

"That's the spirit," said Jesus. "Think positive."

…

The next day Jesus and Mary were casually strolling along the river.

Judas suddenly appeared ahead. He was soaked. He came running over.

"Thank goodness," said Judas. "We need your help. Both of you."

"What do they say about rats leaving the ship?" suggested Mary.

"The Jolly Roger hit a submerged boulder and we think she's done for," explained Judas. "And we've got all that silver bullion on board."

"We can't carry all that," said Jesus.

"No! No! No!" said Judas. "We have a plan."

…

A few hours later Jesus, Mary and Judas had swum across the river and hiked along the bank of a tributary for a few miles. They soon came across the wreck of the Jolly Roger. The Lieutenant and his crew were still busy salvaging what they could.

"The old girls had it," said the Lieutenant as Jesus and Mary approached.

"Where's the silver?" asked Judas.

"We made a depot on the riverbank," said the Lieutenant. "But there's still a good few pounds in the bilges. Unfortunately, the rainy season has just started and the water's rising. I don't think we can get much more from the old girl until the river goes down. But there's more bad news, I'm sorry to say…"

"Tell me," ordered Judas.

"I think we got spotted by a Roman patrol on the other bank," said the Lieutenant. "I told them a story, but I don't think they quite bought it."

"And why would that be an issue?" asked Mary.

Warning: Christians and people who are easily offended should not read this book

"You see, my chaps and I had a bit of a scrap with some Legionnaires a week or two back," explained the Lieutenant, awkwardly. "Friendly sort of misunderstanding you know. Only six or seven killed. The thing is, since then, the old Centurion has been sending patrols along the river looking for a re-match, if you understand. So when those chaps get back to base, he'll probably send a couple of cohorts our way. So we better clear off until the heat's off."

"But there's a village isn't there?" suggested Judas, urgently.

"You see," continued the Lieutenant. "We were planning on hiking over that mountain and following the gorge. There's a village at the other end. We could hide out there for a few months until the river goes down and the heat's off. Technically, this side of the river is Persia so it's outside Roman control. It's just that folks aren't too receptive to a bunch of heavily armed pirates wandering in and taking up temporary residence. So we were thinking of becoming monks and following a travelling preacher, for respectability's sake, just so we can hide out for a few weeks."

Judas and the Lieutenant looked at Jesus and smiled, imploringly.

"Do you all believe in God?" asked Jesus.

"Not really," replied the Lieutenant.

"You might want to reconsider that," said Mary.

"Maybe we will all have a revelation while we're on sabbatical with you," said the Lieutenant. "You know it's important to reach out and save sinners. And my chaps and I have sinned quite a bit. We certainly need saving. Yes indeed!"

"I bet if you guys prayed for forgiveness until the end of time it still wouldn't be long enough," said Mary.

"Quite possibly," replied Lieutenant.

"Let me have a word with my assistant here," said Jesus. He took Mary to one side.

"They've got us haven't they?" said Mary. "And it's all my fault."

"Hook, line and sinker," said Jesus. "I don't buy any of that repentance crap either, but I'm not allowed to judge. Now if you weren't here, I might be able to take a tougher line. But seeing as how you do have some baggage yourself, I can't really abandon them. More joy in Heaven for one repentant sinner than ninety-nine and all that."

"Bah," said Mary. "I knew you'd say that."

They went back to speak to Judas and the Lieutenant.

"OK, we accept," said Jesus. "But you have to listen to my sermons and not fall asleep."

"It's a deal!" said the Lieutenant. He spoke to his men: "Gather round chaps."

Warning: Christians and people who are easily offended should not read this book

The three vicious pirates stopped working and moved closer.

"Brother Jesus and Sister Mary here have generously agreed to lead us into Salvation and the Kingdom of Heaven," began the Lieutenant. "Which is about three day's march over that hill, and beyond the reach of those annoying Roman patrols. So here are some ground rules: 1. Don't kill anyone unless I give you the nod; 2. No bad language, swearing, obscene jokes, threats or curses…In fact maybe it's best that you don't speak at all. Let's say we're a trappist order. 3. Sister Mary is strictly out of bounds to anyone. In fact, avert your gaze if she comes anywhere near you. 4. We have some robes that look monk-like which is good, because we can conceal all our weapons underneath. It's best if we keep all that stuff out of sight. And 5. Don't kill anyone. Now I know I've said that twice, but it is rather important. OK?"

"Aye Aye," replied the three crewmen and returned to packing what they could.

"Now you three," said the Lieutenant. "It can get a bit rough on that mountain pass. So we better tog you out. Have any of you had any military experience?"

Mary raised her hand.

"Well," said the Lieutenant. "I wasn't expecting that. Male chauvinist pig that I am."

He led them over to a cache of weapons. "Take your pick," he said. Mary picked up a bow and some arrows.

"Good choice," said the Lieutenant. "Take a shot at that tree over there."

Mary expertly nocked the arrow and shot it. The arrow quivered as it hit the trunk of a tree almost 100 yards distant."

"Actually, I was thinking of that one," said the Lieutenant, pointing to a tree twenty feet away. "But you've made your point. I suspect you've done this before."

"Once or twice," Mary replied, pulling out some vicious looking daggers to put inside her robe.

"Now Brother Jesus," said the Lieutenant. "You were a carpenter? I think this might suit you." He picked up a shield. Jesus took it and put his arms through the grip. "Technically that's upside down," explained the Lieutenant. "But it's still good. Now…" He handed Jesus a weapon. "This is called a pole axe. If anyone gets too frisky just tap them on the head with this pointy bit at the top and they'll leave you alone. Now Mr Judas," he continued. "You can come with me. You are our secret weapon."

…

The following day the seven adventurers were trekking across a sandy mountain plateau.

A man appeared from behind a rock and approached them. He was wearing dirty robes.

Warning: Christians and people who are easily offended should not read this book

"Welcome," said the man in a foreign accident. "Do you need a guide? It is very dangerous up here. Many bandits!"

Jesus stepped forward with his shield. "God protects us," he told the man. "Are you alone?"

"Yes," said the man. "I am safe here. Bandits no bother me. I have no money. I am mountain guide. You are men of God? Priests?"

"Something like that…" began Jesus.

The Lieutenant threw a tomahawk which buried itself in the newcomer's forehead, felling him immediately. The Lieutenant stepped by the bewildered Jesus and grabbed his shield arm. "Just a couple of inches higher, old chap," said the Lieutenant. Two arrows struck the shield. Mary and the pirates returned fire against three bow wielding bandits who were peering over a nearby rock. An arrow impaled one bandit through the neck, and he fell back stone dead. The other two bandits disappeared and made off.

Jesus looked the Lieutenant in the eye in disbelief. "It's a diversion, old chap," said the Lieutenant. The other three were trying to size us up. I spotted them as soon as this fellow started his nonsense." The Lieutenant pulled up the sleeve of the dead bandit in front of him. There was a short dagger in a scabbard strapped to the dead man's wrist. "He was about to stick you with this and then try and fell me before we knew what was happening," said the Lieutenant. "Bad luck for him but I've done the same trick myself a few times."

"Are you planning on killing everyone we meet up here?" asked Jesus, still shocked.

"I jolly well hope not," replied the Lieutenant. "But up here it's usually best to get the boot in first. Or the knife in this case. Especially with rotters like him. They don't call it bandit country for nothing."

"Goodness," replied Jesus.

"Can I have their knives?" asked Judas.

"Help yourself, old chap," replied the Lieutenant, checking the bodies. "They aren't going to need them anymore."

…

That night in the tent.

"You're still a bit shaken up, aren't you?" Mary asked Jesus.

"I can't remember having anyone cut down in front of me like that before," said Jesus.

"He deserved it," said Mary. "He would have killed you."

"It's a bit of an ethical challenge," said Jesus. "I have to adapt to life in this lawless country."

Warning: Christians and people who are easily offended should not read this book

"We couldn't be in safer hands," said Mary. "Those pirates are the business. Say what you like. No one is going to get close to you with them watching your back. And your front and sides."

"God has a purpose for everyone," said Jesus. "Even cut throats like them."

"He works in mysterious ways," added Mary.

"He certainly does," added Jesus.

…

Jesus and Mary climbed out of the tent the next morning.

Gilgamesh and Judas were trying to bury the bodies of two more bandits who were lying dead besides the holes.

"Just ignore those two," said the Lieutenant. "I think they came back last night looking for their two friends."

"What happened?" asked Jesus.

"Looks like a snake bite to me," replied Lieutenant. "Lots of poisonous snakes up here. Especially at night. They're nocturnal, you know."

"I thought snakes only came out in the day," said Jesus.

"That's city snakes," said the Lieutenant. "Mountain snakes are different. Isn't that so Mr Gilgamesh."

"Aye Aye, Captain," said Gilgamesh. "Snake bite alright."

"Perhaps we ought to avoid anyone else while we're up here," suggested Jesus. "For their benefit as much as ours."

"Suits us," said Gilgamesh.

"No problem," said the Lieutenant. "From now on, all strangers to be given a wide berth. OK chaps. Best foot forward. Tally Ho!"

…

Later that day Jesus, Mary, the Lieutenant, and a couple of his men were peering over a rock. A few hundred yards in front, four armed men were dragging four girls in chains along a track.

"They look like slave traders," said Mary. "Probably on their way up to Jericho or Babylon with their cargo in tow."

"Now," said the Lieutenant. "Those four chaps aren't going to give up those fillies without a fight. In fact, they might just try and help themselves to some of our treasure as well, if they

Warning: Christians and people who are easily offended should not read this book

think we're soft targets. They'll probably just cut our throats just to see what we're carrying. So it's your call? Engage the enemy or beat a hasty retreat and let them pass."

"We can't just leave those girls," said Mary.

"I know," said Jesus. "Let's see if we can talk some sense into them."

"Ok chaps," said the Lieutenant to his men. "We're going for a parley. Lock and load. But try not to repel borders unless they drop the hammer. Move out!"

Jesus, followed closely by Mary and the Lieutenant, approached the caravan. The other Pirates, all with cowls up and avoiding eye contact, were close behind although they quickly took up position besides the other three slavers while Jesus engaged the leader.

"Blessings up on you," said Jesus to the Leader of the slave train.

The slaver smiled maliciously and bowed.

Suddenly Gilgamesh skewered one of the slavers and the pirates downed the other two instantaneously.

The Lieutenant and Jesus grabbed the arms of the Leader. Mary drew a rope and quickly began to tie the slaver leader's arms, as the Lieutenant began searching him for concealed weapons. Mary went to release the four slave girls as soon as the Lieutenant had removed the numerous weapons from the person of the Slave Leader.

"He was goin' for a knife, Captain," shouted Gilgamesh. "I could see it in his eyes."

"Good thinking old chap," said the Lieutenant to Gilgamesh. "Sorry about that," he whispered to the speechless Jesus. "Although Gilgamesh is an admirable fellow, and I wouldn't have anyone else with me in a scrap, he can be a bit trigger happy. Not that that's a criticism. He's bailed me out of a tight spot more times than I care to remember."

A few minutes later, the Slave Leader was securely trussed with his hands tied behind his back. He was sitting and cursing in his own language. He did not seem unusually worried. Jesus was overwhelmed.

"What exactly is this?" said Judas kneeling by the securely bound slave leader, showing him a terrifying razor-sharp curved dagger that the leader had been carrying.

"That brings me good luck," said the slaver. "My mother gave it to me for my birthday."

"That must have been a hell of a party," said Judas.

One of the freed slave girls wandered over.

"You be careful there," said the Lieutenant to Judas. "That chap bites. Keep that letter-opener well out of his reach."

Warning: Christians and people who are easily offended should not read this book

"Three down but one still breathing," said Jesus, recovering his composure a little. "At least the odds are improving."

"If you say so," said the Lieutenant. "It's none of my business but they'll almost certainly hang the old boy when we drag him into town. And that's if he's lucky."

"I see?" asked the slave girl in broken English to Judas, eyeing the knife and beckoning to examine it. Judas stood and handed her the dagger. In one move the slave girl stabbed the dagger deep into the remaining slaver's neck. He gasped and fell, bleeding heavily. Jesus and Judas dashed forward but there was nothing they could do. Blood spurted from the vicious neck wound and the slavers was clearly dead after a few more second. The slave girl spat at him and kicked his still twitching body. Another freed slave girl came over and kicked the body of the dead man as well.

"Well, that's one problem solved," said the Lieutenant. Mary came over, attracted by the commotion.

Jesus, shocked once more, was temporarily stunned.

"A small safety point," said the Lieutenant to Judas. "It might be an idea to check with me before handing out weapons. No harm done this time but just for future reference."

"Sorry about that," said Judas.

"Don't mention it," said the Lieutenant.

"It's him you need to apologise to," said Mary to Judas, pointing to the dead slaver.

"Saddle up!" said the Lieutenant. "No point in waiting round here for any of their chums."

"At least we could bury them," stuttered Jesus.

"Ta Hell with them," said Gilgamesh.

"I speak the girls' language," said Mary. "There were six slave girls to start with. They buried two on the way here."

"That for my sister, pig!" said one of the slave girls, spitting on the body of the dead slaver.

Jesus paused.

"To Hell with them chaps," admitted Jesus, finally. "Buzzards gotta eat."

The party set off again.

...

Three days later the seven descended from the mountain pass to the desert village of Calvera. The village was just beneath the opening of a narrow mountain gorge. A river flowed from

Warning: Christians and people who are easily offended should not read this book

the gorge and snaked past the village onto a desert plane. Jesus led the others. They had their cowls raised to conceal their faces and the girls wore makeshift veils.

"Blessings up on you," said Jesus as he entered the village. One of the Elders came forth and greeted him. "We are pilgrims and weary travellers," explained Jesus. "We would be grateful if we could rest here for a while. We are not beggars. We can pay for our lodging."

"You are very welcome, friends," said the Elder. "We will share what we have. But it is precious little. The harvest was bad. And the rains have only just started. We have many worries, so a holy man and his followers are especially welcome. You will bring us luck. Come!"

The Elder led Jesus and his followers into a large room and summoned some women to make food. Eventually some simple fare was produced. Jesus insisted on giving the Elder a silver coin for his troubles. Other villagers visited the room to examine the visitors. They were surprised to see Mary and the four freed slave girls amongst them, although Jesus explained that they were nuns, and that the other monks had taken a vow of silence and they could not speak other than to pray.

"We have many empty houses," said the Elder. "People are sick of life here. It is hard, especially for the young people, and they leave for the city."

Jesus and the others ate. "So you had a poor harvest?" asked Jesus.

"There is a drought here," replied the Elder. "If you look you can see we had a dam. In the past we had all the water we could use, and more. But the dam broke in a storm several years ago. The King sent timber to repair it, for this is his land, but our carpenters died during the drought, and we have no one to direct. We are simple farmers, not builders."

"It will be our pleasure to help," said Jesus. "Prior to my calling, I was a carpenter, and my followers here are strong but silent. With our help I am sure we can rebuild the dam and your farms will bloom again."

"You are indeed a blessing from Heaven," said the Elder. "I will tell my neighbours. They can make time to help you if you can rebuild the dam. This would be more than payment for our hospitality."

The Elder left the room and began speaking to men in the street.

"What say you, sister Mary?" whispered Jesus.

"This is so cool," she replied. "Being a nun. Do I get my own place – my own convent? What shall we call it?"

"It looks like there's no shortage of bunks for a convent and anything else," whispered the Lieutenant. "Half the houses look deserted. Incidentally, old chap, good thinking with the dam thing. We can drag that out for months. Perfect excuse to stay for a while."

Warning: Christians and people who are easily offended should not read this book

"I had a look at the dam on the way down the mountain," said Jesus. "All the footings are there. We just need to use all those planks and tree trunks to sure up the middle. It means a good bit of sawing and getting those cranes and pulleys up and running. But it shouldn't be too difficult. It's a huge thing though. They'll have enough water for a city once it's done."

"That's it," exclaimed Mary. "Our Lady of the Holy Dam. It's a play on words…"

There was a commotion and shouting in the street. Galloping horses could be heard.

Jesus and his followers dashed out.

Six men on horses were galloping down the main street. Two threw axes which cut down two women who were trying to run. Villagers were dashing for cover into the houses.

Automatically, Mary and the four pirates threw off their robes and drew weapons. The battle-hardened sailors stepped forward as the six invading horsemen careered down the street. The sailors cut down three mounted bandits with swords and throwing axes. Mary shot two horses from under their riders with her bow. A sixth rider collided with a fallen horse and tumbled from his mount. The dismounted rider rolled over but was quickly able to stand. A villager approached him threateningly with an axe. The bandit threw his sword, skewering the villager. The bandit grabbed the reins of his horse and tried to mount it. Judas leapt forward and threw a dagger which impaled the bandit in the back. The bandit gasped and fell, tangling his foot in the horse's reins. The horse panicked and dragged the fatally injured bandit at a gallop, towards the dam.

Jesus and Mary turned to Judas with eyebrows raised.

"I wasn't always a theatrical agent," said Judas, apologetically.

"Backstabber!" said Mary.

"Damned good show, old chap," interrupted the Lieutenant, shaking Judas' hand warmly. "Couldn't have done a better job myself. That bounder richly deserved it." The other three pirates slapped Judas on the back as they returned to the saloon.

The Elder and several villagers approached Jesus, looking bemused.

"Perhaps an explanation is in order," said Jesus, awkwardly.

…

"These bandits come every harvest," explained the Elder, later that day. Several village men were standing around as Jesus and his followers sat at the table. The Elder continued, "But our harvest failed this year. So those six villains were sent in advance to punish us. And when the Chief arrives with his mob, they will expect all our food, even our seed corn. They will leave us to starve. But they will burn our houses and kill us if we do not deliver."

"How many of these blighters are there?" asked the Lieutenant.

Warning: Christians and people who are easily offended should not read this book

"Over a hundred," replied the Elder.

"By the looks of 'em," continued the Lieutenant. "They're a company of cavalry gone rogue from some Arab king – probably decided to go freelance rather than surrender to the Romans."

"How long will they take to get here?" asked Jesus.

"They are probably on route now," said the Elder. "But it will take them at least a month, maybe more, before they arrive. They will raid other villages on their way."

"Thankfully we downed that other chap," said the Lieutenant. "So they won't have any warning. Hopefully they won't be that worried when the advance party doesn't show up."

"The bandits will be furious if they discover their friends have been killed," said the Elder. "And they will torture some of the women to discover where we have hidden the seed corn, and what we saw of their scouts. We have no weapons, and no skill to use them. But you are fearsome warriors. What should we do? We cannot all run. We have nowhere else to go."

The other villagers hollered in agreement.

"Perhaps I could speak to my followers, in private," said Jesus.

"As you wish," said the Elder, waving the villagers from the saloon.

"What do you think?" Jesus asked the Lieutenant and his men.

"'Tis suicide," said Gilgamesh. "A hundred mounted men. We should run while we still have legs." The other pirates agreed.

"Run where?" said Jesus.

Gilgamesh and the others paused.

"We've been running all our lives," said the Lieutenant. "We all know that wherever we go, it will end bloody, or at the end of a rope. Frankly I'm tired of looking over my shoulder all the time."

The men looked at each other, uncertain what to do. There was a long silence.

"May I speak?" asked Mary.

"You speak loud enough for everyone with that bow," said the Lieutenant. "We'll listen."

"You have lots of weapons that you were smuggling on the boat," said Mary. "You can take some of the villagers and fetch those. There's plenty of time to train them. And those of you who survive after the bandits come, they can stay here without fear of being arrested and hanged, like you deserve."

Warning: Christians and people who are easily offended should not read this book

"And you can still collect the silver from the boat when the flood goes down," said Jesus. "So you will be rich men. Even though it is dirty money from slave trading and worse. Best of all," he continued. "If you get killed here, you needn't worry about the Bad Man. It galls me to say this, but self-sacrifice means automatic entry to paradise. That's the rule. You can get straight into Heaven, and you don't even have to listen to me preach."

"How do we fight a hundred mounted bandits?" asked Gilgamesh.

"Military tactics aren't one of my strong points," said Jesus. "But if we fortify some places on the mountain pass, we can cut down the bandits if they try to climb up."

"Good thinking," said the Lieutenant. "Their numbers will be useless. Just like that chap in Sparta. And horses don't count for jack on that footpath. We could hold out there for months. OK, chaps, let's consider the proposition overnight."

"You won't be needing me then?" asked Judas

"We need every man-jack we can get," said Mary.

"Especially you," said Jesus. "With your new-found skill with knives."

"Yes, old chap," said the Lieutenant. "You're a natural-born killer. Just like Gilgamesh here. But not as handsome."

…

"Those old builders were brilliant," said Jesus as he admired the work that several villagers were doing on the dam. Planks and logs were being hauled up on cranes which had been mounted on the rock ledges above the dam. "All we have to do is patch up the centre with these logs."

"Won't it leak?" asked the Elder.

"Sure," said Jesus. "But the leakage will keep the river running. Do you know why it's so big?"

"Legend has it that the King wanted to build a city here," said the Elder. "But that was many centuries ago. The gorge is so narrow that the dam can hold enough water for thousands. But the plan never really worked out."

"The farmland will be excellent," said Jesus. "With irrigation from that dam, you will be able to harvest six or seven times a year and feed a whole city."

"That's assuming the bandits don't kill us all," said the Elder.

"We need to move tents and some supplies onto those ledges soon," said Jesus. "That way we can hold out for weeks."

"Won't they just camp and starve us out?" asked the Elder.

Warning: Christians and people who are easily offended should not read this book

"It sounds like they will starve," said Jesus. "Would you come up that footpath with Gilgamesh and his friends on ledges just over you?"

"I understand," said the Elder.

"The bandits will hang around for a few days, then go somewhere else, where there's easier picking," said Jesus. "Their horses will need fodder as well as the men. It's a matter of logistics. Incidentally, have you posted sentries on the hills to warn of any surprise attacks?"

"No problem," said the Elder. "Mr Adams supervised it himself. May I ask you something?"

"Sure," said Jesus.

"That girl you have," said Elder to Jesus. "Is she really a nun?"

"Of course not," said Mary, who had overheard. "Although I'm coming round to the idea. It would save an awful lot of hassle."

"Who taught you archery?" asked the Elder.

"Artemis," explained Mary. "We used to go hunting. She liked hunting boars best. If you don't fell them with the first arrow, they come at you, and you have to take them hand to hand. Or hand to trotter. It really focuses the mind having an angry 400-pound boar coming at you. Good character-building stuff."

"Good-O," said the Elder, leaving to help with the sawing.

"Do you really want to be a nun?" Jesus asked Mary.

"I knew you'd say that," said Mary.

"And what's the answer?" asked Jesus.

"It's a bit like closing the door after the horse has bolted," said Mary. "Although that's a little bit vulgar. Anyway, my stable door might still be open to the right stallion. Incidentally, did I tell you how macho you looked when you dived in the river to save that Prince?"

"Not that I remember," replied Jesus.

"You were quite dishy," said Mary "Splashing about. Although I had my money riding on the croc."

...

Jesus, Mary, the Pirates, and a few village leaders were in conference.

"I'm a tad worried about those bandits sending another raiding party," said the Lieutenant. "That's what I'd do. Send some chaps on recon if I thought my scouts had gone AWOL."

"We have already posted sentries on the hills," said the Elder.

Warning: Christians and people who are easily offended should not read this book

"I wonder," said Jesus. "If they send an advance force, it will probably be around a dozen horsemen. We can handle that number. Maybe if we send them packing with a bloody nose they might not come back."

"Do you have any ropes and nets?" the Lieutenant asked the Elder.

"Of course," replied the Elder. "We've been using lots of ropes for repairing the dam."

"And we have no shortage of lumber for barricades," said Lieutenant. "You see, the layout of the town makes it a perfect corral. We could lead a small raiding party down the high street into a blind alley and then give them a good drubbing. All we need is a few dozen chaps with pointed sticks. We could put barricades between the houses in the high street."

"We need the raiders to gallop into the trap," said Mary. "That way they won't spot the barricades until it's too late and a lot of horses will shy and throw their riders in the confusion, when they get to the bottleneck. But we need some bait – something to lead them in."

"I notice we have a few horses," said the Lieutenant. "They threw their mounts during the first fracas and they're now surplus to capacity. Can anyone ride?"

"We are all farmers," said the Elder.

"There isn't much call for horse riding in my business," said Jesus.

"And horses are a rich man's sport," said Judas.

Mary cautiously put up her hand.

"Mary," said the Lieutenant. "Do you have some riding experience?"

"The odd gymkhana," said Mary. "And the occasional cavalry charge in the face of the enemy, not more than a few hundred times."

"You never cease to amaze me," said Jesus.

"You're making me blush," said Mary, looking down.

"I can dust off my old riding boots," said the Lieutenant. "So if Mary and I ride out and prod any advance party, we can probably get them to chase us back here, full throttle. And Gilgamesh and you boys can do your stuff and talk them out of making a return visit. Is everyone OK with that? I do feel a bit of a heel taking a lady along but we're the only ones who can ride."

"I can look after myself," said Mary. "And I'm lighter so I can outrun guys on horseback."

"Are you sure?" asked Jesus.

"Sure as sin," said Mary. "Needs must when the Devil drives."

Warning: Christians and people who are easily offended should not read this book

"Don't you worry, old chap," said the Lieutenant. "I'll have her back, safe and sound, before you know it, or my name's not Second Lieutenant Chris Adams. I give you my word as a Naval officer."

"A Naval officer who mutinied," added Jesus.

"Technically correct," said the Lieutenant. "But you can't hold that sort of thing against chap forever. Let bygones be bygones."

"We're keeping Gilgamesh here as a hostage," said Judas.

"That's a fair deal," said the Lieutenant.

…

It was the sabbath, Jesus was asked to address the villagers. His followers were present.

"Considering everything that's been happening," began Jesus. "I thought it would be wise to revisit exactly how things are meant to work. Now, if a man trespasses against you, that means he insults you or cons some money or possessions out of you, or breaks a deal, then go and tell him his fault yourself face-to-face. That does not mean stab him in the neck. Obviously, if he looks anything like our friend Gilgamesh, you might want to go round with a friend. Now if he does not hear you the first time, then take two witnesses. That does not mean that the three of you beat his head in. It means you have two witnesses to remember what you are complaining about. If he still doesn't hear you, then go and tell it to the Church. I know full well that in the big city, justice is often given to the highest bidder. However, in most places, the priest is impartial and has to live with all parties in a disagreement. Furthermore, you will often find that if you have a dispute with a man, many other people have had the same experience, and folk will be losing patience with him. Hence, there is a good chance you will get a fair hearing without having to throw the guy off a cliff. If you still aren't satisfied, try and put the thing down to experience and move on. You won't make the same mistake again. Just remember, you will still have to live with the guy regardless of what happens. This is the word of the Lord."

He paused.

"Now," Jesus continued. "There will now be a minute for quiet reflection so that people may ask the Almighty for forgiveness for their sins."

There was a period of half a minute while people prayed.

Jesus started again: "I don't want to cast aspersions, but some of our maritime friends may want to continue this period of reflection after the service, and for several years beyond that. Now, Sister Mary and her choir will lead us in a hymn: 'By the Rivers of Babylon' which seems unusually appropriate."

…

Warning: Christians and people who are easily offended should not read this book

Mary spoke to Jesus after the service.

"It's harder than you think, isn't it?" asked Mary. "You know, interpreting the commandments and rules."

"You said it, sister," replied Jesus. "It's OK when everyone follows the rules. But it gets really hard to decide what to do when people break the rules, or when the rules aren't enforced. And then money always gets in the way. It's amazing how flexible people can be when they interpret words, especially when there is some cash in it for them."

"Amen to that," said Mary. "Is something else bothering you?"

"I don't like this thing about you acting as bait to lure a raiding party of ruthless outlaws into the town," replied Jesus.

"I don't know what to say," said Mary, taking Jesus' hand. "The Lieutenant and I are the only ones who can ride. And I am a pretty good jockey."

"I still don't like it," said Jesus. "Not one little bit."

"You're not a tad jealous, are you?" asked Mary. "About me and that murderous slave-dealing Lieutenant, dashing and well-spoken though he is?"

"No," said Jesus. "Not at all."

There was a pause.

"Well, maybe a little," admitted Jesus.

"What do they call those promises nun's make?" asked Mary.

"Vows," said Jesus.

"Well fuck those," said Mary. "I just want to screw your brains out right now."

"People are watching," said Jesus.

"I don't care," said Mary. "Poverty and obedience are ok, but my vow of chastity just went AWOL."

"Sympathetic as I am to your position," said Jesus. "It might be advisable to survive your forthcoming encounter with those homicidal bandits before you completely abandon your sacred vows."

"You mean I have to get the bandit recon troop to chase me into town and kill them, before you will shag me?" asked Mary.

"You don't have to kill them," said Jesus. "Just lure them into town."

"Can't I kill a few of them?" asked Mary.

Warning: Christians and people who are easily offended should not read this book

"Only if you absolutely, definitely have to," replied Jesus.

"That spoils the fun a bit," said Mary. "But OK. Why don't you have a word with the horse? He will understand you. You tell the horse, stallion to stallion, how you feel, and he'll take special care of me. And after that, you can come round to the convent, and I can reassure you myself. Hopefully you weren't planning on walking very far tomorrow."

"Isn't that against the rules," said Jesus. "You know, me visiting a convent and all."

"But you can't refuse a condemned man's last wish," said Mary, sniffing. "Or a condemned woman on the eve of battle. Actually, it's so romantic. I'm starting to cry."

"Stop that," said Jesus. "I hate it when women cry."

…

Mary and Lieutenant came thundering down the track with a dozen blood-thirsty outlaws in hot pursuit. The outlaws' horses were tiring but still maintained a good speed being spurred on by riders who were waving swords along with hollering and cursing. They careered into the town and made pell-mell for the saloon, located at the end of the main street. Mary was a nose ahead of the Lieutenant although both horses were flying on the wind. Suddenly the two veered off onto a side track just before the saloon. The outlaws tried to follow but found their route blocked by a dozen wooden barricades, all sporting long, sharpened spears. In the resulting chaos four riders were thrown. High rope netting immediately cut off the escape in all remaining corridors and the dozen mounted riders were subject to a hail of spears and arrows, released from all directions behind strong barricades. Everywhere the bandits turned they faced high barricades, or ropes nets with multiple pikes pointing threateningly in their direction. The remaining mounted horsemen tried to circle but found their enclosure was too limited to maintain any speed, or even to attempt to jump any of the many obstacles that now surrounded them. They ground to a halt and looked round bewildered, expecting a further hail of arrows and projectiles. They were surrounded by villagers with pikes and inanimate barricades which they could neither jump nor threaten.

Jesus stepped out of the saloon followed by a guard of several villagers and pirates armed with spears and bows. One bandit was foolish enough to raise a throwing axe and was felled within seconds by two arrows which found their mark on his chest. The bows were instantly reloaded. Each of the half-dozen mounted outlaws saw spears and arrows marking them in whichever direction they looked. The horses gradually slowed to a standstill, as the men considered their position and desperately sought a means of escape. Several dismounted bandits had to be pulled up so that some horses now had two riders.

"Who speaks for you?" commanded Jesus. None of the outlaws responded. Another volley of arrows descended on them.

"Who speaks for you?" commanded Jesus. One bandit spurred his horse a few feet forward to acknowledge the challenge.

Warning: Christians and people who are easily offended should not read this book

"Do you understand me?" asked Jesus. The outlaw nodded, nervously.

"Leave here," ordered Jesus. "Never come back. Tell your leader you will find nothing here besides Hell Fire, Death and Damnation. Now go!"

A gap appeared behind the scouts as some rope netting was dropped to the ground. What was left of the raiding made off.

The villagers cheered and rounded up the stray horses that were left.

…

Jesus, Mary and the Lieutenant were standing on top of the dam, which was still under construction. Villagers were busy working.

"Good chaps, these farmers," said the Lieutenant. "I admire their enthusiasm."

"No leaks either," said Mary.

"I'm impressed with that as well," said Jesus. "It's like building a boat in reverse. They even have caulking and tar to seal the timbers."

"Couldn't be better if you'd planned it," added the Lieutenant. "By the way old chap, did you mean all that about forgiveness of sins and automatic entry in the event that, you know, me and my boys bite the dust in a fracas with those beastly outlaws?"

"I don't make the rules," said Jesus. "Put it like this. These villagers are God's own children. And those outlaws come and rape and murder and starve them. Now, come judgement day, what's he going to think about you, seeing as how you've been killed defending his children? Basically, you're in the priority lane."

"That's good to know," said the Lieutenant. "Not that it plays on my mind any. Getting whacked is an occupational hazard in my line of work."

"May I ask you a personal question?" Mary asked the Lieutenant.

"Fire away, old girl," he replied.

"I'm not sure of the maritime vernacular, but do you have a woman?" asked Mary.

"Only one," said the Lieutenant. "…In each port! What do you think? Do I look like the sort of chap who wouldn't have a girlfriend?"

"Dashing, handsome, big-spending, psychopath," said Mary. "Now I think of it, you must have to fight the girls off with a stick. Just like my boy, Jesus here."

"Maybe he was a bit of a ladies' man in the past," said the Lieutenant. "But I think that colt is well and truly saddled, poor chap. I guess it happens to us all, eventually. Anyhow," he continued. "I notice there's a cave over there, just above the new waterline. Why don't you two swim over and have a look. It's not visible from the ground and it's the sort of place

Warning: Christians and people who are easily offended should not read this book

someone like me would bury treasure. Go on. I'll help here. You two go exploring. Take your time. I assume you can both swim."

"I haven't brought my bathing suit," said Mary. "But I'm game if you are," she said to Jesus.

Half an hour later Jesus and Mary hauled themselves out of the water and into the secluded cave. They wore a minimum of clothing as they had swum across the new lake.

"Pass me my things from that bag," Mary asked Jesus. Jesus tossed her a few dry clothes from the leather bag he had round his neck. Mary dried herself briefly and started to change. She put her wet clothes on a rock in the sun.

"I bet no one's been in here in centuries," said Jesus. "If ever."

"The dam's really coming along well," said Mary, admiring the construction work and then turning to enter the cave.

"You know," said Jesus, sitting on a rock. "It's easier than I thought, these big construction projects. I mean it's a dam – basically it's just a wall. What could go wrong?"

"I suppose it all depends on foundations," said Mary, sitting by him. "I saw this pyramid once. The bloody thing slipped over. They had to move the whole thing forty miles up the road to Cairo. All because of faulty foundations. And they didn't get the angles right."

"I don't know about angles," said Jesus. "But I know about foundations."

"Remind me," asked Mary, continuing to dry herself and change.

Jesus began: "Whosoever heareth these sayings of mine, and doeth them, I will liken him unto a wise man, which built his house upon a rock: And the rain descended, and the floods came, and the winds blew, and beat upon that house; and it fell not: for it was founded upon a rock. And every-one that heareth these sayings of mine, and doeth them not, shall be likened unto a foolish man, which built his house upon the sand. And the rain descended, and the floods came, and the winds blew, and beat upon that house; and it fell: and great was the fall of it."

"Did you make that up yourself?" asked Mary.

"Of course," said Jesus. "Otherwise, there would be copyright issues."

"It's rather poetic," said Mary. "Although I'm not sure about the Olde English bits – it could do with a bit of modernisation – some urban slang."

"I think it sounds more profound," said Jesus. "'Whosoever doeth this' and 'heareth ye' that. People aren't going to be moved to fear eternal damnation if you start a sentence with 'Now get this' or 'This dude was hanging with his homies'."

"How about starting with, 'I'm serious as cancer when I say…',' added Mary.

Warning: Christians and people who are easily offended should not read this book

"Not a bad idea," said Jesus. "But you need to say something that rhymes with 'cancer'. And rhyming things isn't a very reliable guide to ensuring eternal salvation."

"How about: 'I'm serious as cancer when I say brother Jesus has the answer'?" suggested Mary.

"Actually, I quite like that," admitted Jesus. "But I couldn't say it myself because it's about me."

"Maybe I could introduce you," said Mary. "I could beatbox as well."

"That will really get people focussed," said Jesus. "Especially young people. It's really hard to reach 'the kids'."

"That's 'cos you and me are bogus and sad," said Mary. "But if I beatbox, that will be awesome. You need to speak their language."

"Sure thing, Sista," replied Jesus.

They paused.

"You are such a square," said Mary.

"I know," said Jesus, laughing. "I used to be cool but now it's all strange and frightening. All the kids laugh when I try to get funky."

"You know the solution," said Mary.

"What's that?" asked Jesus.

"Take your top off," said Mary.

"Take my top off!" exclaimed Jesus.

"Yeah!" said Mary. "I know I sound like a tart, but that always gets my attention."

There was a pause.

"Me too," whispered Jesus.

"You mean you've looked," said Mary. "When I take my top off?"

"Oh no!" said Jesus.

There was a pause.

"Well, just a little," whispered Jesus.

"It's OK," whispered Mary. "That's why I do it, especially just now."

"You are a wicked, wicked girl," said Jesus, grinning.

143

Warning: Christians and people who are easily offended should not read this book

"I've been living in a convent for the past month," said Mary. "Something's gotta give. Especially when you asserted yourself with those bandits we rounded up. You really laid down the law. That was so hot! I mean, you were lucky we weren't alone."

"Same here," said Jesus. "When you came careering down that track at full gallop with those guys chasing you. Did it get your motor running? The prospect of imminent death?"

"Anyhow," said Mary. "And you still owe me from that deal we made."

"You said it, baby," admitted Jesus. "Same here…You know, I just wish you weren't so hot."

"Ditto!" replied Mary.

Mary stood up and stood directly in front of Jesus. She looked breathless and was trembling.

"You're shivering," said Jesus.

"Well, I ain't cold," said Mary, making eye contact with him as he looked up.

Jesus put his hand on her hips, and Mary put her hands either side of his head.

"Let's…" said Mary.

"Ahoy there!" shouted Judas, from outside.

"Oh, fuck off!" shouted Mary.

"Sorry," said Judas, hauling himself into the cave. "Bad time?"

"Mary and I were finding some aspects of religious life challenging," said Jesus. "But you've solved that problem for now. Unfortunately!"

"Erm," mumbled Judas. "The Lieutenant said you were over here."

"But he didn't say swim over for a visit, did he?" asked Mary.

"Actually no," said Judas. "I wondered what you were doing."

"We aren't doing anything," replied Mary. "More's the pity."

"I can go if you want," said Judas.

"I know it wasn't deliberate," said Jesus. "But you've rather spoiled the mood. I suspect the Lieutenant sent us here for a reason."

"And that wasn't to explore this cave," said Mary. "The Lieutenant has got that 'night before the battle air' about him. Anyway, what do you want?"

"Actually," said Judas. "I've forgotten."

"You aren't making yourself any friends, you know," said Mary, storming out. "Honestly," she grumbled. "Who'd have thought it was so hard to get laid in a place like this."

Warning: Christians and people who are easily offended should not read this book

…

It was midday a few weeks later. A horn could be heard in the distance. Suddenly a bell began ringing in the village. Everyone gathered in the street, clutching the essential possessions that they could carry. Jesus led the villagers along the riverbank for a few dozen yards, and then up the steep mountain path to the refuge. The Lieutenant and his men were already stationed in their Eagles' lairs and looked down on the villagers as they cautiously made their way up the slippery mountain trail. The pirates and several dozen villagers were fully armed and equipped to repel any onslaught as they peered down the cliffs. The advance guard of bandits galloped into the town as the last villagers breathlessly reached the lowest refuge. Gilgamesh cut some ropes and two wooden step ways crashed down onto the rocks below leaving wide gaps in the footpath.

The horsemen in the village dismounted and began searching the houses. Jesus and the villagers hid. They hoped that the bandits would think the village had been deserted. Gradually other bandits appeared on horses until there were over a hundred milling around the village. One man, presumably their Leader, pointed for some bandits to explore the footpath by the dam. Half a dozen bandits rode over. They dismounted at the bottom of the steep path and searched around. Suddenly one startled. He called the others. They had spotted a villager peering over the cliff. They shouted but were inaudible. After staring for a few minutes, they mounted their horses and galloped back to the village to report to the Leader. They pointed towards the dam and the Leader stared up towards the villagers' hiding places. The Leader summoned his man. After a few minutes they lit torches and began burning the houses.

Jesus, Mary and the Lieutenant had been peering through a gap in the rocks. They saw the events taking place below. The Elder and a few village men scrambled over.

"It looks like we've been spotted," said the Lieutenant. "They're going to torch the village to get us to come down."

"We thought that might happen," said the Elder. "Let them do their worst. If we have nothing else, we have a good supply of timber."

"How long do you think they'll stay?" asked Judas.

"Looking at their numbers," replied the Lieutenant. "I doubt if they could maintain a siege for more than a few days."

"I can't see many supplies," said Mary. "They obviously have to raid places and forage every few days to feed that number of men, especially with horses."

"You'd think the King would do something about them," said Jesus.

"This place is no man's land," explained the Elder. "The Romans could overrun this country at any moment. The King is busy with his campaigns in the East. He isn't going to commit

Warning: Christians and people who are easily offended should not read this book

troops here when the Romans might take the place next month or next year. So we have anarchy."

"I think we can hold out this time," said Mary. "But what happens the next time that lot come back? Will that be in a month, or a year, or a week?"

"That's a good point," said Jesus. "And we need to put out those fires. The town is blazing."

Jesus stood. He took his slingshot and fired a pebble at the wooden dam. There was a low creaking. Then a louder cracking. Then water began to spurt from between the logs. Suddenly the dam broke, carrying the logs and much of the masonry down the valley, engulfing the village beneath thousands of tons of water and washing the village, and bandits, into oblivion.

The villagers stood and cheered for several minutes. The sailors wiped their brows with relief.

Mary looked at Jesus.

"How long have you been planning that?" she said.

"It was a spur of the moment thing," he replied. "But I did notice the dam was filling each day, almost exactly up to the last point we'd barricaded. Anyway, I didn't do anything really. It was an act of God."

"Erm," said Mary. "I'd like to believe you."

"I told you I wasn't a very good carpenter," explained Jesus.

"Remind me never to cross you," said the Lieutenant. "Especially as I don't have an ark any longer."

…

"With God's will, you won't have any problems with bandits now," said Jesus to the Elder. They were in the saloon. The four pirates, Mary and Judas were packed and ready to leave.

"You were sent from Heaven," said the Elder. "You do God's work."

"Sometimes, but not always," said the Lieutenant.

"The Lieutenant and his ahem, 'friends,' have some salvage business back at the hulk of their boat," explained Mary. "But they will be back in a week or so. The four slave girls want to stay here for the time being. They feel safe with Gilgamesh – God only knows why."

"We better escort these three tender-hooves through tiger country," said the Lieutenant.

"I think I can help," explained Judas, beckoning the party to leave the Saloon. "Our friends in the village have collected over a dozen horses. Apparently, horses swim better than outlaws. So the villagers have lent us these steeds on a semi-permanent basis."

Warning: Christians and people who are easily offended should not read this book

They followed Judas outside. Seven horses were saddled and waiting. The villagers cheered. The seven mounted their horses.

"There's a pass through the mountains about two days ride to the north," said the Elder, pointing.

"I can't ride," said Jesus to Judas.

"How hard can it be?" said Judas. "All you have to do is to follow the others until we're out of sight, and then we can walk the rest of the way. We can get a great price for these nags once we're home."

"Just watch me," said Mary, demonstrating on her mount. "Kick to go. Pull back to stop. You'll pick up the rest as we go along."

"After you," said the Lieutenant. "Let's get back to the boat. We've got a withdrawal to make."

"High ho silver!" said Judas. And the seven set off at a gallop.

Warning: Christians and people who are easily offended should not read this book

Part 4 – Preacher Man

He who hath no sin

Jesus stood on the low rock preaching. They were back in Nazareth.

A large crowd of people were captivated – Peter and the disciples were close to the front. Many of the crowd were sitting on the ground. Suddenly Jesus heard a girl crying. A priest was leading two thugs with half a dozen men following. The two thugs were dragging a young woman who was crying and whimpering in terror.

Jesus stood down from the natural platform and walked cautiously across. Mary and the crowd followed closely behind.

"Jesus, The False Prophet," shouted the priest, angrily. "This woman has been found fornicating. She should be stoned for adultery here and now according to the law." The thugs began to bay in support of the priest – not least because he was paying them.

"What would you have us do with this harlot, Jesus?" demanded the priest. "Tell us all so we may witness your judgement."

"She must be stoned according to the law!" said Jesus, clearly. The girl screamed. The thugs moved forward, their blood lust clearly apparent. They began looking round for suitable instruments of death.

Mary began weeping with anger. Jesus' followers became uneasy. The atmosphere was tense.

Jesus stepped forward and knelt before the girl. The thugs released her, and she grabbed Jesus and held him. She feared for her life. The girl was clearly a simpleton – her features appeared odd as she cried. She could barely understand the reason for her plight.

"Stone her!" commanded Jesus, shielding the girl. "And stone me with her. For I would rather die here before I witness such a travesty. For I am a wicked sinner too. We are all sinners in the eyes of God. So let he who hath no sin throw the first stone."

The Disciples understood. Peter stepped forward along with the other men who followed Jesus. Peter eyed the priest's men and smiled. The thugs suddenly became nervous. They stepped back and began to mutter.

"Our law is that she must die," said the priest, defiantly. He glared at Jesus who met his gaze. There was a standoff. Then the priest glanced round. He suddenly realised his men had stepped back from him. They were milling around nervously. One of the thugs beckoned towards him. The priest turned and stepped towards his mob awkwardly. The Disciples stepped forward along with Jesus' crowd. Mary grabbed the hysterical girl and spirited her into the crowd.

Warning: Christians and people who are easily offended should not read this book

"May I suggest we beat a swift retreat, Boss?" said the leading thug to the priest. "Those boys look a bit ugly."

"Come on," said the priest. "Where's your backbone?"

"I think it's about to get stoned," said the leading thug. "I don't fancy our chances against that mob. Have a go if you want but we're out of here."

There was a pause as the priest considered.

"Damn your eyes!" he shouted. He briskly led his mob away cursing.

Jesus stood and watched the Priest fleeing. He exhaled and smiled. Mary appeared next to him. Jesus looked into her face. "That was intense!" he professed and began to laugh in relief. Peter and the other men began to laugh as well. Jesus led them back towards the rock. On the way he turned round, and moon walked across the field.

"Get down brother," shouted Mary in amazement.

"I got that funky rhythm in me, baby," replied Jesus.

…

That evening in Mary's house. The sun was setting. Jesus and Mary were sitting politely on the bed.

There was a silence between them. They both made eye contact and smiled.

"It's getting late," said Mary. "And we have no chaperone."

"I better go," Jesus stood. Mary grabbed his tunic and pulled him back on the bed where he had been sitting.

"Yes," she said. "You should go." She held his tunic so he could not stand. Mary paused.

"You saved that girl's life today," she said.

"I had some help," said Jesus, modestly. "Peter and the boys."

"It was touch and go, all the same," said Mary. "That poor girl. She had no idea what was happening."

There was a pause. Jesus and Mary looked at each other. Mary smiled.

"You were thinking about me when you saved her, weren't you?" Mary asked.

"Maybe," replied Jesus, coyly.

"You should go," said Mary, smiling. Jesus tried to stand but Mary pulled him back on the bed again.

Warning: Christians and people who are easily offended should not read this book

"Jesus," began Mary. "Who invented sex?"

"Ah," said Jesus, looking away. Mary stood. Jesus tried to stand but she blocked him and pushed him back on the bed. Mary knelt astride him and put her arms over his shoulders. Jesus tried to look away but eventually realised that he could not escape. He looked Mary in the eyes and began to smile.

"He which made them at the beginning made them male and female," said Jesus.

"Jesus," Mary began. "Do you really think all the Angels are up there looking down saying: 'Hey Gabrielle. Can you believe what they're doing down there?'"

Jesus laughed. Mary smiled back at him. Her face was close to his. She was looking slightly down on him.

"I know you're conflicted," she whispered to him. "You've had your head filled with all that adultery and fornication stuff. All that hellfire and damnation. Pleasures of the flesh and everything. So you just sit there for a while and have a think. No pressure."

Jesus looked away, embarrassed. He looked round. Then he looked back into her eyes.

"Ok," said Mary. "You've had long enough," she whispered. "Jesus, God wants people to have sex." She paused. "That's why he made it fun. He didn't do that just to make life even more difficult. He already knows people have more than enough problems just surviving, without God trying to make it harder." Jesus looked up at her and smiled, embarrassed. Mary whispered to him. "God wants people to have sex. That's why he invented it. And…" she paused. "You're 30 years old. I know you aren't a virgin. It's just not credible." Jesus smiled and looked away again. Then they made eye contact. Mary kissed him. Jesus smiled. He kissed her back. Mary moved closer to him and whispered in his ear.

"I will be your greatest Disciple," she whispered, slowly. "One day all men will know your name." She paused. "I will love you until the end of time. Now…" she paused again. "Come on baby, Light my Fire!"

Jesus and Mary laughed. There was another more comfortable silence as they gazed into each other's eyes. Mary grabbed Jesus' head and kissed him passionately. Jesus responded. Mary tore Jesus' clothes in a frenzy. Jesus lifted her dress over her head. She leapt on him again and kissed his face and his neck. They were naked. They set the night on fire.

…

Morning had broken.

Jesus opened his eyes. Mary was lying next to him looking into his eyes. They smiled.

"OK," said Mary, suddenly. "You're no use to me now. Clear off!"

"Thanks very much," said Jesus, petulantly. "I'll just get my things." He did not move.

Warning: Christians and people who are easily offended should not read this book

"What God hath joined together, let no man put asunder," said Mary.

There was a pause as they transfixed each other's gaze.

"You certainly practice what you preach," said Mary.

"How's that?" asked Jesus.

"Love Thy Neighbour," explained Mary. They laughed.

"Can I ask you something else?" asked Jesus.

"Sounds interesting," replied Mary. "Go on. I'm up for a dare."

"You remember all that business in the desert?" began Jesus.

"I have a vague recollection," replied Mary, curiously.

"How did you conjure up all those demons and fabulous cities and fire and all those little guys with tridents and horns?" asked Jesus.

"I can tell you," Mary replied. "But you must promise not to tell anyone else."

"OK," said Jesus.

"Magic!" exclaimed Mary.

"Black magic?" asked Jesus, raising his eyebrows.

Mary paused.

"Magic mushrooms," she explained smiling. "It was in the water. I mixed the drinking water with some mushrooms. But you have to be careful to pick the right ones."

"That would explain why I was as sick as a dog," said Jesus.

"Yes," said Mary. "Sorry about that."

"And that explained the eye thing," asked Jesus.

"Yeah!" replied Mary, enthusiastically. "It's good, isn't it?"

"It really gets your attention," admitted Jesus.

Jesus lay on his back looking away.

"It was just an illusion," said Mary. "A hallucinogen-induced trance." Mary blinked twice.

Jesus continued to lay on his back, thoughtfully.

"Just one more thing," he said. "How much do you weigh?"

"That's a very personal question," replied Mary indignantly.

Warning: Christians and people who are easily offended should not read this book

"Stop it!" scalded Jesus. "It's a bit late to start being coy now."

"About 8 or 9 stones," replied Mary.

"Hmmm," said Jesus. "I weigh about twice that." He rolled over and fixed her gaze questioningly. "So how did you manage to carry me up that mountain?"

Mary looked him in the eye.

"I think I'll take the Fifth on that," she replied, meeting his gaze.

"Promise me you will never use witchcraft again," said Jesus. "It's a mortal sin."

Mary held her tongue.

"Promise me," insisted Jesus.

"I promise," replied Mary, eventually.

"Not ever," said Jesus.

"Not ever again," replied Mary.

"Good," said Jesus, relaxing. He was thoughtful again. "Mary," he asked eventually. "What is Hell like?"

Mary paused. "Hell is not a place, Jesus," she explained. "Hell is a time. Like the time I thought I had lost you."

Jesus smiled and put his hands on her cheeks. He looked deep into her eyes. He gradually slid his hands onto her head and stroked her hair. Mary looked back into his eyes. She smiled and waited.

"Jesus," she asked after a minute. "What are you doing?"

"Nothing," replied Jesus.

"You're checking for horns, aren't you?" asked Mary.

Jesus whipped his hands away.

"No, I wasn't," he replied.

"Don't lie," Mary responded. "You were feeling my head for horns."

Jesus looked away uncomfortably. Mary let him suffer for a few seconds.

"Jesus," she began. "If you had found some horns. Would it have stopped you? You know. Doing the nasty?"

"Erm," said Jesus. "I think I'll take the Fifth on that."

Warning: Christians and people who are easily offended should not read this book

Mary began to smile. Jesus laughed in embarrassment.

The mood was suddenly shattered by Joseph the Younger banging on the door.

"Mum wants to see you both in the big house now!" he shouted. "You've been busted! Grace ratted you out."

Mary and Jesus cringed, jumped out of bed, and rapidly dressed.

…

Mary and Jesus walked into the kitchen. Joseph the Elder was eating. He jumped up.

"Morning Mary," said Joseph the Elder, gulping a mouthful of food.

"Morning dad," said Jesus.

"You're on your own this time, son," said Joseph the Elder, patting Jesus on the shoulder as he made his escape. "Good luck!"

Mary and Jesus sat.

Mary, Mother of Jesus, burst in as Joseph the Elder left. The other children peered round the corner of the door, smirking.

"I hope you two are satisfied!" Mary, Mother of Jesus, began. She had a face like thunder.

Jesus and Mary avoided her gaze.

"This used to be a respectable house, but you have brought shame on us," continued Mary Mother of Jesus. "You!" she shouted at Mary. Mary startled. Mary, Mother of Jesus, threw a ring at her. "Put that on," commanded Mary, Mother of Jesus. "It was my mother's ring; God rest her soul. She'll be turning in her grave now. If anyone asks, you two got married in the city. That time when you were 'finding your religion'." She said sarcastically. "A fine story indeed! I bet you were really cavorting around naked in the desert like animals…Shouldn't be allowed." She paused for effect. "Joseph!" she shouted. "You don't have to share with your brother anymore. You can have Jesus' room. He won't be needing it anymore!"

Mary, Mother of Jesus, glared at Jesus. Mary stretched her hand with her new wedding ring on her finger.

Joseph the Younger stumbled in. "Mum, can I keep Jesus' stuff…" he began. "Oh!" he exclaimed as he noticed Jesus and Mary sitting at the table. He paused and stared at them, grinning. Then he began to sing: "Come on Baby Light my Fire." The other children began to laugh out loud. Joseph the Younger continued to sing and gyrate his hips. Even Mary, Mother of Jesus, broke into a smile.

Warning: Christians and people who are easily offended should not read this book

Preaching to the Converted

"We're not reaching the right demographic," announced Jesus as the steering group met at Simon the Leper's House. Jesus, Peter, Judas and Mary were sitting round the kitchen table. It was evening.

"For some reason most of the audience are female," said Jesus.

"I wonder why," said Mary, knowingly.

"And all the older people are already converts," he continued. "Getting the extra hours in while they can. We're preaching to the converted."

"OK boss," said Peter. "What you're saying is that we need to target men aged 18 to 50."

"Precisely," said Jesus.

"Let's just have Mary take her top off at the start of the show," said Judas.

Everyone groaned.

"Judas," said Mary. "That was an important contribution and I'm glad that you felt comfortable to share it with us. But I just want to remind you of the Sixth Commandment: Thou shalt not kill without due cause. Now I really want you to focus on the last three words before saying anything else!" She scowled at him.

"Look Judas," added Peter. "We want them to raise their consciousness to a higher spiritual level – not jerk themselves into a coma."

"That's not quite the way I'd have put it," said Jesus. "But the sentiment is sound. Any more ideas?"

Mary was thoughtful.

"Can we get someone to beat a drum and a few folks to blow some reeds – I think they call it a kazoo?" asked Mary.

"I think we can get that," said Peter. "I know some people."

"Ok," said Mary. "Now I need five disciples to meet me tomorrow morning. I have an idea."

...

Three disciples were standing on the make-shift stage. Mary nodded at Jesus who signalled to the drummer to lay down a beat. People began to look over. After a few bars the kazoos started up. Suddenly the three disciples began to sing and dance in synchrony:

"Young man, there's no need to feel down. I said, young man, pick yourself off the ground..."

A temple priest and a Centurion wandered over and stood either side of the stage, scowling.

Warning: Christians and people who are easily offended should not read this book

"Many ways to have a good time..." sang the Disciples.

The priest and Centurion suddenly burst into life and joined in with the dance.

"It's fun to stay at the Y.M.C.A. It's fun to stay at the Y.M.C.A..."

...

"What a great audience," shouted Jesus as he mounted the stage when the song had finished. The cheers from the now substantial audience began to subside.

The pretend temple priest was the last to leave the stage.

Jesus looked at him. "Hey, have you heard the one about the priest who wanted to become an atheist? He changed his mind when he found out it was a non-prophet organisation."

The audience groaned.

"A priest came round my house last week asking for a voluntary tribute," continued Jesus. "So I gave him two shekels. The next day he sent half a dozen of his lay preachers' round who said they'd lay into me if I didn't stump up another ten."

"Yeah," shouted out a woman. "Fat pigs."

"They wanted a tithe of eight shekels from my brother," continued Jesus. "He couldn't find the cash. So they tithed his wife up until he did."

"You know," continued Jesus. "You've heard it said, 'thou shalt love thy neighbour, and hate thine enemy'. But I say, love your enemies, bless them that curse you, do good to them that hate you, and pray for those who despise and persecute you. Now, I know this is difficult..."

"He's smoking," said Mary to Judas.

"Do you love your enemies?" Judas asked Mary.

"It's never going to happen," replied Mary, scowling. "Not even if you were the last guy in the world."

"Ow!" said Judas. "I'm not made of stone you know."

...

That night Jesus and Mary were together.

"You were on a roll today," said Mary.

"Just playing it by ear," said Jesus.

"I'm worried about something," continued Mary.

"Are you pregnant?" asked Jesus, nervously.

Warning: Christians and people who are easily offended should not read this book

"I hadn't thought about that actually," said Mary.

"Oh, good," said Jesus. "I mean bad. I mean…anyway what are you worried about?"

Mary scowled at him for a second.

"Anyway," she began. "The audience are really stoked on you for sticking it to the temple priests. Especially that Italian one who insists everyone calls him 'Godfather'. But you need to be careful. They aren't gonna like you dissing them all the time and showing them no respect. They're going to come after you."

"I was thinking that as well," said Jesus. "But they've had it coming. Someone has got to make a stand."

"If you insist," said Mary. "But what I was thinking is that the priests run the temple. But who runs the priests?"

"Herod," replied Jesus.

"And who runs Herod?" asked Mary.

"That would be the Romans," replied Jesus.

"Yeah," said Mary. "So the Romans grant the West Bank concession to Herod and he sends the priests to collect the dough so he can build temples and such. Now if you can get the blessing of that Pilate guy. What do they call him?"

"The Gov'nor," said Jesus.

"If you can get in with the Governor," said Mary. "Then the priests can't touch you."

"But the Romans are invaders," said Jesus. "They fought their way in here and they oppress and intimidate us. We were born free, but they tax us to death. They are our enemies."

"Didn't you say we should forgive our enemies?" asked Mary.

"Yeah," said Jesus. "But that doesn't apply to Romans."

"Why?" asked Mary.

Jesus paused. "You're not just a pretty face," he added after some thought. "Won't people think I'm a collaborator?"

"Needs must when the Devil drives," replied Mary. "You need to start thinking about the bigger picture. What's more important: to send out your message or get yourself nailed by some Italian gangsters?"

"How do I get in with the Gov'nor?" asked Jesus, thoughtfully.

"Let's have a think about it," said Mary. "Just you and me."

Warning: Christians and people who are easily offended should not read this book

"Hey Mary," Jesus asked after a pause. "Can you sing?"

"Just because I'm a Black girl you think I can sing," replied Mary. "You should be ashamed of yourself. That is a gratuitous stereotype."

"Sorry," said Jesus.

There was an uncomfortable silence.

"That didn't sound like a 'no'," he added.

"What do you have in mind?" asked Mary.

…

The crowd were cheering as Jesus mounted the platform and Mary took her bows.

"Hey, thanks for coming," said Jesus. "What a great audience. That was, 'I will survive,' a song about the Roman Occupation."

The audience laughed.

"Nah," he said looking at a Roman guard. "I'm just messing with ya. RESPECT! Don't stop believing."

"Now seriously," Jesus continued. "I say love your enemies and do good to them. Bless those that curse you and pray for those who ill use you. And if a man hits you on one cheek offer also the other."

"Now talking of cheek," continued Jesus. "What do you think of that new priest in the temple? What's his name? Tobias? More like Tubby-ass. He's got plenty of cheeks. Now I ain't gonna trash a guy 'cos he's got a weight problem. I mean what's a brother gonna do but go out and eat some more. But he done need to change his lifestyle. Sitting on his big ass all day praying and such and counting all them voluntary donations we give him. It must be hungry work, counting all our money."

The audience were in hysterics.

A temple priest stormed over with some Roman soldiers.

"Hey, smart-ass," said the temple priest. "Tell us this – what do you say about those folks who won't pay their taxes to the Romans?"

Jesus thought for a second: "Give unto Caesar what is his; and give until God what is his – my wife gets what's left."

The audience fell about laughing as the Priest stormed off followed by the Roman soldiers who were sniggering.

…

Warning: Christians and people who are easily offended should not read this book

The steering group met a few evenings later in the house of Simon the Leper.

"Hey Jude," said Jesus. "Why do we always meet at Simon the Leper's House?" he asked.

"He charges the lowest rates," said Judas. "For some bizarre reasons no one else wants to meet at his place. Damned if I know why. Looks like a perfectly nice place to me. It's a demand and supply thing."

"OK," said Jesus. "Now I know you boys have been grumbling about not having much involvement in the show these days."

"Yeah," said Peter. "It's all you and Mary now. We just provide security."

"I can fix that," said Jesus. "I want you boys to start acts of your own. Just a few one-liners at first. And then you can move on to a full set. Once you've got the hang of it you can go on tour. We could cover more ground that way. Take the message out to the provinces."

"Sounds great," said Jude, eyes lighting up. "Jesus and The Disciples. We could set up our own little Empire. Who's up first?"

"We were thinking of you," said Mary. "Lead from the front as it were. Show them how it's done. Let's face it, you're a funny guy."

…

"What a great audience," said Judas climbing on stage at the next show as the applause for Mary subsided.

"Hey," he continued. "Have you heard this one? What's the difference between a beggar's wife and a Jewish wife? A beggar's wife has real orgasms and fake jewellery."

There was not much response.

"What a great audience," said Judas again. "This one's for the Spartans: I had a date with a Greek girl last week – say what you like about Medusa – she gives good head."

Jesus put his head in his hands as the audience began to boo.

"Get off you bum!" shouted a man.

"You're terrible," said another,

"What a great audience," said Judas. "Erm." He looked at the hecklers.

"God must love stupid people," he said. "He made SO many of them."

Jesus mounted the stage and pushed Judas off.

"Hey," said Jesus to the heckler. "Your girlfriend wants you. She's outside grazing."

The audience laughed at the irritated heckler.

Warning: Christians and people who are easily offended should not read this book

"A Centurion went into the Army and Navy store," said Jesus. "'I can't see the camouflage jackets,' he said. 'Yeah,' said the assistant. 'They're good, aren't they?'"

People began to laugh again.

"Moses led his people through the desert for 40 years," said Jesus. "Even back then men avoided asking the way."

"What happened?" said Judas to Mary in the wings.

"You just died," said Mary.

"Now, seriously for a moment," continued Jesus. "I want to talk about the temple priests. You see, the scribes and the Pharisees sit in Moses' seat. That is if they can get their big asses into it...But I say unto them: outwardly ye appear righteous unto men, but within ye are full of hypocrisy and iniquity. You bind heavy burdens and grievous to be borne, with taxes and tribute, and lay them on men's shoulders..."

"Amen to that," started up some hecklers.

"...But they will not work or move with one of their fingers. Ye blind guides, which strain at a gnat, and swallow a camel, lazy and fat, living off our toil," continued Jesus. "Actually, talking about Gnats, does anyone know if Noah included termites in the ark?"

…

Warning: Christians and people who are easily offended should not read this book

Entertaining the troops

"We've struck the mother lode," exclaimed Judas at the steering group.

"Not another leper colony?" asked Peter.

"A pox on you," replied Judas. "We've been hired by the Governor himself to provide a whole hours' worth of family-friendly entertainment to the lonely legionnaires in the garrison. And this pays genuine bone fide gold sovereigns with eagles stamped on the back and endorsed by the Emperor himself, may he reign for a thousand years."

Mary looked at Jesus and tried not to look smug.

"Now," continued Judas. "We've got a small advance so we can up our game. But if we wow them with this show then the world is our oyster. There are hundreds of these USO shows every year – Uber Sacrifice Obligata - that's Latin for bringing pleasure through sacrifice – usually two hours later than ordered. There are Roman garrisons throughout civilisation and all of them have thousands of lonely, homesick soldiers desperate for some adult entertainment."

"I thought you said it was a family show?" asked Mary.

"More of a making-a-family-on-stage show," said Judas. "But don't worry. I was thinking, with our advance we could put on, not just a two-girl show, but a three-girl extravaganza. Girl on girl on girl!"

"That's degrading and down-right obscene," said Mary.

"Five sovereigns a turn," said Judas. "Per girl per appearance."

"The show must go on!" said Mary.

"I see one tiny flaw in your despicable plan," said Jesus.

"Every silver lining has a cloud," replied Judas. "How may I address your concern?"

"The Stern Gang," said Jesus. "If we go entertaining the invaders, those fanatics in the resistance are likely to string us up for collaborating."

"Ah," said Judas. "Let us do some group brainstorming to find a solution."

They thought.

"Double rations!" said Mary suddenly. "All the prisoners in the fort are to get double rations from now until the show. Half of the inmates will be from the resistance and so we will be doing everyone a favour."

"I like what I'm hearing," said Judas.

Warning: Christians and people who are easily offended should not read this book

"And the Stern gang have so many informers in the garrison that everyone will know that their guys are getting extra grub because of us," said Peter.

"Problem solved," said Judas. "I'll speak with his honour the Centurion this evening and we can go live tomorrow. Good work, team."

"What about the two other strippers," said Judas. "I mean tasteful exotic dancers."

"I think I have that covered," said Mary. "Jesus, come with me tomorrow. Bring money."

...

"I feel awkward," said Jesus, as he and Mary sat in the reception room of the House of Esther.

"You mean to say you've never been here before?" asked Mary.

"Of course not," said Jesus, blushing.

"Honestly?" asked Mary.

"No!" replied Jesus.

"Ok," said Mary. "There's no need to get defensive. I believe you. And you're blushing. That's so cute."

"How do you know about this place, anyway?" asked Jesus.

"An old soldier told me," said Mary. "Actually, more than one. Most of the garrison have House of Ether loyalty cards."

"It's all a bit seedy," said Jesus.

"Welcome to my world," replied Mary. "Don't worry, Big Boy. I won't let them hurt you."

Esther suddenly appeared with her maid.

"And what can we do you for?" asked Esther.

"You see, Miss Esther…" said Mary.

"…Madam if you please…" interrupted Esther.

"We were thinking that you may have some exotic dancers we could hire, two to be exact, to put on a show for the garrison," explained Mary.

"Do they need experience?" asked Esther.

"No," said Mary. "Well not at dancing. All training will be provided."

"And the fee?" asked Esther, sitting.

Warning: Christians and people who are easily offended should not read this book

"We were thinking of two sovereign a turn, per girl," said Mary.

"Ten," said Ether.

"Four," said Mary.

"Eight," said Esther.

"Five," said Jesus.

"Done!" said Esther, standing to shake Mary and Jesus' hand.

"Rachel," ordered Esther. "Bring us a drink to celebrate our new business venture."

Rachel, the maid, nipped out.

"Now I can suggest a couple of girls," said Esther. "But feel free to come back and audition them yourselves. They'll all be here just after tea-time when the night shift comes in."

"Many thanks," said Mary. "We may just do that."

"Actually," said Ether. "I used to do a wicked Shimmy myself in my time. And for five sovereigns I could dust off my dancing shoes."

"What a trooper," said Mary. "I'll put you on the call back list."

…

The sun was setting, and various young and not so young ladies began to parade through the reception of the House of Esther as the day shift changed over to the night.

"This is so embarrassing," said Jesus.

"We went out for tea earlier," said Mary. "It was very civilised."

"Yes," said Jesus, "But I've been sitting here for half an hour now. And all the neighbours saw me following you up the stairs."

"You are such a cutey," said Mary.

"What if the punters see me?" said Jesus. "I'll die of shame."

"Don't worry, honey," said Esther, suddenly reappearing. "The clients are brought in by a separate entrance. It's more discreet that way."

"He's a bit shy," said Mary.

"There's a first time for everything," said Ether. She looked at Jesus and smiled at his obvious discomfort.

"Now," said Esther. "Have you seen anything you like?"

Warning: Christians and people who are easily offended should not read this book

"I'm not sure," said Mary. "They are all wearing their robes and hijabs and things."

"Yes," said Esther. "We like our girls to keep a low profile when they come to work. We don't want to upset the neighbours. This is a classy joint."

"I could do to see their figures," said Mary. "And also see how they walk. Poise and grace. That's what we're after."

"Curves?" asked Esther.

"It's a good idea to have a comfortable handful on top," said Mary. "But only in moderation. If you're too top-heavy it all goes swinging around like two sacks of cement and we need to have a free-standing superstructure with no scaffolding."

"More pert and dainty," said Esther. "Rather than big and buxom."

"Ladies!" shouted Esther, clapping her hands. "Please come in here. We have guests."

Around a dozen women and girls of various shapes and sizes appeared.

"Our friends here require two dancers for their show," explained Esther. "It pays five sovereigns a turn minus my commission."

"Five sovereigns?" repeated several girls, in disbelief.

"That's more than some of them earn in a month," explained Esther to Mary and Jesus.

"Now ladies," said Esther. "If you'll just show us your wares and walk up and down. Just like the catwalks in Milan but minus the dresses. Then our impresarios here can draw up a ranking list."

"Oh hell!" said Jesus as the women immediately began to strip without hesitation.

"What's wrong?" asked Mary, knowingly.

"This is so awful," said Jesus. "I'm so embarrassed. Asking these young ladies to strip. It's like a meat market. They're not cattle you know."

"Aw," said Esther. "Isn't he cute. It's his first time, you know."

"Aw," said the girls.

"You just go through into that other room," said Esther, pointing. "And we'll call you when we're done."

Jesus stood up and tried to avert his gaze.

"Gimme some sugar, honey," said Esther, grabbing him as he passed. She kissed him and slapped his bottom as he crept out with his head down. Unfortunately, the girls had lined up in front of him and he had to run the gauntly of passing each one. Most of the women were now only partly dressed. Several insisted on pinching his bottom as he passed.

Warning: Christians and people who are easily offended should not read this book

"Come here, sugar," said an unusually brazen one, grabbing Jesus. She kissed him and turned to Mary.

"Is he yours?" she asked.

"I suppose so," said Mary, showing off her ring.

"If you ever get bored," said the brazen woman. "I'll take him off your hands."

"I'll bear that in mind," said Mary as the girls whooped and hollered at Jesus' discomfort.

…

"You are so adorable," said Mary, as she left the House of Esther an hour later. "Just like a little lamb who got lost in the woods. Anyhow, we've got two girls who can shake their booty and everything. Not that any of them could concentrate after you'd got them all hot and bothered."

"But I didn't do anything," said Jesus. "I just got all embarrassed and dashed out without looking."

"Exactly," said Mary. "It's a good job you got out of there when you did. I don't think I'd have been able to fight them off and they'd have grabbed you and stolen your virtue. You old dog you. Actually, I'm not feeling that virtuous myself. Watching all those girls getting horny with you. I think I'm going to have to stake my claim later. So start your countdown. T minus twenty minutes and counting."

…

Jesus and Mary were sitting at the kitchen table in the Big House. Mary Mother of Jesus came in. "My old friend Ruth has come round," said Mary, Mother of Jesus. "We heard you are putting on a show at the garrison and we wonder if you could help us."

Ruth followed Mary in. They all sat round the table.

"We heard you are going to the garrison, and you might be friendly with the soldiers, particularly the Centurion," said Ruth. "You see my son, Julian, and his friend, Roger, are both in custody and we wondered if you could help get them out. It's an awful place and the guards are so rough. And they're both delicate sorts. And they look after their old mother. And it's terrible…" she began to weep.

"You want us to help break them out of jail?" asked Jesus, in disbelief.

"No no," said Mary, Mother of Jesus. "They've not done anything wrong and it's probably a case of mistaken identities. So if you could just have a word with the Centurion, I know he'll understand and get them out."

"May I ask what they're supposed to have done?" asked Mary.

Warning: Christians and people who are easily offended should not read this book

"It's all made up," said Mary Mother of Jesus as Ruth continued to wail. "They've been fitted up. They're patsies. It's those hill-billy legionnaires. They've had it in for Julian ever since they saw him working in the dress shop."

"When would we ever refuse an accommodation to a friend," said Mary. "Although, and this may never happen, we may want a favour in return."

"Anything," said Ruth.

"You say he works in a dress shop?" began Mary.

"Mary!" interrupted Jesus. "You show me no respect! Of course, we will do this favour. And we do it because it pleases us – not for anything in return."

"I was just asking is all," replied Mary, meekly.

…

"Thank you for seeing us, Centurion," said Jesus.

"I don't usually see reps," said the Centurion. "But the guard said it was urgent military business concerning that 'burlesque' show which you've planned for Saturday night."

The Centurion was sitting behind a desk. He waved for the guard to leave. Mary blew the guard a kiss. The guard blushed.

"The show is all ready to roll," said Jesus. "But we wonder if we could give us some advice on a legal matter."

"I just stack 'em and rack 'em," said the Centurion. "It's the governor who deals out justice."

"I'm sure he's an awfully busy man," said Mary. "And he'll thank you if you can save him some time and take a load of his already troubled mind."

"So you want me to spring one of your friends?" asked the Centurion.

"Goodness!" exclaimed Jesus. "You are a mind-reader."

"Not really," said the Centurion. "I had one of the mothers in yesterday wailing and crying. She said you might be calling. Anyway, these two characters…"

"Julian and Roger," said Mary.

"Yes," continued the Centurion. "Julian and Roger. They look like theatrical types anyway. And they were a bit too theatrical in the public park the other night when two of my soldiers caught them in the act."

"Ah," said Jesus. "I see."

"Unfortunately, they weren't the only one," said the Centurion. "You see one of the priests happened to overhear my boys giving them a dressing down and he insisted they be arrested

Warning: Christians and people who are easily offended should not read this book

and tried for sodomy, corrupting the public morals and bringing down the wrath of God etc. He said we'd all get turned into pillars of salt if we turned a blind eye. So they were brought here."

"What do you think?" asked Jesus.

"I'm not paid to think," said the Centurion. "That's the Governor's job. Personally, I don't give a damn. What another man does with his own bottom is his own affair. I'd as soon give them a slap and turn 'em out – we need the space. And let's face it, that sort of thing goes on all the time in the barracks – we just don't ask, and they don't tell. But the priest is on some sort of crusade and demands justice."

"How old were the two soldiers who arrested the boys?" asked Mary.

"Both died in the wool veterans," said the Centurion. "In fact, one of them has two weeks until retirement. Why do you ask?"

"If they're old," said Mary. "Their eyesight may not be so good. Perhaps it was a case of mistaken identities. And the priest didn't actually see the act in progress."

"And I should care because…?" asked the Centurion.

"Well," said Mary. "If their vision is poor, they will need special treatment at the show. Like front seats and other privileges. And we would be very grateful, the other two exotic dancers and I. I'm sure if you explain to your two subordinates, they will see it our way. Or rather, they didn't see anything much at all because it was dark, and their sight was poor, and they have never seen Julian and Roger before in their lives."

"And the Governor won't be here for every," said Jesus. "And then the Emperor will need a man to take over the Governor's job. A man with experience of the country, and wisdom, and who has the support of the local people. A man who knows how to win favour with the locals can go a long way around here. Especially if people are getting their scribes to write letters of thanks to the Governor. And to the Emperor. May he reign for a thousand years."

"Erm," said the Centurion, thoughtfully. "Leave it with me. But I'm not promising anything."

…

Showtime in the garrison.

"Good evening, Legion X," said Jesus. "And X doesn't mean ten."

"Get off ya bum," shouted the rowdy legionnaires.

"Is this the most X-rated legion in the world?" asked Jesus.

"Yeah!" shouted some soldiers.

"I can't hear you," said Jesus. "Is this the most X-rated legion in the world?"

Warning: Christians and people who are easily offended should not read this book

"Yeah!" shouted some soldiers. "Bring on the strippers," shouted others.

"Later," said Jesus. "You have to earn your fun."

Jesus was on a stage and some of the Disciples were lined up in front so they could provide security. There were a lot of soldiers, but they were unarmed. They had been drinking.

"Sod off," shouted some soldiers.

"What a great audience," said Jesus. "Hey," he continued. "Have you heard this – which of you guys are from Italy?"

Some soldiers shouted out.

Jesus continued: "You know, not all Italians are in the mafia. Some are in the Witness Protection Program. [Boo and groans from the crowd.] Why are there no Jehovah's Witnesses in Italy? The mafia doesn't like witnesses. [More boos and groans.] Ever heard of the Chinese mafia? They made me an offer I couldn't understand. [Food now being thrown at the stage.]"

"What a great audience," said Jesus. "Now your gonna like this one: Did you hear the one about the mermaid prostitute that got on the wrong side of the Mafia? She's sleeping with the fishes now."

"What's in the boxes?" shouted a man in the audience, who had been prompted. There were three upright boxes on stage.

"Do you want to see?" said Jesus.

"Yeah," shouted soldiers. "And get off."

"How much do ya wanna see?" asked Jesus.

"Get on with it," shouted soldiers.

"Perhaps if you threw some spare change, it would loosen the locks," said Jesus. "And that's not all it might loosen."

Some soldiers eventually threw some coins.

"Come on," said Jesus. Glancing at the coins. "These are copper. Give us some real money. It'll be worth it. I promise."

Eventually a few of the soldiers from the more senior ranks tossed some silver-looking coins.

"That's more like it," said Jesus. Some music started playing. "And now for some entertainment I know you're gonna like: Hebrews and Shebrews, Ladies and Legionnaires, Honkeys and Donkeys. I present to you – Mary – Venus – and Vixen."

Warning: Christians and people who are easily offended should not read this book

The three girls burst out of the boxes and quickly burst out of their braziers to howls of lewd approval.

As the first part of the dancing ended, the girls were still on stage. The music finished and the crowd, now hoarse from hollering, were calming down. The Centurion appeared, just to check things were still civilised.

"It's the host with the most," shouted Jesus, climbing back on stage after spotting the Centurion. "Let's give a big hand to the Centurion."

The soldiers cheered and pushed the officer to the front. He reluctantly complied. Immediately Venus and Vixen grabbed him and dragged him on stage.

Jesus hushed the crowd and nodded at them.

"Hey Centurion, when are you coming to civilise my unexplored regions?" asked Venus.

Howls of approval.

"You can bring your sword to conquer my country any time," said Vixen. "And lash me with that Latin tongue!"

More howls of lewd approval.

They let the Centurion go. He scuttled off and tried to appear embarrassed but secretly grinned.

"You know what the ladies say round here," said Jesus. "He rules his women like he rules the garrison – with a rod of iron." Whistles and hoots from the crowd. "And we also have two very special guests at the front," said Jesus.

"Where's Corporal Gaius?" asked Venus.

Gaius was sitting at the front. He looked round and the other soldiers shouted and pointed.

"You look lonely," said Venus. She strode over and sat on his knee.

"Where's Sergeant Agrippa?" asked Vixen.

Agrippa raised his hand expectantly.

"I've got a surprise for you," said Vixen. "But you have to unwrap it first." She handed him the ties to her bikini bottom as she stood next to him and sat on his knee when he'd pulled them loose. "Oh," she shouted suddenly as she jumped up. "I didn't know you'd brought your spear along. I thought big weapons weren't allowed in here."

"Now that we've raised the dead," continued Jesus. "Some more magic." He pulled out a sheet and used it in a disappearing vase trick. This was received with various boos although the audience had warmed to the show by now. After Jesus had succeeded in making various items disappear, Mary reappeared on stage. She was wearing some fleshings. Jesus looked

Warning: Christians and people who are easily offended should not read this book

across. "What shall I make disappear now?" Jesus asked the audience, pointing at the clothes that Mary was almost wearing.

Suddenly the crowd was animated again.

"But first," said Jesus. "A lesson." The crowd booed for a while, although this gradually subsided, as Mary pouted and flexed on stage.

"You heathens have never heard of Daniel in the Lion's den," said Jesus. "So let me tell you a story."

Boos and groans of outrage from the audience although they were running out of steam now.

"If you're quiet he might teach you some magic words that will make all my clothes disappear," shouted Mary.

The crowd were uncertain but decided restraint might be the most productive option. They calmed down.

"Daniel was walking round in the desert, as you do," said Jesus. "And he came across a lion. But the lion didn't try and eat him."

"I hope none of you lions is going to try and eat me tonight," said Mary.

Hoots from the crowd.

"The lion was crying," said Jesus. "Because it had a thorn in its paw."

"Poor lion," said Mary.

"So Daniel went up and pulled the thorn out," said Jesus. "'Why thank you, said the lion,' It was a talking lion. A few weeks later Daniel hadn't paid the Shylocks the money he owed them, so they decided to throw him to the lions."

"Ain't that the truth," said Mary.

"But, luckily for Daniel, the friendly lion was amongst the pride," said Jesus. "And the friendly lion chased all the other lions off. And the Shylocks gave him another month to come up with the cash. The moral of this story is, don't borrow money from Shylocks. And one good turn deserves another. Now Mary," continued Jesus. "Are you going to do a good turn for our guests and protectors here?"

"I might," said Mary, spinning round.

"And what do they have to do in return," asked Jesus.

"They have to be nice and say 'please' and 'thank you' to all the ladies in Jerusalem," said Mary. "For a month."

"Do you think you can do that, you horny sons-of-bitches," said Jesus.

Warning: Christians and people who are easily offended should not read this book

Booing and shouting.

"What's the magic word then?" said Jesus.

"'Please'," replied Mary.

They gradually had the audience begging her with cries of 'please'.

"Ok," said Jesus. "One good turn deserves another. Now I will pull the thorn out of Mary's bra." Jesus pulled one of the straps on Mary's bra and it fell off. "Knock 'em dead girl," he told her as the music started again and Venus and Vixen came back on stage.

...

"Where are Venus and Vixen?" asked Jesus when the show had ended, and they were in the dressing room.

"I think they are escorting a couple of officers to their room for a nightcap," said Peter. "I'll stay here and take them home, if they appear before morning. You should go."

"I've been thinking," said Mary to Jesus. "We went down really well. I bet we can go on tour in most of the garrisons and even further. We could leave here for good."

"But what will the other boys do?" asked Jesus. "Peter and Judas and everyone?"

Peter overheard. "Hey," he said interrupting. "You two get out of here. Don't stay because of us. We'll all be fine. Judas will probably want to come with you anyway. He's getting on rather well with Vixen. And you're on the wrong side of Big Joe and his mob at the Temple. Grab the money and run – that's what I say to you. This place isn't big enough for you anyway."

"Hey," said Jesus. "That's too much pressure at this time of night. Let's talk later."

...

Jesus and Mary arrived in the barn.

"What do you think of the dress?" Mary asked.

"It's very nice," said Jesus. "Is that the right answer?"

"Yes," said Mary. "But it would have been more convincing if you'd have looked at it."

Mary began to take her dress off

"You're looking now, aren't you?" she added.

Jesus sat down.

Warning: Christians and people who are easily offended should not read this book

"Anyway," continued Mary. "This most exquisite dress is from the boutique of Julian and Roger after their grand-reopening following their brief and unplanned holiday care of the Roman garrison."

"What happened at the trial?" asked Jesus.

"It was dismissed," said Mary. "No witnesses. Anyway, come on,"

"Come on what?" asked Jesus.

"Get your kit off," said Mary. "It's bed-time."

"Does it make you frisky?" asked Jesus. "You know, parading about in front of all those horny soldiers."

"No, you pervert," said Mary sitting on the bed, as Jesus pulled off his tunic. "Actually, it doesn't feel like anything. Because it's dark and we were indoors so the stage is lit up and you can't see the audience. You soon filter out the howling and shouting so that you're mainly concentrating on getting the dance steps right and not falling off the stage. In fact, you quickly forget that you aren't wearing very much. It's like being in a dream. And it isn't horny at all. It's just - work."

"But you're horny now?" asked Jesus.

"Why not come over here and find out!" replied Mary.

"Hey," said Jesus. "I'm not a machine. Don't put me under so much pressure."

"What's the useless bit of skin attached to a penis?" asked Mary.

Jesus shrugged his shoulders.

"A man," replied Mary.

"Actually, that reminds me," said Jesus, sitting next to Mary on the bed. "You're a natural at that double act thing we did. You have great timing. I was thinking we should add more of that stuff."

"We will need to add more dirty jokes," said Mary. "All that PG stuff won't wash with the soldiers."

"Go on," said Jesus. "I told you a few gags on the way home. Let's try some out."

"OK," said Mary.

"Did you know that during sex you burn off as many calories as running eight miles," asked Jesus.

"Who the hell runs eight miles in 30 seconds," replied Mary.

Warning: Christians and people who are easily offended should not read this book

"I bet you can't tell me something that will make me both happy and sad at the same time?" said Jesus.

"Your penis is bigger than your brother's," replied Mary.

"What does the sign on an out-of-business brothel say?" said Jesus.

"Beat it. We're closed," replied Mary. Hey, I've got one for you - What's the difference between a woman with PMS and a terrorist?"

Jesus shrugged his shoulders.

"You can negotiate with a terrorist," replied Mary.

"That's cool," said Jesus. "If we practice and try some out each act, we can bump that up to maybe a fifth or even a third of the act."

"Did you know that five out of three people don't understand fractions?" said Mary.

"You're smoking baby," said Jesus. He kissed her. They paused.

"You didn't want me to be vulgar and flirty with the Centurion, did you?" asked Mary. "You know, those gags about unexplored regions and lashing me with his tongue."

"You noticed," said Jesus.

"It's quite sexy," said Mary. "You being protective and all."

"OK," said Jesus, raising his eyebrows. "But those vulgar gags suit the other two girls, Venus and Vixen, better. You see, no offence to those other two, but you are too classy. Crude humour doesn't suit you as well. It just doesn't fit. But those two are naturally brazen. I do not judge them. But they naturally have that vacant look which makes them seductive saying dumb things."

"And they pronounced every syllable S-L-O-W-L-Y," said Mary.

"Actually, I told them to do that," said Jesus. "It gives the impression they are stupid but it also slows down the delivery so people can hear it more clearly. Especially as they haven't done much performing – at least not with an audience."

"Did they know what 'syllable' means," asked Mary.

"I don't know that, do I?" said Jesus. "It's just an act though – them pretending to be stupid. 'Vixen' is an orphan who Esther took in and 'Venus' had a kid but the dad ran off. But you were wrong to avoid telling gags yourself. It may shatter the illusion that you are sexually available, but the guys can fantasize about the other two girls instead."

"But that's not all is it?" said Mary.

Warning: Christians and people who are easily offended should not read this book

"I quite like working with you," admitted Jesus, slightly embarrassed. "It's like we can bond on a level as equals. Sort of creates respect."

"I suspect we're helping with Romano-Jewish relations as well," said Mary.

"Look who's swallowed a dictionary," said Jesus. "'Romano-Jewish'. Go on Professor."

"Sarcasm is the lowest form of wit," scalded Mary. "The more respectful interactions between the soldiers and the population the less easy it is for one to demonise and stereotype the other. So that could potentially reduce the aggression and hatred between us."

"You sound like a hippy," said Jesus. "But what you are saying is you want to be a peacemaker?"

"Yeah," said Mary. "Some guy once said it was a good thing to do."

"Which guy?" asked Jesus.

"I forget," said Mary. "Probably no one important. What about us leaving this place and going on tour, like Peter said?"

"I have all my life here," said Jesus. "And I'm starting to make a difference. You know, exposing corruption in the Church and all that saving souls and stuff."

"You can still do that on tour," said Mary. "In fact, you'd cover a lot more ground if we went round the garrisons doing the act."

"Judas has great plans for our opening night in the city in a couple of weeks," said Jesus. "Let's see how that goes and then decide. I'll do whatever you want. Could that work?"

"Yeah," said Mary. "That could work."

They paused as Mary started looking at Jesus in a superficially disinterested but yearning way.

"Hey," she said suddenly. "Your mum told me a joke. You can use it in the act. You're Jewish, aren't you?"

"Yeah!" said Jesus. "The last time I looked."

Mary began: "A Jewish boy told his mother that he had won a part in the school play. His mother asked, "What is the part you will play, Saul?" Saul responded, "I shall play the Jewish husband," to which his mother said, "Well, you go right back to that teacher and tell her that you want a SPEAKING part!"

Jesus sniggered.

Mary asked Jesus. "I've been thinking," she said. "Do you really need all that God stuff. Those other eight commandments are still good, even without an all-powerful deity."

Warning: Christians and people who are easily offended should not read this book

"Yeah," said Jesus. "But nothing motivates people like that hellfire and damnation stuff. It's a carrot and stick thing: The Kingdom of Heaven is one thing, but eternal torture really gets people listening."

"You have a point," said Mary.

"For example, those demonic man-eating lizards you summoned in the desert, they really focus your mind," said Jesus.

"I can see how they would," replied Mary.

"How many men have you tested?" Jesus asked Mary.

"Do we really have to talk about those things," she replied. "They are in the past. I want to leave that part of me behind."

"You do not have to say anything if it disturbs you," said Jesus. "But you told me about your past life when we were in the desert. I feel you want to share your secrets. Then they will not haunt you."

Mary paused.

"I forget how many men I have tested," said Mary. "But there are more than I can remember."

"Did they all renounce their faith?" asked Jesus.

"Yes, all of them," said Mary. "And usually a damned sight faster than you."

"How long?" asked Jesus. "A few hours. Maybe a couple of days. All except one."

"What happened?" asked Jesus.

"This is strictly need to know stuff," said Mary. "But since we are trading secrets, I'll tell you. You remember hanging off the cliff upside down?"

"Yeah," said Jesus. "I most certainly do."

"I didn't get my grip right and I dropped him," explained Mary.

"What happened then?" asked Jesus.

"What do you think happened?" replied Mary. "He fell half a mile onto some rocks. But I did apologise afterwards. Not to him of course. I got Gabriel to do it. You know, I'm persona non-grata up there."

"So all's well that ends well," Jesus commented.

"Sort of," said Mary.

"What else went wrong?" asked Jesus.

Warning: Christians and people who are easily offended should not read this book

"Believe it or not," explained Mary. "Those archangels are real hard asses. Gabriel made me pay compensation to his family."

"How much?" asked Jesus.

"A thousand camels," replied Mary,

"A thousand!" exclaimed Jesus.

"I thought it was pretty steep as well," said Mary. "I argued him down to 900 but the swine had me over a barrel. And didn't he know it. At least he said he'd keep the whole thing quiet. Anyway, it's your turn now. How did you withstand all that punishment for close on six weeks when most men fold within a day?"

"Actually, I have a secret as well," he said. "I only held up for four days."

"I don't understand," said Mary.

"On day three I began to realise all those bruises and scratches and other injuries magically healed within hours, sometimes minutes," said Jesus. "I got to thinking they weren't real – that or you had some magical healing powers. And then I realised, what good is a dead carpenter to anyone? Then I realised that I was far more use to you alive than dead and you had to keep me alive."

"Very clever," said Mary. "So why did you bother to go alone with things? You know staggering through the desert when you could just have sat there and done nothing?"

"Well, you had put such a lot of effort into it," said Jesus. "I didn't want to disappoint you. And I think better when I'm walking. And I quite enjoyed having you with me."

"What do you mean 'having me with you'?" asked Mary.

"You were with me every second," said Jesus.

"How do you know?" asked Mary,

"I could hear you breathing," said Jesus. "And when it was really quiet, I could even hear your heart beating. I first noticed it during that trek we took in Death Valley. It's so quiet there and you can hear a pin drop. I knew I wasn't alone and you were there protecting me all along."

"Bah!" said Mary. "So I was wasting my time for the best part of five weeks."

"I don't know," said Jesus. "But you are a bit ham fisted and I could feel you pulling me when I went off course in the desert."

"You have no sense of direction," said Mary. "You're a typical man. We'd still be out there if I hadn't put you straight."

"You didn't really need to hold my hand though, did you?" asked Jesus.

Warning: Christians and people who are easily offended should not read this book

Mary scowled at him. "Could you feel that as well?" she asked.

"No," said Jesus.

"How did you know?" she asked.

"I didn't, until now," said Jesus, grinning.

"Shit!" said Mary. "It's my own fault really," she said. "No one ever went more than three days. After that I was improvising. It was uncharted territory. You're bound to make the odd mistake. But if the other girls ever find out my reputation would be dirt."

"I'm not complaining," said Jesus. "It can be our little secret. What are those words? 'I will fear no evil as thou art by my side. Thy rod and thy staff they comfort me.'"

Mary scowled again. "Sarcasm is the lowest form of wit," she said.

"Oh, come on," said Jesus. "You know I love you really." They began to smile.

Warning: Christians and people who are easily offended should not read this book

Let the children come to me

"Do you like children?" Judas asked Mary.

"Yes," she replied. "But I don't think I could eat a whole one."

"What?" asked Judas.

"Never mind," said Jesus. "Why do you ask?"

"Do you think you could do a family show?" asked Judas. Jesus and Mary were walking towards the field where they were preaching that day.

"What do you mean 'family show'?" asked Jesus. "I don't know what bible you've been reading but it's hardly as though the Old Testament is X-rated."

"You know," said Judas. "Dumb it down a bit for the kiddies. Perhaps have a puppet show as well. Maybe some nursery rhymes. I know a great one about a baby shark."

"What he means is," interrupted Mary. "Can we entertain the kids for an hour so he can sell off those barrels of cheap wine to the punters and get them all drunk."

"That's very cynical," said Judas. "And that wine wasn't really that cheap. But it goes off quite fast, so we have to move it in the next few days."

"OK," said Jesus. "We can do the barrel of water trick."

"Excellent," said Judas. "You're a lifesaver. I'll just get the props."

Mary scowled.

"Let the children come to me and do not hinder them," said Jesus to Mary. "Provided they are supervised at all times by an appropriate adult. Now there's a journey we definitely do not want to go on!"

...

Mary had just finished a song.

Jesus stood in front of an empty barrel.

"Ladies and gentleman, boys and girls," announced Jesus. "We now come to the family friendly part of the show. My good friend Mr Judas, has asked me to point out that there are modestly priced refreshments for discerning adults over at the concession stand."

Several of the adults, especially the men, took the hint and set off towards the bar that Judas had set up.

"Now who can tell me who was the strongest man in the world ever?" Jesus asked the audience.

Warning: Christians and people who are easily offended should not read this book

"Hercules," shouted out one child.

"The Emperor," said another.

"Good answers but let me rephrase the question - who can tell me who was the strongest JEWISH man in the world ever?" added Jesus.

"My dad," shouted another.

"Samson," said another.

"Excellent," said Jesus. "Give that young man a prize. Samson was the strongest man ever. Until today. Who thinks I can lift this barrel?" he continued.

"Is it empty?" asked some kids.

"Absolutely," replied Jesus.

"I bet you can," said the kids. He picked it up and put it on a solid wooden stand.

"You aren't strong," said one. "It's empty."

"Ah," said Jesus. "But what if it was full of water? Mary," he said. "How much would this barrel weigh if it was full of water?"

"Ten tons," said Mary. "It would take fifty men to lift it."

"Does anyone think I could lift it then?" Jesus asked.

"No way," shouted out the kids.

"Let's fill it with water and see," said Jesus. "Mary has some buckets. Let's fill it up."

Mary and Jesus led the children a few yards to some water barrels and then they began traipsing back and forth to fill the barrel on the stand.

"Please Miss," said a little girl to Mary. "Why are you a funny colour?"

"Erm," said Mary. "I wasn't expecting that."

"I never saw anyone that colour," said the girl. "Why are you like that?"

Mary looked at Jesus. "Help," she said.

"You're on your own, girl," said Jesus. "I just do the theological stuff." He continued to ferry buckets of water back and forth.

Mary was lost for words.

"Does it wash off?" asked the girl.

Warning: Christians and people who are easily offended should not read this book

"Let's see," said Mary. She put her bucket down and began to wash her hands. The girls and some of her friends came over to help.

"No," said the girls. "It's not coming off. Do you have any soap?"

"Not at the moment," said Mary with relief. Jesus walked past and magically produced some soap. Mary scowled at him as he handed it to the girls. They washed Mary's hands with soap.

"No," said the girls. "It still won't come off. It looks like you'll always be black."

"Right on, sister," said Mary laughing.

A few minutes later the barrel on the stand was full of water. All the children peered in to make sure it was full then Jesus put a lid on the barrel.

"Now children," said Jesus. "Do you think I can lift this barrel, all by myself? All ten tons of it?"

"No way," said the kids.

"I bet you I can," said Jesus. "But first we have to pray. To give us strength."

"Bah!" complained some of the boys.

"Now come on, boys," said Jesus. "If we pray you can see a miracle. All together: Our Father. Who art in Heaven…Forgive us our trespasses as we forgive those who trespass against us…Amen."

Jesus put his hands on the barrel and closed his eyes. Paused. And lifted it clean off the stand.

"Ta dah!" said Jesus and Mary.

"It's a trick," said some of the boys. Jesus put the barrel back on the stand. "Let's see if Mary can lift it?" Mary tried to lift the barrel but couldn't.

"She's only a girl," said the boys.

"Peter," shouted Jesus. "Come and lift this ten-ton barrel full of water."

"I'll try," said Peter. "But it looks really heavy. Only Samson could move that." Peter tried but he couldn't lift it.

"He isn't trying," said the boys.

"You have a go," said Jesus. The children came over and tried to move the barrel but could not. It was fixed down solid.

"You see," said Jesus. "That's the power of prayer."

"Hey, boss," said Judas, dashing over. "We need that barrel."

Warning: Christians and people who are easily offended should not read this book

"Help yourself, brother Samson," said Jesus. Judas picked it up and carried it away with one hand. The children gasped.

"Now boys and girls," announced Jesus. "Sister Mary will tell us the story of Samson and Delilah – first hand."

"I never agreed to that!" exclaimed Mary.

"Just tell it as you remember it," said Jesus.

"Rats!" said Mary. "Well this is the PG version…"

…

It was the middle of the night. Suddenly Mary sat upright in the bed screaming. Jesus jumped up and put his arms around her. Mary was shaking and crying.

"What's wrong?" he asked.

Mary began to compose herself. "I thought this might happen," she explained. "The demons have come back."

"What demons?" Jesus asked.

"A big fat pervert of a palace guard way back in Ramses time," explained Mary. She and Jesus lay back on the bed.

"He did bad things?" asked Jesus. "Before you 'changed'?"

"Yeah," said Mary. "Before I changed."

"What should I do?" asked Jesus.

"You don't have to do anything," said Mary. "Just be there. That's all." She paused. "You know it's odd. I have fought armies of Hittites and hordes of screaming banshees. I've even stood my ground against charging Persian war elephants. And now look at me, I'm scared to be alone."

"We all have our demons," said Jesus.

"Jesus," she asked. "Do you mean all that stuff about forgiving those who trespass against you?"

"I wouldn't say it if I didn't believe it," said Jesus. "I don't work at the Temple - I'm no hypocrite."

"Would that apply to me then? Should I forgive all those men who abused me?" asked Mary.

"Ah," said Jesus. "Now the most important thing when you try and interpret the bible is to apply a bit of common sense."

Warning: Christians and people who are easily offended should not read this book

"How so?" asked Mary.

"What does 'trespass' mean to most people?" asked Jesus, rhetorically. "It usually means some inadvertent slight. Wandering onto someone's land uninvited. Or bad mouthing someone when you're angry. Not mass murder, or rape or child abuse. Does that seem fair?"

"Yes," said Mary.

"And we say, 'Forgive us our trespasses as we forgive those who trespass against us,'" he continued. "Do you think God should forgive those evil men who abused you and killed your mother?"

"No," said Mary.

"If you don't forgive them, then God won't," said Jesus. "And he won't forgive you either for rape and murder of defenceless women and children. Is that fair?"

"I suppose it is," said Mary. "But seeing as how I haven't raped or murdered any defenceless woman or children, not in person anyway, then I don't need to worry about that."

"Exactly," said Jesus.

"What about forgiving your enemies?" said Mary.

"Well," said Jesus. "Sometimes we say, 'love thine enemy as thyself'. It's not quite the same. You can love someone and respect them – most soldiers respect their enemies. But they don't forgive them. If a band of thieves and pirates turned up, God still lets us use lethal force to protect ourselves, other people and our property. I know it's all about the meaning of specific words, but common sense will usually point us in the right direction. And we all know, in our hearts, what is right and wrong. If it doesn't feel right, then it probably isn't. Do unto others what you would have them do unto you."

There was a pause.

"Do you feel any better?" asked Jesus.

"A bit but there has been something troubling me," said Mary. "I am worried about those commandments. One in particular."

"We can go through them if you want," said Jesus. "Do you believe in the one God?"

"Yeah," said Mary. "But there have been issues in the past."

"Well," said Jesus. "God doesn't hold a grudge and you're back on track now. So, hopefully, he'll let that slide. Victimless crime and everything. At least I hope that's the case. Do you blaspheme?"

"Hell no!" said Mary.

"And do you observe the Sabbath?" asked Jesus.

Warning: Christians and people who are easily offended should not read this book

"We have both got extra credits for that," she replied. "What with all that preaching and stuff."

"Right on sister," said Jesus. "Stealing? And lying? And making Craven Idols to worship?"

"Nope!" replied Mary, definitively.

"Honouring thy mother and father isn't really applicable," said Jesus. "Do you covet thy neighbour's wife, or his ox or his ass and such?"

"Not really," said Mary. "Although sometimes I covet your ass. You have hot buns."

"I'm flattered," said Jesus. "But we have a licence, kind-a-sorta, since you started wearing that wedding ring. So that's OK."

"How about adultery?" said Mary, mischievously.

"I refer you to my previous answer," said Jesus. He paused. "I hope we're right about that wedding ring. If not, you and I are in a world of trouble!"

"Damn straight!" replied Mary. "Now let's get to the elephant in the room."

"Thou shalt not kill," said Jesus. "OK. We all have baggage. But try and stay with me on this."

"OK," said Mary, eagerly.

"For roughly how long were you given over to witchcraft and wickedness? How long were you Satan's handmaiden?" asked Jesus.

"Roughly…" said Mary, thoughtfully. "Since they started building the Great Pyramid. That would be about er… three millennia. Give or take a few decades."

"OMG!" explained Jesus. "That's a lot of baggage to carry around. Three hundred years! Well, I suppose the same rules apply. There's no statute of limitations in the bible."

"Jesus," interrupted Mary. "A millennium isn't a hundred years."

"How long is it?" asked Jesus.

Mary mouthed the words: "A thousand!"

Jesus was briefly stunned.

"We're gonna need a few more Commandments," he said eventually. "Anyway, let's do our best with the ones we have. Here goes. Firstly, these armies that you laid waste. Did the enemy soldiers wave swords and throw spear at you and things?"

"Absolute," said Mary. "And not just spears."

Warning: Christians and people who are easily offended should not read this book

"Ok," said Jesus. "So you can claim self-defence. And you were defending your fellow soldiers who did not have the same protection as you. Now, I suspect, given your unusual skill set, that you did the occasional black op. Political assassination and that sort of thing."

"Occasionally," said Mary. "But only two or three hundred."

"And they were evil men? These targets?" Jesus continued.

"You know, assuming they were all men is extremely sexist," replied Mary. "But in the main, they were male. And they were almost always exceptionally wicked. And I don't mean that in a good way."

"And if these evil men had thought that you were a threat to their political aspirations, or if you stood in their way of their ambitions," Jesus asked. "Would they have had any qualms about assassinating you?"

"Not for a second," said Mary.

"OK," said Jesus. "So there are mitigating circumstances. Did you kill anyone before you sold your soul to Satan?"

"No," said Mary.

"And have you killed anyone since you were released by Satan?" he asked.

"No," said Mary.

"So it's just that period when you were under the influence of the Dark Lord that is causing all the bother?"

"Yes," said Mary.

"What would have been the alternative to giving your soul over to Satan?" asked Jesus. "If you had not come under the influence of that Egyptian Queen, what would have happened?"

"I would have been a sex slave to some temple priest or been sacrificed to Ra the Sun God," said Mary.

"Therefore," said Jesus. "I submit that you made the choice under duress. There were three options open to you: death – sex slave – or, deranged homicidal maniac with incredible powers and eternal youth. Anyone could make the same mistake. I think most people would have some sympathy with you."

"I wasn't that deranged," said Mary. "But the other parts are reasonable."

"We cannot criticise the cat for killing the mouse or the bear for killing the salmon," said Jesus. "Or the bee for stinging us. That is in their nature as God made them. The cat and the bear do not hate the mouse or the fish. It is their instinct. And it's likely that your actions were also beyond your control. Ultimately, I cannot forgive you, only you and God can do that. But I know this," continued Jesus. "I see no wickedness in you. To me you are perfect.

Warning: Christians and people who are easily offended should not read this book

A light of goodness shines from you. Even in the desert you stayed with me and watched over me. God has a purpose for you, Mary. I do not know what, but no one ever does. You may even change the world."

"I feel a bit better about my homicidal past," said Mary. "But I'm now a bit worried about having to change the world. It's a lot of pressure to put on someone."

"We'll see," said Jesus. "I'm not infallible, unlike some people. Actually, while I'm thinking, back in the desert I did feel an unusual connection with God – like he was with me. Maybe it was that poison you gave me. But maybe he spoke to me through you."

"I am sorry about that business in the desert," said Mary.

"All's well that ends well," said Jesus.

"I am being punished anyway," said Mary. "This morning I found my first grey hair. I'm starting to age again."

"There," said Jesus. "You destroyed entire civilisations. But now you're going grey. Justice has been done!"

"Amen," said Mary.

Warning: Christians and people who are easily offended should not read this book

Free Food

"I've had another great idea," said Judas at the steering group meeting the next evening.

"Go on," said Jesus.

"That wine sold like hot cakes," said Judas. "So I thought, let's bring some hot cakes for real."

"Who's going to pay?" asked Mary.

"That's the thing," said Judas. "All those rich ladies, who like to watch Jesus, they want to make some donations. And best of all, all that stuff when you stick it to the man – well the fat man – the temple priests, most of the punters think that's great. And lots of them want to make donations to keep you going. Spreading the word and all that. So we can take the money and use it to give away free food to really bring the crowds in. Minus a handling fee of course."

"Oh no!" said Jesus, ominously. "If you're collecting donations, we're getting you audited. Otherwise, you'll skim off the top."

"And the middle," said Mary. "And the bottom."

"Does anyone know any accountants?" Jesus asked.

"Come on," said Judas. "This is the Kingdom of the Jews. If you throw a stick in the air, it'll probably land on some accountant."

"Judas!" said Mary, sternly. "Promoting racial stereotypes does you no credit." She paused so he could reflect. "I've used Levy and Goldman in the past and I've been very pleased with their work," she continued. "But the Cohen Brothers are less pricey, and rumour has it they manage the Emperor's offshore accounts."

…

Mary was just leaving the stage having finished a song.

"What a great audience," said Jesus. "Hey," he shouted. "Isn't that Big Joe Caiaphas over there?" A fat Temple Priest suddenly realised he had been spotted and tried to waddle off.

"Hey Joe," shouted Jesus, pointing. "Thanks for coming. Hey everyone, let's have a big round of applause for Big Joe, the High Priest at the Temple." People began to turn around and clap.

"Hey, Big Joe," shouted Jesus. "It's good to see the diet's working!" He paused so the applause and laughter could die down. "You know," he continued, "Big Joe is High Priest because he has the body of a God. Unfortunately, it's Buddha." Peals of laughter. "That reminds me," continued Jesus. "Commandments are like the courses of a dinner. You can have ten but most people only need two." More laughter at Big Joe's expense.

Warning: Christians and people who are easily offended should not read this book

"So just remember," said Jesus. "Love thy God and love thy neighbour. But try not to love thy pudding too much."

Big Joe finally escaped from the crowd.

"Today," began Jesus. "I thought I'd talk about fornication." Some of the men cheered.

"But that's embarrassing so I'm going to talk about money instead," Jesus added, smiling. The men booed...

...

That night.

"Why is it embarrassing to talk about sex and all that?" Mary asked Jesus.

"Well it's all a bit gross," replied Jesus.

"Good point," said Mary, agreeing.

"Sex is like comedy," said Jesus. "Great fun but it's hard to explain afterwards."

"Can we talk about love then?" asked Mary.

"Help!" said Jesus. "That's almost as hard for guys to talk about as sex. Can't we talk about something else."

"OK," said Mary. "What's the meaning of life?"

"Let's talk about love," said Jesus, changing the subject back. "Why do people fall in love?"

"I know this one," said Mary. "You see guys are total pigs. So they would just run off once they'd got what they wanted and leave us girls to look after the kids. Now you could do a deal and say to some guy – you're cute and you can have your evil way with me, but you have to stay around afterwards and help for the next five or ten years. And they would say 'OK', but they'd still run off the next morning because men are pigs. So God invented love so men don't run off – well not as often or as quickly."

"OK, smart ass," said Jesus. "Why do women fall in love?"

"That's even easier," said Mary. "Only love would make a girl so stupid as to get involved in all the conjugal disgustingness. I mean, it's stomach-churning when you think about it."

"You seem to have all the answers," said Jesus. "How many times have you been in love?"

"Just this once," said Mary.

"Goodness! How's it going?" asked Jesus.

"It's a bit frightening to tell you the truth," replied Mary. "It makes you very vulnerable being so dependent on someone else - especially a man – men are pigs you know."

Warning: Christians and people who are easily offended should not read this book

"I heard," said Jesus.

"How many times have you been in love?" asked Mary.

"Besides now," said Jesus.

"Obviously," said Mary.

"Three or four times," said Jesus. "Although it is terribly bad form to talk about former conquests with a lady."

"Oh, go on," said Mary. "Sharing is caring. Tell me about the first one."

"OK," said Jesus. "But you're not going to go all jealous and have a melt-down, are you?"

"Nah," said Mary. "I can take it!"

"It's just that when most girls have a melt-down they don't talk to you for a few hours. But in your case, it may be the end of civilization as we know it," explained Jesus.

"I'll civilise you," said Mary. "Anyhow I've lost all those powers. Tell me about your first love or no more action for a week."

"Very well, but it's under duress," said Jesus. "Big Sally was her name. 'Big because…'"

"I can imagine," interrupted Mary, wearily. "Double D's no doubt."

"She was the maid down at that huge villa in town," said Jesus. "And I was doing some jobs down there for the mistress of the house. You know, hanging doors. Fixing the roof. Laying down floorboards especially in the bedroom. The mistress was never satisfied in the bedroom. She kept insisting I lay new boards and nail them in. I had to keep ripping them up and laying them down and nailing them one after another. Day in and day out…"

"It's not clever you know," said Mary. "Bragging about scoring with the mistress and her maid. What did your dad have to say about it all?"

"He didn't mind," said Jesus. "We were charging by the hour. But we did keep running out of wood. You know, you need hard wood in the bedroom. You can't lay soft wood on the floor in the bedroom."

"God give me strength," said Mary.

"Well, I could get away most nights to see Big Sally," said Jesus.

"Frankly I'm surprised you had the strength," said Mary.

"I was younger then," said Jesus. "But it was so cool. You know the feeling. You can't stop thinking about someone all day."

"Yeah," said Mary. "I've been there."

Warning: Christians and people who are easily offended should not read this book

"Anyhow," said Jesus. "After a few weeks the mistress rumbled us and sent Big Sally away."

"Were you upset?" asked Mary.

"Devastated," said Jesus. "But life goes on. You say you've only been in love once," he added. "What happened before?"

"During my previous existence," said Mary. "I didn't really have any interest in that sort of thing. It was purely for business. Which is good."

"Why?" asked Jesus.

"Men used to find me intimidating so I wasn't likely to meet someone – not that I was particularly bothered at the time," explained Mary. "You know, being able to destroy entire cities or raise plagues of locusts and things. But that didn't put them off – not all of them. The thing that really put guys off is the fact I earned more than them. That's a real passion killer. I suppose it's like being a supermodel."

"Just out of curiosity," asked Jesus. "How much did you used to earn? With bonuses and tips and everything?"

"About 30K per annum before tax," said Mary.

"Thirty thousand shekels?" asked Jesus.

"No stupid," said Mary. "I wouldn't get out of bed for thirty thousand shekels. Thirty tons of gold."

"Per annum?" asked Jesus, in disbelief. "That's half a billion talons. Caesar can't earn that much."

"If you want the best you have to pay for it," explained Mary. "I've had great references. Moses gave me five stars. He said he was 'extremely satisfied' in his feedback."

"How do you spend five hundred million talons a year?" asked Jesus.

"You know," said Mary. "Winter palace in Cairo, summer palace in Luxor, a yacht to get between the two – nothing fancy – just a hundred oars. A few temples to make things look respectable. But you mainly invest in futures."

"Future?" asked Jesus.

"Yeah," said Mary. "It's real estate that hasn't been conquered. That way the Pharaoh gets his gold back and can recycle the investment. It keeps the economy going."

"And what real estate do you have?" asked Jesus.

"Technically I own Venus, Saturn and most of China," replied Mary.

"What's Saturn?" asked Jesus.

Warning: Christians and people who are easily offended should not read this book

"It's a planet, it's the next one due to be discovered, but I already own it," said Mary. "That's why they're called 'future'."

"It all sounds a bit dodgy to me," asked Jesus. "What about China?"

"That's a bad investment really," said Mary. "The emperors never pay their dues on time. I had to go over one time and boil one in oil just to get the money off him. In fact, I tried my hand at being Empress for a while. But absolute power isn't everything it's cracked up to be."

"How so," asked Jesus.

"You're constantly having to make decisions," said Mary. "The Prince of Zhengzhou says he's also ruler of Henan but he don't have a proper claim and the Shaanxi warlords have put in an objection. Or the Prefect of Canton objects to the Potentate of Macaw letting pirates take refuge in his ports. It's wall to wall hassle. But it's the little things that get really annoying. Like everyone, and I mean everyone, is trying to kill you. Even the imperial gardener will knife you in the back if he gets the chance. So you have to set up a spy network. Which means you have to deal with eunuchs, who are the biggest gossips on the planet. But they bitch like cats on heat. I mean 'meow!' If you turn up at the throne room with a hair out of place everyone in the Forbidden City will know about it by lunchtime. I once mixed brown and orange and I still hold the record as the worst dressed empress ever! Supreme executive authority is a total bummer. Best leave it in the hands of the professionals."

"Well I never!" said Jesus. "So you'd rather be here?"

"Oh yes," replied Mary. "There's the grinding toil and constant risk of starvation but at least no one wants to murder you in your bed. And anyway, I've got me some protection! Haven't I?" She prodded Jesus.

"You don't mind that I have a history," said Jesus. "Romantically?"

"Shall I tell you a secret?" whispered Mary.

"Go on," replied Jesus.

"I quite like it," said Mary. "You know. You being a pistol and all. And no one else can touch."

They giggled.

"Hey," she asked. "Do you like showing me off? You know - like I'm your arm candy?"

"Well," said Jesus. "You are super-hot. And they do say, never hide your light under a bushel."

"That must be some sort of sin," said Mary, smiling.

"Hey, Arm Candy," said Jesus. "Do you want to have a go at the preaching bit? You know, you have so much to say."

Warning: Christians and people who are easily offended should not read this book

"Best not," said Mary. "It's nice of you to ask. But if folks found out about my past then they'd all want to sign up to be 'deranged homicidal maniacs'. It's counterproductive."

"If you change your mind, you can let me know," said Jesus, pausing. "It's nice, you know, talking. Getting to know you."

"I think so too," said Mary. "But some of this stuff, just keep it to yourself."

"My lips are sealed," said Jesus.

Mary kissed him. "They are now," she said.

Warning: Christians and people who are easily offended should not read this book

Five Thousand

"Business is booming," Judas told the steering group that evening. "Now I don't want anyone to panic. But you know that idea we had about free food?"

"What do you mean 'we'?" asked Mary. Jesus put his head in his hands. Peter sighed.

"Collective responsibility," replied Judas. "It seems the free food promotion has been such a success that the next gig is sold out."

"You're selling tickets, are you?" asked Peter.

"Not quite," said Judas. "But the town council, where we've booked the show, has to apply for an event licence. Otherwise, the Romans are likely to read the riot act and set the lions on us. But don't worry. The Governor was very reasonable, and he's granted the licence, but the event is going to be a bit larger than we expected. You see we were planning on three or four hundred."

"How many people does the town council expect to turn out?" asked Jesus.

"All of them," said Judas. "They've declared a feast day."

"What's the population of the town?" asked Mary.

"At the last census," replied Judas. "Five thousand. But some may not turn up."

"Let me guess," said Mary. "You guaranteed free food for them all."

"No," said Judas. "Not at all. That was right out…" He paused and continued, "Actually Yes. It's in the licence - contractually binding and written in stone. On pain of death."

"How much will the current donations cover?" asked Jesus.

"If we stretch out the catering," said Judas. "Maybe six hundred. But I know a guy who can give us a really good deal on fish - so maybe seven hundred."

"What do you suggest we do?" asked Peter. "Borrow the money from those loan sharks?"

Judas looked pained.

"Oh no," said Peter.

"I got a really good deal, ten per cent over base," he explained. "Short-term loan for ten talons. That'll cover the lot - all the catering. And with donations averaging at say, two shekels a head, we'll more than cover the outlay. You have to speculate to accumulate."

"What does the accountant say?" asked Jesus.

"He says it's a good business plan and the numbers all add up," said Judas. "Most of it is tax deductible and we can offset any interest into the next financial year. But there is a problem."

Warning: Christians and people who are easily offended should not read this book

"I should have guessed," said Mary.

"My credit rating isn't that good," said Judas. "You know they rate you as Lombards and Yuppies and such. Well I'm a Neihfo."

"Neifho?" asked Jesus.

"Not Even If Hell Freezes Over," said Judas. "Sacrificial bulls have a higher credit rating than me. But it's not all bad. You see Jesus is a Dinky and Peter is a small businessman with his own house and a yacht."

"It's a fishing boat," said Peter.

"Ya got to embellish things a little," said Judas. "Play the game so to speak. So the shylocks will put up the cash if Jesus and Peter guarantee the loan. Honestly, it's safe as houses."

"So Jesus and Peter are going to guarantee the loan for ten talons," summarise Mary. "And then we can provide free food for the show and pay the money back from the collection and any other donations."

"Exacta-mundo," said Judas. "But it turns out the town councils absolutely hate the temple priests since they closed the local synagogue, and they have to walk five miles to the nearest one. Hence, they admire your work. And they've guaranteed to underwrite half the loan for fifty per cent of any profit."

"So you're selling shares of the profits?" asked Jesus.

"Only for the next ten shows," replied Judas. "Come on, it's a cinch. You're in the big leagues now. Ya gotta see the overall picture. And while I'm thinking, you know that trick you did with the barrel?"

"The one with the false bottom?" asked Jesus.

"Could you do it in reverse?" asked Judas. "So it is a magic barrel what never gets empty?"

"I suppose," said Jesus. "But we'd need some pipe and hide the real barrels behind the stage."

"Lead pipe you say?" said Judas. "I have just the man."

....

Mary and her backing dancers finished their song. A line of Disciples was standing in front of the stage to provide security.

"Thank you, Gaza," said Jesus, going on the stage.

There was cheering all round from the enormous crowd.

"Now can everyone take a few steps back," said Jesus. "Some of the people at the front are

Warning: Christians and people who are easily offended should not read this book

getting crushed."

The crowd shuffled about.

"Ok," shouted Jesus. "Now we have some real magic for you," he continued. "There is free food and drink at the concession stand over to the right. I know it only looks like one barrel and a few baskets but it's a bottomless barrel and those are miracle baskets so there's no need for anyone to panic – there's enough for everyone. Incidentally my associate has pointed out that magic doesn't come cheap and a voluntary donation of two shekels per person may not guarantee you entry into the Kingdom of Heaven, but it will guarantee you entry into the next show - with a wristband. Oh, and no doggy bags!"

Jesus held up some wristbands so people could see what Judas was trying to hand out to those who had paid the donations for the never-ending feast.

"Now I want to take the tone down a bit," said Jesus. "You know, the two most important Commandments are 'Love thy God' and 'Love thy neighbour as thyself'. If you live your life by these two alone then you can enter the Kingdom of Heaven. But do we really need to postpone rewards until the afterlife? If we can all follow these simple rules, we can have our rewards on Earth. The Kingdom of Heaven isn't a way of bribing us to follow the Ten Commandments. The Commandments are advice on how to live here and now…"

…

"Did we clear enough to cover the ten-talon loan?" Jesus asked Mary behind the stage after the show.

"No worries big man," interrupted Judas, counting coins. "And we have some to spare."

"Good," said Jesus. "I was a bit worried about that."

"Me too," said Mary. "Never a borrower or a lender be."

"Sound advice," said Judas.

A man appeared.

"Yo!" said Judas. "This is my good friend Mark, although you might know him as the partner of Mr Spencer, wholesale supplier of food and drink. And here I have the ten talons we owe you." Judas looked very pleased with himself as he weighed two bags of coins in his hands and then tried to hand the smaller of the two to Mark.

"So this is Mr Jesus?" said Mark, holding out his hand for Jesus to shake.

"I've been trying to meet you," said Mark. "It was my daughter you saved from that mob of thugs. The brutes were going to stone her. I was away on business. They'd never had dared if I had been around - I made sure they each one of them got a good thrashing afterwards, I'll say. You showed great courage. I am eternally grateful."

Judas handed Mark the bag of coins.

Warning: Christians and people who are easily offended should not read this book

"No," said Mark. "I won't hear of it. Your money is no good to me. Keep it - no charge. It is reward enough to have met you all."

Mark kissed Jesus on both cheeks and left tearful with joy.

"Now that was a miracle!" said Judas, happily putting all the coins into one bag. "Truly you are the Messiah. King of Kings."

"What do you think you are doing with that money?" asked Mary.

"He didn't want it," said Judas. "So I count it as a donation."

"And what about all that money you swindled out of the audience?" asked Mary.

"They had a good time," said Judas. "And we took a terrible risk. Well Jesus and Peter did. What do you want me to do with it?"

Mary squinted at Judas. "What do you think we should do?" Mary asked Jesus.

"I don't know," said Jesus. "It's all a bit overwhelming. Suddenly having cleared the loan and finding out you saved a man's child from certain death."

"Just remember, before making rash decisions," said Judas. "God giveth and God taketh away."

"Sometimes I wish he'd take you away," said Mary to Judas.

"Peter and I have to go into town tomorrow to pay back the money lenders," said Jesus. "Let's see what happens before deciding what to do with our unexpected windfall."

…

"I've been thinking about magic and miracles and such," said Mary that evening to Jesus.

"That food merchant letting us have all that produce for free was definitely a miracle," said Jesus. "It's as if God hates moneylenders as much as everyone else. Like he's trying to put them out of business."

"The bottomless wine barrel and never-ending bread-basket," asked Mary. "That was all an illusion?"

"Yeah," said Jesus. "There were a dozen barrels behind the stage refilling the wine and we kept exchanging the empty bread-baskets with full ones as the vendors walked round the crowd."

"If people saw a real miracle," said Mary. "Then they would know there was a God."

"Look at the stars or stand on a mountain top or watch the sunrise," said Jesus. "You can see miracles with your own eyes. In fact, the power of sight itself is a miracle. How can eyes and

Warning: Christians and people who are easily offended should not read this book

ears and the power of vision and hearing and speech just grow out of the Earth - just from clay and sand and sea?"

"People don't see it that way," said Mary. "They are desensitised to those miracles. They take them for granted. What they want to see is base metal changed into gold, or people flying through the air, or talking to someone on the other side of the planet or seeing visions of things from the past or future. And machines that think and metal chariots that don't need horses."

"And if they had that power?" asked Jesus. "What would happen?"

"They would believe in God," said Mary.

"Wouldn't they get bored of all those things as well?" asked Jesus. "Or concoct some contorted explanation that hardly anyone understands."

"Actually," said Mary. "You have a point. Miracles would just have to get bigger and better."

"Maybe," said Jesus. "Why doesn't the Devil show himself and do his own miracles? Like blowing up mountains or flooding cities or making earthquakes and such?"

"I know this one," said Mary. "If Satan took credit for disasters, then everyone would know there was a devil. And then everyone would know there was a God. So it might be counterproductive. Actually, the same is true in reverse. If God were to make personal appearances, say at Caesar's Palace every Saturday night, then everyone would assume there was a Devil and some people would seek him out - especially those that couldn't follow the rules."

"It would be a sell-out show though," said Jesus. "They'd need to build a special stadium and hire a troop of cheer-leaders and everything."

"Be serious," said Mary. "God and Satan daren't show themselves any more than they have done because one would confirm the existence of the other. And then there would be a celestial ratings battle to see who could outdo the other."

"Maybe you're right," said Jesus. "But we have to make the best of things as they are, not as we would like them to be. Let's do our best with the people we know and let God and Satan worry about the afterlife. After all, they're the experts."

"Sounds like a plan," said Mary. "It's surprising no one else has thought of it."

"Perhaps one or two folks have," said Jesus. "I think they call them philosophers. I tried to get someone to explain what they said but it's all Greek to me."

"Ha ha," said Mary. "What are we doing tomorrow?"

"Peter and I are going down to that den of thieves in the Temple to pay back the money we owe," said Jesus.

"Are girls allowed in there?" asked Mary.

Warning: Christians and people who are easily offended should not read this book

"Only on weekdays," said Jesus.

"The night is still young," said Mary. "Do you want to take me to Heaven?"

"You bad girl," said Jesus.

"That didn't sound like a no," said Mary.

"Anything that much fun has to be wrong," said Jesus.

"I agree," said Mary. "But what you gonna do?"

Warning: Christians and people who are easily offended should not read this book

Part 5 – Jerusalem

Donkey

Jesus and the Disciples were trekking through the hills approaching Jerusalem.

"Now we need to make a big entrance," said Judas.

"Why?" asked Jesus.

"Marketing," said Judas. "And there's no such thing as bad publicity."

"You would be the expert on bad publicity," added Mary.

"Yes. Well, we need to make a big entrance so everyone will be talking about us and then they will come to the show," continued Judas. "I'll go ahead and get an elephant."

"Elephant?" asked Jesus.

"Yeah," said Judas. "One of those enormous things with trunks. You can't beat an elephant for making an entrance."

"If you say so," said Jesus.

"I'll go ahead," said Judas. "You leave everything to me. Just wait at the gates and I'll come out. Your chariot awaits!"

Jesus sighed as Judas ran off into the distance.

"You can't fault his enthusiasm," said Mary.

"He's got a heart of gold," said Jesus.

"And he's got big pockets to line with the stuff as well," said Mary. "He's been going on about breaking into the Big City for weeks. He wants to make a big impact."

"Elephant," repeated Jesus.

…

A donkey was standing looking bored as Judas introduced Jesus to the animal.

"Now I know it's not quite what I promised," said Judas. "But there are a lot of weddings today and all the elephants were booked."

"What about horses?" asked Mary.

"Have you any idea how much it costs to hire a horse on a Bank Holiday weekend?" said Judas.

"Elephant," repeated Jesus.

Warning: Christians and people who are easily offended should not read this book

"Maybe we can sell it as satire," said Judas, hopefully. "Anyhow the fans are lining up. Let's rock and roll! Jerusalem here we come!"

"You're an idiot," said Mary to Judas, as Jesus set off on the donkey.

…

Jesus and Peter were queueing in the Temple. It was business as usual. There were lots of people and lots of noise and lots of horse trading going on.

"You see," said a man holding up a dove. "The best thing is a bull. We have those but they're really top of the range – big ceremonies and festivals – celebration of major victories and such. And after that, goats. Lots of soldiers buy goats – especially when there's some trouble or they get called up to go to the front. Now bulls and goats is good. But they're expensive. But, for something more in your price range, you can't beat a genuine, thoroughbred, pure as driven snow, dove. That'll put the Gods on your side. Works every time. Here, take a look." He handed the woman a dove. "Beautiful plumage. You see you can't get better than Sacrificial Sam. The Name to Trust for Genuine Offerings and Atonement. Look: beautiful plumage."

"I'm not interested in what your husband died of," said another man behind a table. "You have to come up with the instalments. We lent you the money fair and square. If you don't turn up with twenty shekels by close of business, it's the bailiff for you. And don't come with any of that 'five starvin children' and such: You 'ad 'em. You feed 'em. We've heard it all before. What sort of guy would I be if I just gave money away? I'd be out of business in no time."

"I'm practically giving it away," said another man from behind another table. "Cutting me own throat. Fifteen per cent on the nose. And that's me final offer. Lend you fifty shekels (that's half a talon in new money) 'til middle of next week and you pays me back sixty. It don't come any better than that. That's why they call me Honest John. Although I'll be Homeless John if I keep doing business like this."

Jesus reached the front of his queue. "Here's the money we owe you," he said handing a man behind a table a purse and a piece of parchment. The man opened the purse and counted the money then squinted at the parchment.

"Nah!" he said.

"What do you mean, nah?" asked Jesus.

"Nah!" repeated the moneylender. "This is a day late. You owe us another ten denars in interest."

"But we only borrowed ten to start with!" said Jesus, exasperated.

"Yeah," said the man. "But that was a fixed term loan. Which means the term was 'fixed'. Fixed until yesterday. Now you've gone over we can apply the flexible rate. Which is ten

Warning: Christians and people who are easily offended should not read this book

denars – flat rate for late payment. It says here, look at the small print." He pointed to the parchment.

"You Goddam crooks!" shouted Jesus, losing his temper. He turned over the table. The man dashed off. Jesus stormed round and turned over two more tables. Several cages with doves crashed onto the floor and the birds escaped. Peter tried to restrain Jesus. Some burly men suddenly appeared through a door and began to bear down on the pair.

"Come on boss," said Peter. "We better get out of here."

"But this is a den of thieves," said Jesus. "All of them. Priests and moneylenders. And all this crap with sacrifices. It's blasphemy I say."

"Yeah!" said Peter, dragging Jesus off. "Let's go and do some blaspheming outside though."

Warning: Christians and people who are easily offended should not read this book

Delilah and the Chief Rabbi

"How's my cuddly little Rabbi today?" Delilah asked Big Joe Caiaphas, the Chief Priest in the Temple of Jerusalem. They were in his private quarters.

"Better for seeing you, my little she-devil," said Joe. "What's for tea?"

"Oh, look at you," said Delilah. "Always hungry. I'm having them rustle something up later. You know, you have to keep your strength up. With all that praying and all those dreadful meetings. What do they call that Court thing you have to keep doing?"

"The Sanhedrin," said Joe, sitting down. Delilah hopped up and sat on the table making sure he could see her elegant long legs.

"They shouldn't bother you with so many," said Delilah. "It's not right. A man like you shouldn't have to bother with criminals and heretics and hear about all those wicked folks. Stoning them here and crucifying them there. It just isn't right."

"Amen to that," said Joe.

"Did you hear, there was that awful yob trashing the church today?" said Delilah.

"No," said Joe.

"You see, this guy," said Delilah. "The one who does all those magic tricks – raises the dead and such. He's an awful fraud. Anyhow, he goes to pay the money he owes to the bankers in the church. And, without warning, he goes off on one. And starts pushing the tables over and let all those birds out of the cages. He went 'round calling the place a den of thieves. Thieves I tell you. He was talking about you as well."

"I'm hungry," said Joe.

"Don't worry," said Delilah. "Dinner is on its way."

"Good," said Joe.

"And are you going to put up with that?" asked Delilah.

"Put up with what?" asked Joe.

"That conjuror calling you a thief," asked Delilah. "Loads of folks outside were cheering him on and saying he was right. You know a thing like that can grow arms and legs. You need to nip it in the bud. It's not right. Him casting aspersions on decent hardworking Joe's like you. And do you know something else?"

"What?" said Joe.

"Now I'm not one to talk," continued Delilah, whispering. "But they say he's living with some houri and she's…well I don't like to say it…but…she's not of the white race! You know. One of those escaped African slave girls. There should be a law against it."

Warning: Christians and people who are easily offended should not read this book

"What do you want me to do about it?" asked Joe.

"Crucify him," said Delilah. "Teach him a lesson. Go to the Governor later and get a warrant. And have him crucified. Set an example to the rest. The others will like it – laying down the law and everything. People will respect you. There may even be another promotion in it for you."

"Maybe after dinner," said Joe.

"Ok," said Delilah. "After dinner we can go on down to see the Governor, I've got some things for his girlfriend anyway. And then we can come back for dessert. And what would you like for dessert, my little honey bear?…" She stretched out her legs and smiled seductively at him.

Warning: Christians and people who are easily offended should not read this book

Supper

"How was dinner?" Mary asked. She and Jesus were in the bedroom.

"I thought I would get a load of stick for losing my temper and trashing the Church Hall," replied Jesus. "But they were all pretty stoked on it. Judas said the publicity will bring the punters flocking in – especially as everyone has got it in for the priests and the Shylocks. But Peter caught me afterwards and said I should get out of town."

"He's right," said Mary. "You insist on sticking it to the man in the pulpit. You can't go round messing up their shit. They're gonna smoke your ass even with the Gov'nor on your side. They'll put out a contract on you."

"We're all on lock-down until sunrise," said Jesus. "The city gates are all closed and bolted."

"First thing tomorrow we're out of here," said Mary.

"That sounds like cowardice," Jesus suggested.

"He who fights and runs away lives to preach another day," replied Mary. "And you did fight in the church today. A church of all places! Come sunrise we are gone!"

"If you insist," said Jesus.

"I do insist," said Mary. "This is the big city. The Feds cannot just sit there and do nothing if you go round making trouble."

"OK," said Jesus. He paused. "You can be very assertive you know."

"You don't know the half of it, baby," replied Mary.

Jesus paused.

"What exactly do witches do all day?" he asked, laughing. "Do they go round casting spells and eating babies?"

There was an uncomfortable silence. Mary looked a little sheepish.

"Oh no!" said Jesus, as his face dropped. "You have to be kidding?"

He looked her straight in the eye.

"Tell me it ain't so?" he asked. "Not babies?"

"Well.." began Mary, awkwardly. "I can't say that I've done it myself, but it is in the job description."

"OMG!" said Jesus. "That is bad. I mean really bad. Like…it's the worst thing I've ever heard."

He paused. Mary looked uncomfortable.

Warning: Christians and people who are easily offended should not read this book

"That is really really bad," continued Jesus.

"Well," said Mary. "I never said I was an angel."

"Even so," said Jesus. "That is so bad. The worst thing everrrrrrr!"

"Look at it this way," said Mary apologetically. "If there were ravenous wolves, or jackals or lions. And there was a baby around…"

"That really doesn't help," said Jesus.

"You eat lambs," said Mary.

"That's different," said Jesus.

"The sheep don't see it that way," said Mary.

"But we breed lambs for the slaughter," protested Jesus.

Mary looked at him imploringly.

There was another uncomfortable silence.

"You have to promise me you won't get involved in anything like that ever again," said Jesus. "Like not ever. Not in a million years."

"I think I've lost all my powers anyway," said Mary.

"Don't change the subject," said Jesus. "Promise me you won't use any black magic again ever. Not even to protect me."

"OK," said Mary. "Not in a million years."

"Not even then," said Jesus. "Not ever ever."

"OK," said Mary. "Not ever. Cross my heart and hope to die."

"Good," said Jesus. "The dark arts are evil. One day we will all die – all of us. Even you and me. So above everything else you must save yourself from Hell. You never know when you will be called. And judged!"

Jesus paused and looked at her more sympathetically. "I know you have more reason than most people to be angry with the world. But I don't see any hate in you. Your soul is pure."

"That's nice of you to say so," said Mary. "I don't know why God sent you to save me."

"He does things like that," said Jesus. "And I didn't save you. You saved me."

There was a pause as the mood lightened. They began to smile at each other.

"Hey, you sexist pig," Mary began. "How do you know God is a He?"

Warning: Christians and people who are easily offended should not read this book

"He just is," said Jesus. "I don't hear all your feminists insisting that Satan is a girl."

"She might be," said Mary. "In fact, it might be a ceremonial position. Maybe every four years all the goblins get together in Hell and elect a new one. Like a President."

"God forbid!" said Jesus.

"The angels are all boys though," said Mary.

"How so?" asked Jesus.

"The entire celestial hoard, every man-jack of them, was supposed to be protecting you," Mary explained. "And I just waltz in under their noses. Only a load of guys could screw up that much. Admittedly, things didn't turn out quite as I'd planned them. But either way. Here I am!"

"Yeah!" said Jesus. "I find that a bit odd as well. With all those angels sleeping on the job."

"God works in mysterious ways," said Mary.

"We should give that some thought," said Jesus. "Anyway, we have to get up early tomorrow. It's bedtime."

"It sure is," said Mary.

"Sleep tight," said Jesus.

Mary looked at him and smiled. "I'm not actually that tired," she said.

"Are you sure you've lost all your powers?" asked Jesus, squinting at her.

"I think so," said Mary. "Well, all the best ones."

"You're a black magic woman," said Jesus. "You're trying to make a Devil out of me."

"I put a spell on you," said Mary. "Because you're mine!"

...

Jesus, Mary and Peter looked out of the doorway. They were each wearing tunics with hoods. People began passing up and down the street indicating the gates to the city were now open.

"Ok, boss," said Peter. "Word on the street is that Big Joe has got a warrant out for you after the clever way you trashed the synagogue yesterday."

"If we keep our heads down, we can make it out the gate without the Feds bothering," said Mary. "If anyone stops you, I'll create a distraction and you run for it."

"This all seems a bit cloak and dagger to me," said Jesus. "But if that's what you want."

"That's what we want," said Peter.

Warning: Christians and people who are easily offended should not read this book

They pulled their hoods up and walked briskly down the street and mingled with the populace. As they rounded the corner, they saw a gate. Roman soldiers were standing around, trying to appear like they were checking for contraband and troublemakers but really they were doing as little as possible.

Mary and Jesus followed an empty cart towards the gate. Peter was close behind. The cart stopped suddenly. Mary led Jesus pass it. They were amidst a throng of people bustling in and out – some carrying goods into the city – others leaving with farming instruments. There was a crash. Everyone startled and looked round. A large jar had fallen off a cart and smashed, flooding the street with oil. "Come on," whispered Mary. She dragged Jesus by the arm. The soldiers looked up but were focussed on the smashed jar. Mary and Jesus were just reaching the gate.

"Hey, Jesus," shouted Judas who had just come through the gate. "I got you that elephant."

The soldiers looked directly across. They were suspicious. The Centurion appeared from the guard house. He spotted Jesus. He stepped across and grabbed Jesus' arm. He vaguely recognised him, but he was uncertain. The soldiers followed him.

"What's your name?" the Centurion asked.

Jesus said nothing.

"It's Peter," said Peter.

"Not you," said the Centurion. "Him."

"Sorry, your honour," said Peter. "He's a bit deaf. He's called Peter."

"Not 'Jesus'?" asked the Centurion.

"No," said Peter. "Definitely Peter."

"Are you sure?" asked the Centurion.

"Certain," said Peter. "His name's Peter. Not this Jesus guy."

"Why did that guy call him Jesus then?" said the Centurion.

"Mistaken identity," said Peter. "We get that a lot. This guy is called Peter."

The Centurion looked suspiciously at Jesus and Judas.

"Bring both these two," ordered the Centurion. The guards grabbed Jesus and Judas by the arms.

Mary shrieked. She grabbed a dagger from one of the soldiers and tried to stab the Centurion. He dodged her and the dagger clipped his ear.

Warning: Christians and people who are easily offended should not read this book

The Centurion grabbed his bleeding ear. Mary was about to make another lunge when Peter grabbed her and pulled her back.

"No!" shouted Jesus. "Thou shalt not kill. Control yourself, Mary. You anger me."

Mary looked at him in desperation. The guards began dragging Jesus and Judas off. Mary shouted. "Don't say anything. They'll use your words against you. Say nothing. I got this!"

Peter had wrestled the dagger off her and handed it to the Centurion.

"She doesn't know what she's doing," he told the Centurion. "She's upset. You know women. It was an accident."

The Centurion held his ear but could not see how bad the wound was.

"Look," said Peter to the Centurion. "Take me. Let her go. She didn't mean anything."

"Damn the lot of you!" shouted the Centurion. He spat at Peter's feet and set off after Jesus and the guards.

…

"Jesus of Nazareth," announced Big Joe, Prosecutor and Chief Priest of the Temple. Jesus was standing in chains before the Governor, Pontius Pilate, who was seated. The accusing Priests were sitting at a table. The public were watching from a safe distance in the city square behind fences. Roman soldiers had formed a barrier.

"You have been convicted by the most Merciful and Wise House of Judgement, of blasphemy, sedition, heresy, defiling the Holy Temple, raising rebellion, breach of the peace, and conduct unbecoming to good order. Do you have anything to say?"

Jesus remained silent with his head bowed.

"You don't have much to say for yourself, Preacher," said Pilate. "Centurion. You know this man. Tell the Court of his crimes."

"He caused a disturbance at the temple and did shout and behave most unbecoming, accusing the Priests and moneylenders of being 'thieves'," replied the Centurion.

"I can understand why they might be upset," said Pilate. "And sedition?"

"I heard him say of the Priests, that they work like gnats and eat like camels, and he has been most insulting to them," continued the Centurion.

"Much to the delight of the people, I hear," commented Pilate. "And Raising Rebellion?"

"I know not," said The Centurion. "Although I did hear him preach and he has said strange things to the great displeasure of the Priests."

"Pray tell," said Pilate.

Warning: Christians and people who are easily offended should not read this book

"He said things such as 'Love thine enemies' and 'If a man strike you then turn thine other cheek'," replied the Centurion.

"I hear he also made some comment about tax evasion?" asked Pilate.

"You are well informed my Lord," replied the Centurion.

"I have to be in this job, Centurion," said Pilate.

"The Priests asked him whether the people should pay the Roman taxes and he told them, 'Give unto Caesar what is his.'" replied the Centurion.

"And you heard this?" said the Centurion.

"With mine own ears, My Lord," the Centurion Replied. "Well, my own ear."

"And that scratch," asked Pilate, pointing to the Centurion's wound. "Did he give you that?"

"No, my Lord," admitted the Centurion. "That was some Hell cat. And the accused did reprimand her most severely and said to her, 'Thou shalt not kill'."

"Well Preacher," said Pilate, looking towards Jesus. "There is more to you than meets the eye. Now," Pilate directed his questions to the accusing priests. "The accused has grievously insulted you priests accusing you of 'biting like gnats and being fat as a camel', how do you plead?"

The onlookers began to giggle.

"It was actually 'working like gnats' and…" Big Joe began to whisper. "'Eating like camels'."

"Shame on him," said Pilate, sarcastically. "And you priests are positively wasting away before our very eyes."

The audience began to laugh.

"All this talk of starvation has made me hungry," said Pilate. "I grow thirsty." Pilate clapped his hands. "What other heinous crimes has he committed?" Pilate asked the accusers. Big Joe and the others looked at some parchments frantically. After a pause Big Joe began to read.

"He doth consort with a harlot and does fornicate with her and she is not of the white race, thereby corrupting public morals and bringing the wrath of God upon us," said Big Joe, looking up and smiling smugly with self-satisfaction.

Governor Pilate held a newly filled cup. Jezebel, the African slave girl stood next to him looking exceptionally tall and glamourous. She held a gold decanter in one hand. She had her other arm draped round Pilate's neck. Pilate was patting her free hand which rested on his shoulder. Pilate looked up at Jezebel who blew him a kiss and strode off. Pilate turned his gaze onto Big Joe. The Governor did not look pleased.

Warning: Christians and people who are easily offended should not read this book

"Shit!" whispered Big Joe as he took in the situation.

"Perhaps we were rather premature with the last charge," said Big Joe, apologetically. "I think we may have been a bit harsh. We seek your leave to dismiss the charge of fornication."

Pilate scowled and picked up a parchment.

"Let's see what sentence your kangaroo Court has pronounced on this 'fornicator'," he said reading the document.

"Crucifixion!" Pilate shouted. "Rabbi," he asked in disbelief. "Have you been smoking the incense again?"

The onlooker began to fall about with laughter.

Big Joe and the other accusers began looking at each other nervously and began whispering. Suddenly another priest stood up.

"With your leave, your honour," he said. "We are at grave fault and beg your indulgence. This offence was committed under ecclesiastical law and the accused is a citizen of Nazareth not of this city. We should have put this case before Herod. We ask the Court to forgive us for wasting their time and petition to remove the accused and bring him before the Royal Court instead."

"Case dismissed!" pronounced Pilate to cheers from the crowd. "Take this fornicator to Herod. And give my regards to him and his new wife."

...

Big Joe and the accusing priests sat at a table in the open Court in Herod's throne room. There was a big audience of eager spectators. Herod and the Queen were sitting on thrones. Jesus stood before them in silence. His chains had been removed.

"It is a privilege to appear before you, your Highness, and know that we can receive wise and merciful justice here at the Court of King Herod the Great..." began Big Joe.

"Just a second, counsellor" interrupted Herod. "As a point of order, Herod the Great was my father. And I'm no longer a King. I'm what is called a Tetrarch. It means I rule a quarter of my father's Kingdom. Thank you for reminding me. You can call me Your Honour, or 'Herod The Not So Great' as you please."

"That wasn't the best start," whispered an assistant to Big Joe.

"Many apologies, Your Honour," said Big Joe. "The man before you, Jesus of Nazareth, has been convicted by the most merciful and wise House of Judgement, of blasphemy, sedition, heresy, defiling the Holy Temple, raising rebellion..."

"Yes, yes, yes," interrupted Herod. "Get to the fornication bit."

"We have dropped those charges," said Big Joe.

Warning: Christians and people who are easily offended should not read this book

"Well pick them up again," commanded Herod.

Big Joe was flustered but quickly composed himself as an assistant passed him a parchment.

"The accused was charged with fornicating and consorting with a harlot and houri and woman of ill-repute…" said Big Joe.

"Three at once!" interrupted Herod. "Good work!"

"No, your honour," explained Big Joe. "The same one, but on several occasions. And she is not of the white race and their lascivious behaviour doth therefore endanger public morals and bring the Kingdom, I mean Tetrarchy, into disrepute and angers the wrath of God, or Gods, as you see him, or them."

"Goodness!" said Herod, standing and walking towards Jesus to take a closer look. The Queen accompanied him. Herod addressed the accusers and the audience. "And where is this evil woman, this adulteress, this vile creature who degrades man and leads those of weak character and feeble morals to eternal damnation? Show her to me."

Mary pulled back her hood and raised her hand awkwardly, Herod made eye contact. Mary smiled at him and waved, knowingly.

"I know her," blurted out Herod.

"We believe she used to work here as an….erm… 'chamber maid'," said Big Joe.

Herod suddenly remembered. "Well, boys will be boys, eh," he said awkwardly. "No sense in getting too carried away. What do you think my dear?" he asked, turning to face the Queen. "Is he everything they say about him?"

"Oh yes," the Queen replied. "He is super-cute. I mean Damn girl! He's sex on legs."

"No! No! No!" shouted Herod as the audience began to snigger.

"Can we keep him?" asked the Queen untying one of the straps on Jesus' tunic. "I want to cross examine him later."

"Do you have anything to say for yourself, Preacher?" Herod asked Jesus in resignation.

Jesus remained silent and looked at the floor.

"Don't worry," said the Queen to Herod, beaming. "He's probably the strong silent type."

"Well, he doesn't look like he can raise the dead, or raise a rebellion," pronounced Herod. "The only thing he seems to raise is the Queen's temperature. Take him back to the Governor."

"Bah!" said the Queen. "You never let me have any fun!"

…

Warning: Christians and people who are easily offended should not read this book

"Be upstanding! The Imperial Court of Judea is now in session. His Honour Governor Pontius Pilate Presiding," the crier moved aside as Pilate strode onto the platform in the public square. He casually waved the assembled throng to be seated if they had chairs.

"What's he doing here?" demanded Pilate as he saw Jesus standing before him.

"The Honourable Tetrarch, Herod, has sent him back," replied the Centurion. "Apparently he's too hot to handle."

"That is just typical of Herod The Not So Great," grumbled Pilate, sitting. "Wanting me to do all his dirty work. Rabbi," he said to Big Joe, who was seated at a table with the other accusers. "Have you reconsidered your position?"

"They still demand Crucifixion," interrupted Centurion.

"You are hard men," observed Pilate. "This is an innocent man. Why do you persecute him?"

Big Joe stood. "He doth blaspheme and offend our God most grievously," said Big Joe. "He claims to be the Messiah. King of Kings."

"That was part of a conjuring act," snapped Pilate.

"The House of Judgement has ordered that he must die," argued Big Joe. "And we humbly request that the law be applied and the governor order execution for, as we all know, only the Imperial Court may enforce such a sentence."

Pilate paused for thought.

"He has caused much nuisance and disturbed the public order," said Pilate. "He shall receive a dozen lashes. He shall then be brought before this Court on the morrow so that the House of Judgement may reconsider their sentence. And I advise them that posterity will lay judgement upon them for their actions."

"As you command," replied Big Joe, deferentially.

"Take him away," Pilate ordered the guards, in exasperation.

…

"What troubles you, my lord," Jezebel asked Pilate that evening in his chamber. "It grieves me to see you tortured like this."

"It's that damned preacher," Pilate replied.

"Execute him and be done with it," advised Jezebel. "He is but a conjuror and a carpenter. What of it?"

"He has caught the public imagination," explained Pilate. "And the Emperor's spies are everywhere. This conjuror leads the people against those bloated fat fools in the Temple. While their energy is directed towards the Priests, the people here make less rebellion against

Warning: Christians and people who are easily offended should not read this book

Rome. And the Preacher says, 'Give unto Caesar what is his.' I would be a poor governor if I were to kill any man who preaches peace with Rome. He is a friend to us. We must encourage him and his kind to spread their message of cooperation. And the Emperor will be most displeased if he should hear otherwise."

"Why do you put such importance on the sentence of the priests?" asked Jezebel. "They are conquered men and your servants."

"I have but a few legions to keep peace in these rebellious lands," said Pilate. "It is the temple priests and their men who administer this province. They collect the taxes for themselves and for us. They keep the order. I must do their bidding if it does not conflict with our ambitions here. That is the law, and that bloated Rabbi knows it. If I defy him, he will appeal to Rome, and it will go badly for me. I may never get out of this cursed backwater."

"I can see this problem troubles you," said Jezebel. "I am a simple servant. But I love my lord greatly. May I make some small suggestion?"

"If it pleases you, my dear," replied Pilate.

"The Emperor celebrates a great victory in Rome," suggested Jezebel. "In honour of this, let the People choose between this Jesus and another man, some hideous murderer. Pardon one and execute the other. Thereby you have honoured the emperor, the People will be satisfied, justice is done, and the priests cannot be seen to oppose you, without incurring the wrath of the people and the emperor."

Pilate thought.

"That is an excellent idea," he said eventually. "In fact, it is inspired. I will do as you say."

"You are too kind," said Jezebel. "With your leave a servant of the High Priest has come to collect some things. I must attend to her briefly."

"Go," said Pilate. "But no for too long." He smiled at her as she left the room.

...

The Imperial Court had reconvened once more in the City Square. Pilate was presiding. The Priests were sat in the place of the accusers. Before Pilate, Jesus and another man were being held in chains. Jesus' tunic was torn. He had been lashed. The crowd was unusually small, and the Priest's henchmen were prominent amongst them.

"This day the Emperor celebrates a great victory," Pilate pronounced. "Not just for Rome but for the world. In celebration we make an offering to you, his loyal People. One of these men will be pardoned. Here stands Jesus of Nazareth, Preacher. Accused of blasphemy and sacrilege. I have already punished him for his crimes. But the temple priests still demand his life. And next to him stands Barabbas. Murderer! Which of these men shall be freed? Jesus?"

Warning: Christians and people who are easily offended should not read this book

Mary and a few disciples who had run the gauntlet of the priests' thugs, cried "Release Jesus!"

"Or Barabbas?" Pilate asked the crowd.

"Release Barabbas," shouted men in the crowd, including all the Priests' henchmen.

Pilate was bewildered.

"I ask you once more," Pilate commanded in confusion. "Which of these men shall be freed? Jesus of Nazareth?"

The disciples screamed "Release Jesus." But they were quickly drowned out by men shouting "Barabbas. Barabbas is innocent. Free Barabbas. Crucify the heretic."

Pilate peered into the crowd. He saw the priests smiling to themselves. He saw some of their henchmen handing out coins to those who shouted in favour of the murderer.

"I am unclean," shouted Pilate, angrily. "Bring me water."

Pilate stood in fury as a servant brought a water jug. "Pour it," ordered Pilate holding his hands out. "I wash my hands of you," he shouted to the crowd, finding it difficult to control his temper. "I am innocent of this man's blood. Crucify the Preacher. Release the Other. A curse on you!" In his anger, Pilate threw the washing bowl over and it smashed on the stone.

The guards drag Jesus away as Pilate leaves.

…

Jesus cried out in agony as the iron nail was cruelly driven into his wrist, and through his flesh, and into the wooden cross beneath. He lay on the cross which lay on the ground. He wore only a loincloth. Several guards held him down. Soldiers held the small crowd back. There were intermittent screams of pain as other prisoners were nailed to their crosses. Mary, Mother of Jesus, Joseph and some Disciples stood amongst the crowd. Most were kneeling and crying. Mary, the African slave girl, was absent.

A second nail was hammered home. Mary Mother of Jesus fainted. Peter held her in his arms and cried. The onlookers watched in horror. Jesus fainted as the nails were hammered through both his heels. Their grim task accomplished, the guards lifted the cross using ropes attached to the cross bars and slotted it into a hole driven into the ground and lined with wooden braces.

Jesus moaned as the guards left to attend to another victim. The soldiers allowed the onlookers to move closer but kept them several feet from the cross and threatened those who came too close with spears. Many fully armed soldiers and officers stood watching the crowd, anxious to intervene at any sign of trouble.

Jesus hung on the cross. He wailed. His body went into involuntary spasms occasionally. The onlookers fell and prayed.

Warning: Christians and people who are easily offended should not read this book

Time and agony drew on. Minute by minute. Hour by hour. Unending.

After an hour, a soldier came up to Peter. "We can end this," he told Peter.

"What do you mean," asked Peter.

"After sunset the other guards will go," said the soldier. "It doesn't have to go on any longer. No one is going to be too bothered if he's hanging there dead at sunrise. And we have sharpened spears. But there is a risk. If my men and I are caught, we will be flogged. So you have to pay us for our mercy."

"How much?" asked Peter.

"How much have you got?" the soldier replied.

"How long does it usually take?" asked Peter. "To die. Like that?"

"A couple of days, usually," said the soldier. "If you watch you will see they can't breathe properly when they are hanging by their arms. So they have to push themselves up with their legs and their heel bones grind on the nails. And that goes on hour by hour until eventually their legs are too weak. And they suffocate."

"And you approve?" asked Peter.

"Better them than me," said the soldier. "I am a coward. I do what I have to, and survive. Just like everyone else. The priests wanted to make an example of your boy there."

"Is he a threat to the state?" asked Peter.

"Of course not," said the soldier. "The Governor would have had him beheaded there and then in the square if he'd been a threat to the Empire, not have him hanging there for days in full view of everyone to incite riots. No. He's just made enemies of the wrong people. Anyway, if you want our help, you know where to find me."

The soldier went to join the other guards.

Time and agony drew on. Minute by minute. Hour by hour. Unending.

Eventually, in mid-afternoon, the Centurion came through. He looked uneasy. Jesus began moaning then began to whisper. Mary Mother of Jesus went to the Centurion and knelt at his feet. "Let me speak with my son," she begged. The Centurion looked down at her, pitifully. "Let her pass," he ordered the guards eventually. The soldiers moved aside as Mary staggered through. They quickly reordered and took position to keep the other onlookers away. Mary crypt to the base of the cross and knelt. She looked up and prayed. Jesus began to speak.

"I cannot hear you, my son," said Mary Mother of Jesus.

Jesus spoke again.

Warning: Christians and people who are easily offended should not read this book

Mary, Mother of Jesus, looked pained. "Merciful Lord," she prayed out loud. "Give my son the strength to speak."

"Mother," gasped Jesus. "Find Mary. Tell her: Forgive them. For they know not what they do."

Jesus collapsed into unconsciousness. Mary, Mother of Jesus, ran from the evil place sobbing. Peter and Joseph followed here and tried to provide comfort. The Centurion took a spear from one of the soldiers. He hurled it true and straight. It ran through Jesus' chest and he fell limp and silent. Free of pain.

...

"Centurion, we have a problem," said Jezebel, as she walked into the guard room of the Palace with Delilah.

"We hear that there is trouble brewing because of this preacher that you've crucified," added Delilah.

"There is always talk of rebellion," said the Centurion.

"This is different," said Jezebel. "People are sick of idle priests taxing them and calling it a donation."

"And then sitting on their fat backsides and doing nothing," said Delilah.

"And they charge extortionate rates for weddings and funerals and any other service," said Jezebel.

"That preacher has got everyone going," said Delilah. "And now they're coming here for some payback."

"I better call out the guard," said the Centurion. "Does the Governor know?"

"He's likely to join them," said Jezebel. "He's no friend of the House of Judgement. Not after they embarrassed him like that in public."

"I better check," said the Centurion as he got up and left.

Jezebel turned to Delilah. "Have you seen Mary recently?" she asked.

"She's dropped out of sight," said Delilah. "Not a sound."

"That's what bothers me," said Jezebel. "I think rebellious subjects are the least of our worries."

...

Warning: Christians and people who are easily offended should not read this book

Night fell. Mary, the African slave girl, knelt in the room. Her eyes opened with a start as the first moonlight appeared. She blinked and her eyes glowed demonically. She turned and strode towards the city. As she walked, she tore her clothes.

As the moon rose, distant thunder rumbled. The soldiers were lined in formation in front of the high city walls. The fortifications were strong – several feet thick at the base. The soldiers held shields and weapons. Before them stood Jezebel and Delilah in the armour of Warrior Maidens. They held spears. They looked up. The moon glowed red.

Jezebel and Delilah smiled at each other as they saw Mary striding down from the hills. Mary moved quickly, although she only appeared to walk. As she came into range, Jezebel and Delilah nodded at each other and threw their javelin with supernatural force, straight and true towards Mary. Suddenly the javelins rose up in the air and circled overhead. They flew in a huge arc and then hurtled down to Earth. There was a deafening thunder strike. The two javelins impaled Jezebel and Delilah vertically. They were both consumed in flames. A second later the soldiers fell to their knees and held their ears as deafening screams the rent the night. Jezebel and Delilah were impaled on burning crosses before them.

Mary continued onwards. The soldiers panicked. They scattered. Many soldiers ran within the safety of the city gates. Other soldiers ran forward from within the citadel and slammed the enormous gates shut. They quickly sealed the gates slamming heavy bolts home and lifting huge tree trunks into place into iron clasps set into the thick wooden gate posts. The soldiers stepped back as the barricades fell into position.

A second later the enormous gates were blasted into splinters. The soldiers were thrown to the ground. Mary strode through. A large cohort of defenders were standing in formation before the steps of the huge stone keep. Mary approached. Spears and arrows fell on the ground before her in mid-flight. Mary made a sign. The enormous battlements and heavily fortified walls collapsed into rubble behind her. Men charged forward but were tossed back by invisible hands yards away from Mary as she strode steadily onward, irresistible. Many of the soldiers fled in terror as she came closer. Others froze in fear. The Centurion knelt before her as she approached. "Hell hath no fury," he whispered as he cast his sword down and bowed his head awaiting death.

Mary lifted the Centurion bodily with one arm by his neck and carried him up the stone stairs of the keep. She held out her hand and a discarded sword flew from the ground into her grip. She pinned the Centurion to the wooden door of the gates. He squirmed, gasping as she pulled back her sword arm about to strike. Mary, Mother of Jesus, threw herself bodily between the she-Devil and the soldier. "No!", she screamed. Mary, Mother of Jesus, grabbed Mary's head. "You must forgive him," she begged. "The Lord Commands it. Thou shalt not kill." Mary held the Centurion against the door by his neck, her terrible fury visible to all. Then she gradually relaxed and let him fall. He scrambled away, clutching his throat. Mary stabbed the sword into the thick wooden door three times shattering the oak with each blow. She turned. Her eyes glowed. She pointed towards the blood red Moon. The skies darkened.

Warning: Christians and people who are easily offended should not read this book

The soldiers fell on their knees. A shadow appeared over the Moon. The skies darkened as the Moon's light was slowly extinguished into black. Darkness fell on the land.

Warning: Christians and people who are easily offended should not read this book

Mary and Judas

Judas was nervous. It was night. He could not sleep. Eventually he climbed out of bed and found a wooden club to protect himself. He slammed the club into his palm to ensure it was solid. Then he lay back and closed his eyes. He rolled around for a few minutes and slept. He heard a noise and opened his eyes.

Mary was leaning over him with her face a few inches from his. Judas shrieked and scrambled across the bed to the wall.

Mary continued to scowl at him. She held up the club.

"Expecting someone?" she asked.

"No," Judas lied.

"Come on," said Mary "Get your things and bring a shovel. We have work to do." Judas scuttled across the room and collected a bag and a shovel

Mary walked towards the door. "Bring that blood money too," said Mary. "We can use that."

Mary and Judas walked up the path towards the tomb. The Centurion with the cut ear was walking down in the opposite direction. Mary smiled at him as they passed and tossed him the purse which contained Judas' money. The Centurion saluted and continued to walk down, ignoring them.

Mary and Judas approached the tomb. Two guards were lying close by. They were both snoring loudly. Judas walked over to one of the guards. He picked up the flagon that the guard had dropped.

"Leave that alone," said Mary. "You don't need to worry about those two. They're out for the count."

Mary and Judas approached the heavy stone that sealed the crypt. Judas used his spade to tap the seal.

"No man is going to move that," said Judas.

"I am no man," replied Mary, taking hold, and rolling the heavy stone aside.

…

Mary and Judas stood over the open grave on the hilltop.

Mary was speaking in Hebrew: "um btsernu ubbdidesnu ubrgey hshmmh shlnu, elinu lstes mmekb khr s'h, hu ezub esnu l, rueh nmn, l nkrb esnu l s'h" [*]

Judas looked bewildered. He looked at Mary in puzzlement.

"Didn't you know I was Jewish?" asked Mary.

Warning: Christians and people who are easily offended should not read this book

"I never really thought about it," replied Judas.

There was a pause, as Mary whispered some prayers.

"Mary," Judas began. "How did you move that enormous stone?"

"All Black people can do that," said Mary. "We're stronger than you White folks."

"Come on," said Judas. "Be serious."

"There was an earthquake," replied Mary.

"I didn't feel any earthquake," said Judas. He suddenly fell over as the ground shook. Some nearby buildings collapsed.

"How about that one?" said Mary, glaring at him. "That's called an aftershock."

Judas staggered to his feet. He appeared nervous as he stood by the grave.

"Do not test me, Judas," Mary warned him. "Anyway," she continued. "You can relax. If I wanted to kill you, you'd be dead already."

…

[*um btsernu ubbdidesnu ubrgey hshmmh shlnu, elinu lstes mmekb khr s'h, hu ezub esnu l, rueh nmn, l nkrb esnu l s'h

And if in our grief and loneliness and moments of desolation, we should stray from following Thee, O leave us not, faithful Shepherd, but draw us near unto Thee.]

…

A few days later Mary was trimming Judas' hair and applying some makeup to his face. They were in his room.

"Damn I'm good," Mary said as she admired her work. "I've not quite got the eyes right but it's good enough."

She motioned for Judas to stand.

"Now just exchange a few pleasantries with him and keep moving," ordered Mary. "Then meet me at the next turn off." She led him out of the house and looked down the road.

"Show time!" she said as she peered down the lane.

Judas briskly wandered down the road. Peter was leading a donkey. He seemed upset and preoccupied with his own thoughts. The donkey was agitated and was pulling at the reins. Judas had just reached Peter.

"Morning Peter," said Judas.

Warning: Christians and people who are easily offended should not read this book

"Morning Jesus," replied Peter, trying to calm the donkey

"Just on your way to Damascus I see?" added Judas.

"That's the plan," replied Peter. "If this beast will let me."

Peter suddenly paused. The donkey reared up. By the time Peter had reigned the animal in Judas had disappeared.

…

By the sea of Galilee.

"Ok," said Mary to Judas, as they peered over some rocks. "They've just cast the nets. Go along the beach like I told you."

Judas strolled out and walked up to the seafront where the water lapped the sand. He waved and shouted over to the fishermen who waved back. He smiled and walked along the beach for a few yards, then headed back into the dunes and disappeared. He could hear them shouting.

Once behind the rocks Judas went up to Mary. "This way," said Mary. "We'll be gone by the time they get back on land."

"I've been thinking," said Judas as they walked.

"That's good," said Mary, sarcastically.

"Well now," continued Judas. "Seeing as Jesus is gone. I wonder, you know, if you and me-?"

Mary stopped for a second. She handed Judas a flagon to drink from.

"I do NOT believe this!" she said, exasperated. "What is it that you don't understand about the concepts of Furious Anger and Terrible Vengeance."

"It was just an idea," replied Judas, awkwardly, taking a drink.

"You know," said Mary. "You remind me of a guy I once met in a place called Pompei."

"Wasn't that place incinerated by a volcano?" asked Judas.

"That's what they say," said Mary. "But that's actually what they got for pissing me off!"

"I daren't think what you must be like with PMT," added Judas, trying to lighten the mood.

"Oh, God help me!" exclaimed Mary. She paused. "What we got here is a failure to communicate," she said eventually. "Say 'Hello' to my little friend." She smiled and pointed for Judas to turn round as a Tyrannosaurus snapped and almost bit his head off. Judas dashed off with the terrible lizard in pursuit.

Warning: Christians and people who are easily offended should not read this book

…

Mary and Judas were strolling in the hills down to Jerusalem. Judas was nervous.

"Now we're just going to have a little walk round town, to show you off, sort of thing," explained Mary.

"Do we have to?" asked Judas. "The city is full of Roman patrols."

"They think you're dead, so they won't be expecting you, or rather him," replied Mary.

"I think I'd prefer to face that dragon again," said Judas.

"Your wish is my command," replied Mary and whistled. "Hey Bonzo, here boy," she shouted.

"No! No! No!" exclaimed Judas. "I didn't mean that."

"Now don't you worry," said Mary. "I'll be with you every step of the way. We'll be in and out in five minutes – ten tops. We can even hold hands if you want. But don't get any ideas."

"I don't like this one bit," said Judas.

Mary pulled out her hand and a gold coin magically appeared. "There's a dinar in it for you," she said.

Judas looked conflicted.

"How about two dinars?" said Mary, as two coins appeared.

"Now you're talking my kind of language," said Judas, reaching out.

Mary tossed one coin to him. "Half now, half later," said Mary.

After a minute Judas spoke once more.

"I didn't mean to rat him out you know," said Judas. "It was an accident. And they put us straight in the cells and he told me to take the money and run. Save yourself he said, 'It's me they're after. There's no point in both of us going down'. Anyway, he told me, Mary's got it sorted."

"I know, Judas," said Mary. "You don't have to explain to me," she smiled at him. They walked in silence.

After a minute Judas began to cry. Mary stopped and took him into her arms. She looked into his eyes.

"Jesus loves you, Judas, nothing else matters," she told him. "You must be strong now. We have great work to do. And no one must ever know. That is your punishment."

They walked a bit further.

Warning: Christians and people who are easily offended should not read this book

"I'm frightened," said Judas.

"Have faith," said Mary, smiling at him. "While you are with me not even the Devil himself can hurt you."

"What if a Roman patrol stops us?" asked Judas as they approached the gates.

"I'll think of something," explained Mary. "Destroy the Temple or block out the sun. Nothing too big. Just something to get their attention."

They walked straight past the guards at the gate and into the street where people were milling around.

"You see," said Mary. "That wasn't too bad after all. Now Big Joe is making some public pronouncement at lunchtime, and we wouldn't want to miss that. Seeing you will really mess up his shit. And that nice Centurion I met says he can sneak you onto the platform with all the big knobs."

"You said we'd be out of here in five minutes!" exclaimed Judas.

"I have no recollection of that," said Mary, smiling. "Anyhow, you're free to go. If you want to summon up some demons or have the fires of Hell rain down from the skies, when you next run across a Roman patrol, then be my guest. I'll just be over there shopping."

"Bah," said Judas.

"Can we go shopping?" asked Mary. "We've got loads of time. And I need a new outfit. What do you think: black or red?"

"Black," replied Judas. "Like your heart."

"I agree," said Mary. "Black goes with anything. And then there's a couple of shoes shops I want to check out. Only six or seven. There's these wonderful sling-back sandals I've had my eye on."

"Have I already died and gone to Hell?" asked Judas.

"Jesus used to take me shopping," argued Mary.

"He told me," added Judas.

"What did he say?" asked Mary.

"If all else fails," replied Judas. "Cyanide."

"Bless him," said Mary. "Jesus used to pay as well." She looked at Judas and smiled imploringly.

"I don't have any money," said Judas, firmly.

"What about that gold dinar I just gave you?" asked Mary.

Warning: Christians and people who are easily offended should not read this book

"Bah," said Judas, tossing the coin back to her.

"I knew you'd see it my way," said Mary. "People usually do." She reached out and took his hand.

Warning: Christians and people who are easily offended should not read this book

Judas and Aphrodite

Judas, Mary and a beautiful Greek woman were sitting in a room at a table.

"Now Judas," said Mary. "My friend, Aphrodite, and I are going to give you instruction in the most terrible weapon that man will ever know."

Judas' eyes gleamed in anticipation.

Mary smiled knowingly, and then held up a quill.

Judas' face fell.

The beautiful Aphrodite moved to sit next to him, pulled out some parchment and began to write saying out loud: "A is for alpha, B is for beta..." she paused and smiled at Mary.

"Now Judas," Mary began. "You are going to write a Gospel. An account of Jesus of Nazareth, as you knew him. I have chosen you for this task because you are special."

"How is that?" asked Judas.

"Those other boys," said Mary. "They're sort of, how shall we say, 'puritans'. And I need someone who can be somewhat selective with the truth. You see, the dark arts must end with me. There is no place in this world for them now. And we don't want generations of people trying to raise demons or consort with witches. It would be bad! So what you are going to do is to side-line me. Focus on Jesus and The Message. Make me into a footnote – something you might put in that bit at the back that no one reads. Like the acknowledgements."

"So I'm not to mention that business when you rolled that two ton rock?" asked Judas.

"No," said Mary. "It might also be best to gloss over all that stuff with maidens and lusty widows as well."

"I understand," said Judas.

"Excellent," said Mary. "Now once you've finished, knock up a few copies and post them out."

"Where?" asked Judas.

"Everywhere and anywhere," said Mary.

"That will cost money," replied Judas.

"Now I'm glad you mentioned that," said Mary. She pulled a sheet off a large cauldron that was brim full of gold coins. "This should keep you going for a while."

Judas picked up a handful of coins in disbelief.

"If I cut some corners and I'm careful, maybe I can spin this lot out to two or three hundred years," he said, trying to look like he was haggling in the market and had been beaten.

Warning: Christians and people who are easily offended should not read this book

"That's the spirit," said Mary.

"Ok," began Judas enthusiastically, dropping the coins back into the cauldron. "Gospel of Judas, chapter 1."

"Now," interrupted Mary. "Don't take this personally. But 'Gospel of Judas' doesn't scan right. Purely from a marketing perspective. You understand?"

"How about I use my middle name," said Judas, enthusiastically. "Gospel of Matthew."

"Booyah!" exclaimed Mary, standing to leave. She paused. "Now are you sure you have everything you need?"

Judas looked at the coins and then at Aphrodite, who smiled back.

"I'm good," he said.

Mary leant over him.

"I'm going now," she said. "I've put it around that you hanged yourself. Which is better than you deserve. So don't make a liar of me. No guest appearances. Ok?"

"OK," replied Judas.

"Judas," whispered Mary. "If I hear you've been showing up in Judea or anywhere else, it won't be just your wardrobe that malfunctions."

"OK," replied Judas, nervously.

Mary kissed him on the forehead and left.

Warning: Christians and people who are easily offended should not read this book

Twenty years later

Peter and Mary reached the brow of a hill. Peter was old and grey. They looked out. The Eternal City of Rome lay in front of them.

Mary turned to Peter and said: "I must leave you now, Peter. Remember what we talked about."

"So you cannot come any further?" asked Peter.

"Best not," said Mary. "If I go down there everybody will see me. And then the Paparazzi will be after me. And you know what they're like. You can't even go out for a cup of coffee."

"Mary," asked Peter. "I've been meaning to ask you about that. You haven't eaten anything."

"I'm just not a breakfast person," replied Mary.

"Well now," continued Peter. "You see. I've known you on our travels these past twenty years. And throughout that time, I haven't seen you eat anything at all ever."

Mary looked uncomfortable.

"The truth is," she said, thoughtfully. "I'm on a diet. You know, a second on the lips. A lifetime on the hips. A girl's gotta keep in shape."

"Oh," said Peter hesitating. "And I have never seen you sleep either."

Mary paused. "I power nap," she said, suddenly. "Half an hour here. Half an hour there. Just enough to recharge my batteries. Just enough to keep me young and beautiful."

"Oh," said Peter hesitating thoughtfully and looking carefully at her. "Now you mention it, I've aged these past years. Wrinkles, grey hair, and all that. But you don't look a day older than when we first met."

"I can explain that," said Mary, desperately. "Cleopatra taught me this trick with hair dye and ass's milk."

"Ass's milk?" repeated Peter.

"Ass's milk," confirmed Mary. "You should try it. Does you the world of good. Cleopatra swore by it."

"Cleopatra's been dead almost fifty years," said Peter. "Which means you aren't a day under 70. That's remarkable. Did you know the Hebrew word for 'virgin' actually means 'young woman'?"

"I did not know that," said Mary, relieved he had changed the subject. "But there are so many Marys round here that people could easily get confused."

"I can see how they would do that," said Peter.

Warning: Christians and people who are easily offended should not read this book

"Anyway, a lady never discusses her age," said Mary, reaching out and shaking his hand. Peter turned and began to leave.

"Oh," shouted Mary, as Peter began to march off down the hill. "I've got some money for you. I'll get someone to come by and drop it off. You can buy yourself some new shoes…or build a church ... or something." Peter turned and waved in acknowledgement.

"Goodbye Peter," shouted Mary. "May the Lord be with you."

"And also with you," said Peter, smiling as he turned to walk away.

After a few seconds Peter descended into a valley and was lost from sight.

"That was close," said Jesus' voice. "Do you think he bought it? He's an awful loudmouth."

"He suspects but I think I nailed it," replied Mary, still looking in Peter's direction.

There was a pause.

"Why didn't you do the eye thing?" asked Jesus.

"Ahhhh!" exclaimed Mary. "I was trying to keep him on message. Not give him a heart attack! You know: 'Jesus: Lamb of God,' not 'Mary: Destroyer of Worlds'!"

"You didn't destroy that much," added Jesus. "Even on Good Friday."

"I was having a bad day," responded Mary.

"Except for those two witches," said Jesus.

"Yeah!" said Mary, grinning. "I really lit them up!"

There was a pause as they turned and began to walk away together.

"You know that thing you did with the moon was super-awesome," said Jesus.

"Yeah!" said Mary. "That was cool. I didn't know I could do that. Anyway, where are we going?"

"I fancy going to Mecca," said Jesus.

"Why Mecca?" asked Mary.

"There's a guy there that I want to meet," said Jesus. "Apparently he's giving away virgins like they're going out of fashion."

"What is it with you guys and virgins?" asked Mary. "Tell me, how many virgins is enough?"

"Mary," began Jesus. "Virgins are like camels. One is good but it pays to have a couple of spares."

"You know," said Mary. "I feel exactly the same way about men!"

Warning: Christians and people who are easily offended should not read this book

There was an uncomfortable silence.

"Shall I drop the virgin thing?" asked Jesus.

"Hallelujah!" replied Mary.

There was another uncomfortable silence.

"Will you do the eye thing for me?" asked Jesus, trying to get back into Mary's good books.

"No!" she replied petulantly.

"Aw go on!" protested Jesus. "Come on! Do the eye thing to the next people we meet. It really puts the fear of God in folks."

"OK," said Mary, reluctantly. "But only if you're good! Hey, can we go via Babylon? It's on the way."

"We do have a bit of time," said Jesus. "Actually about 500 years. What's in Babylon?"

"Just some woman I once met," said Mary, nonchalantly.

"Are you on some sort of witch hunt?" asked Jesus, suspiciously.

"What if I am?" replied Mary. "If you know anyone better qualified, I'm all ears!"

THE END

"Messiah" is based on a true story.

Warning: Christians and people who are easily offended should not read this book

Appendix

Believe it or not, this story is a genuine attempt to spread the word of Jesus Christ – "Love thy Neighbour as thyself - Do unto others as you would have them do unto you." Not because I am a Christian (which I aren't really) – but because the world will be a better place because of this message. (Love the Lord thy God with all thy heart … Love thy Neighbour as thyself… There is none other commandment greater than these. Mark 12:29-12:31)

My principal motivation in writing this story was the murder of my friend Sir David Amess MP who was stabbed to death at his constituency surgery by a previously law-abiding young man who seems to have become a religious fanatic. I therefore began to write a story about the life of Osama bin Laden – the jihadist who masterminded the 9/11 attacks which lead to the murder of around 3000 American civilians who neither knew Osama bin Laden, nor al Qaeda, nor did they bear him any ill will. It gradually became clear that Osama bin Laden, and his millions of supporters, are motivated by religious zeal – bin Laden genuinely believed he was doing God's work and would be received in Heaven for his atrocities. It occurred to me that nothing motivates people more than religion, and no one is a greater motivator than Jesus Christ. Hence this story – a fictionalised exploration of the exploits and motives of The Christian Messiah.

Jesus spoke in parables so that the audience at the time could understand him. This story is an attempt to send his message in a way which is accessible in a modern, post-industrial, secular society.

For avoidance of doubt, "Judea" is now in modern Israel. It was known as the Kingdom of Judea at the time of Christ. The Arab people who lived there were called "Jews" and their state religion was "Judaism". I am English, my religion is (notionally) Anglicanism and I was born in the Kingdom of England – same thing.

There will be many crackpots and fanatics who cannot resist seeking vengeance and retribution against me for the blasphemies within this book. To them I say: Damn the lot of you! (Although Salman Rushdie and the Charlie Hebdo journalists probably had similar dismissive sentiments when they published their work.) There will be some genuine Christians and other people of a delicate disposition who will be genuinely offended. To them I say: Why in God's name have you read this book? Every page has a warning that it contains blasphemy! This book is not aimed at the converted – it is not for Christians. If you are a Christian do not read it! This book is aimed at the unbeliever – the vast multitude of atheists / agnostics who inhabit the brave new world of the Western Democracies in the post-industrial age. To them I say: Love thy Neighbour as thyself / Do unto others as you would have them do unto you. If you want to know more – go into any Church and ask.

Was Jesus a celibate? Who knows! Does it really matter? Is it honestly any of our business?

Warning: Christians and people who are easily offended should not read this book

Did Jesus exist? Definitely! Even an atheist like me can see there is overwhelming historical evidence to support his existence. Does that mean there is a God? No.

Does God exist? Who knows? Does it matter? It matters to Christians and religious people. But regardless of this, Jesus' message remains entirely valid - Love thy Neighbour as thyself.

Even if there is a God – the existence of Jesus does not make that God (or Creator) either benevolent (kindly), omnipotent (having unlimited powers), rational (logical as we understand things) or infallible (incapable of making mistakes).

Jesus was a blasphemer – he was outspoken – he did not shy from controversy – indeed Jesus courted controversy – this explains why he had so many followers who were equally annoyed with idle Temple Priests taking their money as forced donations to line their pockets. It also explains why the priests had Jesus killed – to silence him and make him an example to anyone else who might be so outspoken.

Jesus said: "Woe unto you, scribes and Pharisees [a religious sect at the time], hypocrites! Ye fools and blind. which strain at a gnat, and swallow a camel [the Priests were lazy and well fed]. Ye serpents, ye generation of vipers, how can ye escape the damnation of hell? Ye devour widows' houses, and for a pretence make long prayer: therefore ye shall receive the greater damnation" Matthew 23:2-23:39

This is pretty courageous stuff! It's actually surprising Jesus survived as long as he did – would you go round Russian or China or Tehran today and denounce their Leaders as blind fools, hypocrites, vipers and gnats? The priests in Jesus' time had presumably become lazy and corrupt. There was clearly a lot of anger at the time directed to the Church from the local people – this happens every so often in many organised religions – especially Christianity – and even in any State monopoly where there is no competition. Let's face it that's why Martin Luther invented Protestantism and why Margaret Thatcher privatised the mines and railways and everything else.

Jesus also became a political activist. He led a protest movement against abuses in the established Church of the day. What we forget, in our Modern Era, is that the Church used to be a branch of the government. The Church was enormously powerful and influenced every aspect of people's lives every day. Church attendance was compulsory, and it raised money by compulsory donations (taxes) and land ownership. The Church even had their own Law Courts throughout the pre-industrial world. The Church was the only form of mass communication, and it was a principal actor in international diplomacy. (Marrying princes to princesses between neighbouring states is a lot cheaper than military conquest.)

Pontius Pilate (the Roman governor of Judea) was a smooth operator. As was Herod Antipas (Ruler of Judea and, presumably, a Roman collaborator when Jesus died). (Herod the Great, he of the fictional massacre of the innocents, was Herod's Atipas' father.) Pilate and Herod must have been very sophisticated men. They were ruthless and powerful and doubtless would not be concerned for the life of a local Carpenter, especially a troublemaker who verbally attacked the Church and who upset the existing order of things. Yet Pontius Pilate

Warning: Christians and people who are easily offended should not read this book

bent over backwards to protect Jesus. Why? Because Jesus was a supporter of the Roman occupation – "Render therefore unto Cæsar the things which are Cæsar's" Matthew 22:21.. "Love your enemies, bless them that curse you, do good to them that hate you, and pray for them which despitefully use you, and persecute you" Matthew 5:44. This would be music to the ears of the Roman Governor. Jesus was very sophisticated by invoking the protection of the Romans while he attacked the Church. Pontius Pilate and Herod would immediately see through the ruse the Priests were promoting that Jesus was a heretic. They would recognise this as a cynical attempt to silence one of their critics who, presumably, expressed the reasonable view at the time that the Church had become corrupt. Promoting Christianity, or allowing it to spread, would therefore be to the advantage of the Roman occupiers who were trying to quell a rebellious province like Judea.

Are organised religions (like Christianity) bad? No. All organised religions, like many state monopolies, have phases of controversy and corruption (dare we mention child abuse). But organised religions are usually a force for good in the modern world. Not only do they spread the word (Love thy Neighbour as thyself) and support charity, but they act as a force for Justice (at least some of the time). Organised religions help to stop fanatics perverting their religious beliefs and then undertaking ridiculous Crusades – it became clear from my studies of Osama bin Laden that he, and his followers, had managed to convince themselves that they were doing God's work by murdering thousands of innocent civilians who bore them no ill will. This is entirely contrary to Islam and the Quran – just read it if you don't believe me. Organised religion can help reign in crackpots and fanatics – the sort of people who started the Crusades and the Spanish inquisition etc etc. Organised religion has to have some rituals – people cannot be expected to sit around in a church and chat for an hour. Some religious rituals also make people feel better, like Christenings, weddings, funerals etc. It's just that some of the rituals are a bit daft – like the symbolic cannibalism of Holy Communion (eating the bread and drinking the wine – the flesh and blood of Christ). What nonsense!

Is the Christian Bible (and this book) antisemitic? No. Christians worship a Jew! The Disciples were Jews. Most of the New Testament was produced by Jews (using Greek scribes). It's just bad luck that the Temple Priests at the time of Jesus were Jewish (because that was that state religion) and they were corrupt.

Those who compiled the Gospels did a good job. They studiously appear to have collected, as near as possible, eyewitness accounts of the life and speeches of Jesus, as best they could within a century of his death. (Jesus died on Friday 3 April 33 AD – when there was a partial eclipse of the Moon visible in Jerusalem – there may also have been an earthquake around the same time.) Those who collected the Gospels published four of them in The Bible – presumably the Gospels that covered most of the action. Some others have also survived.

There were actually very few miracles reported in the Gospels: which is good because miracles (fairy stories) put people off religion in modern society. Insisting that Jesus fed the five thousand or raised the dead or walked on water has become a public relations disaster in the 21st century. You have to move with the times! It's just a shame Jesus wasn't literate. (Incidentally Jesus told everyone to go forth and "raise the dead" – Matthew 10:5-10:42 -

Warning: Christians and people who are easily offended should not read this book

clearly there has been something lost in translation.) Many people can heal the sick and cleanse the lepers. On a good day some people can even cast out devils. But raising the dead! Incidentally it also seems Jesus was only spotted alive on a few occasions after the Crucifixion (by Mary Magdalen and St Peter amongst others) although that would be an ecumenical matter.

Occasionally, even today, sometimes people suddenly become blind, or lame, or comatose (in a stupor) or mute, and they do suddenly recover – although these are not common causes of these symptoms. These are so called "catatonic" or "dissociative" states (terms and disorders invented by Freud who, paradoxically, was also Jewish). At the time of Christ, it must have been easy to believe that people who were having epileptic fits, or people variously described as 'insane', as being possessed by demons.

Hallucinogens include naturally occurring drugs that can certainly cause visions (including seeing Demons). However, in Biblical Judea the likely source would probably be cacti rather than "Magic" mushrooms. Many contaminants in rotten food are also hallucinogens. Dehydration, sleep deprivation, infections and fevers frequently cause visual hallucinations (e.g. alcohol withdrawals or "delirium tremens").

Black slave girls (dare I say 'sex-slaves') would be common through the Arab and Roman world, including Judea at the time of Christ. Was Mary Magdalen a black slave girl? If she was, and became the wife of Jesus, it's not likely that the Disciples or the Gospels would want to record this – Censorship and Taxes are even older than Christianity. Similarly, was Jesus a virgin? Once again, it's not likely that the Disciples or the Gospels would want to record this. However, quite frankly, it's none of our business anyway. But Jesus was fun! (See how often he laughs in the Gospel of Judas.) He was not schizoid or anodyne (dull, boring and avoiding controversy) – he had great social skills. He must have had tremendous charisma and he could certainly work a crowd, and then some! Jesus was the Billy Graham of his day! (How's that for blasphemy!) Apparently, Jesus had many female followers – many of whom gave him money!!! It is reasonable to presume he had a normal sex drive and would require some sexual outlet (like all men – brute beasts with no understanding). The idea that Jesus was celibate may be comforting to the delicate sensitivities of many people who would be embarrassed by the idea that Jesus, or anyone else, had sex. However, religious celibacy has generally caused more problems than it has prevented. (Catholics can criticise Judaism and Islam but at least these religions are sensible enough not to require their priests to be celibate.)

Here is a synopsis of story in this book for dummies (and for those ranting fanatics who will condemn the author without bothering to read the book): Mary (Magdalen) is an African slave girl who has become a witch employed by queen Cleopatra. Being a witch, Mary has tremendous powers and super strength. Hence, she and her coven (with Delilah and Jezebel), are able to help Cleopatra and Mark Antony defeat the rebel Roman Generals, Brutus and Cassius, at The Battle of Philippi (which actually happened!) They see the Star of Bethlehem indicating the Birth of The Messiah. Cleopatra, at the behest of Satan, sends Mary and the girls to destroy The Messiah. (Satan is a jealous God and dislikes competition.) Mary is sent

Warning: Christians and people who are easily offended should not read this book

to discredit Jesus and expose him as a False Prophet. After 30 years in King Herod's Court, in Jerusalem, Mary eventually locates Jesus in Magdala (a fishing village in Judea which is still there – 'Magdala' = 'Magdalen'). Mary is a sexy African slave girl – a dancer. (Incidentally Cleopatra actually knew Herod the Great in real life!)

Jesus is a bit of a crook and not a very good magician, but he is so handsome and charismatic that no one cares! He does a magic act on weekends with his Disciples to earn some cash. This includes an illusion of raising the dead and a disappearing act which takes advantage of the fact that his best friend, Judas, looks like him – at least from a distance. Mary is destitute. Jesus takes the beautiful Mary home with him. Mary's parents go ballistic but give in because they feel sorry for her. She joins the Act. Mary is a big hit because she is superhot! The audience love her! Kerching!

Jesus and Mary get into various scrapes together. As the act progresses Jesus notices that preaching is a crowd pleaser. He starts thinking he can do more than simply entertain people as a conjuror. After a near death experience in a storm, and a scam where he appears to raise Lazarus from the dead (to claim his own inheritance), he is eventually baptised by John the Baptist and decides to become an itinerant (travelling) preacher. He goes into the desert to find his religion where he finds Mary the Witch waiting for him. She tries to bribe, seduce, and torture him, using witchcraft, so he will admit he is a liar and False Prophet and renounce his God and then she can expose him as a fraud. He resists. The harder she tries the more convinced he becomes that he is right, and his Faith becomes stronger as his body weakens. (He is fasting in the desert.) Eventually Mary gives up. Mary returns to the Temple to speak with the two other witches. They cast her out because she has failed. She loses her powers.

Mary is destitute again. She is sexually abused in the streets and becomes an outcast – she is Black, and she is a harlot. Jesus comes and finds her and forgives her. He baptises her but recognises she has been treated abominably. "This woman was born into slavery. Her virtue was taken from her by evil men as a child. She had but one choice: to sell her body or starve. Her sin is that she chose to live." He kneels and begs her forgiveness for his own sins and hypocrisy.

Mary and Jesus have a shotgun wedding. Jesus continues to preach. He is furious with the priests and also moneylenders. His popularity increases because everyone is sick of the corrupt priests exploiting them. Eventually Jesus enters Jerusalem, the biggest and wealthiest city in the area. He loses his temper with moneylenders and the Priests in the Temple. The Priests want to silence him. They accuse him of blasphemy. Jesus tries to escape but Judas inadvertently identifies him to the guards. He is tried by Pontius Pilate (the Roman governor) and Herod, and then Pilate again. Pilate tries to protect Jesus (Jesus was a friend to the Roman occupation and preaches to their advantage). Eventually Pilate gives in to the Priests and Jesus is crucified. Jesus dies to save Mary's soul. Only he and Judas know she is a witch. Jesus had forbidden her to use witchcraft.

Mary is consumed with anger and is about to destroy the world. (She is a witch.) She causes an eclipse of the Moon. Mary, Mother of Jesus, prevents her from killing the Romans and

Warning: Christians and people who are easily offended should not read this book

everyone else! Jesus has ordered her to forgive her enemies and has saved the world. Mary and Judas convince the Disciples that Jesus is the Messiah and help them spread His word. Mary teaches Judas to read and write and begins the process of compiling the Gospels. Mary does exactly the opposite of what the Devil sent her to do. But she warns that Judas must write her out of the Gospels, otherwise everyone would want to learn witchcraft.

As to blasphemy? Is it really so bad to suggest a Black woman can save the world? Damn - it's political correctness gone mad!

Some people say: "The Devil can cite scripture to his advantage". I say: "He certainly can!"

Email: eleni.lee@yahoo.com

Printed in Great Britain
by Amazon